the
Royalist's
Daughter

Other books by E.B. Wheeler

The Haunting of Springett Hall
Born to Treason
No Peace with the Dawn
(with Jeffery Bateman)
The Bone Map
Bootleggers & Basil
Utah Women: Pioneers, Poets & Politicians
Wishwood

the Royalist's Daughter

E.B. WHEELER

Rowan Ridge
Press

Cover & interior photos: Portrait of Dorothy Osborne by Peter Lely, and Cromwell at Dunbar by Andrew Carrick Gow
Formatting by LJP Creative
Editing by Chadd VanZanten

Published by Rowan Ridge Press
North Logan, Utah
Originally published as Yours, Dorothy © 2018 by E. B. Wheeler

First printing: April 2018

ISBN: 978-1-7321631-5-7

To the real Dorothy and William,
I hope you would be pleased with how I told your story.

Author's Note

DOROTHY OSBORNE IS CELEBRATED AS one of the earliest writers to elevate letters to an art form, and in a century when most women were illiterate and female authors were unheard of. We are fortunate to have her letters from 1652 to 1654, and I have incorporated portions of some of them into the text. Few of William Temple's letters from the same time period survived, but I have quoted a few short pieces of his writing as well. All other letters from William, and all letters from outside the 1652 to 1654 time period, are of my own invention.

This book is a work of fiction, but it attempts to follow as closely as possible the real events of Dorothy and William's lives. More extensive notes at the end of the novel explain which parts of this book were fabricated to fill in the gaps in our information.

1645

·

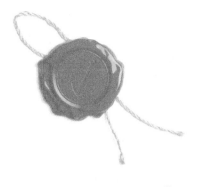

Chapter One

Dorothy Osborne held her family's fortune—and their future—in her hands. Her arms ached at the weight of the leather trunk she cradled, heavy with her father's best clothes and some linens embroidered by her grandmother in the reign of Henry VIII. The musty scent of the second-hand clothes in the shop tickled Dorothy's nose. She shifted her grip, and her fingers dug into bare leather. The trunk had displayed enamel-work lions until she'd been forced to pry them off and bring them before the merchants to feed herself and her mother.

Wooden shelves of drawstring purses, sword belts, and plumed hats crowded Dorothy, as if watching with her as Aunt Gargrave stood across the counter from the French merchant, bartering away the last of their family's pride.

"You are robbing us." Aunt Gargrave thrust a doublet under the merchant's pointed nose. "This one has real pearls." She yanked a blue doublet from the trunk. "And this is silk."

Dorothy rebalanced the trunk, blocking the sight of her shamefully plain wool dress. Her father, Sir Peter, had looked so handsome and brave in the blue silk doublet, a rapier clanking at his

3

side. A true cavalier, a knight of proud King Charles. Someday, when the king put down Parliament's rebellion and regained his throne, her father would no longer be held under siege and could wear his fine clothes again. Dorothy wanted to snatch the doublet back from the grasping merchant, savor its scent of family and home. But they were doing this for her father, and for their rightful king.

"They are beautiful." The haberdasher studied the doublets with his jeweler's glass, his fingers lingering over the pearls on the collar. He pushed it away. "But I already have more doublets than I can sell. Every Royalist who flees to France is selling, selling, selling, and who will be left to buy?"

Who indeed?

Dorothy tried to keep her face composed, but her fingers trembled. The French merchants had grown used to taking advantage of desperate Royalists, but they had never met Aunt Gargrave.

"Wars don't last forever," Aunt Gargrave said. "The king will retake his throne, Royalist lands and fortunes will be restored, and people will buy again."

The merchant frowned.

Aunt Gargrave added, "Or perhaps the Royalists will lose."

Dorothy gave a start, wanting to scold her for such talk, but Aunt Gargrave went on.

"It may be that Parliament will win this war. Some of them are Puritans, aye, and may turn their noses up at fine ornamentation now, but when they are in power, do you think they will deny themselves and their wives the chance to flaunt their position?" Aunt Gargrave smiled. "And do not forget the French nobility. They will soon realize that the spoils of war are sitting on their coast, and they don't have the Puritan's dislike of finery."

The merchant shook his head. "I cannot pay what you ask."

An icy wind slithered under the shop door, around Dorothy's ankles. How cold her brothers must be on the frozen battlefields, and her father in Castle Cornet, under siege by Parliament's forces on the island of Guernsey in the English Channel. He and his men survived on a single moldy biscuit a day and whatever rats they could catch. They tore up the floors to burn for fuel. Dorothy imagined her father huddled by a tiny fire and trying to warm stinging cold fingers while he starved for the king. King Charles's forces were too busy fighting Parliament to come to Sir Peter's aid. The Osborne women were the only ones left to save him.

"Wait!" Dorothy hefted the trunk onto the wooden counter. A gold ring with an emerald rested on her finger. It had been her grandmother's, and Dorothy had hoped to someday give it to a daughter of her own. She slid the ring off and held it out.

"Dorothy!" Aunt Gargrave pulled her back. "Think of your future."

Dorothy met her eyes. "I am. A future with my father safe and my king back on his throne." What more could she hope for? She clutched the ring. "This is my duty, Aunt. Let me do my part for my family."

Aunt Gargrave stepped aside.

The merchant stretched out his claw of a hand. Dorothy rubbed the smooth metal of the ring one last time, then let it fall into the man's palm.

"And these."

Her fingers were shaking so hard she struggled to unclasp her pearl brooch and remove the gold signet ring from her other hand. The last of her dowry. But what were her own little dreams compared to the service she could do for her family and her country? She dropped the jewelry on the counter, the dull clunk echoing in her chest.

The merchant touched the brooch, his yellowed fingernail caressing the riches that would have gone to Dorothy's husband. She forced herself to watch, thinking of her father's dire conditions and not whatever hazy future she might have known if the war's muskets and cannon had not torn holes in her world.

5

"Let me see the rest of it." The merchant gestured to the trunk.

Aunt Gargrave took over the haggling, offers and counteroffers flying like tennis balls in a match.

"Done!" Aunt Gargrave exclaimed, a smile of triumph turning up her lips.

Dorothy held her breath as the merchant counted out his coins: reliable French écus and Louis d'or, none with the uncertain image of the English King Charles. The merchant finished all too soon, leaving Aunt Gargrave with a small pile of coins. The Osbornes were nearly beggars now. Dorothy tried to accustom herself to the sound of the word, but it rang tinny and flat. They would save her father and deal with the rest when it came.

Aunt Gargrave weighed the coins in her palm, then slipped them into her pocket through a slit in her skirts, out of sight of cutpurses and the many pirates who had found haven behind Saint-Malo's walls.

"Is it enough?" Dorothy asked as they exited the shop. The cold sea breeze buffeted her with the scent of brine.

"'Twill have to be. I've already engaged the ship. Now we will fill its hold."

Aunt Gargrave sailed down the narrow cobble streets, the crowds somehow parting to let her venerable, gray-haired figure through. Dorothy dodged fishmongers, sailors, and musketeers to keep up. The maze of streets ran through stone buildings crowded behind the town walls. The tall homes of wealthy merchants peeked over the shoulders of smaller shops, as though spying on the curious mix of humanity passing beneath them.

Dorothy kept her gaze down as she walked, aware of the many eyes watching. Her dress was sadly out of fashion, yet its puffed sleeves and low bodice announced that she was no Puritan, but a fallen Royalist, another victim of Parliament's war on the king.

A few men loitering outside a tavern leered at her over their tankards of ale. They dressed in the most extreme of cavalier fashions: brightly colored doublets with trails of lace hanging from the sleeves, buttons left undone, and long hair laboriously styled to look carefree. She wished for the luxury of a mask to hide from their leers.

"Keep up!" Gargrave called.

"Coming, Aunt." Dorothy picked up her step.

"Why are you blushing like a naughty child?"

Dorothy's face burned warmer. She kept her voice low. "Those men are staring at me."

Gargrave shot them a look that made them suddenly interested in their ale or the clouds drifting overhead. She sniffed. "Shameless, but 'tis to be expected. You're a lovely young woman."

Dorothy shook her head.

Aunt Gargrave rolled her eyes. "Don't be such a milksop, niece. This false modesty is what comes of keeping girls locked up in their homes and refusing to educate them."

"I'm educated!"

"In what? Dance and embroidery? A little French, and that only because you sat in on your brothers' lessons. When I was a girl, I learned Latin, geography, and astronomy, too. 'Twill make a generation of silly girls, mark my words, if you don't give them anything but fluff to fill their brains. When Elizabeth sat on the throne, we knew what it meant to be a woman."

"Aye, Aunt Gargrave," Dorothy said, hardly attending the lecture she'd heard so many times.

Her aunt stopped and forced Dorothy to meet her serious gaze.

"Listen, niece. We cannot afford girls who 'Aye, Aunt Gargrave' their way through life. It was one thing when we had a strong king on the throne, but now our men are gone and we're all that's left. No matter what they tell you, do not forget that women know how to work, and how to fight too."

Dorothy nodded, then smiled mischievously. "Aye, Aunt Gargrave."

Aunt Gargrave laughed. "There. I knew you had some spirit in you. Hold on to it. We'll need it in the coming days."

Dorothy fell into step with her aunt, keeping her head high despite the stares of passing men. Before the war, she never would have been in the streets without a male relative. But Aunt Gargrave was right: Fortune had placed her in this position, and she would serve her country and her family just as her father and brothers did.

"I suppose I'll not marry now, anyway," Dorothy said, testing out the idea. She loved the warm security of home and family, but she had seen enough women yoked to tyrannical brutes or dead in childbed to know the risks of marriage.

"You're only eighteen. Hardly a spinster."

"My dowry is gone, and unless—*until*—the king is restored and we can return to Chicksands, we have nothing but our good name—our Royalist name—to recommend us."

"And your pretty face and refined manners. Don't underestimate those. They'll be your best weapons in the hunt for an influential husband."

"You think I'll snare one?" Dorothy teased, but Aunt Gargrave did not change her serious tone.

"I think you must. What else will save your family now? You and your brothers—if God wills that they survive this war— must marry well. The recommendation of my traitor brother may endear you to some sniveling Parliamentarian, or your father's loyalty may win the admiration of a Royalist who is not so impoverished as we are. Or even a Frenchman," Aunt Gargrave mused.

A Frenchman would not be terrible, but a Parliamentarian! Dorothy wrinkled her nose at the idea. Yet her Uncle Danvers, who had turned against the king to support Parliament, was the only one in the family who prospered, or who might introduce Dorothy to a wealthy suitor.

Once they secured a supply of dried meat, salted fish, ale, and barley, they left the safety of the town walls for the port. Dorothy stared over the deep blue channel waters. There, across the Bay of Saint-Malo's, was the island of Jersey—firmly in the king's control—and beyond that, Guernsey, where her father held out for the sake of the king and his family's honor, waiting for her and Aunt Gargrave to ease their suffering.

They made certain the supplies for her father, Sir Peter, were stowed below deck, and then boarded the little two-masted ketch. Dorothy gripped the railing of the quarterdeck as the boat rolled underfoot. Sea travel was yet another thing she never would have experienced if King Charles were still on the throne where he belonged. This was a man's world. Boats were called "she," but Dorothy thought the ocean must be masculine: mysterious, free, and capable of turning deadly. She huddled into her cloak, hypnotized by the onslaught of the waves against the little vessel as it pushed out to sea.

The wintry wind caught the sails, and the boat made good time skittering over the open water. Dorothy closed her eyes and inhaled the salty air, saving the memory. Soon, the king would defeat Parliament, order would be restored, and she would be allowed to return home to the quiet halls of Chicksands. There would be no more talk of marrying her to a stranger. She'd be safe again with her own gardens and books, but she did not want to forget the smell of the ocean.

Saint-Malo faded into the horizon, and the bitter chill seeped through Dorothy's cloak as the hours crept by. She strolled in circles to warm her numb feet, trying to watch the men's work without being obvious in her curiosity. The sailor nearest her tensed, and she followed his gaze across the choppy sea. A chorus of shouts rang out among the crew, and Aunt Gargrave rushed to join Dorothy at the railing.

"What's happening?" Dorothy asked.

"Pirates!" the captain called. "We'll try to outrun 'em."

He ushered the two women down to the main deck. They pressed against the stairs, out of the way of the sun-burned men adjusting sails and readying muskets.

"They're gaining on us," the captain called down. "At this rate, they'll catch us before we make it to Guernsey or back to Saint-Malo. We can stand and fight, or else try to lose them in the rocks ahead." The captain squinted over the sun-flecked water. "We're more maneuverable, but 'tis risky."

He and Aunt Gargrave turned to Dorothy for a decision, but she shrank from their gazes. How could she know what to do? She did not want blood on her hands.

A distant boom echoed over the waters from the pirates' boat.

"We should … we should run for the rocks," Dorothy croaked over the rough calls of the sailors.

The captain gave a curt nod and shouted orders to his crew. The tenor of the men's voices changed. The boat's sails caught the wind, and the boat edged to the right.

Dorothy wished for something to hold on to. She could not swim. Nothing would save her now except God and the experience of the captain and his crew.

The sound of cannon fire continued, but it grew more distant. The boat jolted over the choppy sea. Dorothy and Aunt Gargrave huddled beside the stairs as sailors rushed past or surveyed the shallow waters. Sharp rocks waited below, eager to claw through the thin wooden hull and drag them into the cold embrace of the sea.

The captain jogged down the stairs, the sticky scent of his sweat mingling with the tang of salt in the air. "We've outrun them, m'lady, but they'll be waiting for us if we change course for Guernsey again."

Dorothy and Aunt Gargrave exchanged a look of frustration. What good did the relative safety of the rocks do them if all their plans and efforts rotted in the hold?

"We could make for Jersey," Aunt Gargrave said slowly. "Beg Colonel Carteret for an escort."

Dorothy frowned. "He's done little enough thus far."

Colonel Carteret was the king's governor on Jersey, which remained staunchly Royalist, yet he cowered in safety on the island and had stopped his ears to Sir Peter's cries for assistance.

The captain cleared his throat. "They say Colonel Carteret has his own pirates."

"To attack Parliamentarian ships," Dorothy said.

The captain looked skeptical, and Dorothy's stomach went cold. Certainly, the king's governor wouldn't attack his allies. It was just a rumor, and Dorothy knew how little faith to place in those.

"We'll ask him to put his pirates to good use." Aunt Gargrave nodded to the captain. "Take us to Jersey."

The boat wended its way through the rocks. Dorothy inched closer to the railing and watched dark, jagged shadows pass beneath them. Finally, the vessel pulled free and danced across the waves again.

A smudge on the horizon resolved itself into an island with castle walls curling around its highest point like a serpent sunning itself on a rock. Jersey. The castle loomed above them as they thumped up alongside the dock. Dorothy followed Aunt Gargrave down the gang-board in time to meet an official in Jersey's livery striding toward them.

"We're here to see Colonel Carteret," Aunt Gargrave announced.

"And who are you?" the official asked, taking in their worn gowns. His doublet and hose were in fine fashion, decked with clean, white lace.

"Lady Katherine Gargrave, sister-in-law to Sir Peter Osborne, the king's governor on Guernsey. And this is Sir Peter's daughter, Mistress Dorothy Osborne."

The official frowned. "Very well."

He led them higher through the series of walled defenses, until the island's green fields and snug homes stretched below them to the west. Dorothy paused to catch her breath. Did her father have a similar view from Castle Cornet on Guernsey? Of course, there was no peaceful village and fields of cattle surrounding him, but an angry town keeping him under siege. Still, the king had ordered her father to hold the castle, and therefore hold it he would—honor demanded nothing less.

A guard met them outside the great hall of the castle.

"Colonel Carteret is in his council chambers, and he invites you to join him."

The guard led them into the chambers, a long room hung with rich red tapestries displaying the golden lions of Jersey. A dais elevated the colonel's carved wooden chair above the rest of the council members. None of them acknowledged the two women when they entered the room. Their attention was on a man in chains in the center of the room.

"Geoffrey Fitzgerald, we find you guilty of espionage against your rightful king." Colonel Carteret's voice rolled through the room, and the council members nodded.

The chained man raised his head. "A king ceases to be a rightful monarch when he taxes his people without the consent of Parliament—"

"We sentence you to be hanged." Colonel Carteret waved a jeweled hand to the guards.

"—introduces ungodly foreign influences in his country and church, wages war on his own subjects—"

Dorothy edged away from the raving prisoner as the guards hauled him out of the chamber. She narrowed her eyes. The king might not be perfect, but he represented law and tradition. It was Parliament that had dragged the kingdom into war.

"Lady Katherine Gargrave and Mistress Dorothy Osborne," the guard announced.

Dorothy and Aunt Gargrave stepped forward into that ring of curious, accusing stares.

"Lady Gargrave, Mistress Osborne." Colonel Carteret nodded to each of them in turn. "What brings you to Jersey?"

"We have come with supplies for Sir Peter at Castle Cornet on Guernsey," Aunt Gargrave said. "We seek an escort from Jersey to help us make it past the pirates and Parliament's forces in the channel."

Carteret sipped from his goblet of wine, then dabbed his lips with a linen cloth. "I understood that Sir Peter's properties had been sequestered and his family was impoverished."

Dorothy winced at the word.

Before Aunt Gargrave could respond, he went on, "I also hear that some of Sir Peter's family have been living with one of Parliament's most vocal supporters: Sir John Danvers. Your brother, I believe, Lady Gargrave."

Aunt Gargrave straightened. "My sister, Lady Osborne, did seek refuge from our traitor brother for a time, to spare her children from starving. But we women have movable assets we can sell to support our family and the cause of our king, even when Parliament drives us from our homes."

"Family is all we have left," Dorothy added quietly. "And all that matters."

Carteret's attention snapped to her. "And what would you do to save your father? How am I to know you haven't betrayed the king to buy these provisions for your father? Or agreed to spy for Parliament?"

Dorothy opened her mouth to object, but Aunt Gargrave put a warning hand on her arm.

"I have heard it said, Colonel, that we often accuse others of that which is in our own heart. We have sacrificed everything for the king's cause. Can you say as much?"

Angry red spots lit the colonel's cheeks, and he smiled grimly. "Who but a traitor would accuse the king's loyal governor of not giving his all? I'll have you removed from this island immediately, so you'll not have a chance to gather information for your Parliamentarian relatives." He smirked. "And I'll keep the provisions aboard your boat, in case they are ill-gotten gains."

Dorothy tried to object but choked on the words. Aunt Gargrave let out an exclamation of rage, but soldiers with muskets surrounded them, pushing them to the door. Dorothy burned in anger and humiliation at their forced parade back down the hillside.

At the port, the precious supplies for her father sat on the docks, never to reach Guernsey. Her father would continue starving for his honor and loyalty, while Colonel Carteret wore jewels and sipped wine. Dorothy had sacrificed her dowry for nothing.

On the boat once again, with Jersey to their backs, the fire burning in Dorothy dwindled to ash. Her teeth chattered at the bitter wind, and she leaned on the railing. The salt spray from the ocean wet her face in place of the tears that wouldn't come.

"It is not over, Niece," Aunt Gargrave said, her voice as chilly as the sea.

"Aye, we'll keep fighting," Dorothy said. But she'd had a bitter taste of her own helplessness. How was a woman to survive in a world thrown all out of order?

By marrying well, she could almost hear Aunt Gargrave remind her. Perhaps even to some unprincipled brute like Colonel Carteret. The thought turned her stomach more than any seasickness from the rolling waves. She would help save her family, but it might cost her everything to do it.

1648

THREE YEARS LATER

Chapter Two

Isle of Wight, England

WILLIAM DOFFED HIS HAT IN respect as he passed beneath the looming portal of Carisbrooke Castle. It was, after all, the prison of a king. The dark arrow slits glared at him from the towers, as though challenging his intentions. He did not ask for much from this visit, though: just answers, understanding, illumination.

Two guards with rapiers and muskets stepped into view.

William stopped and held out his hands to show they were empty. "William Temple to see Colonel Robert Hammond."

"State your business with the colonel."

"He's my cousin. I'm here to pay my respects." William saved the real reason for his visit for his cousin's ears.

The guards regarded him warily, taking in the cavalier style of his long hair and the lace at the cuffs of his shirt. One of them confiscated William's rapier and searched his person for other weapons. Looking disappointed when he found nothing, he called for a fellow guard to fetch Colonel Hammond.

As William waited, the clank of metal chains echoed in the courtyard. A fair-haired man in mud-splattered breeches and doublet marched across the green bailey between two guards, his hands manacled behind him but his pace quick, as though trying to outpace his guards and go of his own accord. He noted William's cavalier fashion and flashed a wry smile before entering the stone belly of the gray castle.

Robert Hammond emerged a few minutes later from a nail-studded oak door across the bailey. Last time William had seen his cousin, Robert had worn the cavalier fashion himself, but now he was a perfect Puritan—a Roundhead—in dark doublet and breeches, a simple felt hat without a single merry plume, and hair cut short.

Most of the men in William's family changed allegiances as easily as they changed fashions, chasing whatever cause offered wealth and security. William feared that the only thing that saved him from being just as unsteady was that he had never decided whom he should be loyal to. He hoped to find that answer today, and then he would know what sort of man he was.

"Cousin William?" Robert asked, clasping William's hand and guiding him away from the guards. "What brings you here?"

"I'm off to start my Grand Tour."

"You finished at Cambridge?"

"More like Cambridge finished with me." William tried to laugh off his failure, but it rang flat to his ear. "Father has banished me to France."

"Ah, well, I didn't get my degree at Oxford either. The connections you make there are more important than whatever Latin or Greek they try to stuff into your head."

Connections! Well did William know it. He had found little to love in the stiff Puritans who surrounded him at the college, but those were the men his father expected him to befriend. And he was certain to marry one of their dour-faced sisters—one with a good fortune to her name—if his father had his way. Maybe it was the right thing to do. He would throw his lot in with the Puritans and Parliament, if only he could see the honor in their revolution against the king.

"Come, Cousin, 'tis not like you to frown," Robert said. "What's troubling you?"

"Can I see him?" William asked quietly.

Robert looked confused for a moment, then he rubbed his tired eyes. "He's not an exotic animal on display."

"I did not mean it like that. I just...I want to understand. I want to know what people have found worth fighting and betraying and dying for."

Robert studied him. "Very well," he said quietly. "I cannot let you speak to him alone or give him anything, though. We just foiled a plot to sneak him out the window. I think you saw one of the conspirators, Richard Osborne, just now. He's from a family of Royalist trouble-makers, and some of them are probably still lurking about."

"I understand."

Robert grunted and motioned for William to follow. They made their way down long, stone corridors, past guards standing at attention.

"He's in the constable's chamber," Robert said. "It was the only room..."

"Fit for a king?" William muttered.

Robert shot him a warning look and took an iron key from his belt to unlock the great oak door. William stood straighter, his pulse hammering in his ears. Civil war tore his nation apart, and the man behind that door was the reason. William wasn't sure if he wanted to love the king or hate him, but he wanted to feel *something*.

Robert beckoned him into a spacious antechamber. A large writing desk spread with books and letters dominated the room. The tapestries had been stripped from their rods, but cushioned chairs softened the starkness, and a single portrait of the queen, Henrietta Maria, brightened the white plastered walls. Newly-installed iron bars hampered the view out the window.

Charles Stuart, by the grace of God—or so the Royalists said—King of England, Scotland, and Ireland, stood to greet them. The top of his head did not quite reach William's, but he surveyed William with the critical eye of a lord and commander. His chestnut hair hung in long curls, his white lace collar showed not a fleck of dust or soot, and his graying beard, though a little shaggy, still came to a neat point.

"One of your subjects wished to meet Your Majesty," Robert said. "May I present William Temple."

William bowed, and King Charles returned the gesture with a nod.

"William Temple. I know that name, but I do not believe you have been presented to me before." The king placed a hand absent-mindedly on a book of catechisms on his desk. William smiled when he recognized the volume, written by his favorite of his mother's brothers.

"I believe my uncle, Henry Hammond, is well known to Your Majesty."

"Of course. You are the nephew he raised—his late sister's eldest son?"

"The same, Sire."

"And how fares my servant Henry?"

"In prison, Your Majesty," William said quietly. "And very sorry to be driven from the work in his parish."

King Charles nodded. "This is how our times reward loyalty. Those who break faith seem to be rewarded on every side, while men of honor languish in prison." His Majesty gave Robert a pointed look. "But God, who knows the heart of every man, will reward us all according to our works." He turned his gaze on William. "I hope you are at peace with what He will find in your heart."

William gave a start. How could the king know his own inner struggles—the revolution of his feelings against the duty laid before him by his father?

"This interview is at an end," Robert said, his voice acid.

"Thank you for your time, Your Majesty," William said.

"I have nothing but time to give my subjects," Charles said, his tone sad and a little defiant. He turned to stare out the barred window.

William and Robert bowed their way out of the room.

"Well?" Robert asked once the door was secured.

"He's...a man," William said.

Robert nodded. "Nothing more."

"Perhaps a little more," William mumbled. There was something about the king: a noble air to inspire men. But it was not enough to inspire William. The answer—the purpose he sought—was not here in Carisbrooke Castle. Perhaps there was nothing in the world—no cause or force—worth devoting himself to. He said to Robert's back, "You once saw something to love in him, though."

Robert whirled on William. "Do you think I enjoy this position? Aye, I once promised to serve King Charles. And he fled to my doorstep, hoping for protection. What was I to do? I had a duty to Parliament as well."

"And how do you decide, when duty calls you in two directions?"

Robert's gaze darted around the corridor, as though afraid of spying shadows. "I have tried to serve both duties, but eventually, you have to choose a side. We cannot all be Uncle Henry, confound him and his simple faith, making the king think all the Hammonds would stumble over ourselves to go to prison or be executed for him. He's the reason I'm in this hopeless position!"

William's hackles rose at the curse directed to Henry Hammond. Simple he might be, in his faith and service to others, and in his loyalty too. But he had taken William in when his mother was dead and his father had no time for him. "I would count myself fortunate to have Uncle Henry's simplicity. To know where my duty lay, and to stick to the course, come what may."

21

"Oh, I meant no insult to our saintly uncle. But you must be a realist, William. Honor only gets you so far, and then you have to be practical. The Royalist cause is gasping its last."

William grunted. Maybe Robert was right—Robert, and William's father, and all the others. Parliament had won the war, and the army ruled the country. When the world turned upside down, maybe the most reasonable thing was to stand on one's head. Befriending Parliament was the path to success—to finally winning his father's approval.

Yet the idea of giving in to the voice of the crowd dragged at him like a dark anchor. Would doing so lessen him in Uncle Henry's eyes? In his own? He tended to think that Parliament was too heavy-handed with the king, but he did not feel strongly enough to fight them over their defense of what they saw as the freedoms of Englishmen, any more than he was willing to persecute or kill Royalists for supporting law and tradition. If he did not choose a side, he was trapped between them both. Perhaps he was fated to be the disappointment—the failure—his father thought him. Perhaps Uncle Henry had been overly kind when he said he saw something great in William.

William rode back to the inn at Newport, his mood as heavy as the gray clouds hanging over the English Channel. The common room of the inn was dim and subdued. A few members of the company drank and gossiped, enjoying an excursion to France, but most huddled in defeat: the jetsam of war washed from the shores of England.

One young lady wore the universal attire of Royalists—once fine clothes now worn to almost thread-bare shabbiness—but unlike her fellow refugees, her back was straight and her gaze determined. She turned a thin leather book over in her hands.

William took a seat near the window, not far from the young lady, and rested the back of his head on the cool glass. With his eyes closed, the voices in the room closed in on him.

"I could not even get a message to Cousin Richard," the young lady whispered to her male companion.

"We knew it was likely a lost cause," the young man said. "Our family is expert in those."

"There must be something—" the lady pleaded.

"Hush! Not here."

The silence stirred William's curiosity, and he opened his eyes. The young lady glanced in his direction. Her dark hair blended with the smoky dimness of the room, but her large, heavy-lidded eyes caught William's, and their sorrowful expression stirred in him a sense of companionship.

As if realizing that she had held his eyes too long, the young woman quickly looked away. The momentary brilliance of her gaze was gone, plunging the inn back into gloom.

William leaned his head back again, watching her from the corner of his eye. He considered asking the host for her name, but why? Disgraced Royalists were not the good connections his father expected him to make on his tour of the Continent.

She whispered something to her companion. The young man shook his head, hunching to hide his disgusted expression.

William's pang of jealousy surprised him. He did not even know this girl, but he wished to be the one whose ear she whispered in. He compared her and her companion: the same dark hair, thin faces, and large eyes—though where hers were soft and sad, his darted about with the nervous energy of a cornered fox. William relaxed against the window. Of course, a young woman of gentle breeding would be traveling in the company of her brother.

A porter announced the boat for France, and the travelers shuffled to their feet. The young woman and her relative stayed seated as the others exited. The young man moved his hand against the window while she tugged urgently at his sleeve, pulling him after the crowd.

William glanced over to see what the young man had done to the window. The glass bore an etched message: "And Haman was hanged upon the gallows he prepared for Mordecai." It was from the Biblical story of Queen Esther, who saved her people from Haman's scheming, but why was it significant?

William strolled behind the pair, earning a wary look from the young lady.

The party gathered at the dock, waiting for the captain to invite them onboard. Ropes creaked with the waves, and the wind whipped the scent of salt around the anchored boats.

Running footsteps approached behind them. William turned to be swarmed by soldiers with swords and muskets. Everyone in the traveling party drew closer together, and William found himself arm-to-arm with the young lady with the luminous eyes.

"This party is under arrest for treason," one of the soldiers declared.

The young lady trembled slightly against William's arm.

William stepped forward, partially blocking her from the soldiers' view. "Who accuses us?"

"You'll answer to Colonel Hammond and no one else," the soldier said and marched them all back into the town.

William trotted along with the frightened flock of passengers herded into the town square, carried by a dreamlike sense of detachment. This morning he'd met the king, and now he was going to stand before his cousin accused of treason. Had something happened at Carisbrooke Castle? A bolt of excitement shot through William at the thought of the king escaping. But if Robert thought he had something to do with it, William faced prison or even execution. He smiled wryly at the irony of his father sending him abroad for his safety.

The look on his cousin's face doused the last flickers of William's amusement. Robert gave William a searching look and addressed the party of travelers.

"I know there are Royalist plotters among this party. I will ferret them out, or all of you will be placed under arrest."

Murmurs rolled through the other travelers, and most looked frightened or confused. All except the pretty lady and her brother, who both stood very still and pale. A cold chill crept up William's neck at the thought that his presence might have endangered them, and the other travelers as well.

"Cousin Robert, why do you suspect us of conspiracy?" he asked. "Most of us never met before this day."

"We found the etchings your party left on the windows of the inn."

William tensed but stopped himself from glancing at the young woman and her brother.

The brother shifted, but the pretty girl put her hand on his arm and stepped forward.

"I wrote those words," she said in a clear, determined voice.

"You?" Robert scoffed.

"I did. You doubt me? I am Dorothy Osborne, the daughter of Sir Peter Osborne, lately His Majesty's servant under siege at Guernsey."

"Osborne," Robert said. "Then Richard Osborne..."

"Aye, Richard Osborne, Gentleman Usher to His Majesty, is my cousin. He's rotting in prison for nothing more than trying to free our rightful king." She lowered her voice. "My family has given everything for His Majesty's cause, even the life of my elder brother. Being this close to the king, I thought of the tale of Esther, a woman who saved her people from usurpers, and etched the ending to that story into the glass: 'And Haman was hanged upon the gallows he prepared for Mordecai.'"

She carefully pronounced the name "Haman" so it sounded like "Hammond," and her soulful eyes flashed with defiance. Robert placed a hand on his rapier.

William glanced between them. Would Robert execute a woman? Likely he would only imprison her, but women had proven to be capable spies during the war, so he might not be lenient. Dorothy's brother watched with stupefied horror.

In the silence, William laughed. It was a false laugh, a little too high pitched, but it did not matter. It broke the deadly tension between Dorothy and Robert and drew his cousin's gaze to him.

"You find this threat to our family amusing?" Robert asked.

Dorothy gave William a disgusted glance and edged away from him.

William pretended not to care. "'Tis a clever play on words, is it not?"

"Clever!" Robert's face reddened.

"Come now, Cousin, do you really expect this young lady to build a gallows and haul you up on it—stout fellow that you are?"

A couple of the soldiers smirked.

William stepped closer and whispered to Robert. "Angry words are like a kettle giving off steam—the pressure is reduced, and no harm is done. Is the king secure?"

Robert hesitated, then nodded.

"We don't want the Hammonds to be known as men who persecute women or turn our swords on our enemies when they have already fallen."

Robert held William's gaze, and William did his best to keep his expression light, though he feared his cousin would hear his thundering pulse.

Robert sighed and studied Dorothy. "Who is your escort here?"

"My brother. He warned me to stop, but I refused to listen."

She lied calmly, reversing her actions with her brother's. William should not have admired it, but he had seen so little courage and self-sacrifice since Uncle Henry went to prison.

Robert considered her defiant expression. "You would do well to heed your guardian's advice in the future. Women are too often stepping out of their places in the late disturbances, and it only leads to trouble and foolishness like this." He scanned the men of the party. "Which is this brother of yours?"

The young man stepped forward, his face pale. "I am, Sir. Robin Osborne."

"You are young to have charge over a headstrong girl. Keep better control over your sister in the future."

"Aye, Sir," Robin replied.

"Go, leave this island and do not return."

The party relaxed visibly and made their way back down the street. The soldiers followed, no doubt to be certain they boarded the boat. Most of the other passengers avoided the brother and sister as if they had the pox, but William stayed as close to the young lady as he dared. She was everything his father's plans would keep him from: assertive, destitute, Royalist. If he was to please his father and make something of his life, there was no room in it for a Dorothy Osborne. Yet she was someone who knew what it was to feel, to drink deeply from life. He only had the crossing from the Isle of Wight to France before he lost her forever, but he had to find a way to speak to her before she was gone.

Chapter Three

The English Channel

DOROTHY WATCHED THE ISLE OF Wight fade to a smudge on the horizon and then vanish. An endless parade of waves rolled toward the boat, pitching the deck high then slamming it down in a dizzying fall. A cold, salty spray misted over Dorothy, and she clutched the rail.

"Another opportunity to serve family and country gone," she whispered to Robin.

"I warned you there would be nothing we could do."

"But Parliament has no authority to imprison their king. *Our* king. Might does not make right." Dorothy leaned heavily on the rail. "Or it should not."

The sea shushed around the boat, whispering: *Hush, hush. It doesn't matter. Nothing you do matters. Rest, sleep, don't bother opening your eyes.*

Robin's rasping cough jerked her awake. Poor Brother! He sat hunched under his cloak. The sea breeze touched Dorothy lightly, but Robin seemed buffeted by a crueler wind. His sapling-thin frame had gained a little weight since returning from Guernsey with their father, but there was still a hollowness about him, and his breath rattled in his chest. If she and Aunt Gargrave had been

29

able to get the supplies to Castle Cornet, would it have made a difference?

"You should be out of this cold air, Robin. Let's move to the cabin." Dorothy put a hand on his arm, but he shrugged her off.

"Stop mothering me!"

Dorothy caught her breath and pulled her cloak tighter.

Robin stared at her with wide eyes. "I did not mean that. Truly, Sister." He buried his face in his hands. "I cannot bear to be confined. Please, don't ask me to go in."

Dorothy nodded and swallowed the hard knot in her throat. She and Robin had always been inseparable as children, the two youngest in the family, but the war had taken him somewhere that she could not follow.

Robin shuffled over to sit with a group of young men playing cards on a wooden crate. As though the Osbornes had anything left to gamble.

Dorothy navigated the rolling deck to sit by Robin, but someone stood between them—the dark-haired young relative of Colonel Hammond. Why was he following them? It must be some new Parliamentarian trick—trying to get in their good graces and spy on their family.

She skirted around the spy and found a bench where she could sit within sight of her brother. A piece of lace had snagged on the weather-roughened wood. She picked it loose and wound it into a tight ball. It could be useful as a bookmark or lining for a purse or doll's dress. She stuffed it in the pocket in her skirts. With an uneasy glance at Robin bent over the gaming table, she opened her book and prepared to forget her worries for an hour's time.

Colonel Hammond's young relative strolled over. He kept his distance, but he was not stealthy—the worst spy Dorothy had ever seen. His dress imitated the cavalier style, but he was no Royalist: his doublet and breeches were too new. He wasn't a Roundhead either, dressed as he was in bright reds and golds. That only left one other category, as far as Dorothy was concerned: opportunist. Well, he would find no opportunities with her.

She tried to focus on the French passages of her romance as the young man's footsteps approached. He loomed silently over her, his shadow blocking her light. She snuck a glance at her brother's back. What a dreadful chaperone! Whatever game this stranger was playing, she would not join in.

"You enjoy romances," he said.

Dorothy lifted an eyebrow but did not look up from her book. "As you see. And I dislike being interrupted when I read."

He perched on a crate next to her. "Of course. How obnoxious it must be to try to lose yourself in some tale of great deeds and heroes and have some idiot prattling on as if he, a mere mortal, could hold any interest compared to the heroes of those stories."

She glared at him, and he flashed a grin. The corner of her mouth twitched, but she dropped her attention back to the pages. He was handsome, with his long, black curls and sea-gray eyes, but she could hold her own against the advances of a pretty fop.

"Indeed," she said. "But I wonder if the prattler realizes that he is one. For certainly, if he were wise, he would know when to hold his tongue."

"In the face of wit, beauty, and courage combined in one woman, all men become either prattling idiots or else dumb-struck ones. And now you know which sort of man I am." He stood and bowed. "William Temple, at your service."

Flustered by the compliments, Dorothy snapped her book shut and rose to leave. "You are a flatterer, Master Temple."

"Don't go!" He rose along with her, all joking gone from his expression.

She clutched the book to her chest. "What do you want from me?"

"Only to speak with you."

"So you can report back to Colonel Hammond?"

He looked sincerely stung by the accusation. She had not thought him a good enough spy to be able to act.

"Truly, I have nothing to do with my cousin and his politics, Mistress Osborne." He reached out imploringly.

Dorothy backed against the rail. "You have nothing to do with politics at all, I wager. You care for nothing but your amusements and your fine clothes."

"It is a well-cut doublet, is it not?" He brushed imaginary dust from the velvet and held out his sleeve. "And have you ever seen such pretty lace?"

Dorothy stared, uncertain if she should be horrified or amused by his vapid response.

The laughter in his gray eyes faded. "Aye, I'm ridiculous. Especially compared to your courage and passion. If only I knew how to be the kind of hero in the books that so captivate your attention."

"Heroes exist only in stories, Master Temple." She caressed the leather cover of her novel. This stranger claimed she had courage, but what was bravery when it accomplished nothing? Only foolishness. "I begin to fear all the noble virtues and achievements are confined to fiction."

She expected a retort to her sharp words, but he turned to watch the waves roll away from the boat. After a moment, he spoke in a careless tone that did not match his troubled expression. "I think I don't care for romance novels."

"Have you read many?"

"One or two, translated from the French."

She wrinkled her nose. "No one translates them well. How can you know you don't like them when you've read so little, and none of them good samples?"

"Is there one you would recommend to me?"

"How is your French?"

"I have not studied as I ought to, but it is passable."

"Then I would tell you to look for the volumes of Seigneur de la Calprenède's *Cassandre*."

"I will." He straightened. "In fact, I will make you a bargain. I will apply myself to a fair-minded study of romances, overlooking the poor examples I have seen thus far, if you will grant the same courtesy to my sex."

Dorothy regarded him carefully. His tone was still light, but his gaze pled with her. "Why do you care?"

He gave her a crooked smile. "I hope to find that you are mistaken."

"You mean, you hope *I* find that I am mistaken?"

"Nay, I hope that we both may discover that men are not always as bad as the extremes of war make them seem. That there is something of goodness left in men. Left in myself."

She almost dismissed it as another ploy, but he met her critical stare with an earnest gaze. The distance between them dissolved, and the creaking of the boat faded. She caught her reflection in his gray eyes. Perhaps the war had reached him as well.

"Very well, Sir," she said, her voice strangely breathy. "I accept your bargain."

"You will loan me one of your romances, and you will give us mortal men a chance to prove ourselves?"

"I will."

"I'm glad. And I hope I may come to know you better in France."

He stepped closer. Too close. His kinsman was jailer to the king, whom her family had broken themselves for. She turned away to point at the lonely little island peering over the waves.

"Look, we're already passing Herm!" Soon she would be in France again with her family and fellow refugees.

He looked at her in surprise. "You know it? Have you traveled this way often?"

"On occasion."

"You must be even braver than I thought. Are you not afraid of pirates?"

"We have outrun them before." She kept the memories of that harrowing day out of reach and enjoyed William's admiration.

He shifted so they stood side by side staring out over the water. "Herm looks lonely."

"That is not always a bad thing."

"'Tis peaceful, I suppose."

"And free," Dorothy said, surprising herself.

"Is that what you want?" He glanced at her. "Freedom?"

"I want my family to be safe."

"But what do you want for yourself?"

The wild sea wind whistled around them, beckoning. Dorothy turned her back to it. "Only to know I have done what's right."

"Hmm." William leaned against the rail. "If you could live on that island, what do you imagine it would be like?"

Dorothy let her gaze wander over the lonely stretches of sea grass. She could not afford to forget the realities of her family's situation, yet for a moment her fancy slipped its reins.

"I would have my own little cottage, with some hens for company and a great hound to ward off strangers. In the morning I would garden and in the evening I would sit in the sun and read." She paused, itching to pick up a pen and write out the bucolic scene as part of some heart-rending romance. But even alone on an island, some things were too far-fetched. "And I would dress like a milk-maid—no tight stays, hooped skirts, or lace that must stay clean."

She stopped, certain William must be laughing at her. He was smiling a little, but his eyes were focused in a dreamy daze on the island. She blushed to think of him sharing in her daydream, walking somehow in the corridors of her imagination.

"And what about you?" Dorothy asked softly.

"I think if I were dressed as a milkmaid, I would look much less pretty than you."

She pulled back with a frown, and he hurried on. "There's my problem. I'm not sure how to answer seriously because I don't know what I would hope for from an island paradise." He rested his hand on his rapier hilt. "But I would want it to be something..something that mattered. Something that would make my father proud."

"You think he is not proud of you?"

"I lack his ambition. I lack the resolve to do what it takes to succeed. You may have guessed my father is for Parliament."

The last fragile threads of the daydream snapped. "You will have to join their camp as well."

"Must I?" His voice was pleading. "'Twould be simpler if I did, but I cannot seem to commit to either side. I sometimes wonder if the king did betray our country by trying to rule without Parliament's input, but then I question if Parliament really has the right to raise an army against the king and anyone who speaks in opposition to them." He sank against the railing. "My father thinks I am a ne'er-do-well, not serious about anything, and I begin to fear he is right."

Dorothy studied the lines of his handsome face. She might have labeled him a shiftless rogue an hour earlier, but now she glimpsed more beneath his flattery and foppish dress. Something fierce and intriguing. "I think he is wrong. I think your problem is that you are too serious."

"You are the first to ever accuse me of that." He chuckled.

"But if you were not serious, you would not mind taking up a cause you did not believe in."

"I hope you are right." He turned but did not step any closer. "And I hope I may see you again, when we are in France? Otherwise, I'm afraid I will believe this boat ride was merely a dream."

Dorothy gripped the boat's rail, the rough wood biting into her palm. Gannets wheeled overhead, their wings black-tipped flashes of white as the birds plunged to the sea and soared up again. But when they returned to land, they would crowd into their rocky nesting grounds without even enough space to stretch their wings. Freedom was for the sea. She shook her head.

"At least, I will need to return your book." William held out his hand for the volume.

Dorothy held the book closer. There was no one she could trust—only her family. But there could be no harm in loaning a book. Slowly, almost against her will, she placed it in William's hand. Her fingers brushed his, sending tingles racing to her chest. Her arms felt empty after carrying the book so long, but also pleasantly free.

"Then we will meet again in Saint-Malo," she said.

Chapter Four

THE SEA OFTEN BROUGHT STORMS to Saint-Malo, but the sun smiled on Dorothy and William as they strolled the beach with Robin as chaperone. The bright blue waters had retreated for low tide, leaving a damp, sandy path like a bridge for them to cross to the rocky little islands in the harbor. Dorothy leaned on William's arm to keep the soft sand from swallowing her boots. The contact filled her with fluttering warmth.

Saint-Malo was the site of the Osborne's exile and humiliation—a foreign prison—yet the last two months, with William there, Dorothy had not noticed the bars of her cage. As long as she had him with her to climb the stone walls of the city and look out over the forest of masts in the port below or stroll through the peaceful green farms of the countryside, she was as free as the dolphins who glided and leapt through the bay.

She paused to rescue something glinting by her boot: a button. She brushed off the clinging sand, revealing fine enamel work in red and blue. It must have come from the doublet of some nobleman or officer. Royalist or Parliamentarian? Regardless, the button was worth a shilling or two and would help buy bread for her family. She slipped it into her drawstring pouch, hesitating to meet William's eyes.

"My lady?" he offered his arm again.

His expression carried no judgment or disgust for her scrounging: only a hint of sorrow. Even the silliest notion that sprang from Dorothy's thoughts to her lips found a safe harbor in William's confidence. She smiled shyly at him, and his face lit with a grin.

Dorothy took his arm but held his steps back as she searched for her brother. He had fallen behind again.

"Robin, have we tired you out?" she called. He had acted as chaperone many times as she and William explored the city, trudging behind like a thin shadow.

He gave her a wan smile when he caught up. "I enjoy the exercise."

William gently urged Dorothy forward. A pair of roguish men swaggered past, and Dorothy leaned into William's protection. He smiled down at her.

"Pirates, I'll wager." His gray eyes lit with mischief. "Friends from your seafaring adventures?"

"Naturally." She chuckled. "I'm obviously not choosy in my acquaintances, if I can associate with a Parliamentarian."

"You've been associating with a Parliamentarian?" William put a hand on his rapier. "Name the villain, and I'll call him out for a duel."

Dorothy laughed, scouring away some of her lingering worries. "I cannot allow that. You are too fierce, and his life is precious to me."

"He is your devoted servant, madam, and would gladly lay down his life in your defense."

Dorothy met his earnest gaze. "I only ask that he guard it carefully."

He caressed her hand and raised it to his lips. The warmth of his soft kiss sent tingles up her arm that lingered as they strolled on.

They reached a wide tidal pool and peered in to see starfish and cone-shelled limpets clinging to the rocks. A silvery bass darted about, seeking an escape from his prison.

"Poor thing," Dorothy said, trailing her fingers in the cold water, "caught up in something he does not understand. One moment he was free, and the next his whole world was gone."

"The tides will change again," William said gently.

"True." Dorothy dried her fingers on her wool skirt and glanced over the sand to where the sea waited to surge back. "But when they do, we will not be able to stand here together, will we?"

"By then, I hope we will be somewhere else. Somewhere safe." He squeezed her hand, taking away the chill in her fingers. "For now, shall we enjoy this walk?"

Dorothy nodded.

They reached the island and climbed the rocky rise while Robin stayed below, his cough rasping over the cry of gulls. The salty wind buffeted them, but Dorothy squinted and tried to imagine the shores of England across the channel, green and inviting. William guided Dorothy off the summit, out of the wind.

"I finished the next volume of *Cassandre*," William said.

"And you enjoyed it?"

"More than I expected. I'm left to lament over my poor French, though. I understood the main threads of the story, but some of the word play was lost on me."

"That's why I dislike the translations. A lack of skill in French is easily remedied, though, especially for a young man with the opportunity to travel abroad."

"True. And no knuckle-rapping teacher ever inspired me to learn the language as your passion for literature has."

How bold he made her sound! A doctor had warned Dorothy's mother that reading too much could addle the female senses, yet William admired her for it. He brushed back a loose strand of her hair, distracting her from her embarrassment.

"And what of your end of the bargain?" he asked softly. "Have you found any hope for us poor males?"

"I have always thought my father heroic. He gave everything he had for the king. He would have given his life had His Majesty allowed it." She touched her thin pouch with its scrounged buttons and coins. "But what good has it done him? Until His Majesty regains his throne, we are trapped here in exile."

William dug at the sand with the toe of his boot. He uncovered a broken spiral shell and a brass buckle. Wiping them clean, he handed them to Dorothy for her little collection. Free from the grasp of sea and sand, the inside of the shell shimmered with a pearly brilliance.

"The problem, then, may not be a lack of heroes, but the treatment they receive at the hands of the world," William said.

"Perhaps." Still holding her treasures, she let William guide her along the shore of the island, where the waves licked at the sand.

"My father changes course with every shift in the wind, swearing allegiance to the king then turning against him for Parliament. Now he's rewarded with a seat in the House of Commons for his inconsistency." William squinted at the sun flashing off the water. "Meanwhile, my uncle Hammond, the man who raised me and showed me what Christian love and devotion should be, is driven from his parish and in hiding for staying true to his duty."

"It seems a man's conscience is a troublesome thing," Dorothy said quietly.

"Would you have him give it up?"

"Not at all! But Fortune is cruel. They say she favors the brave, but it often seems she truly favors the unprincipled. The happiness of this world is for those who live by its rules, and God will reward his own in the next."

"I hope that is not entirely true. Surely there are heroes in this world. Those who persists in the face of opposition? Even against Fortune herself?"

"Only in the tragedies," Dorothy said.

William opened his mouth to protest but closed it again and frowned. "I believe the tide is turning. We'd best hurry back."

They caught up with Robin and made their way across the narrow sand bridge, the roar of the sea closing in on them. By the time they reached the French shore, the water lapped at Dorothy's boots, and the sea had already washed away their footprints.

Robin escorted Dorothy home in a silence born of long companionship. Yet Dorothy felt the contrast—her own quick steps against his faltering ones, her cheeks burnished bright by the salty wind, while his bore red fever spots.

He paused at the door.

"You must be exhausted," she said, hesitating to release his arm. "Are you not coming inside?"

"I cannot bear it. I must feel the sunshine while it lasts." He closed his eyes and tilted his face so the light shone past the brim of his hat.

She reached for him but pulled her hand back without touching his threadbare doublet. Her brother bore wounds she could not heal, burdens she could not lighten. She pushed open the door. The little house her family rented was dim, and it took her eyes a few moments to adjust. The stale odor of old smoke and ill bodies hit her as she stepped into the parlor.

Her father, Sir Peter, huddled behind a screen that shielded his eyes from the faint glow of the fireplace. Her mother, Lady Dorothy Osborne, would be in bed, too weak to come down the narrow stairs.

Sir Peter blinked slowly and looked up to Dorothy. The smoky glow of the embers brightened his wrinkled face. Dorothy placed her treasures from the beach into a tin cup on the mantle and adjusted his blanket. His hand rested on the arm of the chair, his fingers clutching a worn letter—the one signed by the king, releasing him from his duties at Castle Cornet.

"Are you comfortable, Father? Do you need to be closer to the fire?"

He patted her face. "There's my girl. You smell like the sea."

"I've been out walking."

"A young, healthy girl should not be locked in this gloom all day."

"We can open the curtains."

Dorothy moved to the window, but a figure stepped from shadowy staircase leading to the bedrooms. She gasped, then laughed off her surprise.

"Oh, Harry. 'Tis only you."

"The light irritates Father's eyes." Her brother moved over to the fireplace and placed a heavy hand on their father's shoulder. Sir Peter nodded, and his tongue lolled over his lips a few times before he settled down to stare into the dimness again.

"Of course," Dorothy said.

"You've had a letter, my sister." Harry produced a folded parchment and smiled. "Guess who it is from."

"Lady Diana? Is her family escaped from England?"

Dorothy reached for the letter, but Harry kept it just out of reach.

"No word from your pretty friend yet. This letter is from London."

"Aunt Gargrave, then?" She dropped her voice. "Uncle Danvers?"

Her mother's brother had been a great friend to them in their distress, but her father did not like to hear the name of their Parliamentarian relations.

"Not unless one of them has taken to writing you love poems."

"Oh!" Dorothy folded her arms. "That coxcomb Sir Thomas." Her cousin had been persistent in his interest, though she'd heard little from him since her family's fall from grace.

"Worse!" Harry handed her the letter. "'Tis from Henry Cromwell."

Dorothy blushed and almost dropped the paper. Henry Cromwell, son of Lord General Oliver Cromwell, had befriended her when she found refuge with Uncle Danvers in London. She had not expected his ongoing correspondence.

"Cromwell!" her father rasped from his chair and struggled to rise. "Not in my house! Never speak the name of that traitor in my house!"

"Shhh." Dorothy set the letter aside and helped her father sit again. "Of course not."

"You would not want your daughter courted by such a powerful man?" Harry asked.

Dorothy shot him a warning look, but too late. Her father shook his bony hand, further crumpling his worn letter from the king. "No Parliamentarian will ever have my daughter! Not for all the gold and power in the world! Traitors! Traitors!"

Dorothy flinched as the reality of his words crashed through dreams she had not acknowledged even to herself of a life with William. Her father would never let her marry a man whose father sat in Parliament and whose cousin kept the king's prison.

"And yet Brother John married a Danvers." Harry spat in the fireplace. "Your own heir allied himself with a Parliamentarian."

"You have no brother called John! I do not wish to hear the name of traitors in this house!" White spittle flecked their father's lips. "Now, Charles was an Osborne! He died for his king! Oh, Charles, my son, my son." He covered his face. The dim light of the fire highlighted the blue veins in his skeletal hands. Tears glistened on his cheeks when he looked up and whispered, "Nay, Harry, you are my eldest." He stretched trembling fingers to Dorothy. "And my daughter will never betray me."

"Father, you have nothing to fear," Dorothy whispered, soothing back his thin, white hair. "I'm not going anywhere. We will all return to Chicksands together someday, when this war is over."

Her father leaned back heavily in his chair. Gloom settled over the little parlor. Dorothy squeezed her eyes shut and for a moment imagined she was walking again with William in the sunlight.

Back in his chambers, William sprawled on his bed with the next volume of **Cassandre**. He still felt Dorothy's light touches on his arm, and her honeysuckle scent lingered on his clothes as though she were in the room. Their strolls could never be long enough. He wanted to feel more of her soft warmth. He longed to sneak a taste of her strawberry-colored lips. She was better than the finest wine or a perfect summer day in a country garden. If only he were a poet, he might find the words for his delicious intoxication.

He grinned stupidly at the wooden ceiling beams before he remembered the book in his hand: his solace when they were apart. Perhaps that was because a certain pair of sad, brilliant eyes had scanned these same lines and seemed to stare back at him from the imagined face of every heroine.

A letter sat on the washstand beside his bed. Another message from Dorothy already? He broke the red wax seal without paying attention to the crest. His father's handwriting blared from the page.

> *It comes to my attention that you are still in Saint-Malo, wasting your time on an undesirable connection. I expect you to remember the duty you owe this family and your responsibilities as my oldest son. You must put any ridiculous notions out of your head and continue at once to Paris.*

William read it several times. The message could not be real. **Wasting time. Undesirable.** He ripped the letter into shreds and tossed it in the fireplace, stabbing it with the poker until the pieces were ash, but he could not burn away the words he had read.

How had his father known? William had been discreet in his attentions to Dorothy and had no acquaintances in Saint-Malo. Someone had betrayed him. But who was his enemy? A fellow suitor?

He could ignore the letter, fling defiance in the face of his father and his duties. Dorothy would not approve, though, and he could not—would not—hide the truth from her. He had to speak to her.

He grabbed his hat and went out. The sea had blown in another storm, and William splashed through the puddles gathering on the cobbled streets. When he neared the Osborne's lodgings, he was not surprised to see Robin outside, huddled under the overhang of the upper story. William's steps faltered. Could Robin be the one who had turned on him, weary of playing chaperone? The young man glanced up.

"Good morrow, Robin," William said cautiously.

Robin nodded, but a wet cough interrupted his greeting. His covered his mouth with a handkerchief, and spots of blood bloomed on the white linen. Robin staggered a little, and William caught his elbow.

"You need a physician," William said.

"Too late for that," Robin mumbled. "We are ghosts, you know. The Osbornes died at Castle Cornet."

"Don't think that way." William turned to take some of the battering of the rain driving against Robin's pale face.

"'Tis too late for all of us. Except perhaps Dorothy." Robin met his eyes. "Do what you can for her, Master Temple."

"Of course. What I can." What would that be, with him banished to Paris? "Can I see her?"

"I'll bring her to you. My father is feeling especially vehement against Parliamentarians today. Wait for us at the Sign of the Hart down the street."

William nodded and hurried away to reserve a parlor for them at the inn. Then he sat plucking loose straws from the rush mat and slowly twisting them into knots.

A rap sounded at the door. William was surprised to see Dorothy enter the room alone. He tossed a straw into the fire and stepped forward, stopping just short of taking her hands, though he longed to feel the touch of her fingers again.

"I have bad news," he said.

"Oh." Dorothy went rigid, and the deep sadness returned to her eyes.

William could not do it. He could not hurt her. Could not leave her. He would ignore his father and stay forever in Saint-Malo by her side if she asked him to. But he valued her too highly to deceive her.

"My father has requested that I continue my journey to Paris. He wants me to further my education."

"He has heard about me and my unacceptable situation." Her voice was matter-of-fact, her eyes downcast.

"He does not know you, Mistress Osborne. If he did, he would understand."

"He is only guarding your interests," she said. "We both have duties to our families, and you have a Grand Tour to complete. You are learning nothing in Saint-Malo."

"You are wrong. I have learned more here than I ever did at Cambridge. I have learned about goodness and sacrifice. I have learned that there are things in the world worth being inspired about."

Dorothy squeezed her eyes shut and shook her head. He stepped closer. Dorothy's chin quivered. William's own voice trembled with grief and frustration.

"You think me a fool, but I have never been so serious."

"I think you are young and unschooled."

"I am twenty, madam, and I have been to Cambridge. Certainly, I am your senior."

She smiled sadly. "I am older than you by almost twelve months, and I have lived lifetimes in the last few years."

"Then be my teacher, my muse." William fell to his knees. "I will be your disciple."

"Make me no promises," she whispered.

"I want to promise you everything." He took her hand.

"And yet, your father serves Parliament, and mine the king. Even if your father would relent, mine would not. There can be no happy outcome to such a situation." She gently pulled her hand away, and her voice caught on a sob. "I am glad to have been your friend, but you have more to do in the world than scrounge the beach for stray buttons. You must go."

William stood. There was something to what Dorothy said. He had to do something more with himself to truly help Dorothy—to bring her home to him someday. "You banish me from your presence, but I will not be exorcised entirely. If I write, you will respond?"

"The Osbornes are not fit company for a young man of significance."

"Yet, if you don't write back to me, whom will I have to talk to about the romances I read? I'm determined to perfect my French, and I'm afraid my peers will laugh at me if I try to discuss the latest affairs of Cassandre or Britomart with them." He placed a hand over his heart. "Not that I would be ashamed, but I would miss the intelligent conversation."

A flicker of a smile reached Dorothy's eyes. He would do anything to see that light there always.

"I suppose," she said, "if you write to ask my opinion on literature, I could not refuse to respond."

"Then I will be able to go, knowing I will have your letters to carry me on, that I will not be forgotten."

"Never, Sir," Dorothy said.

William caught the wistfulness in her voice and clung to it, the only hope he had to guide him forward.

1649

SIX MONTHS LATER

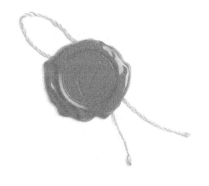

Chapter Five

THE GRAY OF JANUARY HUNG over Saint-Malo and drizzled from the clouds, turning the streets to filthy rivers and confining Dorothy to the parlor. She prodded at the gristly piece of mutton stewing over the fire. It might never be tender enough to eat, but at least it would flavor the watery lentils and barley. When the rain stopped, she and Robin would have to scour the gutters for anything they could sell. The hunger cramping their stomachs left little room for pride.

Smoke from the fireplace stung her eyes. Coal was too costly, but she'd scrounged some driftwood to burn. At least the smell was more pleasant: smoky and sweet instead of oily. She had also collected an armful of the long, grassy leaves of rushes to dry, peel, and dip in melted fat saved from the mutton. The resulting rushlights would serve in place of candles through the long winter evenings.

She straightened and shook the newest treasures from her tin cup onto the mantel. A couple of pewter buttons and a chipped glass bead. She placed them in order from largest to smallest then with the two gray buttons framing the green of the glass. No matter how she arranged them, they were not worth enough. The soft gray of the buttons reminded her of William's eyes. The hollow ache in her stomach spread to her chest, and she swept the baubles into the tin cup.

The rattle roused her father. "Dorothy?"

"I'm here, Father." She took his hand, and he relaxed back into his fitful dozing.

The door slammed open, and Sir Peter cried out in alarm. Harry hurried in, his wide-brimmed hat dripping water. Robin sulked behind him. The dull orange glow of the fireplace framed Harry as he wrinkled his nose at the stew and turned to face his father and Dorothy.

"I have found a position for Robin, working as a clerk in the household of a wealthy French merchant," Harry said. "It pays little but provides room and board for him."

Sir Peter nodded, but Dorothy looked from one brother to the next. "A position for Robin? But, he's not well. Surely, he should not—"

"'Tis already settled," Harry said.

"It will help the family," Robin added. Dark circles hung under his eyes. Dorothy relented. At least he would have solid meals and a warm bed.

Robin gestured Dorothy into a huddle with him and Harry.

"There's more news," Robin whispered.

"Parliament is debating whether to convict King Charles of treason," Harry said a little too loudly.

"Treason?" Dorothy whispered and glanced over to the fireplace, but her father had not heard. "They cannot mean it!"

"They'll use it as an excuse to keep him under house arrest permanently and force him to bow to their will," Harry said. "Once they've settled everything, we'll finally be able to reclaim our home."

"Return to Chicksands?" Dorothy asked. Memories of sleeping in her own chambers or reading in the gardens under the hawthorn tree seemed like the tattered fragments of a dream.

"Aye," Harry said, but Robin looked skeptical.

Harry moved to the fire, and Robin sat next to Dorothy on the stairs, shoulder to shoulder, as they had when they were children studying French or arithmetic.

"You doubt Harry's optimism?" Dorothy asked in a hushed tone. Harry was eight years her senior, and she could not help feeling a little in awe of his age and experience, but Robin knew him better.

"Why would Parliament return Royalist lands when they control the king?" Robin asked. "They're selling off the estates they seized to fund their army."

Dorothy squeezed her eyes shut, trying to block the image of some stranger digging up her gardens and sitting by her hearth.

"But it is not all bad news for you today." He passed Dorothy a letter.

The sight of William's familiar handwriting drove away her terrible visions of Chicksands in Parliament's hands.

"Thank you, Robin," she whispered.

She hurried up the narrow stairs, tiptoed past the room where her mother slept, and climbed a ladder to the garret. An occasional ping of water dripped from the sloped ceiling into tin cups spread around the floor, but Dorothy settled by the dormer window, pulling her knees up under her skirts to warm her legs.

The dim light played over William's quick, slanting words and brought him into the room with her. She skimmed the introduction, anxious to escape into his stories of Paris.

I met a cousin of yours, Sir Thomas Osborne.

"I'm surprised you can tolerate his company," Dorothy whispered.

'Tis strange, how one greets a fellow countryman in a foreign country as a friend, when in your homeland you might have nothing to do with one another. Though this countryman has something else to recommend him: a well-loved surname.

She smiled and read on about the fine gardens he visited and all he had seen in Paris.

> *I stopped in a bookstore to purchase the next volume of Cassandre. I did not even blush when the other men stared. Are you not proud of how I have taken to romance? I also asked the shop owner, if I was to read the works of one Frenchman which it should be. He answered Montaigne, and so I bought one of his works as well.*

> *It is good that I did, for there is trouble in Paris, and I have spent a great deal of time confined to my chambers.*

Dorothy held the letter closer.

> *The Parlement of Paris and some of the nobles demand more limits on the power of Anne of Austria, the queen regent, and her advisor Cardinal Mazarin. With royal troops returned from the war in Spain, the queen regent seems unlikely to give in to their demands as she has in the past.*

> *From my window, I can see crowds gathered, shouting and slinging stones at the mounted guards. The royal guards slowly fall back under the assault. Soon, I fear the whole world will burn with revolution. My father sent me on the Grand Tour in part to protect me from the upheavals in England, but he has tossed me into the fire. At least I shall have plenty of time for reading.*

"Oh, William. Take care!"

Perhaps spending time with Montaigne will not be such a poor way to pass my days. My groom brings with my breakfast the news that the Queen Regent and Cardinal Mazarin have fled the city.

I also hear the army has purged the English Parliament of its more moderate members—my father included—and put King Charles on trial for treason. Can a king be a traitor? Have the French queen and cardinal betrayed their own people? I look out at the people starving behind the barricades, and I am not certain. I wish you were here so we could discuss it, but then I would fear for you, too. Royal troops are attempting to establish control, but the forces of the nobles and the Parlement of Paris are prepared for a siege. And so am I.

Dorothy wished she could reach through the letter and pull him to safety.

You and Montaigne are my only companions. When I worry over the fate of parliaments and kings, he tells me, "On the highest throne in the world, we still sit only on our own bottom."

Dorothy chuckled.

He also whispers wisdom to me. He says, "The greatest thing in the world is to know how to belong to oneself."

Dorothy stared out over the sluggish storm water draining through the streets. It was fine for a French philosopher to speak of belonging to himself, but what of the rest of them? Even if Montaigne meant all men to be independent, he couldn't mean women as well. Dorothy would always belong to her family—her desires bent to their needs. She slowly returned to William's words.

Do I belong to myself? I don't think so. I belong to my father and my duty. And yet a part of me belongs to a pair of pretty eyes I hope will honor these lines by reading them. I don't wish to be an unprincipled man, but is there a way for me to follow my own desires and still be true to the honor I owe my family?

"I don't know." Dorothy's words came out a whisper.

And what does that honor mean? My father swore allegiance first to the king and then to Parliament, and how has Parliament rewarded him? He voted for compromise with the king, so Colonel Pride barred him and all the other moderates from taking their rightful seats in the assembly. What will our nation come to, when the army persecutes those who seek peace?

Harry seemed so certain that Parliament and the King would come to an agreement, but if only revolutionaries were left in Parliament, the King's cause was grim.

I wish I could hear your opinions on these matters. But Montaigne whispers, "When I am attacked by gloomy thoughts, nothing helps me so much as running to my books." You have advised me to read Cassandre, and so I will, remaining ever, your faithful,

W. Temple.

Dorothy read the letter again and again, trying to draw more from each word—some reassurance that William remained safe and well after the letter left his hands. There was nothing she could do. Nothing but write back and pray for his safety.

As she searched through her carefully hoarded scraps of paper for one with some space to scrawl a letter on, an anguished cry echoed up from the parlor.

"Father?" Dorothy nearly tumbled down the stairs in her haste to reach him. Dimly, she knew her mother had roused herself and stumbled along behind.

She reached the parlor and found Harry supporting their father while Robin leaned heavily in the doorway, a letter clutched in his hand.

"What has happened?" Dorothy asked.

Robin met her gaze, his eyes dull. "The king. They have beheaded King Charles for treason."

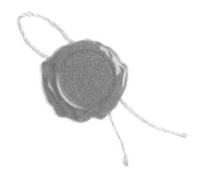

Chapter Six

SAINT-MALO, FRANCE

A KNOCK SOUNDED ON THE front door, and Dorothy flinched. The few visitors who came to the Osborne house in the month and a half since the king's execution rarely brought good news.

Lady Osborne rested her needlework on her lap, a faint tremor twitching her fingers. "Answer that, please, Dorothy. Maybe some-one has more work for us."

"Aye, Mother." Dorothy was happy enough to set her own needle aside. The little money they earned mending shirts kept them alive, though she still had to scrounge with Robin when his work could spare him.

She opened the door and gave a start. A ghost! How else could this pale apparition of her friend Lady Diana be standing in her doorway?

"Dorothy!" Lady Diana stumbled forward.

"My lady!" Dorothy embraced her friend—thin and cold, but substantial after all—and guided her inside. "How do you come to be here?"

"My father." Lady Diana's voice trembled. "He's been executed. We had to flee."

"Oh, my lady." Dorothy smoothed back her friend's coppery curls as hot tears soaked her shoulder. Lady Diana's father, Henry Rich, Earl of Holland, fell as another defender of King Charles.

When Lady Diana's sobs abated, Dorothy gently guided her friend upstairs to her chamber.

"Try to rest," Dorothy said. "There's not much comfort here, but there's safety."

"That's the best comfort," Lady Diana muttered, curling up on the straw-stuffed mattress.

Lady Diana kept to Dorothy's chamber the next day. Over watery porridge and stale bread, she poured out her story of fleeing in the night when her father was convicted of high treason for fighting against Parliament in the war.

"Treason! For choosing the cause of his king." Lady Diana's eyes flashed fury. "And when the army overcame him and he surrendered his sword, they promised to spare his life. Such are the promises of Parliament."

Dorothy shook her head in disgust. "What of the rest of your family?"

"We have all gone to ground or escaped. I expect to meet up with some of my brothers here in Saint-Malo. Then when things settle down, we must find our way back."

"You're returning to England?"

"Of course. The army's puppets in the Rump Parliament have abolished the monarchy, but young Charles Stuart, the Prince of Wales, still lives, so there is hope for our cause." Lady Diana wrinkled her forehead. "You are not planning to stay as exiles in Saint-Malo forever?"

"I... I don't know. We have nowhere to go."

"You have your Uncle Danvers. He has always been kind to your family."

"He signed the king's death warrant!"

"All the more reason that Parliament will listen when he asks for Chicksands to be returned to your family. He cannot wish to see his sister wasting away in poverty."

Dorothy sat back, her mind churning. Where did her duty lie? Uncle Danvers had sheltered her and her mother when Parliament seized Chicksands. But could he help them now, when Royalists faced the axe for treason? And even if he could, was it right to turn to such a man for help?

"What other options do you have?" Lady Diana asked quietly.

Dorothy pondered that question over the next several days as she mended worn clothes and scavenged the beach for driftwood in the biting sea wind. It should not have been her decision alone, but Harry was too proud to surrender, and Robin too defeated to fight. By the pale glow of a rushlight, she poured out her worries to William.

> *Sir,*
>
> *You honor me with long letters, and I repay you poorly with this one, which will be short. The troubles you face in Paris make my own seem small, since Saint-Malo is as peaceful as ever, though dull since you went away. Yet, I do not think we can stay here forever. I believe I have a duty to see to my parents' well-being when they are both ill, yet can I ask their enemy for aid, even if it is to protect their health? I cannot bear to see suffering, especially in those I love, and I fear it will lead me to compromise where I should remain stubborn.*
>
> *Yet rest assured that I will never compromise in being*
>
> > *Your faithful friend,*
> > *D. Osborne*

The next morning, Dorothy delivered the letter to the postmistress at the White Hart, praying that her message could make its way past troops and barricades.

"You have time for letter writing?" Harry asked when she returned. "I wonder if your time is misspent here. Perhaps we could hire you out as a gentlewoman's companion or a teacher of young girls."

"I don't know—"

"Don't worry yourself over it. I'll arrange everything."

Dorothy wandered upstairs in a daze.

"My dear, what has happened?" Lady Diana asked.

"Harry thinks I ought to work as a companion or tutor to girls. It would make me less of a burden, and I want to do my duty." She met her friend's eyes. "But to be forever a servant in someone else's home?"

"You could escape by marrying."

"Who would have me? I have nothing to offer." She conjured the image of William's stricken countenance the day his father sent him away. That path was closed to her. Instead, she thought of her mother's care-worn face and her father's broken-minded stare. "But if I leave, who would take care of Mother and Father?"

"Your uncle still might be able to help," Lady Diana said.

Dorothy nodded slowly. If they could return to Chicksands, all would be well for her family again. "I have to do what's best for them."

"What's best for whom?" Harry asked, stepping into the room. He bowed and gave Lady Diana his most winning grin, though she kept her eyes downcast.

Dorothy stood. "Lady Diana suggests that we appeal to Uncle Danvers for help in recovering Chicksands."

Harry frowned. "I had considered that, but I wanted to be sure his position was secure so we could be certain of success. Perhaps it *is* time we were returned to our rightful place. We have lived like beggars for too long."

"We will have to go begging to Uncle Danvers."

Harry dismissed the notion with a wave of his hand. "He is family. 'Tis the duty he owes us."

Dorothy cast a sidelong glance at Lady Diana. "Do you think he can protect Father?" She would not see Sir Peter brought to the executioner as Lord Holland had been.

"We can make Father behave himself. Keep his head down and his neck from the axe."

Lady Diana flinched and tightened her grip on the book in her lap.

"But what will such a compromise do to Father?"

Harry sat beside her on the bed. "He deserves better than this life—we all do. Father is a noble soldier, and I served with Prince Rupert himself in the war. With Chicksands restored, we can move our family out of this hovel and wait quietly until England comes to its senses and young Charles Stuart retakes his father's throne."

Dorothy glanced at Lady Diana. "I suppose you are both right."

"Mother will not have any objection, but you will need to break the news to Father," Harry said. "He'll take it best from you."

"Am I to use Father's affection to manipulate him?"

"'Tis for the best, my sister," Harry said.

"Very well. I will speak to him. Only, give me some time to think of what to say."

Harry left Dorothy and Lady Diana alone.

"I feel like a traitor," Dorothy whispered.

Lady Diana squeezed her hand. "We must make difficult choices in times of war."

Dorothy bowed her head. All of their suffering for the king, and now they were turning to his enemy for help. After all her talk with William of heroes, she felt like a villain. But villains had conviction. She would be something worse: just another opportunist. Yet if young Charles Stuart did return to England, he would need those loyal to the throne to greet him. Her family did no one any good hiding behind the walls of Saint-Malo. Her parents and Robin could recover their strength at Chicksands. She just had to ease the blow to her father.

After spending some time rehearsing, steeling herself to her father's anger and devastation, Dorothy descended the stairs. Sir Peter stared into the fire, clutching his tattered letter from the king. She nodded to Harry and knelt by her father's side.

"Father," Dorothy said gently.

He looked up, his eyes watery in the firelight.

"Father, I think it is time we returned home."

"To Castle Cornet? But the king has dismissed me." He held up the letter. "You see? He wrote to me himself."

"I know." She rested a gentle hand on his arm. "I don't think he meant for you to remain a refugee in France after your loyal service. 'Tis time to return to Chicksands."

Lady Osborne looked up from her mending, her gaze suddenly sharp.

"Chicksands?" Sir Peter asked. "'Tis in the hands of Parliament."

"I believe Uncle Danvers could use his influence to have it returned. You have been a loyal servant to your country and deserve to retire to the peace of your own estate."

"Danvers? The regicide?" There was no venom in his voice, just hollow curiosity.

"Aye, the regicide. He is still family, and he would not like to see his sister and her children starving and exiled for the rest of their lives."

Sir Peter did not answer but turned back to the fire and petted the frayed edges of his letter.

Lady Osborne straightened. "Dorothy, I will dictate the request to my brother, but you must write. My hands are too shaky."

Dorothy took up her quill and copied her mother's words, but in the scratch of the pen on paper, she could only hear *traitor, traitor, traitor.*

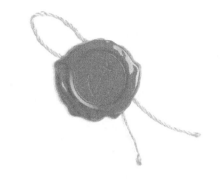

Chapter Seven

CHICKSANDS, ENGLAND

DOROTHY PEEKED OUT THE WINDOW of the coach Uncle Danvers had loaned her family, keeping the damask curtain half-closed to conceal the scenes of southeast England from her parents as much as possible. The slighted walls of castles and cities lay in heaps of rubble, and weary villagers shuffled past gaping holes where cannonballs had torn through their shops and homes. In the countryside, ancient homes with shattered windows and walls blackened by fire watched over battle-trampled fields with the empty stares of the dead.

The Osbornes skirted well around the Parliamentary stronghold of London to reach Bedfordshire. The closer they came, the tighter Dorothy clutched her little pouch of shells and stray buttons from Saint-Malo. Her mother, sitting across from her, squeezed her eyes shut, and her father continually flicked his tongue over his lips. Here were fields Dorothy remembered as plowed and green, now overgrown or churned to mud. Was there no refuge left in the world for them?

The red sandstone All Saints Church heralded the village of Campton, a familiar anchor in a landscape awash with destruction.

Stone and brick cottages with thatched roofs clung to the sides of the gentle hills like ships on a rolling sea.

The carriage turned north and clattered over the bridge crossing the River Flit. They climbed the wooded road leading to the Osborne's estate of Chicksands Priory. Dorothy watched through the treetops as the many brick chimneys appeared, followed by an intact roof, then the ancient priory walls.

Dorothy sank against her cushioned seat. The roof and walls appeared undamaged. Everything else they could manage. Yet, it looked wrong. No candles shone in the windows, no sheep grazed in the pastures, and the gardens were trampled to mud. It should have felt like home, but it exuded a lifelessness equal to the nearby ruins of the old priory hospital.

The coach rocked to a stop in front of the brick building. Its square façade stood solid and dependable as it had for five hundred years, sheltering Gilbertine nuns and canons until Henry VIII had driven them from his shores and seized their houses to sell off.

Harry opened the coach door and helped Dorothy down, then their mother and father. Robin dismounted slowly from his borrowed horse, struggling to keep his balance, and trailed behind them like a wraith. Lady Osborne clung to Sir Peter's arm. He tried to stand straight, but his back hunched as he surveyed his once proud estate. Dorothy took his other arm. If only she could do more to help him bear the weight of defeat.

"Well, we had best see what's left of the place." Sir Peter tried to smile, but his voice cracked.

Harry pushed the wooden door open, and it groaned on its hinges. A stale smell rushed over them like a foul yawn.

"I suppose Collins hasn't had time to get all set to right," Sir Peter said.

Lady Osborne pressed her lips together and stepped into the house over which she had once presided. Her footsteps echoed on the stone floor. Dorothy followed, catching a cobweb in her hair. She brushed it away with a shudder.

The great hall was empty of furniture, leaving the ribbed vaults of the ceiling to hover over an empty room. Dorothy paused by the window where her favorite bench had once stood angled just right to catch the morning sunlight for reading or stitching. Weak flames crackled in the hearth, but the rush-light torches were out, and a lingering animal smell hung over everything.

"What have those villains done?" Lady Osborne said.

"We cannot stay here," Robin said quietly.

Dorothy was afraid he might be right, but this was their home. They had tossed aside their principles and crawled back to Parliament to beg for it.

"Uncle Danvers spent a great deal of money to help us reclaim it," Dorothy whispered, making certain her father did not hear. "And where else could Father go?"

"It would be beneath our dignity to abandon it now," Harry said.

Robin shook his head.

"Collins!" Harry called.

"Coming!" The young manservant's voice echoed down the bare hallway.

Collins scurried into the doorway, bits of straw stuck to his brown doublet, and ashes smudging his bright, round face. He bowed. "Begging your pardons. I've been working nonstop." He straightened and looked around the room. "I was unable to finish before you returned."

"You'll need more help, no doubt," Lady Osborne said wearily.

He looked chagrined. "It was a bit worse than we expected, but I'll manage."

"Are all the rooms like this?" Sir Peter asked.

Collins hesitated and glanced at Harry, who nodded. "Aye, Sir. Some a bit worse. I've been working to make the bed chambers fit for living in, and the kitchen. I thought those were the main priority."

Lady Osborne nodded. "Are there any furnishings left? Or pots or pans for the kitchen?"

Collins cleared his throat. "I've arranged some straw pallets for the bedchambers until the beds can be replaced—"

"They stole our beds?" Lady Osborne asked.

"Chopped them up for firewood, by the looks of it, m'lady."

Lady Osborne's eyes narrowed, but Sir Peter nodded, his eyes distant. Probably thinking of tearing up the floorboards in Castle Cornet for warmth. Dorothy took hollow comfort from the thought that the Parliamentarians had suffered, too.

"I'll see to the kitchen," Dorothy offered. She could put off retiring to her chamber and finding what was once her refuge now decorated with nothing but some straw stuffed in a sack.

"Good girl," Sir Peter said.

Harry smiled crookedly. "'Tis a good thing you are such a good girl, and pretty as well. 'Twill take a husband with connections and a fortune to restore us to our proper place." Harry leaned closer and gestured at the empty room. "Perform your part well, or we will be trapped living like this."

Sir Peter and Lady Osborne took his comment in stride, but Dorothy's steps faltered as she headed for the kitchen. Harry—and Robin, if he recovered—would have to marry girls with large fortunes to help secure their futures, too, but her part was to find a husband who could help them keep up appearances and meet the right sorts of heiresses. Someone like Henry Cromwell would do, if her father could overcome his prejudice against Parliamentarians. But never William Temple. His father was a less successful traitor than Lord General Oliver Cromwell. How long did she have until she was sold off as a sacrificial lamb?

She stopped in the doorway of the kitchen. A lingering stench that suggested someone had used the fireplace as a latrine had replaced the scents of yeast and roasting meat. Collins had swept out what he could, though, and there was no evidence of rats or mice. A few pots with poorly mended handles sat on the block in the center of the kitchen. It was a start.

Dorothy's stomach rumbled. Her parents would be famished, and they could not afford to suffer more.

She pushed her way out the back door and stared at the ruins of their estate. The barns and coops stood empty, the doors removed and probably burned. The gardens were trodden under and turned to rot. Splintered stumps stood in the place of apple trees, the orchard's annual bounties sacrificed for a bit of winter's warmth—or just for spite.

A sound behind her made her jump. She turned to find Collins standing with his head down.

"You startled me," she said.

"I'm sorry, m'lady."

She took a deep breath. "'Tis no matter. You've faced a difficult task here."

"I've failed."

"Failed?" Dorothy glanced around at the destruction. "No one could have expected you to fix all of this. You've done well, Collins. Thank you."

He bowed his head.

"What is left to us?" Dorothy asked.

He hesitated and glanced over his shoulder.

"You don't need my brother's permission to speak to me. My mother is ill. Management of the household will fall to me. Tell me what I have to work with."

"Aye, m'lady. The house is bare of furnishings, as I said. I have only a little left to buy with."

"Start with beds for my parents and Robin, then for Harry and me. And we'll need some benches, at least, for the front room if guests come to visit." She bit her lip, thinking. "The benches are cheaper than beds, and mother will want someplace to sit. Get those before the beds for Harry and me."

Collins hesitated, then nodded.

"I see we have a few pots."

"Aye, m'lady. I found them scattered about the yard and cleaned and repaired them. I suppose the soldiers did not steal them because they were broken."

"How fortunate for us." Dorothy smiled wryly. "And what of the property?"

"As you see. And, Parliament did not return all of the land."

"Our land? Furniture and sheep I can understand, but how do they steal our land?"

"They gave it to their loyal followers. One neighbor, Colonel Samuel Luke, received a large portion."

"How much is left to us?" Dorothy asked, her voice small.

"About a tenth of the former estate."

Dorothy braced herself on the doorpost. Only one tenth of their property. They had entered the war fairly wealthy, the estate bringing in four thousand pounds a year. A tenth of that? Four hundred pounds a year? It was little to live on, and that assumed they could make the land profitable again.

"The tenants?" she asked, afraid of the answer.

"They are glad to have Sir Peter back. They long for stability. They have little to pay with, so I accepted rents in eggs and peas. I sold some, which is how I got the money I did."

"You did well," Dorothy said. "I am going to—to see what's left."

Collins bowed before returning inside.

Dorothy tiptoed through the sticky mud, surveying the ruins of her childhood home. The apple trees she had played under, the gravel paths she had run down to gather daisies for her mother, all were gone. The muddy fields were in no condition for planting. Her family had suffered in Saint-Malo, but those who stayed behind must have starved as well, letting the animal needs of the present devour any thought of the future.

A low whining drew her from under the heavy shroud of her thoughts. From among the ruined trunks of the orchard, a mud-encrusted hound gazed up at her. Its tail thumped dully against the ground, and ribs showed through its dirty coat.

"Poor thing!" Dorothy knelt by the dog, but it whimpered and backed away. She pulled her hands into her lap. "Did one of the soldiers leave you behind? I don't have much to eat myself, but I will try to bring you something. Chicksands can be your refuge now, too."

The barley porridge she and Collins scraped together for dinner was filling, but nothing more. Dorothy doubted the dog would be interested in it, but he licked the pewter plate clean and whined for more.

"I have nothing else to give," Dorothy said quietly.

That night, before the sunlight failed her, she sat to write to William that she had made it home.

> *Your father was wise to send you away. England is not what it once was. But my family is together, and therefore all is well.*

The words came out a little wobbly, as though her pen tripped over them, but she pressed on.

> *I could wish that you were here, but 'twould be selfish. I will be content instead to imagine you walk with me as you did at Saint-Malo and to know that, if rumor may be believed, Paris is quieter now and you are safe.*

And what good would it do if William were in England? Harry had made it clear: she was to be sold on the marriage market, probably before William made it home. She would only ever walk

71

with him again in her imagination. She signed the letter *Your humble, D. Osborne* and delivered it to Collins, who would be going to London and could put it in the hands of the post.

The next day she wandered the paths of the garden. There was so much to be done she could not pick a starting point, and so she did nothing.

Soft footfalls padded behind her. The lost dog. She held still and he approached, hesitantly nosing her hand. She slowly moved her fingers over his short coat and brushed away some of the mud, revealing the black-and-white spotted coat of a carriage dog.

"You're a noble fellow under all of this filth." The dog whimpered and licked her hand as she checked for injuries. "I shall call you Ulysses, because I'm sure you've had some adventures."

He cocked his head at her voice, so she rambled on.

"The only one who recognized Ulysses when he came home was his faithful dog. But his wife, Penelope, waited for him, too. While Ulysses was off fighting and feasting—and frankly being a rake at times—Penelope had to remain at home for twenty years and protect his throne. She tricked all of those who tried to force her to marry and lose her husband's kingdom, and she and Ulysses were reunited at last."

Dorothy rubbed behind the dog's ear, and he seemed to grin up at her.

"There's something to be said for Penelope, is there not? Women can sometimes follow their hearts, if they are clever enough."

Dorothy dusted off her hands and walked farther through the ruined orchard. Ulysses trotted along behind her. The skeletons of trees surrounded her, but the breeze brought the faint, mossy scent of water and life. She turned towards the little brook that crossed the property. A flash of shimmering green leaves ahead caught her eyes. She gathered her skirts and jogged as well as she could, encumbered by petticoats and stays. The dead, broken trees gave way to living comrades.

She stopped herself by throwing her arms around the trunk of one of the trees and laughed at the sight of rosettes of leaves shimmering with fat, white blossoms. Bees hummed around her, and the brook sang by. She lifted her face to the sun and said a silent prayer of gratitude.

"We'll bring Collins to see," Dorothy said. "'Twill take some pruning, but it looks like we'll have apples and plums. Oh, and apricots!"

Glossy, green unripe fruit adorned the apricot branches like tiny beads. Dorothy's mouth watered at the thought of biting into soft, sweet apricots, but in the meantime she had work to do.

Each morning, with Collins or without him, she came out to cut away dead branches and make sure the channels were clear so the water could reach the trees. As the apricots grew fatter, she turned her attention to the gardens. She could not plow a field, but she could plant seeds and nurse the herbs that added flavor to their meals and made healing brews for her mother and father.

William wrote that he had left France for Italy, and Dorothy sent a note in return with real enthusiasm for the life returning to Chicksands.

As she stooped to trim back some fennel one morning, Ulysses' ears perked up.

"What a fine sight you are, my sister, with dirt under your nails."

She looked up at Harry, who carried a basket of fish from the river, and laughed. "There's not anyone here to impress, and our meals taste better for it."

"True enough. Your industry does you credit, and I'm certain we'll find you a husband who appreciates your skills at housewifery."

"Not anytime soon."

"Sooner is better than later." He took the fennel from her and tossed it aside. "Do not forget your duties, my sister."

Dorothy watched him go and clutched her empty fists.

"Duty!" she said to Ulysses. "Is it not also my duty to help feed my family?"

But she was not certain. Would she serve them better by marrying someone—anyone—who could provide connections and wealth to help rebuild Chicksands?

She escaped to the orchard to let the cool, wet scent of the brook soothe the heat pounding in her head. She helped to bring the trees back to life, but how long would she be at Chicksands to enjoy the harvest?

A quiet cluck came from the branches of an overgrown plum tree. Dorothy bent down to see two brown and white speckled hens roosting in the tangled shelter.

"Who are you?" Dorothy asked. "I think your noble forbearers must have lived in my coop. You're very brave to have survived out here, but would you not like to come home? Here chick, chick, chick."

The hens cocked their heads but did not leave their safe haven.

Dorothy considered grabbing for them but did not want to frighten them away. She grubbed around in the dirt for a fat, wriggling worm and held it out.

"Chick, chick, chick."

One of the birds stretched out its neck.

"Come here, pretty hen," Dorothy said, keeping the worm out of reach.

The hen flapped out from her roost and landed heavily on Dorothy's arm. Ulysses barked, but she shushed him and pinned the hen against her chest. Dorothy backed away, and the other hen clucked unhappily and followed. She led her odd parade up through the orchard and back to the coop. She tossed the first hen inside, and the other fluttered in after.

"I'll find you some grains," Dorothy called in, and found a loose board from the barn to block the coop door.

She raced into the kitchen, Ulysses bounding behind, and startled Collins by grabbing a handful of barley and running it back out to the coop. She tossed it inside to the offended hens, and they settled down to scratching. After a few days of that, they would think of the coop as home and come there to lay their eggs if she made a nest for them. Then there would be eggs to add to their meals. A rooster! If she could find one, they would have more chickens—meat and eggs to sell.

She smiled and leaned against the weather-beaten coop. Perhaps she could still prove herself useful to her family through her thrift and industry instead of on the marriage market. Then— maybe then—Chicksands would remain her safe haven, and she could save herself from being sold to the highest bidder.

1650

ONE YEAR LATER

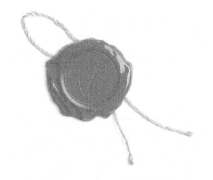

Chapter Eight

LONDON, ENGLAND

WILLIAM HOPPED OFF THE THAMES ferry as soon as it touched the wharf. He bounded up the riverside stairs. Home at last after two years abroad, surrounded again by English voices and English manners. A haze of oily coal smoke hung over the city, obscuring the many church steeples and even the battlements of the Tower. Hackney carts crowded the streets, but William set off at a walk. He was once again treading the same ground as Dorothy Osborne.

He dodged his way down narrow streets. The buildings' upper stories overhung the road, blocking sunlight and rain alike. Had the city always felt so wobbly, like it was about to tumble down around him?

"Fresh fish!" A girl shoved her basket of wares toward William.

He escaped her but barely missed being knocked in the face by a chimney sweep's dirty brush. In the last two years, he had lost the rhythm of London's streets.

He found his way to his father, Sir John's, new hired lodgings in Covent Gardens. When William had last been in London, it had been a fashionable quarter, but now merchants took the place of the fleeing nobility. Like any gambler, Sir John Temple's luck had run out. He had misjudged the strength of Lord General Cromwell and his army.

William rapped on the door, and a housemaid opened it.

"William!"

His sister, Martha, raced down the steep stairs and flung her arms around his neck. She was tall enough now to do so, and, at age twelve, almost too old for such exuberance. The little girl who idolized him was growing up, and he was missing it.

"Martha." He gently tugged one of her curls. "You're looking like a young lady. How do you fare here in London?"

"I'm learning the lute!" She led him inside by the hand. "Would you like to hear me? Oh, but I want to hear all about France. Did you really see the uprising in Paris?"

"Aye, I had an excellent seat for the performance. Let's hear your music, and I'll tell you tales of France."

She played her selection of love songs decently enough, and William imagined that each was about Dorothy. Then, while Martha rested her fingers, William told her stories about the barricades in Paris and the beauty and stubborn pride of the French queen.

"Did Father really send you away to protect you from a romance?" Martha asked, dropping her voice to a conspiratorial whisper.

The reminder of the reality of his situation struck him like a blow to the chest. "I suppose he meant to protect me from my own heart. There was no need. Her family would have forbidden the match as well."

"*Her* family would have forbidden the match? Certainly, you were good enough for her!"

"In some ways I never could have been," he said with a smile. At least in one person's eyes, he could do no wrong. "There were political objections."

"I don't think she could have been good enough for you either, then."

"And why is that?" William fought the impulse to defend Dorothy.

"If she were, she would not let politics stand between you. She would climb down a rope made of bedsheets in the night, and you would elope together to France."

William chuckled. "You've been reading romances."

"I saw that in a play!" Martha cradled her lute. "If she loved you, she would never love another. Like Father. He never remarried."

"True." It was strange that their pragmatic father had never ceased mourning their mother. William stared at the beams of the ceiling.

Martha perked up. "You're still thinking about her, are you not?"

"I admit I do think of her—rather often. I've written to her, but 'tis a hopeless cause."

"Did she write back? Is she betrothed or married?"

"She does write, but her family are Royalists, ruined by the war, and I must marry well."

Martha wrinkled her nose. "Just promise me you will not marry someone dreadful."

William forced a smile. "I will promise you that. Whomever I marry must meet with your approval."

They passed the morning in pleasant conversation, but after a light dinner of trout and boiled greens, William dressed to go out.

"Where are you going?" Martha asked.

"To play tennis. I need some exercise."

"I don't think you should."

"Why not? It looks like a pleasant day."

"Those Puritans don't like it. Father says we should not upset them."

William frowned. "If the tennis courts are still open, I see no harm in it. But thank you for your warning."

She continued pouting as he readied himself to go, and he almost gave in, but he could not stay locked inside. He had to see what opportunities London might offer him. Certainly, there would be some employment for an educated young man that did not require loyalty to the army and their Rump Parliament.

The bustle of the street testified that life went on. Yet an odd sort of homesickness settled over William, like he was visiting another foreign city. Soldiers marched past on patrol, and he kept his head down. A stench hung over the streets in the neighborhood of St Paul's Cathedral. Fashionable young men still thronged to the nearby inns and eating-houses to dine and smoke, but they had given up strutting in the streets to show off their finery, and if they gambled, they did so discreetly. Parts of the cathedral roof had decayed and teetered on the edge of collapse. Soldiers lounged outside the church, and some led their horses inside.

William pulled up short. The Puritans might not like the ostentation of the old building, but could they not have found it in themselves to respect a holy building?

"Master Temple!" a familiar voice called.

William turned to see Sir Thomas Osborne striding toward him through the crowds. The tall young man's mane of blond curls made him a strange contrast to the dark, short-cropped soldiers milling about, like a lion pacing through a pack of wolves.

"Sir Thomas, what a delight to find you home in London."

"Those protests in Paris were so bothersome. The opportunities are all here in England. Where are you headed?"

"I was hoping to play tennis."

"Many of the courts are closed now. The Roundheads don't like anything that smacks of nobility or enjoyment." Sir Thomas gave him directions to one that was still open despite Parliament's disapproval. "Watch your step and you'll have no difficulties. Your family chose the right side in the late troubles."

"And how fares your family?" William asked, pretending nothing more than polite interest.

"Getting back on our feet. My cousins are in town." He grinned, showing his teeth. "I'm thinking that my cousin Dorothy would make me a nice little wife."

"Ah." William's heart lurched, and the colors of the city faded to gray. "May I offer you my congratulations?" he choked out.

"Well, nothing is official yet, but it will be soon enough. They're in no position to turn me down."

"I see." Did Dorothy want to marry her pompous cousin? She had not mentioned him in her letters, but her family might push her into the match regardless of her feelings. Was there anything William could do to stop it?

"I would enjoy seeing Robin again," William managed. "Where is he staying?"

"Danvers House." Sir Thomas gave him the address in Chelsea, west of London proper, and continued on his way. William wandered to the tennis court and lost several bouts, unable to focus on the arcing path of the ball.

That night, William met his father over supper. Sir John Temple wore his graying hair short, more out of political expediency than any religious conviction.

"You look well," Sir John said, though he frowned at William's cavalier looks.

"Thank you, Sir. As do you." It was not entirely true. A sort of restless frustration hovered in the set of Sir John's lips and the creases in his forehead. William went on, "How is my brother John?"

Sir John's face softened into a satisfied smile. "Very well. He finished at Oxford, and he's been admitted to Lincoln's Inn."

"So, he's to be a barrister," William said. His brother John completed college and was well on his way to a prosperous career, despite the troubles of the times. He succeeded in every way that William failed, and the contrast showed in Sir John's face when he leveled his gaze at his eldest son.

"And what are your plans now, William?"

"I was hoping to find a career in the city." Yet the idea had already begun to sour in London's sooty heat. This was the army's England now.

Sir John nodded. "You have been quiet during the troubles, so you might be able to find favor with the Lord Generals. They're not as extreme as some of these soldiers who want to pull all of society down on our heads. Give landless laborers and even beggars a say in the government of the nation? It can only lead to chaos."

"Hmm." William might find something useful to do for Parliament, some way to help his country heal after nearly a decade of war. Yet, after seeing England under Parliament, William hoped young Charles Stuart reclaimed his father's throne soon.

"Your first priority will be to marry," his father added. "Find the daughter of one of the army officers, and you'll be settled. Choose one with an estate, or at least a respectable fortune. That's the only way to stability." Then he added quietly," You never know when politics will turn against you."

William set down his knife. Was this his future? To become his father, chasing the political winds like a stray piece of paper? Sir John advised William to seek stability, but how could a hollow man living a hollow life ever be stable? At least his father had loved his wife.

"I wonder if I should return to the continent before I settle into anything." He was running again. A coward. But he could not face the dull, gray course his father plotted for him.

"And why is that?"

William thought quickly. "To learn Spanish. Even my most demanding teachers would be pleased with my French, but I feel my education is incomplete without mastering Spanish. It would make me a more valuable asset to the nation."

"Hmm." Sir John stabbed a piece of mutton, not quite looking at his son. "You would travel to Spain."

"To the Netherlands. Spain still has a hold on its provinces there, and what better place is there to study science and art?"

"The Dutch Republic has made a name for itself, too. It could be instructive to spend some time there." Sir John fixed his gaze on William. "But when this trip is finished, it will be time for you to settle down to your role in this family and fulfill your duties."

"I understand, Sir."

This was his last reprieve, and then he had to find a career he could stomach and marry some Puritan heiress. But he could not do so in good conscious while still harboring dreams of Dorothy Osborne. She was forbidden to him, yet she was the light and hope on his dim path. He had to see her.

The next day, he set out for the home of the regicide, Sir John Danvers. He escaped the crowds of London proper and into the fairytale lands of Chelsea: a village made, it seemed, of castles and palaces. Only money and political favor could buy such wealth, and the house of Sir John Danvers was a pearl among the rest.

The fine house rested amid beautiful gardens, the equal of many William had seen on the continent. Evergreen bay laurels—a symbol of victory—and rose bushes just beginning to leaf out made neat geometric patterns, a perfect display of man's control of his world. Dorothy's family had hovered near starvation in Saint-Malo, while at Danvers House, even the fruits and herbs bent and bloomed to please their master.

William knocked at the ornately carved door, and a stern-faced manservant answered.

"William Temple here to see Master Osborne," William said. It seemed a safer course to start with Robin.

The manservant bowed him inside a cavernous great hall accented by sweeping staircases. The servant left William to study the tapestries of hunting scenes softening the walls. Determined not to fidget, William clasped his clammy hands behind his back and stood as still as the embroidered boars facing off against the hunters' spears.

After a few minutes, heavy footsteps echoed off the high ceiling. Harry Osborne strode into the room and looked down at William like a mighty lord meeting his most humble tenant.

"I understand you wished to see me, Master Temple," Harry said.

William met the man's condescending gaze. "My apologies, Sir. I meant to call on Master Robin."

"Robin? What can *he* do for you?"

"I only wished to see how he did, since I was in London."

"I see." Harry smirked. "I'm certain my *brother* would be happy to see an old acquaintance. I'll see if he's well enough to receive a visitor."

Harry left him with those foreboding words.

The window behind William stood open, and the sweet scent of rosemary drifted in with the sun-warmed breeze. Behind there came a low female voice, richer than any notes from a harp or viol. Dorothy. William could not make out her words, but a deep male voice answered her, and she laughed in response. Jealousy sent its tendrils to squeeze William's chest. Who made her laugh in his place? Did her eyes brighten for someone else as they once did for him?

"Master William?"

William gave a guilty start and turned to face Robin. Dorothy's brother had always been thin, but he had grown even more gaunt, with dark bags under his eyes.

"Master Robin! How goes it?"

"As you see." Robin's smile hovered on the edge of grimace. "But what of you? Are your adventures on the Continent come to an end?"

"I'm only stopping over before heading back."

86

"I'm sorry to hear that," he lowered his voice and glanced at the open window. "And I will not be the only one."

William hesitated, wanting to feign ignorance, but this was what he most needed to know. "Do you think so?"

Robin's smile softened the weary lines on his face. "Let me show you around my uncle's garden. I could use the sunlight."

William had to slow his steps to keep pace with Robin's lagging gate. Robin spoke haltingly of his new clerk position and his dislike of the city. Despite his concern for his friend, William struggled to attend his words, knowing every step took him nearer to Dorothy. Then they exited the back door and burst into the bright light of the garden.

He knew her immediately, framed beneath an arbor of dormant grapevines. Her face was turned from him, but a dark curl escaped from her up-swept hair, and her gown poured over the gentle curves of her figure.

She was not alone, though. A young cavalier with long, fair hair and a surprisingly pointed nose leaned close to speak to her. Cold shot through William, too thick to be dispelled by the sun's rays. But Dorothy stepped away from the cavalier and shook her head, and then she looked up.

Her eyes met William's.

For a moment her expression was blank, unrecognizing. Then it lit with surprise, and her pink lips formed an "O" of wonder.

She left the cavalier and stepped lightly toward William, the basket of white and yellow daffodils on her arm swinging. The time and distance between them melted away and took everyone else with it.

"Master Temple! How delightful to see you here! You are returned from France." Dorothy reached out for him, then seemed to think better of it and instead plucked another daffodil from the garden bed. "To stay?"

She was so close, he could smell the sweet scent of her hair, like honeysuckle. He bowed to stave off his desire to pull her closer.

"Unfortunately, no. I travel next to the Netherlands. But I needed to see you—how you were."

"I am well enough. It is good to be home." She glanced up at him again with a sad smile. "I've appreciated your letters. I hope you will continue to write?"

Footsteps crunched over the gravel path as Harry approached with the pointy-nosed cavalier.

"Dorothy," Harry chided. "Whatever is keeping you? Master Cromwell is leaving soon, and for some reason he seems to prefer your company to mine."

He chuckled then gave William a smug glance.

William ignored him, trying not to gape at pointy-nosed young Cromwell.

"Master Temple," Harry said, "perhaps you are acquainted with Henry Cromwell, son of Lord General Cromwell? A good friend of our uncle's."

Cromwell gave him a polite bow, which William barely managed to return. The young man evaluated William for a moment, then returned a warm gaze to Dorothy, who smiled at him.

The ground threatened to crumble beneath William. Henry Cromwell, courting Dorothy? Apparently, her family's objection to Parliament was overcome by enough money and a high enough position. But what of Dorothy? William could not read enough of her face to know her feelings about the man.

"Dorothy, let's walk on," Harry said.

"I was just renewing an old friendship," Dorothy said quietly, her eyes fixed on the yellow flower twirling between her fingers.

Henry Cromwell cut off Harry's protest. "We'll leave you to your conversation." He bowed again to William and led a reluctant Harry away. Courteous. Because he had no interest in Dorothy, or because he was secure in his position?

"I should sit," Robin said, and lowered himself onto a stone bench a respectful distance from Dorothy and William.

Dorothy gave William an apologetic look. "You were going to promise to write to me, I hope?"

"Will you have time to read anything I send?" William meant for it to sound teasing, but there was a bitter edge to his words.

"Of course! You doubt my friendship?"

"Nay, but I know we cannot—that is to say—you have duties to your family."

"My parents are both ill. I have been caring for them, and for Chicksands. Those are duties indeed, but your letters are a pleasure. Sometimes the only pleasure I have."

William winced inwardly. He had let his words sting her when she already struggled. "Of course, I will write. As long as you want me to. I only wish…"

He dared not voice his longing, but he grabbed her hand and held it lightly. She sighed, a sound so filled with heartbreak that William grasped her hand more tightly, and her fingers curved around his as if they belonged there.

"Yet what are we to do?" she asked quietly. "Fortune is against us."

"We defy her." William took her other hand and squeezed them both. "Let the world hold us under siege. We will triumph."

Dorothy's eyes brightened, but then the flicker of hope faded. "I have seen men broken by sieges. They may not surrender, but their minds and bodies are shattered." Her hands rested heavy in William's, the daffodil crushed in her grip. "Yet, I can endure much."

William released her hands. The bruised daffodil drifted to the ground. "I am speaking foolishly, of course. You must follow the path that will bring you happiness, Mistress Osborne."

He caressed her name as he spoke it. She was too precious to see hurt, especially for his own selfish ends. And what could he offer her? His future was so bleak even he was fleeing it.

"Happiness?" she repeated, her eyes uncertain. "I'm not sure happiness belongs to this world."

"I would see you happy." He plucked another daffodil and handed it to her. "Settled in your own home, with your hounds and your books, and your children gathered around you."

She shook her head. "I see no such future for myself. My family's position is still...tenuous. My father only allowed me to visit Uncle Danvers because of the great debt we owe him. These times are so uncertain." She met his gaze again. "I worry for you, traveling as you do, but I suppose it cannot be helped."

"It is for the best, and I am improving myself. You saw in my letters that my French is better."

She laughed a little. "Aye, and you seem more serious now."

"Do you approve?"

"I would not want you changed in essentials, but I think you will do great things when you find your way."

"I hope to prove you right, but I cannot find a path that allows me to prosper without compromising what seems right."

She met his eyes. "You are brave. You will return a triumphant hero."

It was more praise than he deserved. More than he could carry. He shook his head. "I'm afraid by the time I do, you will not take much notice."

"And why would I not?"

"Certainly, you will be married long before then. My career can hold little interest for you."

"I have no plans for marriage, not anytime soon. My parents need me, and... and I don't want to marry where there is no affection or understanding."

"You have a good heart. Affection will find you." William glanced up at the garden, where Henry Cromwell emerged from the shadows of the arbor in close confederacy with Harry Osborne. "I'll wager ten pounds that, before I return to England again, you're happily settled."

She gave him a look of hurt and confusion, and he bowed to the other young men as an excuse to avoid her eyes.

He left Danvers House sincerely hoping that he would lose his bet, but he could not expect Dorothy to hold out for a hopeless relationship. His only chance was to somehow become like Henry Cromwell or Sir Thomas Osborne: too influential for either of their families to object to. The Netherlands seemed like a poor place to do that, except...young Charles Stuart, the would-be king of England, had taken refuge in neighboring Holland. If William could make himself useful to King Charles's heir, he might find favor with Dorothy's family and be the hero she believed him to be.

William picked up his step. He had a trip to prepare for.

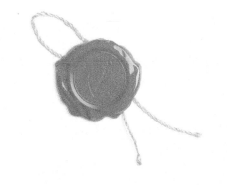

Chapter Nine

BREDA, DUTCH UNITED PROVINCES

WILLIAM SAT OUTSIDE HIS LITTLE apartment overlooking the main canal in Breda. The water rippled like silk as barges slid over its quiet surface. Neat brick houses and shops pushed right up to the waterfront, their stair-step facades casting wavering reflections on the river. In the cobbled streets, the plumes of cavaliers and the somber felt hats of Puritans mingled with women's silk hoods and laced bonnet, nun's veils, and the simple black caps of Jews. The distant call of merchants hawking Flemish lace or porcelains imported from foreign shores floated on the morning breeze.

Since the Dutch had driven the Spanish from their eastern provinces, trade here had flourished, but this was more than prosperity. Calvinists and Catholics, Puritans and Presbyterians, Humanists and Jews—all came to Holland to exchange goods, money, and ideas. Tolerance. That was the key to Dutch wealth and peace. William wished it could be exported to England as easily as linen and lace.

He caught a glimpse of a dark-haired woman in the crowd and straightened, but of course it was not Dorothy. Each time he smelled honeysuckle, he imagined the rich sound of her voice.

Echoes of her chased him through Saint-Malo, Paris, Brussels, and now here. Her absence was the only thing that made Holland less than perfect, and his mind gnawed over the words in her latest letter.

I pray that you are well. I have not received a letter from you for some time.

And then nothing but silence. It was the only word he'd had from her in the two months since he'd left. He wrote each week, trying to bring her closer by recounting everything he saw, yet apparently none of his letters arrived. Had more fighting disrupted the post, or did Fortune play games with them? William rested his chin on his hand and glared at the stone walls of Breda, as if Dorothy's letters might be piling up just outside the gate.

The solid square outline of Breda Castle peeked back at him through the stair-step roofs, the sunlight glinting off its many windows. Inside, young Charles Stuart, heir to the thrones of England, Scotland, Ireland, and Wales, kept his court, such as it was, composed of exiled Royalists, spies, and impoverished opportunists. Thus far, William had not found his way past the entry hall, much less into a position where he could serve the would-be king.

He spotted the face he had been waiting for and sprang to his feet, dodging his way into the flow of the crowds. The streets in Holland felt so different from London; the buildings stood straight and tall instead of leaning out over the roads, allowing sunlight to pour over William's path.

"Master Poole!" he called.

The Irishman turned, and his face lit with a grin. "William Temple!" His brogue rang in the street. He grabbed William in a rib-crushing embrace then stepped back to look him over. "I have not seen you since before Cambridge. I recall you'd just gotten into some trouble over releasing an angry rooster into a crowd watching a cock fight." He laughed. "And I wager you still play the jester for the ladies, with those pretty curls of yours."

William's smile tightened. "Actually, I hope to take on a more serious role."

"That ought to please your father at least."

"Not at all, I'm afraid. I want to join Charles Stuart's court."

Poole shook his head. "Rebellious as always."

"This is not about my father. I have chosen my side."

"I'm sure our young king without a country would appreciate the gesture."

"'Tis more than a gesture. I wish to do something useful."

Master Poole met William's gaze, and William flinched at the pity he saw there. "Do you have an army?"

"I have my sword. I can fight."

"Charles Stuart needs more than one sword. He needs money, soldiers, horses, cannon, all ready to stand against the training and experience of Parliament's New Model Army. He needs powerful politicians and diplomats who can argue his case before ministers and kings. He needs spies with the right connections who can find the weaknesses and divisions among his enemies. Have you any of those things?"

William hesitated then shook his head very slightly, trying not to dislodge all of his dreams.

"Here, lad, cheer up. I'm trying to persuade Charles Stuart to use Ireland as a base of operations in retaking his father's throne. We'll have him crowned again before the year is out."

"May I join your cause?"

Master Poole gave him a half smile. "Temple is not a popular name in Ireland these days. That pamphlet your father wrote about the Irish Royalists... The English Army used it as an excuse to take retribution on the Irish."

William gritted his teeth. His father had been thrust from his position of Master of the Rolls in Ireland during the war, and apparently, he had burned William's bridges on his way out. "I am not my father. Let me atone for his mistakes."

Master Poole's shoulders rose in a sigh. "I cannot promise anything, but if I'm successful with Charles Stuart, I'll see what I can find for you."

"Thank you, Sir!"

William accompanied Master Poole toward Breda Castle.

"How are you enjoying Holland?" Poole asked.

"Very well. There's a lifetime of art and philosophy to study here, and 'tis peaceful."

"Peace is good for trade," Poole said. "The Dutch must be the most pragmatic people in the world and look how it benefits them."

William considered that. His father was pragmatic, but he was not certain the Dutch had much in common with Sir John Temple. The Dutch stubbornly held to their principles, while his father stubbornly refused to hold to any. If the king were restored, his father would switch sides again. That would bring William one step closer to Dorothy, but if her family saw him as an opportunist, they would sneer at his suit for her hand. He had to prove his loyalty while Charles Stuart was at a disadvantage.

They did nothing at Breda Castle but mingle in the lower halls with other would-be courtiers and diplomats hoping for an invitation to climb the stairs to the grand hall above where the would-be king kept his motley court. William joined Master Poole again the next day, and many days after, for more of the same. Charles Stuart might be in exile, but his claim to the throne still drew throngs of men like wasps to fresh meat. The French, Scottish, English, and Irish, each with their religious differences and competing goals, hovered around Breda, vying to convince the king that they were the ones who could return him to his throne.

"'Tis foolishness," William said to Master Poole one evening as they walked through the peaceful cool toward Master Poole's lodgings on Charlottestraat. "If all of these factions worked together, the young king would be on the throne already."

"If all of these factions could work together, the old king would still have his throne." Poole shook his head. "I would be satisfied with tolerance for Catholics, and let the other churches do as they will, but the French would make everyone Catholic, the Scottish would make everyone Presbyterian, and I do not think the English know what they want, except to be rid of the Puritans."

William frowned at the soft babble of languages filling the street. The Dutch were not perfect in their tolerance, but why could no one else see how much better their system worked?

William would not be the one to point this out to the king—that became increasingly clear as the days passed. The Irish were losing their fight against Lord General Cromwell's armies, so the king had little time to speak to anyone connected with Ireland. Every man who crowded into Breda Castle's long, columned halls had something to offer: money or land or armies. William had nothing but his mind, and the king already had one of his own.

Still, William returned to the castle each day. He wandered the halls of his luxurious waiting room, admiring the art adorning the walls.

One morning, he nodded to another waiting courtier—a Scotsman, Master Jaffray, who paced the corridor with a rolled document in his hand.

William paused before a painting of a beautiful woman with hair the color of Dorothy's. Jaffray stopped nearby and studied a painting of the crucifixion.

"There's no finer place in the world to see art than Holland," Jaffray said. "This Rembrandt, he seems to capture light with his brush."

"Indeed." William glanced away from his dark-haired girl. "He draws the light from the darkness."

"That's often the way of it," Jaffray said as much to himself as to William. "Light and darkness—they usually come together." He stepped farther down the hall. "Did you know this one is painted by a woman, Judith Leyster? Her father lost his fortune, so she turned to painting, and now she's a member of the guild and has apprentices of her own."

William studied the painting, a simple domestic scene of a mother caring for her children painted with understanding and honesty. What freedom these Dutch women had! Dorothy's painting was not at this level, but her writing—William treasured each word she sent, and while he would be jealous to share her letters, he thought it a shame that the world could not enjoy her ease with words and lively wit. If only there were a respectable way she could earn her own way. He turned his attention back to the portrait of the dark-haired woman.

Jaffray smiled at William. "By the way you're staring at that painting, I'll wager you're not thinking about brushstrokes. You have a dark-haired girl at home?"

William shook his head. "She is not mine."

"Then you'd better make her yours, my lad."

"I was hoping to find a way to do that here, but it seems if I cannot help the king, I cannot help myself."

The Scotsman gave him a curious look. "Well, there's often more than one way to a goal. You do not have the look about you of Charles Stuart's other courtiers."

"I am not. Not one of his courtiers, I should say."

"Then what brings you to Breda?"

"I am in exile myself, I suppose. My father is a Parliamentarian and displeased with me for not submitting wholeheartedly to his values."

Jaffray nodded. "You are a Royalist."

"I favor the rule of law over the rule of the rapier and musket. A strong monarch, established by long tradition, brings stability."

"And what do you think of our young king?"

"He is...the only one with a rightful claim to the throne."

Jaffray laughed. "You are an honest fellow, but you have a diplomatic tongue." He tightened his grip on the paper in his hand, crinkling it slightly. "Then give me an honest answer to this: who sins more, the one who offers a bargain he knows will not be kept, or the one who accepts it, knowing he will break it?"

William glanced at Jaffray's paper. He could not make out the words at that angle, but the writing was formal, weighty. Official. William did not know what prompted the Scotsman's question, but the burden of it showed in Jaffray's troubled eyes. "I suppose one sin might be greater than another, but I would leave it in God's hands to judge. I can only account for my own decisions with any fairness."

"And how would you judge yourself, then, in the same situation?"

William fidgeted with the coin in his pocket: a rose farthing, minted under King Charles. And who made England's coins now? Did Oliver Cromwell's warty face appear on them? At least there were coins to trade and food for all to buy with them.

"I would weigh the good that would come against the imperfections of the arrangements," William said.

"Imperfections!" Jaffray exclaimed, but he turned the papers around in his hands again and studied them, the lines in his forehead relaxing. "Interesting perspective, young Master Diplomat. I might be able to find a roll for you in Scotland, if you have Presbyterian sympathies."

William glanced again at the document in Master Jaffrey's hands. A treaty with the king, perhaps? If Charles Stuart was going to Scotland, William wanted to be there too. It was a small lie, to pretend to be Presbyterian, since he did not favor any of the sects. His gaze traveled back to the portrait of the dark-haired woman. She seemed to frown at his deceitful thoughts.

William shook his head. "I appreciate the offer, but I cannot pretend to be something I am not."

Master Jaffrey nodded. "Very well. I wish you luck, then."

They parted with bows.

Two days later, William heard the news: the king had joined an alliance with the Scots, promising to adopt Presbyterianism for himself and his whole nation in return for the backing of the Scottish army. William sat on the edge of the canal, skipping rocks over the gentle waters. Charles Stuart was no Presbyterian; Master Jaffray was right to distrust his promise. But now the exiled king had his army and a potential path to the throne. William hoped he retook it soon to end the bloodshed and political turmoil, but William would not have any share in the triumph.

He trudged home, his whole world shrouded in gloom. He wanted to write to Dorothy, but what could he say? He had let hope get the better of him, and he failed again. He had nothing to offer Dorothy or anyone else. He picked up a volume of romances, but the stories rang false. What were wizards and false knights against the pain of real loss?

William tossed the book onto his mattress and picked up a quill. Ink was a dangerous weapon, as his father's writings against the Irish had proved, but it might be put to safer uses. It was unfair to write to Dorothy when he had nothing to give her, but at least he could vent his sufferings on paper. He would write stories meant only for her. She might never see them, but he would do his best to capture his heart on paper for her, and along with it, preserve his memories of her for the lonely days ahead.

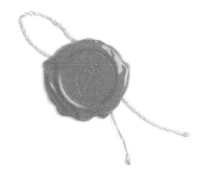

Chapter Ten

CHICKSANDS, ENGLAND

DOROTHY STUMBLED ON THE STEEP stairs at Chicksands, sloshing beef broth over the edge of its pewter bowl. She ignored the warm stain seeping into her dress. Her mother was finally feeling well enough to eat. Everything else could wait.

Lady Osborne sat where Dorothy had left her, propped up on her mattress with bolsters and pillows. She smiled wearily and reached for Dorothy.

"My good girl. You did not have to fetch that yourself."

Dorothy sat the bowl on the bedside table and took her mother's hands. Her skin felt cool and as fragile as paper, still marked by callouses from long days and nights of sewing and gardening, of tending ill children, and of scrounging for food and supplies when Parliament threw their family out of Chicksands.

"I am happy to do it, Mother." Dorothy gently squeezed her mother's hands and released them to hold the soup bowl.

She counted each sip of broth her mother managed to swallow, each little bit of strength and nourishment. Before the bowl was empty, her mother put down the spoon.

"That is all, thank you."

"Just a little more?" Dorothy held the bowl up.

Lady Osborne hesitated then shook her head. "I simply cannot. I'm sorry, dear."

Dorothy set the bowl aside. Her mother did not need to know that the beef bone they used to make her broth was the last meat in the house. Dorothy would find something in the garden to sell or trade, and they always had the eggs from her hens.

"Would you like me to help you to your chair? You could look out the window. 'Tis a lovely day."

"I am so tired." She met her daughter's gaze and managed a thin smile. "But a view outside does sounds pleasant."

Dorothy helped her mother to her chair—an easy task, as Lady Osborne felt no heavier than an autumn leaf. Her mother gave a rasping sigh as she settled into her seat. Dorothy hurried to drape a blanket around her thin shoulders. She unplaited her mother's silver-streaked hair and brushed it smooth, longing, for a moment, to feel gentle hands soothing her aches and fears. She rebraided the brittle hair and tried to remember a time when her mother's hair had not been laced with gray, but those memories were from before the war and hard to distinguish from fragments of old dreams.

"Dorothy, dear, there's a velvet bag in the trunk by my bed. I want you to have it."

"Mother, you are going to get strong again."

"Fetch the bag, child. I have no use for the contents, but you may."

Dorothy found the velvet bag and shook a pair of pearl earrings into her hand: at this point, no doubt the finest things in their home.

"I had hoped to give you so much more," her mother said, her eyes brimming with tears. "At least I saved these. Something I would not let anyone take away. They were my mother's."

Dorothy imagined her mother hoarding the precious earrings while they starved in Saint-Malo, but she could not be angry with her. There was something empowering about having a secret treasure that belonged to you alone.

"Oh, Mother." Dorothy embraced Lady Osborne. "I will cherish them. But you have given me much through the years."

Her mother squeezed her eyes shut. "I think I will doze here awhile. Why don't you get some rest as well? You've been working so hard."

"I can stay here, in case you need anything."

"You are young. You need to be out of this stuffy room. Go along now."

"Aye, Mother."

Dorothy kissed her mother's cheek and left, keeping the door open a crack in case Lady Osborne called for help. Ulysses rose from where he'd been napping and trotted after her, tongue lolling. She placed the earrings alongside the collection of buttons and shells on her bedside table then wandered the halls like one of the ghostly nuns said to haunt the priory, not certain what to do with herself. Collins brought welcome relief.

"Pardon, Mistress, but there's a visitor for you."

"For me?" Dorothy's first thought was of William, but he had not written for some months. She let out a slow breath. "You may show him—or her—to me."

"He said it would be better if you met him out of sight of the house. He's at the old hospital ruins."

"William." Dorothy hurried to the rubble walls east of the house with Ulysses bounding after her.

But the figure waiting for her had fair hair, not William's dark curls. Dorothy stuttered to a cautious walk. The young man bowed, and she recognized his distinctive nose from a distance.

Dorothy approached and curtseyed, smiling to hide her quashed hopes of William. It was good to see a friend—any friend.

"Master Cromwell. What brings you to Chicksands?"

"You, of course. What else?" Henry's grin kept the flirtation from sounding too serious. "I must return to Ireland soon, but I could not miss the chance to visit you while I was in England."

"I'm glad you did."

Dorothy sat on one of the crumbling walls of the old priory hospital and gestured for Henry to join her. He sat near enough for private conversation, but not close enough for scandal.

"Tell me about Ireland," Dorothy said, hushing the voice in the back of her mind that said she was only interested because William's father had been Master of the Rolls there before the war.

Henry poured out a sad story of the hardships of war on the rebelling Irish, the destruction of homes and fields. His eyes were distant, and he rubbed Ulysses' spotted head. Dorothy sensed he was holding back, not giving her the whole gruesome truth.

"I can well imagine the suffering of the families," Dorothy said.

"You have experienced a taste of it yourself." Henry glanced back at Chicksands. "But you seem to be recovered now."

She thought of the long nights at her mother's bedside, and her father pacing the halls with the worn fragment of his letter from King Charles. "The war's toll continues long after the cannon have fallen silent."

"I'm sorry." He said it as though he felt responsible. Considering his father's position as Lord General, perhaps he did.

"I suppose we cannot help what side of a conflict we are born on, only what we do with the position we find ourselves in," Dorothy said.

Henry shifted as though the smooth stones of the wall they sat upon suddenly felt uncomfortable. "Unfortunately, the war is not over in Ireland or at home. The political situation is delicate. Unstable."

Dorothy watched him, sensing he had more to say. He met her gaze.

"I want to be sure you're safe. I have always been fond of you, Mistress Osborne."

She flushed a little. "You are a good friend, Master Cromwell."

"I could be more to you." This time there was no teasing in his expression.

Dorothy studied her hands where they rested in her lap and spied the broth stain on her bodice. Of all the ridiculous sights. She was hardly better than a poor serving maid. How could Henry even think of this?

"I doubt your father would approve," she said. "Or my father either, for that matter."

"My father could be brought to see the light. Your father showed himself a loyal and honorable man, even if the king's cause was the wrong one, and your Uncle Danvers is a firm ally of Father and of Parliament. Besides, you are charming, and would make a wise and loving wife." He grasped one of her hands. "I could help you and your family."

This was Dorothy's part. Her father would hate a Cromwell as a son-in-law, but few men were in a better position to protect her family's interests than Henry, and she enjoyed his company. Yet she could not make herself speak to accept his proposal.

"Certainly, I am not so odious that poverty is more preferable," Henry said with a sad smile.

"Of course not! 'Tis only—I don't know if I would be comfortable—Do you truly believe in your father's cause?"

"Will you like me better if I do not?"

"I will like you better if you give me an honest answer!"

"I cannot refuse you that, but I don't have a simple answer. I think the king was a tyrant, but I am not proud of my father's role in his execution. And I fear a Catholic uprising, but I hate seeing the violence my father's army inflicts on Ireland."

"Then why do you return there to fight? How can you ignore what your conscience tells you?"

"'Tis my duty to my father, and now to my country. It makes me sick, but I cannot trust my own scruples above the wisdom of others."

Dorothy turned away.

"You think me unprincipled?" he asked quietly.

"Nay, you are a good man."

"Might I make a good husband as well?" he asked.

Dorothy stared across the countryside. William had predicted her marriage. Where was he? Why did he not respond to her letters? Henry's family was as objectionable to her father as William's, but Henry had two things William did not: the confidence to stand up to his father, and the means to help her family.

Yet she could not quite respect a man who went against his conscience. William refused to bend to the political winds and lived in exile because of it. She could admire his resolution, but she was not allowed to love him, no matter what her rebellious heart whispered.

"I don't know, Master Cromwell," she whispered. "The future is still too uncertain."

"I will give you time, Mistress Osborne. Not all the time in world, because I do have my duty to my family, but I respect your need to think on it."

"Thank you."

Henry Cromwell took his leave. Dorothy sat alone on the ruined wall stroking Ulysses' broad head.

"What was I supposed to do?" she asked the dog.

A growl rumbled in his throat.

"You did right," said a voice from the shadows behind her.

Dorothy gave a start and found Harry standing over her. "How long have you been there?"

"I could not let my sister visit with a young man unchaperoned." Harry sat beside her. "You have made another conquest, and your finest one yet."

Dorothy shook her head.

"There's no need for false modesty with me. I have wondered what game you are playing with the suitors you have turned down, but now I see that you have higher goals in mind."

"I did not care for the other suitors."

"I don't fault you. They were Royalists, true, but their estates were ruined by the war. With someone like Henry Cromwell, your future would be secure."

"That's not—"

"Oh, I understand. Cromwell might not be a good choice. If the political tides turn once again, the Cromwells will fall hardest and be washed out to sea with the Parliamentary dross. You don't wish to be like Icarus, flying too near the sun."

"I could not marry a Parliamentarian and break Father's heart." She stood. "And Mother and Father are ill. They need me."

"Of course," he said, sounding amused. "This is not the right time. I did not give you credit for much sense before, but now I see that you have been playing a deep game."

Harry gave her an approving pat on the shoulder and strolled off, leaving Dorothy more confused than before. Was he saying she could marry a Parliamentarian and still preserve peace in the family? If Harry were her ally, they might convince her father that William Temple was not his enemy, that she and William could marry. That moment was not the right time to broach the subject, as Harry said, but hope made her steps lighter as she crossed the lawn to the house.

Dorothy resumed her bedside vigil. There seemed to be less of Lady Dorothy Osborne as each day passed. Deep lines drew maps of pain across her forehead and puckered her pale lips. Every breath sounded more fragile than the last, and Dorothy found herself filling her lungs along with her mother until exhaustion overcame her.

The rushlights burned low as Dorothy dozed by her mother's bedside. Collins came to replace them and bring Dorothy supper: cold pigeon and weak ale. He gave Lady Osborne a concerned look and left the room, his quiet steps barely crunching on the rush mat.

Dorothy woke to a strangled rasping from her mother's bed. She grasped her mother's hand. It was cold as an icy stream. As death.

"Collins!" she called. "Bring Father."

"Dorothy," her mother whispered, pulling her closer.

"I am here, Mother."

Her mother squeezed her hand. "My good girl. How you have suffered."

"Not more than others. Not more than you."

"Aye, this life is the time for suffering. Do not expect otherwise."

"Don't say that. For all we suffer, does God not give us an equal measure of happiness and grace?" Dorothy clung to her mother's chilly hand.

"Mankind has shown its true face to us in our sorrows. No matter how poorly you think of people, they will prove themselves even worse. But at last I escape it all."

"Mother?" Dorothy tightened her grip. The candle wavered, and the grasping shadows hovered closer. "Please don't go!"

"Dorothy." Her father's voice called her from her dread. He stood in the doorway behind her. But he was not speaking to her. He only saw his wife, Dorothy Danvers, Lady Osborne. He crossed the room and fell at her bedside to clutch her hands. Lady Osborne did not look at her husband, but kept her gaze fixed on Dorothy as a long, groaning breath rattled in her chest and the light dulled in her eyes.

The room grew still.

"Dorothy!" Sir Peter howled his wife's name, collapsing against the mattress.

Dorothy sank back. Pain tightened her chest, but no tears came to match her father's. Numbness dulled her vision, stilled her thoughts, made her arms too heavy to lift.

Then duty and tradition took control.

She comforted her father and mumbled instructions to Collins. He brought a basin of water and a cloth so she could wash her mother's body and wrap it in a woolen shroud. It was only a hollow shell, and Lady Osborne's parting words made Dorothy wonder how long her mother had been empty.

Once, in the early morning hours, she glanced up and saw Harry standing in the doorway, his face in shadow so she could not read his emotions. He gave her a curt bow and left.

Without the benefit of more than a few moments of rest, Dorothy sleep-walked through the rituals of the funeral at the little parish church.

Harry attended to each mourner as they expressed their sorrow, nodding solemnly and dabbing his dry eyes with a handkerchief. Dorothy sank further with each moment, as though she were watching Harry and the others from under a murky lake while her lungs filled with water. She would never feel her mother's gentle caresses again in this life nor hear her voice, except the dreadful last words that echoed around her. *No matter how poorly you think of people, they will prove themselves even worse.* Neighbors expressed condolences, but their empty words floated away like ash on the breeze.

"I am sorry for the loss of your wife," one silver-haired gentleman said to her father.

Her father, who had been nearly limp throughout the burial, suddenly tensed.

"Get out," Sir Peter whispered to the man. Then he raised his head, and his shoulders straightened. "Get away from me, traitor! How dare you appear here! How dare you desecrate my wife's funeral!"

His words reverberated off the windows of the church, bringing a hush to all assembled.

The silver-haired man bowed stiffly to Sir Peter and Dorothy and backed out of the chapel. The whispering returned with increased intensity. Sir Peter blubbered, tears finding their way along the wrinkles in his cheeks. Dorothy numbly wrapped an arm around his shoulders.

"That was Colonel Samuel Luke," Harry whispered to Dorothy. "I don't know what he thought, appearing here after using the war to gobble up our lands."

Dorothy stared after the man. So, he was the one who bought their sequestered lands and brought her family to their reduced state. Yet, he had seemed sincerely sorry for her mother's death.

"I hope I might call on you soon, Mistress Osborne," said another neighbor, Master Beagle, his fleshy cheeks wobbling. "To offer my condolences." His eyes showed no sorrow.

"My sister is in mourning," Harry said sharply, then he lowered his voice. "There will be time for other considerations soon enough."

Dorothy's stomach squirmed. It would not be long before she would be forced to make a choice for the sake of her family.

Henry Cromwell's face swam into her imagination, but it felt like a betrayal of their friendship to marry him for his position and not out of any real respect. She imagined William again but reluctantly swept his image aside. William's father had banished him from the country, and his family was not well off. They also sought an alliance for power and money. Love had no place in the struggle for survival.

1652

SIXTEEN MONTHS LATER

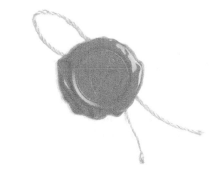

Chapter Eleven

CHICKSANDS, ENGLAND

"I WORRY FOR YOU, DAUGHTER," Sir Peter said, studying Dorothy across the supper table. "You look so pale."

"'Tis those mourning clothes," Harry said. "Time to put them aside, my sister. It has been over a year since Mother's death. I'm weary of seeing you in black."

Dorothy set down her spoon. No matter what color she wore, the ache of loss still rose up at unexpected moments to strangle her.

"Aunt Gargrave has invited you to London," Harry said. "I think we should accept. You need a woman's guidance. Motherly advice."

Dorothy cringed. Aunt Gargrave was many things, but motherly was not one of them. "I prefer the quiet of Chicksands. I like to be of use to you and Father."

Harry waved her concerns away with his linen napkin. "I am overseeing everything here, and I have Wright to help me now. You are not needed. And in London, you have the opportunity to make a good match. Who could you choose here in Chicksands? Master Beagle? Ha! Not worthy of my sister."

Dorothy toyed with the mutton on her pewter plate. "I had not thought of marrying soon."

"We don't want you to end up a spinster. Do you wish to find yourself in Hell, mending bachelors' smallclothes and leading apes on a chain?"

"I already mend *your* smallclothes, and many of the suitors you have introduced me to are hardly less foolish than apes."

"All the more reason to go to London."

"All I'm likely to find there are richer apes."

"At least you can buy them golden chains."

"Enough." Their father's weary voice cut through their jibes. "Dorothy, I think this is for the best."

She bowed her head. "Aye, Father." She had survived war, poverty, and piracy; certainly, she could survive London as well. "How shall I travel there?"

"Jack Peters offered to make his coach available to us," Harry said.

Dorothy groaned inwardly. The Peters were the most gossipy and interfering of her circle of cousins.

"Peyton writes that he is going to London soon," Sir Peter said. "I will ask him to bring Dorothy."

Dorothy could be satisfied with that. Thomas Peyton, the husband of her long-dead eldest sister, was a favorite of hers, and his seriousness would be a good match for her somber mood.

Collins approached the table. "Letter, Miss."

"Thank you!" Dorothy snatched it from his hand. Had William finally written?

The handwriting was Lady Diana's.

Harry sliced his mutton with heavy strokes of the knife, but his narrow gaze rested on the letter. Dorothy placed it aside for later. Unshed tears burned in her eyes, and she squeezed her lids shut.

After supper, she retired to her room to read Lady Diana's gossipy letter then pack a traveling trunk. No sense in delaying, and no knowing how long she would be gone. She brushed the dust off the baubles on her bedside table and held up the shell to watch the light roll over the pearly luster inside. Had she once stood on the shores of France with William Temple? Were it not for the shell, she might doubt it was anything but a dream.

Ulysses pawed at her skirts and whined, making her feel like a traitor for leaving him.

"I wish I could take you with me." She packed the shell in her trunk and rubbed the dog's spotted head. "You would not like London. 'Tis busy and loud, yet one can still feel all alone. You are allowed to stay here and roam the fields." She sat heavily on her straw-stuffed mattress. "Solitary is not necessarily the same as lonely, is it?"

But she did not have the freedom of Ulysses, so not many days after, she found herself bundled away in Thomas Peyton's coach. They traveled in companionable silence, watching the countryside give way to tight clusters of wooden houses. Wagons hauling coal or garden produce crowded the road. London's smoke-scented haze crept over them and smothered the brightness of the afternoon.

The carriage slowed and finally rolled to a stop in the tangle of London hackneys and wagons.

Peyton groaned. "Now 'twill take us as long to get through London as it did to make the journey from Chicksands."

A pair of soldiers with muskets held over their shoulders outpaced the crawling vehicles. Peyton flicked the curtain over the window, plunging the carriage into twilight dimness. Dorothy sat back, trying to hide herself in the upholstered seat.

"They are everywhere now," Peyton whispered, glaring at the curtained window. "Ready to pounce on anyone who does not conform to the will of the army. Rabble! They'll turn everything on its head."

Dorothy glanced at the thick velvet curtain standing between them and the light and dust and soldiers of London. Muffled shouts and whinnies still filtered through the barrier. It would do nothing against a sword or musket ball.

"What are we to do?" she whispered. The army had murdered a king and led Parliament by the nose. A few disgruntled Royalists, stripped of land and influence, hardly seemed formidable against so great and terrible a power.

"We are not wholly defeated. There is still the younger Charles, waiting in Scotland for his opportunity." Peyton fell silent, staring off at a spot above Dorothy's head with his brow furrowed. He spoke again slowly, "Most of our plans are of no concern to a young woman, but you might think of the fortune your father is able to provide for you. How much is it?"

"Four thousand pounds," Dorothy said. "Though much of that is through Uncle Danvers's generosity."

Peyton gave her a conspiratorial grin. "All the better to use that traitor's blood money against his own cause."

"What do you mean?" Dorothy asked.

"Your father has given his all to the king's cause and should be allowed the peace of his retirement, but there are other Royalists—younger men—who still have the fire to see order restored to the country. Marry one of them and you, and your fortune, can aid in the cause."

"I see." Dorothy stared absently at the curtains. Could her marriage really make a difference on the grand stage of wars and politics? She longed to ask William, to feel his reassuring touch, but he had not written for almost two years.

This life is the time for suffering. Do not expect otherwise. Her mother's whisper pushed other thoughts away. Perhaps God was showing her where her duty lay. Her father would be proud to see her married to a Royalist and advancing their family's cause.

By the time the coachman lowered the steps and Peyton escorted her to the door of Aunt Gargrave's London home, Dorothy was determined to find an acceptable partner among her Royalist suitors. She tried to quiet the heavy ache in her chest with a reminder that this was the noblest thing she could do with her life.

Dorothy descended the stairs, dressed in her gray satin gown for yet another supper party. Aunt Gargrave waited by the front door, casting glances at the iron chamber clock ticking impatiently from the side table. The Puritan army had shut down the theaters and forbade most public entertainments, so private parties were the only social activities available. No matter how the events exhausted Dorothy or wore on her nerves—always having to be on stage and on guard—she was not in London to stay holed up in her chambers with a book. At least tonight there would be music.

When Dorothy reached the bottom of the steps, Aunt Gargrave gave her dress a quick inspection and straightened her white linen collar.

"Very good," Aunt Gargrave said with a smile. "Master Bowman and your cousin Sir Thomas will not even notice any of the other ladies. I shall be shocked if you don't make at least one conquest tonight."

Dorothy forced a smile. There was no one at these parties she wished to see as her doting servant, but what she wished hardly mattered. This was her duty. "I don't believe you can be shocked, Aunt."

"That's because I'm always right."

Dorothy chuckled and followed her aunt onto the streets. It would be less dusty to take a hackney coach, but with the crowded streets, it was faster to walk. Dorothy lifted her gray skirts just enough to protect them from the refuse cluttering the road and hurried after Aunt Gargrave. In a quarter hour, they arrived at Lady Whitsand's home and a manservant showed them into the parlor.

Her cousin, Sir Thomas Osborne, was not present, which allowed Dorothy to relax a little. His attentions had grown wearisome over the past two years. It was a match that everyone would accept—everyone except herself—but she saw no advantage to family, king, or country in marrying a silly ninny and letting him fritter away her fortune on tobacco and horse races.

Master Bowman approached her. She gave him her best smile. His thinning blond hair did not cooperate well with the cavalier fashion for long curls. He had a decent enough face, except for the large wart near his upper lip. She was very careful not to focus on it while they exchanged pleasantries.

"Have you heard the latest news?" Master Bowman asked.

Dorothy heard bits of rumor and gossip every day, but she could not be sure of the truth of any of it, so she shook her head.

Master Bowman led her aside and lowered his voice. "The Royalist stronghold in Galway is fracturing. 'Tis our last foothold in Ireland, and the Parliamentarian siege is breaking it." His voice was rough with frustration.

"We must not give up hope." Dorothy repeated the platitude with little sincerity.

"We must seize our hope. We must fight for it."

He thumped his fist on the back of a chair and swept off his hat. Wisps of fair hair straggled across his balding scalp, making him look like an old man playing at being a dashing cavalier. If only he could keep the hat on always.

He gave her a look full of meaning. "May I visit you at your aunt's house tomorrow?"

"Aye," Dorothy said.

His words should have filled her with thrills or nervous flutters, but instead they made the night's music sound flat. Her father had starved and broken himself at Castle Cornet, though; certainly, she could sacrifice as well.

The next morning, Dorothy stood like a doll as Aunt Gargrave's maid laced her into her second-best dress and fussed with her curls. A dull, gray rain trickled down the window, smearing the view into colorless confusion. Dorothy tried to take calming breaths, but her stays stifled her. She would have to bear it.

She awaited her fate in the parlor, passing the time by starting a letter to Lady Diana. Master Bowman was a Royalist with acceptable connections and an estate that had survived the war, and he was attentive toward Dorothy. He would help her family, give her a respectable position in society, and do his part to support young Charles Stuart. Dorothy's father, Harry, Brother Peyton—all would be happy. She would try to be as well.

The maid entered the room. Dorothy took a shaky breath and stood.

"Mistress Osborne. Master Bowman to see you."

Dorothy managed a weak smile to greet him. Was it her imagination, or had the wart on his lip grown larger?

He strode across the room and took Dorothy's hands.

"I have spoken to your father."

"Oh?" Dorothy swallowed a sob of despair. This was her place in life. Her duty. She stared at the wart, unable to meet his eyes.

"I think we will deal well together, but Sir Peter was stubborn. He says he will give me four thousand pounds and no more. If only he would make it five thousand, I would happily take you for my wife."

Dorothy pulled her hands away. "The war has been hard on my family. Surely you must understand that."

"We all must give a little more."

"My father has given his fortune and his health." She took a steadying breath. "Could we not do as much good with four thousand pounds?"

"Do good with it? I suppose. But can you really expect me to marry you for less than five thousand? 'Tis merely a thousand pounds more."

"I begin to think that a thousand pounds less would still be too high a price for a husband such as you."

Master Bowman stared at her for a moment, as if trying to work out the insult in his head. Dorothy helped him along.

"You may look elsewhere for your five thousand pounds, but I pity the lady that has them. Good day, Sir."

Master Bowman snatched up his hat and stormed out of the room. Dorothy collapsed on her chair and laughed for the first time in weeks.

"Well, my lady," she said to the unfinished letter to Lady Diana, "I do indeed have a tale to tell you."

William would laugh to hear of it, too. The thought drained away Dorothy's smile. Though she tried to regain some of her mirth in writing to Lady Diana, a dullness weighed down her words, and she was afraid the story came out more pathetic than amusing.

"You must give up this moping, child." Aunt Gargrave glared at Dorothy over her plate of brown trout and parsnips. "After supper, take one of the maids and go walking in Hyde Park."

A trickle of cold rain dripped from the eaves beyond the window.

"Aye, Aunt, if the weather breaks." Dorothy picked at the limp vegetables on her plate and forced herself to take a bite. Nothing. They tasted like nothing. She pushed the plate away.

"If you're going to sulk over Master Bowman, you should not have sent him away."

Footsteps approached up the stairs before Dorothy could muster a defense.

"My sister!" Harry called. "Come, greet your favorite brother."

Dorothy rose and gave him a curtsey. "Harry! I did not know you had business in London."

"I understand my sister is not receiving her due from these city rascals. I'm here to take over matters."

Aunt Gargrave looked to be on the verge of a pithy comment on Harry's matchmaking skills, but he cut her off.

"I brought another surprise for you, Aunt. Master Jack Peters lent me the use of his coach, and I escorted his dear wife here with me. Mistress Peters will be inside shortly."

"Yoo-hoo!" Cousin Peters called, pushing her way past Harry. The long plume on her enormous hat threatened to knock pictures askew on the wall. "'Tis been an age since I've been to London, and I know the town must miss me."

"Hello, Cousin," Aunt Gargrave said. "I suppose you also need a room?"

"A room, aye. I know you would not have me stay elsewhere." Cousin Peters grinned.

Dorothy stood close enough to Aunt Gargrave to hear her huff of disdain.

"I will leave you ladies to your gossip," Harry said, bowing his farewell. "I'll be staying with Robin, but I'll be here often to check on you, my sister."

"Dorothy Osborne!" Cousin Peters exclaimed. "My, how you've aged. I hardly recognize you!"

Dorothy pressed her lips together, not certain if she should thank her cousin for the observation.

Cousin Peters turned to Aunt Gargrave, and Dorothy had to duck to avoid a tickle from her plume. "And what are we to do with this niece of yours, now that she has cast off Master Bowman?"

"I suppose she will have to marry Sir Thomas. More's the pity," Gargrave said.

"Aye, more's the pity," Cousin Peters said, studying Dorothy. "She has such a serious, melancholy face. That will scare the young men away." Her expression brightened, and she flapped her white handkerchief in excitement. "But perhaps not an older one."

"You are thinking of a widower?" Gargrave asked. "We considered marrying her to Peyton when poor Elizabeth died, but Dorothy was so young at the time, and, unfortunately, he has—"

"Has remarried to that Cecilia creature, aye. Oh, but I know just the man for Cousin Dorothy! Sir Justinian!"

"Sir Justinian Isham?" Aunt Gargrave looked thoughtful. "I thought he was in prison."

"In prison for debt," Cousin Peters said. "Debt he accrued in service to the late king. But now that he has inherited the baronetcy—"

"It would be unseemly for a baronet to be in prison," Aunt Gargrave said. "Though I wonder how long that will be true. The Puritans are determined to grind us all down until we're licking up the dust of their feet."

Cousin Peters waved away her concern. "Sir Justinian is quite a scholar, Cousin Dorothy. He has an extensive library and patronizes many men of letters."

"Oh?" Dorothy asked politely.

Cousin Peters turned back to Aunt Gargrave. "We must arrange a meeting. I have heard that he's in London looking for a wife. He could do no better than the beautiful Dorothy Osborne."

Dorothy was certain such a paragon *could* do better, but she would obediently make the acquaintance of Sir Justinian.

A week later, she found herself at a musical party where the widower would be present. At least Dorothy could attend with Harry instead of her aunt and interfering cousin. She and Harry ascended the stairs to the portrait gallery above, where a group of empty chairs faced a harpist in the long process of tuning her instrument. At a whispered word from Harry, the host, Master Durham, guided Dorothy to where the guests were admiring the paintings. Master Durham halted in front of a small group of men and caught the eye of one of them with a meaningful glance.

"Mistress Dorothy Osborne, may I present Sir Justinian Isham. Sir Justinian, Mistress Osborne."

Dorothy curtseyed. Sir Justinian looked to be in his forties—not as old as Dorothy had feared—and he dressed in the somber colors the Puritans made fashionable, though he wore his brown hair long. His face, though, was…unfortunate: rather puffy and red, especially around his eyes.

Sir Justinian made a grand bow to Dorothy and took her hand. His flesh was too warm and soft, like rising bread dough. Dorothy steeled herself to refrain from whisking her hand away and wiping it clean.

"How fortuitous to make your acquaintance, Mistress Osborne."

"Indeed," she said, lowering her eyes to hide her amusement at his pompous words. She was glad to have her hand back to manage her skirts.

They stood awkwardly for a moment.

Sir Justinian cleared his throat. "By the increasing temperature, I surmise that summer is flying toward us on her golden wings."

"It is getting warmer," Dorothy said. The poor man must be very awkward with women. He could not possibly speak that way all the time. "I understand you have an impressive library."

His puffy eyes brightened. "Indeed, I cherish knowledge, and I have collected an extensive repository of erudite volumes."

"I enjoy reading very much."

"Oh, mostly romances I would venture to guess." His condescending tone raised Dorothy's hackles as he went on. "I prefer more worthwhile subjects. History, poetry, natural sciences." He must have caught a glance of Dorothy's expression, because he hurried to add, "But of course, romances are fine for young ladies, provide they do not read overly much and strain their intellects. I keep my daughters sequestered at home to protect them from the tumults of society, but I do allow them the occasional novel."

"How kind of you," Dorothy said, letting her voice drip with false sincerity. "Do tell me more about your daughters."

He blinked his puffy eyelids, as if unprepared for the question. "What is there to tell? Four pretty girls with nice manners. As I said, they have not been out much in society yet."

Dorothy pictured four children in white dresses staring longingly out the window of the country estate where they were jailed, and her heart softened toward them. "How old are they?"

"Oh, quite nearly your age. They should fetch good husbands and be out from underfoot soon once I bring home a new wife." He smiled indulgently.

"I see." Dorothy's picture of the girls' setting shifted to something more like the dank dungeons of her novels, with the poor damsels in gray rags.

When the music started, Dorothy escaped to sit with Harry.

He leaned over to whisper, "What do you think of Sir Justinian?"

She huffed quietly. "He's aptly named. He's a pompous, Byzantine tyrant."

"The resemblance is not all bad," Harry said, a smile in his voice. "I seem to recall that the Emperor Justinian was ruled by his wife, Theodora."

"You think I would wish to rule over my husband?"

"What could be better? Marry the old fool and use his position and estates to our family's advantage."

Dorothy shook her head at her brother's silly talk. "He keeps his daughters confined like nuns in a convent. I hardly think I would fare better."

"He would not dare. You underestimate your family's power and connections. After all, I served with Prince Rupert in the late troubles."

Dorothy thought Uncle Danvers might be a more useful connection in the current climate, but she tried to focus on the harp's bell-like tones. Still, the conversation with Harry troubled her. In the course of a few years, she had gone from a refugee searching gutters for lost coins to an actor in political games. Yet she did not know what part she was supposed to perform.

The following weeks descended into a blur of nightly suppers, musicals, card parties, and even a play staged in the drawing room of an earl's wife. Sir Justinian and Sir Thomas Osborne crowded into every moment Dorothy appeared in public.

When her aunt was not parading her around town, Dorothy hid in her chambers with a collection of Montaigne's essays. She stared at the pages, but instead of weaving worlds for her to escape into, their words stayed dead on the on paper, as flat and gray as her meals, the weather, the air in her lungs. She should have been flattered to have two illustrious men vying for her affection, yet her reflection in the window looked pale and drawn. Her suitors continued to tell her she was glowing, beautiful, rapturous, as if they could not really see her.

The maid knocked lightly on Dorothy's door and entered with a folded paper: another invitation. Dorothy took the paper with a mumbled thank you, wishing she could toss it in the fireplace.

As soon as the maid was gone, she paced the room, twisting the invitation around in her hands. Her family pressured her to pick a suitor, and each evening's entertainment brought her closer to the day she would have to make that decision, like a traitor approaching the gallows. Sir Thomas or Sir Justinian? Arrogant youth or arrogant elder?

She paused at her bookshelf and rearranged her precious volumes by height, then by title. A headache prickled behind her eyes. There were no answers in her books. She broke the blue wax seal on the invitation. A masque, given by Lady Havershire.

Dorothy groaned. A masque meant elaborate costuming and acting by all the attendees, herself included. She would have to draw on whatever good spirits remaining to her and pretend to enjoy herself. If she could just pick a suitor, it would end the ceaseless rounds of loud, late nights in other people's homes.

The invitation weighed heavy in her hand. Lady Havershire's masque revolved around Charlemagne and his knights, and Dorothy was to dress as a dryad. She sorted through her collection of beads, buttons, and ribbons to see what might make a good headdress. Her touch lingered on the shell William had given her at Saint-Malo. She traced the smooth, pearly interior then drew her finger back, afraid she would wear away its beauty. The shell did not fit with the theme, but she found a place for it, dangling by her ear.

By the evening of the ball, Dorothy was already tired of Charlemagne, dryads, and knights.

"Hold your head up, niece," Gargrave reminded her as she led the way outside and summoned a pair of sedan chairs carried by porters. The house was not far, but Aunt Gargrave wanted to protect their pale linen dresses.

Dorothy straightened and stepped into the enclosed chair. The porters lifted it and trundled down the street past coaches and pedestrians. Each uneven step jolted through Dorothy like imps prancing on her aching head. It was all she could do to exit with grace when they arrived at Lady Havershire's west London home. Aunt Gargrave emerged from her own chair and guided Dorothy inside. Sir Thomas was at her side before she had grown used to the brightness of the beeswax candles.

"My dearest cousin!" he said.

Dorothy was forced to look up to meet his gaze, and the glare of light through his ridiculous profusion of blond curls gave his angular face a devilish look.

"I hope you will allow me the privilege of staying by your side tonight," Sir Thomas said.

"That will depend on the actions of the masque, will it not?" His shimmering green and gold costume, topped by a hat with a fountain of purple feathers, did nothing to help her headache.

"Your part is not important—I made sure of it. You can wait in attendance on me."

Dorothy pressed her lips together and allowed him to lead her to their places. She reluctantly went through the moves of the dance when the masque called for it, but otherwise ignored the complex and meandering story that seemed designed mainly to let all the men have a noble role. As they played their parts, she scanned the crowd, wondering what William would think of the performance.

"He is not here," Sir Thomas whispered, leaning close enough that his fair curls brushed Dorothy's face.

"What?"

"That old fool who's been paying court to you."

"Sir Justinian? I did think he would be attending. I hope he's not unwell."

Sir Thomas smirked. "Nothing of the sort. His coach was in no condition to travel tonight, so he could not attend."

"Rumor flies quickly."

"'Tis no rumor. I made sure of it myself, with the help of one of Sir Justinian's footmen who wanted a temporary increase in income."

Dorothy stared at him in horror. Sir Thomas seized her hand.

"I want you to see that I am serious in my affections for you."

"This is cold-hearted."

He gave her a condescending look. "You cannot tell me you care for that old man."

"I don't like to see anyone tricked."

"But the poets tell us, *'the rules of fair play do not apply in love and war.'* And we live in a time of both."

"All the more reason to rise above it. To do what we know is right regardless of—"

Sir Thomas chuckled and covered her mouth with a velvet-gloved finger. "When we are married, you may preach your morals to the children, but I will abide by my own strategies. I hope to see the king restored, whatever the cost, and plan to rise far in his rightful government."

Dorothy shook her face free of the musty stench of his glove. *"When* we are married?"

His eyes turned harder. "'Tis time to stop playing games, Dorothy. You are enjoying this season of allure before age dims your beauty, but you cannot mean to marry Sir Justinian."

"You are an unprincipled scoundrel! I would rather die a spinster than marry a—a rakehell like you!"

Dorothy's voice had slowly risen in volume and pitch until the actors stopped, and everyone stared at her and Sir Thomas. Her cousin forced a dry laugh, but the room broke into astonished murmurs. Dorothy wished for a moment she were one of the heroines in her novels and could faint away and let the whole mess be sorted without her. Despite feeling hot, though, she was not the least bit light-headed. If anything, she was in danger of screaming at her cousin again.

Aunt Gargrave. She needed Aunt Gargrave.

Or to be like her.

Dorothy held her head high, letting her dark curls frame her flushed face, and walked boldly into the crowd. Women in masks and men in crowns and colorful armor parted the way for her, and she passed without looking down or making eye contact. The shell dangling by her ear clanked against a neighboring bead like a slow applause.

Aunt Gargrave met her at the end of her procession and escorted her outside. The cool, smoky London air hit Dorothy like ocean spray, waking her from her trance. To her surprise, her hands did not tremble, and she had to stop herself from giggling.

"Are you unwell?" Aunt Gargrave asked.

"Not at all. In fact, my headache is much improved."

Her aunt smiled a little. "That is good, because tomorrow it will likely become much worse."

The next morning, Harry joined them for breakfast.

"I understand you decided against our cousin last night," he said, taking a mouthful of ham and eggs.

Dorothy prodded at the preserves on her plate with her spoon.

"Don't misunderstand me," Harry said. "I think you did right. Perhaps not to berate him in public, but to choose Sir Justinian. A connection with him will be much more advantageous to our family. I would not part with you to someone who was not worthy."

"And Sir Justinian is worthy?"

"He is wealthy and foolish. What more could we wish for?"

Dorothy set down her spoon. "I don't know that I have chosen Sir Justinian."

"Last night's display could mean nothing else. Do you have any other suitors—serious ones?"

"Not at the moment," she admitted quietly. *If only William would return*, her heart cried out, but she smothered the false hope.

"All men are about the same, my sister, and you have run out of choices. You don't know that a better bargain than Sir Justinian will appear again soon, and you are not as young as some of the other girls looking for husbands."

To avoid responding, Dorothy forced herself to take a bite of toasted bread, the preserves cloying on her tongue. She did not think all men were the same, though those willing to marry her shared a number of unfortunate traits. William had been different. Or was that only what she imagined?

A clamor of feet and voices sounded from the portrait gallery.

"I will see them now!" a female voice called.

"I believe Lady Osborne has arrived," Aunt Gargrave muttered.

Dorothy cringed to hear her mother's title, but that voice belonged to Anne Osborne, another Danvers cousin who had married into the Osborne family, and the mother of Sir Thomas.

Anne Osborne sailed past the servants and stopped to loom over Dorothy.

"Is this some kind of ploy?" Anne's glare took in all three of them.

"A ploy?" Aunt Gargrave asked.

"Publicly humiliating my son! What do you hope to gain from this?"

"Nothing, Aunt Osborne," Dorothy said. "I don't wish to marry him."

Anne Osborne whirled on Harry. "What do you mean by this? It was practically settled between them."

"My sister is a very desirable match."

"As is my son! We must keep the wealth and influence of our family joined and strong!"

"I believe it would aid my family more to extend our connections beyond our cousins," Harry said. "I'm sorry, Aunt, but I support Dorothy's decision. This discussion is over."

"Stubborn, unnatural girl!" Aunt Osborne flung at Dorothy on her way out of the room.

No one contradicted it. Dorothy sank back in her chair, her hands shaking. Was she stubborn and unnatural? She should be happy for marriage to a well-positioned man such as Sir Justinian, but her wicked heart thumped with dread at the thought of it. Her father would not force her into the match, but he insisted that she marry someone. What if she had run out of choices?

The heaviness that had momentarily lifted at her freedom from Sir Thomas crashed back over her, bringing with it a crushing headache. Aunt Gargrave's prediction from the previous night had proved true. At day's end, Dorothy dragged herself up to her chamber and collapsed into bed without bothering to do more than peel off her petticoats and stays. She faded in and out of sleep, worry kneeling on her chest. Her mind slipped between the bleakest days of Saint-Malo and dark futures without gardens, fresh air, or sunlight. Through it all echoed her mother's parting message: *This life is the time for suffering.*

When the maid appeared in the morning, Dorothy banished her from the room. The dim light of another rainy day pinned her under the refuge of her blankets.

Aunt Gargrave appeared in her doorway. "Why are you still in bed?"

"I'm so weary. I ache everywhere." How did anyone manage to rise day after day? And to what purpose?

"I don't have time to coddle you. Sit up."

Dorothy pushed herself up, her body as uncooperative as a pile of sandbags. When she managed to sit, her ears rang with pain.

"There. Now to get you dressed."

Dorothy shook her head. "I cannot bear it. The stays. I cannot breathe."

Aunt Gargrave felt her forehead. "You're not feverish."

"But I'm not well." Dorothy slumped back into the bed.

Her aunt regarded her for a long moment, then exited. Dorothy passed the hours watching the dim light from the fireplace flicker across the plaster wall until Aunt Gargrave returned with a physician. He checked her eyes and pulse and looked in her throat then asked Aunt Gargrave a series of questions that Dorothy could not hear.

"'Tis her spleen, I have no doubt," he finally said aloud. "Her humors have become unbalanced, and the excess of black bile from her spleen has pushed her into a fit of melancholy. 'Tis a common affliction, especially in women."

"How do we treat it?" Aunt Gargrave said.

Dorothy sat up to catch every word of his response.

"Black bile is cold and dry, so she should eat warm, moist foods. Keep her inside. Confine her in this chamber if necessary. Don't let anything excite her or strain her mind."

Dorothy drew her blanket tighter. Was she to be a prisoner, then?

"What about taking the waters at Epsom?" she asked hoarsely. Lady Diana had mentioned that she planned to visit there.

The doctor frowned. "Some have found relief from them, but the journey might be too taxing."

"I can endure it." Dorothy sat straighter, though it caused black spots to flash across her vision. "I will rest once I'm there."

The doctor shrugged a shoulder and gathered his satchel.

Aunt Gargrave gave Dorothy an exasperated look. "I suppose it will do you some good to get out of London. You have been pale lately. Heaven knows who will be able to escort you, though."

"Harry will take me."

"We'll see." Aunt Gargrave's forehead wrinkled in concern, and she escorted the physician out.

Dorothy sank back into her pillows with a frown. Why would Harry not take her to Epsom? He wanted her to be well and seeing Lady Diana there might cheer her up. But Dorothy would bear anyone's company—even gossipy Cousin Peters—if it meant she would still have sunshine and fresh air. Her headache finally eased enough to allow her some sleep, and she dreamed of the light glittering off a dark blue ocean and pearly shells washed to shore.

Chapter Twelve

Epsom, England

"Sister, dear, don't lean so! You'll upset the carriage."

Dorothy hid her smile from Brother Peyton's wife, Cecilia, and moved away from the window. "I'm just anxious to see Epsom. You've been before?"

"Oh, aye. I love the dining and the dances, and all the people to watch. I find it the best of things when my spirits are low." She beamed at Dorothy from across the coach, her pink cheeks dimpled.

Dorothy could not imagine Cecilia feeling low, but she welcomed her sister-in-law's abundant cheer, especially since it required little of her.

Cecilia's dimples faded. "Is the luggage balanced, do you think? I thought it was balanced, but are we leaning? Scoot over a little farther, Dorothy, dear. Wait. Too far. There! Stay just where you are and, heaven willing, we'll make it safely to Epsom."

Dorothy folded her hands in the middle of her lap, and looked straight ahead, lest the movement of her eyes send the coach swaying to one side or the other. Hedges and farmland flashed by on the edge of her vision.

"There! 'Tis Epsom. Now, dear, don't look out the window. We'll tumble to our deaths!"

Dorothy suppressed her smile and contented herself with turning her head ever so slightly to see the little town famous for its mineral waters peek up from the green, rolling landscape.

"'Tis not very crowded," she said.

"I told you it would not be."

The carriage finally bumped to a stop in front of a coaching house marked by a sign with a white pony. The dull ache behind Dorothy's eyes eased once the jostling stopped. She disembarked, envying all the more her brothers' freedom to ride when and where they pleased and avoid the discomfort of the coach.

The innkeeper showed them to a room on the upper floor. Cecilia inspected the mattress for lice and fleas and unpacked her own linens for the bed. Dorothy sat on a stool by the window overlooking the valley. In the distance, a wooden hall housed the well with its healing waters. Goose girls herded their charges down the dusty High Street, past newly-built inns and houses.

"I hope you're not moping, dear," said Cecilia. "We cannot have you giving in to your melancholy."

Dorothy forced a smile, but a prickling fear stirred in her chest. The melancholy was always there: a wolf stalking in the darkness. How could she fight it? She clutched the windowsill. She could not triumph when her own mind and body worked against her. The waters at Epsom would help. Perhaps they would keep the wolf at bay.

"I would like to find Lady Diana," Dorothy said, her breathing tight. "She's staying at the White Pony as well."

Cecilia was busy stripping off bed linens and other suspect items and discarding them in a pile. "That should be fine, dear. Just stay inside. Oh, and do not speak to any strange men until I join you."

"Aye, Sister."

Dorothy hurried down the hall and knocked on Lady Diana's door. An older woman in simple but well-made bodice and skirts answered. Behind her, Lady Diana lounged on a chair reading.

"Dorothy, my dear!" Lady Diana set her book aside and beckoned her friend into the room. She motioned to the woman who had answered the door. "Cousin Ann, allow me to introduce Dorothy Osborne. Ann is acting as my chaperone."

Dorothy returned Ann's curtsey, and the older women sat again to her embroidery, leaving the younger ladies to gossip. Dorothy told Lady Diana about her public refusal of Sir Thomas, and her friend convinced her to laugh at the memory. Then Lady Diana expounded on her many suitors, including Dorothy's cousin Henry Danvers.

"I am flattered by the attention," Lady Diana said, "but I needed this rest. My eyes give me a great deal of trouble."

"Your eyes?" Dorothy studied the bright, witty gaze of her companion.

"They often pain me. I've tried many cures, all to no avail. We are creatures made to bear with suffering, are we not?"

"I suppose it is so we don't become too attached to this mortal life," Dorothy said quietly.

"Perhaps," Lady Diana said. "I have wondered, though, why God would give me such a cheerful humor if he did not mean for me to be happy."

Dorothy had no answer to that, though if Lady Diana's bright personality meant that she was supposed to be happy, perhaps Dorothy's melancholy one signified a sorrowful fate.

Cecilia tracked them down and insisted they move outside.

"You need to see people and be seen. Especially you, Dorothy. Jovial young company—that's the cure for your sorrows. Dance, flirt, gossip, and we'll have you right in no time." She turned to Ann. "Don't you agree?"

The older woman gave a bemused nod.

"You see? Move along now. Oh, wait. Don't forget your hats. There, perfect!"

Cecilia shepherded them outside. She let the two friends walk arm in arm, while she chatted incessantly with Ann, who quickly developed a glazed expression under the onslaught of jabber.

"Have you heard about Lady Sunderland?" Lady Diana asked.

"I don't think so, but I know her," Dorothy said. "Her parents—the Sidneys—live not far distant from Chicksands." They were staunch Royalists as well. Lady Sunderland's husband, Henry Spencer, was killed riding into battle with King Charles.

"But you have not heard that she married again?"

"You cannot mean Dorothy Spencer, Lady Sunderland?" Dorothy's pace lagged. "But she was so in love with Lord Sunderland. She swore she would never love another." The poet Edmund Waller had even written adoring poems praising her wit and beauty, but her unfailing devotion to her husband's memory never faltered. "Whom would she marry?"

"Nobody, at least according to her family. A Robert Smith of no account and no lineage."

"I don't understand it."

"She says she did it for pity, since Master Smith was so persistent in his love. Her family is furious, and London is buzzing with the gossip."

Dorothy shook her head. "Is love always so unsteady?"

Over the following weeks, Dorothy and Lady Diana took the waters and attended musical performances and a few private parties—for if Cecilia did not already know everyone in Epsom, she soon would. Yet there were no expectations for Dorothy to meet, no one telling her what to wear or where to go. She found herself smiling more often.

As she and Cecilia were out walking one morning, hoofbeats trotted up behind them, and a familiar male voice called, "Hello, my sister!"

A shadow blocked the morning sunlight, and Dorothy blinked up at Harry, whose fine doublet and polished boots clashed with the casual, bucolic scenery.

"You look much improved," Harry said as he dismounted and embraced her.

From the difficult squeeze of her brother's too-tight arms, Dorothy examined her heart. The wolf still lurked there, but quietly. "I suppose the waters are helping."

"I'm glad to hear it. We'll have everything right again soon. Sir Justinian is still pining after you, and I spoke to him of you to keep your memory fresh." He took her arm and guided her away from Cecilia. "I was concerned that you were wasting away over William Temple, but I can see you are past that. That pup was not worthy of your troubles over him."

Dorothy winced and pulled away. "He was not a bad young man, Harry. You know I don't like to hear ill spoken of my friends."

His eyes darkened. "Friend? Ha! If he were such a friend, would he not have made the effort to visit?"

"He has been detained on the Continent, furthering his studies."

"If that were true, I would not have seen him in London last month."

"William Temple was in London?" It could not be. He might neglect to write if he were travelling, but how could he refuse to send her word when he returned to England, after all his protestations of undying friendship?

Harry's hand on her arm braced her up. "I'm sorry you must learn of this, Dorothy. It is as I have said: men are unsteady, unfaithful."

"Even you?" Dorothy yanked her arm away.

"I am not just a man. I am your brother. Ties of blood are the only ones you can count on. We—our family—must hold together in the face of whatever the world will throw at us. We will come out on top again, against Parliament and war and unfaithful friends. Rely on me, my sister, and all will be well."

He patted her cheek, his dry fingers cold on her skin.

"Perhaps he was distracted. Or did not know where to find me."

"Who, Temple? He greeted me, my sister. Gave me the coldest bow I have ever received. As if he were somehow above noticing me! And after I served with Prince Rupert in the late troubles. But he spoke not a word about you, not even to ask how you were."

The birds seemed to stop their singing, and Dorothy's legs turned unsteady. Her mother's warning had been right. She would live to see everyone betray her.

"I'm fatigued," Dorothy murmured. "I would rest."

"Of course, my dear sister. I will leave you to your peace for now." He studied her for a moment. "When we return to Chicksands, I am going to hire a companion for you."

"A companion? But I am always with Father or the servants. I hardly think—"

"I want someone to watch you. Watch out for you, I should say. Because of your ill humors. We cannot trust you to be aware of your own best interests."

She did not know what to trust. If everyone else would betray her, might she also betray herself?

"Brother Peyton spoke of sending his eldest daughter for a visit," Dorothy said. "She would be good company."

"I have already chosen for you: Jane Wright. Her brother is proving an excellent steward for Chicksands, and her sister is married to the rector, Master Goldsmith. She will be ideal to guard you through your fits of melancholy."

"Oh." Was Jane to be her companion, then, or a nurse of sorts? Or a spy for Harry? But that was an uncharitable thought after all her brother's concern.

She sank onto a low stone fence overlooking the fields. How bright the rolling pastures looked, with the golden sun playing over the grasses and the sheep and cattle browsing on the gentle hills. Yet she was in the shade. Somewhere out there, William was alive and happy, and she was glad for him. By now, he must have given his heart to someone else. That would explain why he cut her off. Searing pain tore through her at the thought that she no longer had any place in his life. Her world grew smaller and more constrained, while his expanded forever away from her.

Chapter Thirteen

BEDFORDSHIRE, ENGLAND

THE HEDGEROWS IN BEDFORDSHIRE WAFTED the scent of honeysuckle, and William felt as though Dorothy were waiting around each new bend in the road. It did not help that she—or at least her home at Chicksands—was achingly close. He urged his mount to a canter. Whether a thousand miles away or in the same room, Dorothy was forbidden to him. He had to forget her.

His horse stumbled, nearly throwing him from the saddle. William regained his balance and swung down to calm the prancing animal.

"What's wrong, girl?" he asked, scanning the horse and the ground.

There it was. A pulled shoe. It would cost him at least an extra day to get his horse to a blacksmith, and if she was injured, he'd have to find another way back to town. Another day of freedom was not such a bad thing, though. His visit to his family's Yorkshire properties had been refreshingly free of nagging, but he could not stay there long. He could not stay anywhere long, since he had no means to support himself.

He led the horse to the nearby village of Bedford, found a farrier, and arranged for a room at the Boar's Head Inn, hoping it was not infested with fleas.

"Anything else, Sir?" the innkeeper asked, passing William a mug of ale.

William shook his head, but as the innkeeper turned back to other customers, William called, "Wait! How far is it to Chicksands?"

"Chicksands? A healthy walk that direction."

The innkeeper pointed to the southeast. William nodded his thanks and swirled the ale in his mug. He had done his duty: stayed out of Dorothy's way. Why must Fortune tease him this way? He sipped his drink, but it seemed to vanish too quickly. He lacked the money and the stomach for the cockfighting going on in the inn's courtyard, so he stretched and wandered the village. Brick and timber houses gave way to thatched cottages as the dirt road moved from the town center. Sheep trotted past with barefoot shepherd boys.

William's feet turned to the southeast almost against his own will. What did he expect to find at Chicksands? Nothing promised Dorothy would be home. She might be married and established elsewhere. The innkeeper probably knew, but William did not quite have the courage to ask. It would serve him right, after neglecting her. As long as she was married to someone who made her happy, someone who appreciated her wit and could bring a smile to her eyes. He bent over, hands on knees, feeling that he might lose his ale on the dusty road.

What had he done? Had he lost his chance of happiness for a sense of duty? Yet the cause had been hopeless. He picked up a stick and flung it into the woods, sending birds chittering into the air.

He turned away from Chicksands and trudged back to the village. He was still the failure his father saw, and not the potential hero

Dorothy had admired. What could he have offered her? A family reduced to scrounging for heiresses to survive, no prospects for a career, no future.

He slept fitfully that night, knowing it was probably the closest to Dorothy he would ever come again.

The next morning, he continued on his way, returning to London resigned to whatever Fortune held in store for him. Outside his father's lodgings in Covent Garden, he had to skirt around their landlady, Mistress Painter, who was sitting in the dim sunlight reading a romance. William tried to see the title, wondering if it was one Dorothy had read, but he shook the thought away and went inside.

"I'm glad to see you back, boy," his father said. "Clean yourself up. There's someone I would like you to meet this evening."

His father's tone set off a warning in William's mind. "Of course, Father. Who is it?"

"Her name is Agnes Claybourn. She is a delightful girl, and an heiress. Five thousand pounds and an estate. An alliance with her is exactly what our family needs, and her parents look kindly on the match. They're seeking ties to a family with an old, respectable name."

"I see," William said, managing no enthusiasm. When his father gave him a sharp look, he added, "I will be happy to meet her."

His father nodded and clapped him on the shoulder. William went upstairs to change out of his dusty riding clothes. Five thousand pounds and an estate. That was the price for which he was to be sold. At least in this he could finally be useful to his father and his family. With an estate, he could live the life of a gentleman and not worry any longer about chasing the possibility of a government appointment. The changing political tides would not affect their family so much. Perhaps he could imitate his uncle's simple life and spend his time helping poor tenants. Withdrawing from the world had its appeal.

Of course, he would be admitting he was a failure at doing anything but holding an old name and not being too hideous for a young heiress. So much for the potential Dorothy had imagined in him.

That night, his father took him to dine with the Claybourn family. They sat on benches along a wooden table surrounding a peacock that had been plucked, roasted, and presented with its tail replaced. The feathers with their shimmering blue and green eyes drooped over William's plate as the conversation droned on.

The Claybourns seemed unexceptionable: polite, sturdy, surviving the difficult times by keeping their heads down and plodding forward. Agnes Claybourn was pretty enough, with her fair hair, but her eyes lacked any deep expression.

"Do you enjoy reading?" William asked her.

"Reading? Mother always warned that too much reading would spoil my mind." She quickly added, "I can read, of course, though I spent more time learning dance and embroidery." She finished the statement with a pretty, well-trained smile.

"Have you ever thought of traveling? I just returned from Holland, and it is a delightful country."

"Traveling?" Her forehead wrinkled. "I suppose I prefer to remain at home. But I would be delighted to hear about your travels, Sir."

She did not look delighted. She looked polite. She had been groomed to make an ideal wife. Her mind was not empty, but easily moldable to fit her husband's interests and desires. She would keep house prettily, entertain guests, rear children, all while smiling. Was that all she wanted, though?

William gently pried into Mistress Claybourn's thoughts as the servants carved the peacock and served it with gravy, but he found only a girl who was anxious to please and conform, one that would never challenge him to be more, and never think him a failure as long as he managed to meet the simple, basic requirements of society. He saw a dull, quiet life stretching before him. Perhaps that was all he was suited for, but something different still burned in him: his dreams of an active, meaningful existence.

Dorothy had kindled those dreams, and perhaps they were as unobtainable as she was. But even as he continued to meet with Mistress Claybourn over the following weeks and his father planned his harmless future, the call of the life he had hoped for would not be silenced.

"You like Mistress Claybourn?" his father asked one night over a game of backgammon.

"Does it matter?" William rolled a two and a three and clicked his pieces forward on the board. "Have you not already arranged everything?"

"Her parents hesitate. They would see her marry someone who has some affection for her, to make sure she will be treated well."

"Treated well? I would never mistreat my wife!"

"There is a difference between not mistreating someone and treating them well." His father picked up the dice.

William stared at the sharp black and white points painted on the board. Agnes Claybourn acted so complaisant, he had nearly forgotten that she must at least desire a husband who would regard her with affection.

"I suppose I don't yet know her well enough."

"Hmm. See that you get to know her better, then."

William watched his father move the pieces ahead of his own. "Is it settled, then? Is Mistress Claybourn to be my future?"

His father glanced up at him. "I will not force you to marry her. I know you are too stubborn for that. But someone like Mistress Claybourn would be ideal for you—for all of us. Given how little we have to offer, I hope that you will not let the opportunity pass by too easily."

"I understand," William said.

He lost the game and ascended to his chamber to stare out the window, which looked at nothing but the brick wall of the adjacent house. He knew what was holding him back. Dorothy still haunted his dreams, and her opinions guided his choices, even when he dressed in the morning. The only way to let her go was to know for certain that she was already gone.

William took a deep breath and pulled out a sheet of paper. With his pulse pounding in his throat, he addressed a short note to Dorothy—one that would be enough to confirm that all was lost and let him commit to a future with Agnes Claybourn.

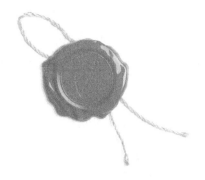

Chapter Fourteen

CHICKSANDS, ENGLAND

DOROTHY SAT DOWN TO SUPPER with only her old bachelor cousin Henry Molle and mousy Jane Wright for company. Harry was in London and her father was ill, but Cousin Molle insisted on dining in state. With his bandaged foot propped on a cushion, he reigned over the room from a high-backed chair at the far end of the table from Dorothy and Jane. Empty vases and silvery-polished pewter cluttered the board between them. The room was gray with winter light, but this stiffly formal dinner was the closest Dorothy would come to any holiday festivities, since the Puritans had banned the celebration of Christmas.

"Eat some of this leek soup," Molle called from the other end of the room. "'Tis warm and moist—exactly what you need. Now, I am supposed to avoid things that are moist since I have this infection in my foot. The pus was quite profuse."

Dorothy grimaced and pushed her greenish soup away. "Perhaps you would prefer some pheasant, Cousin?"

"Pheasant. That does sound delicious. Oh, but what are the properties of pheasant? Warm or cold? Dry or moist? Do you think your cook knows? How does he prepare it?"

Dorothy caught Jane trying not to laugh and quickly looked back at Molle. "He makes an excellent gooseberry preserve to serve with it."

Cousin Molle frowned. "I cannot recall the properties of gooseberries, either. I must not take anything that will upset my stomach. 'Tis delicate, you know. More wine!" he called to Collins.

Dorothy sighed and cut off a piece of the pheasant. Warm, cold, dry, moist. To her, it simply tasted bland.

Cousin Molle watched her eat with the expression of a hopeful puppy. "If only I could recall what the physician said about gooseberries."

Dorothy was tempted to invite the neighborhood physician to dine with them—he spent so much time at Chicksands attending her father anyway—but an evening with her cousin might frighten the good doctor away.

As Molle ate some delicate white bread—without butter, because he could not decide if it was fresh enough for his sensitive stomach—he rambled on about his gout. Dorothy did her best to nod politely while not really listening.

Collins slipped back into the room and presented Dorothy with a folded letter. She took it and opened the wax seal without looking at it, but when she noticed the handwriting, so familiar and dear that the looping circles seemed to draw the words onto her heart, everything in the world went still. She heard nothing more of Cousin Molle's complaints, only William's sweet voice reaching through the paper.

I can only beg you to forgive me for my inconsistency in writing, but I am now returned to London and my mind often turns to you. Though I was not a faithful correspondent, you have remained in my thoughts.

A friend reminds me that you once made a wager with one who would be your devoted servant for the

amount of ten pounds on the occasion of your mar-
riage. He wonders if that debt has come due. I hope to
hear from you and find that you are well. Know that I
remain

Your humble and obedient,
W. Temple

Dorothy set the letter down, nearly missing the table. He wanted to know if she was married. Their situation was no more hopeful than it had been. She could write him a cold letter, say she remembered no such wager, and be done with it. That was the wise thing to do. But she grew weary of being wise. What would happen if she teased him—flirted a little? It seemed that he would respond in kind. At least she would have a like-minded person to write to.

"Cousin Dorothy? What news?"

Dorothy looked down the long table at Molle, who watched her with a sharp eye. Next to her, Jane cast sideways glances at the letter, as though trying to steal some of the words from it.

Dorothy's hands trembled as she refolded the paper. She scrambled for an innocuous answer. "News from a friend."

"A friend?" Cousin Molle smiled. "Well, cousin, you'll keep your own council, I suppose, and young people will have their romances, but remember where your duty lies. An excess of passion is very disturbing to the humors, moreover, and—"

Dorothy nodded as Cousin Molle lectured on, but her attention was focused on the folded paper in her lap. She traced the seal over and over, the wax soft under her fingers. He had not forgotten her. A warmth settled over her and spread down through her body, tingling to her fingertips. The birdsong outside the window trilled, it seemed, for her.

Now it was just up to her to answer. He had not written in years. Was it possible he would neglect her again? She knew she should not commit herself, not show him what his letter meant to her. Not until she could be sure of him. She would control her passions and not let her heart overrule her head. But outside the window, the bird song continued.

Not forgotten. Not forgotten. Not forgotten.

As soon as she could escape from Jane's watchful eye, Dorothy sketched several drafts of a letter.

Too long.

Too flirtatious.

Not flirtatious enough.

She tossed each unhappy result in the fireplace and scowled at the ashes. She needed advice. Lady Diana was staying nearby with a gentlewoman known for her excellent cures for eye troubles, so Dorothy fastened on her hat and set off to visit her friend.

"What shall I do?" Dorothy asked as she and Lady Diana studied William's letter by the light of the fireplace.

"You cared a great deal for this William Temple?"

"I... I do. I did." The log crackling in the fire popped, and Dorothy gave a start. "That is, if circumstances were different—"

"Ha! Circumstances! My dearest, you rely too much on Fortune. She is no friend to anyone—capricious wench! But you cannot let such an opportunity pass."

"Is it wrong to correspond with him?"

"If you don't, I will, and tell him I am packing your bag so he may elope with you to the Continent."

"My lady! I would never... the scandal of it. And how would we live? I don't know that he has established himself enough to have a respectable occupation yet, especially not without his father's approval."

Lady Diana grinned and lazily twirled the signet ring she wore on a chain—the latest fashion from London. Dorothy realized how much of her heart she had already revealed. Her friend was right. There was no sense in denying what she wished to do the most.

"Don't be too dour in your response," Lady Diana said, bending to stir the low flames with a fire iron. "Tease him a little. If you cannot see him often, these letters are your chance to keep his interest."

"If he is interested elsewhere, I have no right—"

"Hang your rights, for once, my sweet Dorothy. If he was not already fairly captivated with you, he would not have bothered to write again. Whatever may come of it, think of this as a courtship."

Dorothy glanced again at the letter in her hands. William had cared enough to write to her again. She did not know what prompted it, but should she not take the risk of opening up to him a little? If Dorothy found someone she cared for more, she would have lost nothing by the comparison. And if she did not? Well, if she never found anyone to equal him, why would she want anyone else?

She accepted a fresh sheet of paper from Lady Diana and penned a new reply. This time the words came more easily.

Sir,

You may please to let my old servant (as you call him) know that I confess I owe much to his merits and the many obligations his kindness and civilities has laid upon me; but for the ten pound he claims, it is not yet due, and I think you may do well to persuade him (as a friend) to put it in the number of his desperate debts, for 'tis a very uncertain one. In all things else, pray say I am his servant.

And now, Sir, let me tell you that I am extremely glad (whosoever gave you the occasion) to hear from you, since (without compliment) there are very few

persons in the world I am more concerned in. To find
that you have overcome your long journey, that you
are well and in a place where it is possible for me
to see you, is such a satisfaction as I, who have not
been used to many, may be allowed to doubt of. Yet I
will hope my eyes do not deceive me, and that I have
not forgot to read; but if you please to confirm it to
me by another, you know how to direct it, for I am
where I was, still the same, and always
Your humble servant,
D. Osborne

There was nothing more to write. It was now up to William, to see if he would truly continue the correspondence. With a fluttering in her stomach, she sent the letter off with Collins and waited to hear how William would respond.

1653

THE NEXT MONTH

Chapter Fifteen

London, England

January dug its chilly claws into London, but William whistled on his way to play tennis. Dorothy was not married, and she had not cast him off. William just had to convince his father to trade an heiress for a Royalist. If Dorothy's inheritance could not offer the stability that Sir John desired, William would find a way out of the proposed alliance with the Claybourns and forge his own future. He trounced a line of opponents at the tennis courts as he worked out a plan.

That night at supper, he waited until the servant had placed the stewed hare on the table then addressed his ideas to his father.

"I want to be doing something, Sir. You have educated me—given me opportunities to travel—and the thought of retiring to an estate at this point in my life feels like exile."

"Ah, is that what's been troubling you?" His father set down his knife and turned his full attention to William. "You've shown no aptitude for academics or religion, and politics are an uncertain game. I assume that means you wish to pursue law?"

His father looked so hopeful that for a moment William considered agreeing. Yet the law now served the Rump Parliament and the oppressions of the army. That was not the path to becoming his own man—to belonging to himself, as Montaigne advised.

"I had something else in mind," William said. "Something in diplomacy."

His father leaned back and crossed his arms. "You wish to leave the country again."

"Not permanently, but I want to be moving—to be doing something useful."

"Huh. I wonder if I have addicted you to travel after being forced to send you abroad for so long. Life is not one long Grand Tour, William. You must learn to settle down and shoulder responsibility."

"I understand that, Sir." William struggled to keep his voice steady. "My time in Holland opened my eyes. I saw a country prospering in science, in literature, in art, and people of different faiths living in relative peace. I want to teach England what Holland knows: that tolerance brings peace and prosperity. War has destroyed so many lives in our country, and if I can help spare us from that again, I would consider my life well spent."

He held his father's thoughtful gaze.

"Perhaps time abroad did you some good after all. Your ambitions show youthful over-optimism, but you might make a useful diplomat, and heaven knows that Parliament will need men to help smooth over their rashness in executing the king." Sir John sighed. "Very well. I do not have the influence I once did, but I will see what I can find out about diplomatic positions."

"Thank you, Sir!" William's airy dreams were taking solid form. He could almost touch them.

That night, William avoided a dinner party where he would be expected to dance attendance on the Claybourns. He knew his father expected him to stay in their good graces, but he shirked his filial duty and instead wrapped himself in a blanket against the lonely winter chill and reread Dorothy's latest letter.

Her family pressured her to accept Sir Justinian, her arrogant "Emperor," and she jokingly promised William one of Sir Justinian's grown daughters as a wife if her family forced her to marry the old man. William chuckled in spite of the reminder of the obstacles that stood between them. He began his reply, imagining that Dorothy sat at his side, taking away the sting of the cold.

> *If I were an emperor, I would still be your humble servant. My entire kingdom—even my head—would be yours for the asking.*

William wrote on like a babbling fool, yet he did not want his imagined time with Dorothy to end. He set the page aside and pulled out a fresh sheet of paper, creamy and smooth in the smoky light of the tallow candle. How to use it? A few sheets of paper could never hold everything he wished to tell her—but especially of the places he wanted to show her in Holland and the Spanish Netherlands. He wrote as the bellman rang the hours of the night and sent the letter off with the early morning post-boy.

A few long days later, a carrier brought Dorothy's response.

> *I humbly thank you for your offer of your head; but if you were an emperor, I should not be so bold with you as to claim your promise; you might find twenty better employments for't. Only with your gracious leave, I think I should be a little exalted with remembering that you had been once my friend; 'twould more endanger my growing proud than being Sir Justinian's mistress, and yet he thought me pretty well inclin'd to't then.*

After dashing off a reply, William joined his father at breakfast.

Sir John waited until the manservant left the room, then fixed his gaze on his son.

"I understand you've been sending a great number of letters."

"Now that I am back in London, I have many friendships to renew," William said, trying to sound careless.

His father slammed his palm on the table, rattling the pewter plates. "Do not assume me an idiot, boy. I know you've been writing to that Osborne girl you met in Saint-Malo."

"*Mistress* Dorothy Osborne, the daughter of Sir Peter Osborne."

"Whatever her family's previous station, they are outcasts now. Mistress Osborne can only drag you down. Do you hear me, Son? You are not to have anything to do with her."

William stared at the plate in front of him, unable to make a promise he would not keep.

"Stubborn fool." Sir John rubbed his eyes wearily. "If all goes well, it will not matter. I have talked to my old acquaintance Lord Lisle, and he is to head up a diplomatic expedition to Sweden to earn their recognition of the government of Parliament. He will take you along."

William drew a long breath. He had no interest in Sweden, but it was a chance to gain experience and perhaps secure a permanent diplomatic position. A step toward a future with Dorothy.

"Thank you, Father," William mumbled.

The next morning, William dressed before dawn and tiptoed past his father's chambers and down the stairs to ease the door open. He knocked on the neighboring door and asked the servant for his landlady, Mistress Painter, knowing the old lady to be an early riser and suspecting her to have a kindly heart.

"Aye, what is it?" the harried landlady asked, stuffing a rebellious strand of gray hair back under her cap.

"Will you send this this letter out with yours when the postboy comes?"

She wiped her hands on her apron and gave him a confused look as she took it.

"And," William went on quickly, "may I have the reply sent to you, and I'll pick it up here?"

An amused gleam lit Mistress Painter's eyes as she glanced at Dorothy's name on the address. "Ah, that's the way of it. Well, I enjoy a good romance novel at times. Aye, you can send your letters through me." She wagged a finger at him. "Just see that you leave enough to pay the postage."

"Thank you, Madam!"

William counted out the coins into her hands and bounded off. Writing letters was not enough. He had to see Dorothy before Lord Lisle took him to a long exile in Sweden.

In the meantime, Dorothy had mentioned an interest in the new fashion for collecting antique signet rings and brass seals, so William headed for the London markets.

Chapter Sixteen

CHICKSANDS, ENGLAND

DOROTHY SAT MENDING STOCKINGS BY the large, square window of the great hall when Collins brought the post from London and a small leather sack.

"What's this?" Dorothy laid the mending aside.

"For you, Mistress." Collins grinned as he handed her the post and the sack.

She set the letters atop the mending and shook the sack out. Antique seals poured onto her lap, some sliding down her skirts to clink on the floor. Some were set in signet rings, while others were affixed to knobs of brass, pewter, wood, or even silver. She laughed and gathered them up.

They came with a note:

I sent you all I could find, except one I kept for my own. -W.T.

She glanced again at the wax seal on the note. It was stamped with a heart and anchor. Dorothy smiled as she traced her finger over the symbol of faithfulness.

William must have hunted all over London for the seals, as he had once helped her comb the shores of Saint-Malo for buttons and shells. Even Lady Sunderland, who had started the trend of wearing antique seals on ribbons, did not have a collection like this.

"What have we here? Love letters?"

She jumped at the sound of Harry's voice. Before she could object, he snatched a folded letter from the stack beside her. Ulysses mumbled a growl, but Dorothy silenced him with a touch and reached for the letter.

"Please return that. I've not read it yet."

Harry kept it from her and scanned the lines.

"Oh, 'tis bad news, I'm afraid." He shook his head and allowed Dorothy to take the letter.

She tried not to let her agitation show. Bad news? From William? But the letter was not from William. It was filled with Henry Cromwell's careful script. He rambled on about a Mistress Elizabeth Russell and asked Dorothy to congratulate him on his upcoming happiness.

Dorothy looked at Harry in confusion. "This is wonderful news."

"Wonderful news? Your mind is addled. Your suitors are falling away like pikemen before cannon fire. First Sir Thomas and now Henry Cromwell. You need to act quickly, or you'll lose Sir Justinian as well."

If only Fortune would smile on her so.

"I did not want to marry Cousin Thomas or Henry Cromwell."

"Then I don't understand why you hesitate to secure Sir Justinian." Harry yanked Henry Cromwell's letter from her and crumpled it.

"Harry!" Dorothy snatched it from his hand and smoothed it out. "How am I to write back if you destroy his letter?"

"You have no need to write back. He is only teasing you with the knowledge that he is beyond your reach now."

"Henry Cromwell is my friend. I am happy for him and glad that he continues to write."

"Are you mad, little sister? A successful, intelligent man is not interested in being your *friend*. You cannot possibly offer anything in conversation or counsel that he wishes to hear."

Dorothy grabbed the bag of seals and her other letters and marched from the great hall, Ulysses in tow. She spied Jane pacing in front of her bedroom door, so she turned to sneak down the back staircase and escape Chicksands Priory. She found refuge under her hawthorn tree and hunted through the packet for another letter with the heart and anchor seal. There it was!

She lifted the red wax and smoothed out the neat folds in the paper to read William's words.

> *I hope you may come to London soon. I must see you before I am banished from your presence once again. And who knows what may happen on such a long journey as mine?*

But how was she to get there?

"Perhaps when Lady Diana is well enough to travel," Dorothy whispered to the letter.

She sorted through the rest of the post and found a series of short romances written in William's hand. She did not recognize the titles: **The Constant Desperado, The Labyrinth of Fortune, The Incautious Pair.** Had he been translating for her? He knew she would be a heartless critic when it came to translations. She read the dedication:

> *I must only ask your pardon for entitling you to the disastrous chances of love and fortune. You will not be displeased, since I thereby entitle you to my whole life, which has hitherto been composed of nothing else; but whilst I am yours I can never be unhappy, and shall always esteem Fortune my friend, as long as you shall esteem me your servant.*

Dorothy leafed through the pages again. William had written these! During his exile, he had produced a volume of romances dedicated to her. She leaned against the twisted hawthorn trunk and read. They were varied and entertaining, nearly as good—she thought—as the best French romances, but they each ended tragically, with lovers separated or dying violently.

She read until the light grew too dim then hid the pages behind a basket of turnips in the kitchen—a place Henry would certainly not look. After supper, she snuck the manuscript to her room and stayed in their company late into the night. The emotion-laden pages were more than just stories; they were pieces of William's heart and mind given to her while they were apart. But did their tragic endings mean he saw no hope for them, too?

She woke the next morning much too late for breakfast. A short note from Lady Diana waited for her on the table. Dorothy read the light-hearted gossip with pricklings of guilt. She should not neglect a friend for a lover; she owed Lady Diana a visit. Taking a light cloak, she slipped out the back door with only Ulysses as a companion. Dorothy breathed the crisp scents of meadows and sheep, and she let her fingers trail over Ulysses' black-and-white spotted coat. Harry would be angry and insist she take Jane next time, but Dorothy did not want the little shadow sent by Harry creeping after her and ruining her blissful hours of freedom.

Lady Diana stayed confined to her chambers at Mistress Wentwood's house. The curtains kept the room in constant duskiness. Lady Diana smiled when she recognized Dorothy, but her bloodshot eyes no longer brightened like they once had.

"I'm glad you've come," Lady Diana said. "I can only read for a short time before my eyes tire, and it is so dreary is this little room."

"Do you feel much improved?" Dorothy asked.

"Not at all. In truth, I only stay because I enjoy your company." Lady Diana's smile faded. "And I am afraid of the reception I will receive in London. My suitors will desert me when they see the sorry state I've fallen to."

"Nonsense! Your eyes will recover, and in the meantime, the beauty of your mind will attract the suitors worth having."

"Ah, Dorothy. You are ever my valiant knight." Lady Diana laughed fondly.

Dorothy gave her a crooked smile. "I shall duel any man who dares insult you."

"I almost believe you would dare. You are stubborn, beneath your quietness."

Dorothy lost her smile. "Is it stubbornness that afflicts me? Harry says I am mad, and sometimes, when my mind is in disorder, I wonder if he is right."

"What does Harry know?" Lady Diana squeezed her hand. "Did I show you what he sent me?"

"My brother is sending you presents?" Dorothy would love to have Lady Diana for a sister, but the idea of Harry courting her sat in Dorothy's stomach like a bit of rotten meat.

Lady Diana produced an antique seal with a silver handle. "Look at it by the window so you can appreciate it."

Dorothy did so and gasped at the sight. Her brother had sent Lady Diana a hideous seal, with the face of some pagan idol glaring from the silver. Had he been trying to woo Lady Diana or insult her?

"Have you ever seen anything so ugly?" Lady Diana asked with a laugh.

"What was he thinking? You ought to throw it back at him."

Lady Diana giggled. "Nay, I'll keep it. 'Tis so hideous, it will make me look like a rare beauty by comparison. But a brother with such poor taste cannot be trusted in his opinions. Don't let his teasing bother you." She pointed to the signet ring Dorothy had placed on a ribbon around her neck. "I see you have joined the rest of us in following Lady Sunderland's fashion."

Dorothy rubbed her fingers over the smooth brass and confessed to Lady Diana about William's gift and his letter.

"We must get you to London, then," Lady Diana said.

"You are still not well."

"I fear I am only delaying both of our destinies. Write to Master Temple and tell him you will see him soon."

Lady Diana's coach deposited Dorothy at Aunt Gargrave's house near Charing Cross. Harry insisted that Jane come along, and Aunt Gargrave gave the girl a straw pallet next to Dorothy's bed. Dorothy was to have no privacy. Not even a few moments to sneak a message to William.

After breakfast the next day, Aunt Gargrave and Cousin Peters cornered Dorothy in the parlor. Aunt Gargrave's expression was pinched with concern, but Cousin Peters' eyes sparkled with the wicked joy of gloating over troubles not her own.

"I'm glad to see you've given up your moping," Aunt Gargrave said.

"I was not moping," Dorothy said quietly. "I was ill."

"You don't have the luxury of being ill. Sir Justinian is anxious to see you. If you don't convince him of your affection, he may look elsewhere."

"Aye, elsewhere." Cousin Peters nodded her agreement so enthusiastically, it endangered her broad-brimmed hat.

If only he would look elsewhere! If Dorothy could outlast all her suitors, perhaps her family would accept William.

"We need to get you out of the house," Aunt Gargrave said.

"What about Spring Gardens?" Dorothy asked.

Aunt Gargrave frowned. "'Tis not the most reputable place."

"Not the most reputable place, aye," Cousin Peters said, "but the Roundheads have not closed it down yet. We will wear masks, and no one will know who is who."

"I'm not sure Sir Justinian will approve of meeting his future bride in such a place," Aunt Gargrave said.

"Oh, he will not want to look like a fussy old man, and he'll enjoy throwing defiance in the teeth of Parliament," Cousin Peters said with a laugh.

"Very well." Aunt Gargrave settled back in her chair. "If Sir Justinian does not object, we will go."

Dorothy glanced at Jane, sitting beside her as always. She had to find a way to tell William where to meet her. "I think I'll invite Lady Diana."

"I thought she was still recovering," Aunt Gargrave said.

"Such a shame," Cousin Peters put in. "She was quite a beauty. And now—"

"She is still beautiful," Dorothy said.

"Still beautiful. Of course, of course," Cousin Peters said hastily. "And a mask might hide her eyes."

"We'll invite Harry and Robin as well," Aunt Gargrave said.

Dorothy would be glad to see Robin, but Harry's watchful eye would make it harder to meet with William. She had to hope the confusion of masks and crowds would give her a chance to avoid Harry, Jane, and Sir Justinian. Dorothy sent a note off to Lady Diana, knowing her friend would pass the news on to William for her.

They donned cloaks and black velvet masks that evening as the early dusk of winter fell. Robin declined the invitation, but everyone else would meet at the gardens. For Dorothy and the others at Aunt Danvers's house, it was a short walk through the Charing Cross neighborhood to the gardens.

A few people still bowled on the open green, but most had abandoned their games in the gathering darkness. Instead, people swarmed into the walled park, escaping the memories of war and the oppression of the Roundheads for the evening. Within the harbor of the walls, viols and lutes played a dance suite, and vendors sold food and drink to the masked crowds wandering the garden paths or admiring the fountains. Dorothy clasped her hands over her fluttering stomach. Somewhere in this swirl of disguised faces, William waited.

It could not lead to anything, of course. William was just a friend. But still her heart beat a faster tempo than the musicians' gigue at the thought of being near him once again, at the memory of his gentle touch on her skin. She scanned the crowds. How would she recognize him? Behind their masks, everyone looked strange, even frightening.

Then a voice whispered French into her ear. "Do not fear, Mistress Osborne. I am here."

She whirled to gaze into a pair of gray eyes behind a simple black mask. She broke into a smile. Before she could say anything, William had taken her arm and whisked her away from her family's party. She should have objected, but she felt truly free for the first time since her mother had died.

He led her into the dancing, and she let him guide her through the quick steps. Her cheeks warmed at each brush of his fingers, as though she'd been sipping sweet wine.

"I'm glad you were able to come," William said, his voice low. "I feared it was just a dream that you had actually written to me."

"That part, at least, is not a dream."

"Nor is this." William drew her aside and trailed his fingers over her cheek. Longing brightening his eyes: a desire far beyond friendship. It stirred in her, too, and she tilted her head back to meet his gaze, then caught herself and quickly looked away.

"It will feel like a dream when it is over," she whispered. "It cannot last."

He gently turned her back to face him. "Then let us enjoy it while we may."

She took his arm, and they strolled through the fairyland of the masque, the people in colorful clothing, the torch light driving away the darkness. Dorothy tried to absorb every moment of it, but especially the warmth of William's touch and the scent of his doublet.

"Meet me tomorrow morning in Hyde Park?" William asked.

"Aye," Dorothy said before she could question the wisdom of it. One more day to bask in the dream she could not keep.

She parted reluctantly from William and wiggled her way through the press back to her party, all on the lookout for her.

Harry gripped her arm. "Where have you been?"

"I saw an old acquaintance," Dorothy said.

"What will Sir Justinian think of you?" Harry hissed in her ear. "You must secure his commitment to you."

Harry released her arm, leaving it stinging. Dorothy's head was so full of William, she could speak pleasantly with Sir Justinian even when he said such ridiculous things as, "The music doth pay homage to the pulchritude of the night."

She avoided dancing with him, though. She could not bear the thought of even the mildest of his touches after William's caresses.

The next morning, she nearly floated down to breakfast and greeted everyone with a smile.

"I see you enjoyed yourself last night." Aunt Gargrave watched her suspiciously.

"I had a lovely time. 'Tis good to be out in company again."

"Indeed," Harry said, not looking up from his eggs and ham. "Did you have a pleasant time with Sir Justinian, then?"

"Pleasant enough."

"You are being too careless, Dorothy. Don't overestimate your charms."

She looked down, hiding the rebellion in her eyes.

"I think we should stay away from masques in the future," Harry said to their aunt.

Aunt Gargrave nodded. "They are risky anyway, with Parliament shutting down all the public amusements."

"If that is the case," Dorothy said quietly, "I would like to walk in Hyde Park today." She glanced up to meet her brother's narrow gaze. "Certainly, that cannot be objectionable?"

"Of course not," Aunt Gargrave said. "Provided you take an escort."

"Sir Justinian would be more than happy to play that role," Harry said.

Dorothy frowned. "I will hardly be able to relax and enjoy the exercise if I'm entertaining Sir Justinian."

"Yet it is an opportunity to secure him. He is wealthy, he is old, and I believe you will be able to manage him quite handily."

Dorothy gave Harry a curious look. She had often thought he was teasing in the past when he spoke of controlling her husband, but his statements had moved past joking.

"Do you mean in the same way he manages his daughters?" Dorothy asked. "He keeps them locked away. I could not abide it. I think him a secret tyrant, and I don't wish to fall under his management."

Harry looked thoughtful. "It would not do to marry you to a man who was not tractable. You should keep him dangling, though, in case a better option does not present itself soon. Unlike his daughters, you have other protectors who will not allow you to be locked away. I would make certain it did not happen to you."

Dorothy shook her head. "Were I married to him, he would be my lord and master. Even you would not be able to override his commands."

"That is a troubling notion. Very well. You may go walking with Jane today if you like."

Dorothy glanced at Jane, who gave her a weak smile. Dorothy relented. It was better than Sir Justinian.

They dressed and walked the short distance to the former royal grounds of Hyde Park. Parliament had sold it, but the new owner kept it open to those able to pay for admission. Luckily, Harry gave Dorothy a small allowance for London. Dorothy considered pretending she could not pay for Jane as well, but she could not walk on alone. She would have to lose the girl in the park.

The open green was crowded with people in their finest, riding horses or coaches or simply walking. Their slow pace was better suited to display than exercise, but the brisk air woke Dorothy's troubled thoughts. This meeting might be a mistake. What could Harry do to her, though, for greeting an acquaintance? With everyone in London here, it would be no surprise that she saw an old friend.

A few family friends greeted Dorothy, and she nodded as she passed, her eyes always scanning. Finally, they came to rest on the figure she'd been searching for, and her whole body felt lighter, as though she might float to William's arms. Then she remembered Jane at her side. Jane, whom her brother sent as her companion. Jane, whom she knew so little of.

William's gaze locked on her, his posture casual, but his eyes bright and alive with interest. If Jane was paying attention, she would not fail to miss that.

"Spring must be coming," Jane said. "I see some crocuses there in the lawn. Do you like them, Mistress Osborne?"

Dorothy gave her a quizzical look and glanced at the little yellow flowers she indicated.

"They're so lovely, I would like to pick some," Jane went on. "It would be proper, don't you think, if I gathered a few while you waited on the path? I would not want you to ruin your fine slippers in the mud here."

"Aye, I think it would be perfectly proper," Dorothy said carefully. "You will not be out of sight, after all."

Jane nodded and stepped just out of earshot to fuss among the flowers as William approached. He took her hand and squeezed it, then lifted it to his mouth with a lingering kiss that sent tingles up her arm.

"Master Temple. How pleasant to meet you here."

"And you, Mistress Osborne. How fortunate to find you alone for the moment." His lips quirked in a smile.

"Aye, I believe we have at least one friend," Dorothy whispered.

"I hope not just one. Your father still does not look favorably on us?" William asked.

"Nay. And yours?"

"He is anxious to see me away to Sweden. I don't know how long it will be until we can meet again."

Dorothy clung to his arm. "The trip will be dangerous. I would not have you go."

"It is only for a time, and it will help advance my career. With a greater income and the favor of those in power, it may be possible for our situation to change. You would still like that, would you not?"

"I would," Dorothy breathed out. "But please, don't pin your hopes and your future on something that might not happen. I don't wish you to waste—"

He ran his finger over her lower lip, and she shut her eyes, melting into the sensation.

"Don't call this a waste. No matter what may happen, this moment is not a waste, and I will not have you call it such. For now, just promise you will not cease to write. That you are still my faithful friend?"

"I am," Dorothy said.

"And I yours. It is enough for now. And I cannot believe that God would be so cruel as to keep two kindred minds and hearts apart forever."

"God is not cruel, but Fortune is, and Fortune rules in this world."

"We shall see." William smiled, then straightened with a look of alarm.

Dorothy turned to see Harry approaching on the path behind her, his eyes narrow.

Before Dorothy was aware of what was happening, Jane was at her side again, and William was bowing and disappearing into the crowd. The warmth of his fingers lingered on Dorothy's skin, while the cold stare of her brother turned the rest of her to ice.

Harry closed the distance between them in long strides, and Dorothy found herself being dragged off the path into the shadows of the trees.

"What is the meaning of this... this flirtation?" Harry hissed.

"Master Temple is an old friend."

"If he were your friend, he would not be distracting you from your duty and the path that will lead you and your family to security. Can you think of no one but yourself?"

Dorothy tried to object, but no words would come.

"Do you think you are invisible?" Harry went on. "This is Hyde Park! Look at who else witnessed your misbehavior."

She scanned the crowd, and gave a start when she recognized William's cousin, Colonel Hammond, watching her with narrowed eyes. She had thought she was going to face prison or execution under his hand on the Isle of Wight, and here he was, ready to condemn her again. From his expression, he had not forgotten who she was. Had she harmed William's chances? Would her family pay for their entanglement? Uncle Danvers had arranged for their past to be forgotten, but they were still Royalists, and her brothers had futures to think of.

"I am sorry," Dorothy whispered. Not sorry for seeing William— she could not feel any regret for those few moments of happiness. But sorry she had not been more cautious.

"I hope we will not all be." Harry guided her on, with a glare at Jane. Dorothy dared not look at her companion. The girl had shown herself to be something of a friend, but now Harry might take that away, too.

That night, they had supper with Robin. With him, at least, she felt no condemnation. Seeing Colonel Hammond again reminded her of their adventures together, and she longed for her childhood companion. Yet he was not the Robin of her youth. His cough was a constant interruption now, his eyes were dark, and when Dorothy gently embraced him, his thin bones bit into her arms.

"Don't look so alarmed, Sister," Robin said, pulling her aside. "I shall not suffer much longer."

"Oh, Robin." Dorothy wanted to tell him he was wrong, but she knew he spoke the truth.

"You need not mourn for me," Robin said. "But I want you to live for me. Don't let anyone hold you back."

Dorothy shook her head, and Robin took her hand, his skin feverishly warm against hers.

"Don't feign ignorance." He met her eyes. "This war has leaked poison into our family. You know it is true. I would not see you eaten alive by it as well."

"Family is all we have," Dorothy said. Yet the war had shredded her family. Her father still would not speak to her eldest brother John. Robin was dying, and her mother already gone. It seemed most days to be only her and Harry.

"Will you let your own family suck the life from you like marrow from a bone? That is not what family is meant to be."

Dorothy had no answer. The king was gone. War had left bleeding wounds in villages and between neighbors. Parliament and the army strangled the life from England. Where could one turn but to family? And, physically weary as she was from caring for her father, she was proud to be the daughter of a man of integrity and loyalty, and she felt honored to serve him.

Yet she caught Harry watching her with his calculating gaze, and she felt for a moment like she was at sea again, the deck tossing beneath her feet and nothing stable to grasp.

Chapter Seventeen

CHICKSANDS, ENGLAND

HARRY HAULED DOROTHY BACK TO Chicksands like one bringing a condemned debtor to Fleet Prison. At least, if Chicksands were Dorothy's prison, she had the "Liberty of the Fleet" and could roam the estate. She had to keep Jane close as her warden, but that no longer seemed so terrible.

"Thank you for what you did in Hyde Park," Dorothy said to Jane as they strolled through the orchard.

"What did *I* do, my lady?" Jane asked with a sly grin. "I only stopped to admire the flowers."

Dorothy chuckled. Had she thought Jane a mouse? More like a watchful cat.

When she returned to the house, she searched for the romance she had been reading, but it was not in the great hall where she'd left it. Jane helped her look, but they came up empty-handed.

"Have you seen my book, *Cléopâtre*?" she asked Harry when he came in from inspecting the fields. "It was in the great hall."

Harry searched the house and came back carrying the volume. "'Twas in the kitchen. I don't know what you were thinking."

175

Dorothy stared at the book. Had she taken it to the kitchen? Not that she could recall. But who would have moved it there?

A few evenings later, over a supper of chicken pie, Harry said, "Our Cousin Thorold has announced her intention to visit. I believe she is making the circuit of relatives to gloat over her recent widowhood."

Sir Peter nodded absently, but Dorothy sighed. It would fall to her to entertain Cousin Thorold.

In a few days' time, Cousin Thorold descended on them like a queen on a visit of state. Her black silk gown draped low on her shoulders in the latest fashion, and pearls accented her long, thin neck. With her beady eyes and prominent nose, she looked rather like a goose dressed in mourning clothes.

"Move those chairs in the great hall," she said to Collins, pointing out Dorothy's favorite reading spot. "I do not like the way the light falls across them. And bring in a table for cards." Cousin Thorold smiled at Dorothy. "You do play at cards, do you not, Cousin?"

"Of course," Dorothy said.

"That is good," Cousin Thorold said, running a finger over a painting to check for dust. "I was afraid the Puritan disdain for anything amusing might have infested your household."

Dorothy wanted to remind her cousin what price her family had paid to fight the Roundheads, but she held her tongue.

Sir Peter visited with Cousin Thorold for a few minutes after an early dinner, but complained of fatigue and retired, escorted by Harry. Dorothy wished she could do the same, but instead she was left to a never-ending series of cribbage games.

Thorold smiled too sweetly at Dorothy as she moved her peg up on the board and placed another sixpence on the table—one of those minted by Parliament, boasting the laurel leaves of victory. "Of course, Cousin, you'll have to come and stay with me when your father dies."

Dorothy nearly dropped the cards she was shuffling. "Pardon?"

"Well, 'tis inevitable, is it not? At my age, I'm not one to mince words. You are not married. You chase off every man who gets close to you. What do you expect to happen?"

Dorothy dealt their cards. "My father's health is poor, but there's no reason to plan for the worst."

"You must always plan for the worst." Thorold thumbed through her cards and selected two to toss in the crib.

Harry came in and greeted their cousin warmly. She turned a flirtatious smile on him, and Dorothy suppressed an eye roll.

"Mistress?" Collins approached Dorothy with an envelope. She recognized William's seal and pulled it under the table, turning it over before Harry could see the address. Despite her efforts at nonchalance, Harry watched her suspiciously.

"Excuse me," Dorothy said. "I seem to be running low on coins. I'll get more so we can continue our game."

Dorothy hurried to her chamber and opened the letter to drink up William's words.

> *I am anxious to be on my way to Sweden to prove myself, yet I hate being so far from you. I would like to visit Chicksands before I go, if you think it possible. If not, at least promise me your thoughts for one hour of the day.*

Dorothy jumped at a knock on the door.

Jane poked her head in. "Your brother is coming."

Dorothy nodded and slipped the letter under her sheets on her way to grab a few groats and threepenny coins from her dressing table.

Harry stalked into the room. "Dorothy, why have you left your guest alone? You've been gone fetching coins so long, you could have minted some new ones in the time since you left."

"I did not leave Cousin Thorold alone. I left her with you. I thought you might enjoy the chance for some private conversation."

"Me?" Harry looked taken aback.

"She is wealthy. You must plan on marrying as well."

"I personally served with Prince Rupert in the war. You could hardly expect me to stoop to Cousin Thorold." His look of distaste faded. "But you see what wealth has bought her. Her crassness would be ridiculous in a poor spinster, but it is smiled on with indulgence in a wealthy widow. Consider that as you plot your future course." He scanned her room. "Come, you must return to our guest."

Dorothy headed back to her card game, where Thorold accosted her with gossip.

"Lady Sunderland and her Master Smith are the biggest fools in town. She should never have married again. As a widow, she was admired and respected. But now? Ha!"

"Oh?" Dorothy asked. A nasty part of her wanted to hear that Lady Sunderland was regretting her ill-advised remarriage after swearing her love for her first husband.

"Aye. Master Smith makes a fool of himself for her every whim. He went from a respectable man to a clown. He was seen rolling on the ground with his lady's dog, trying to teach it a trick to amuse her." Thorold shuddered.

Dorothy frowned at the image. Devotion was admirable, but Dorothy would not want her husband laughed at for her sake.

"That's what comes of flaunting the opinions of family and society." Thorold took a sip of ale. "Have you ever heard of a love match that ended happily? The passion fades in any marriage, and those that only had passion to begin with are left without the other comforts they might have enjoyed: wealth, rank, respectability."

"You don't believe affection plays a role in marriage, then?" Dorothy asked.

Thorold looked at her in surprise. "Of course not. Do you think I married for love? Ha! My husband was a bore. But now he is gone, and I am a merry widow. This is the best part of a woman's life. Marry an old man, my dear. Aim for a short role as a wife, and a long, comfortable widowhood."

Thorold continued pouring her gloomy philosophy in Dorothy's ear. Dorothy wanted to refute her, but the only cases of unfading devotion she could recall came from books. As soon as Harry escorted their cousin away, Dorothy hurried upstairs to read William's letter again. Certainly, Thorold must be wrong, and Lady Sunderland, too. Love could last. Respect and affection could endure. It could not all be a passing illusion. Yet her mother's warning about happiness whispered in the draft slithering across the floor, and Dorothy shivered and hunted for William's letter as a talisman against ghosts.

It was not under the linen sheets where she'd left it. She searched under the bed and lifted the straw-stuffed mattress. Nothing. She combed the rest of her room, checking in her trunks and under the rug. The letter was gone. Dorothy paced the room a couple of times and shook out her sheets again, then chased down Jane in the garden.

"Have you moved my letter from William?" she asked.

Jane stood, her face paling. "Nay, my lady. But I thought I saw..."

"What?" Dorothy asked.

"I thought I saw your brother's groom in the hall outside your chambers."

Dorothy sat hard on the garden bench. "You think he took the letter? But it was hidden, and nothing else was missing from my room." She hesitated. "Could Harry have asked him to find it?"

"I cannot say, my lady. But I think he is strangely jealous of you."

"He wishes to see me happy and secure," Dorothy said. "Could it be that William will not provide those things for me?"

"We can never see what the future will bring, but I like Master Temple." Jane rested her hand on Dorothy's arm. "God willing, all will be made clear."

Dorothy nodded. She would have to confront Harry about his groom. Since her brother was gone, she took a few minutes to respond to William before she forgot everything he had written.

You make so reasonable demands that 'tis not fit you should be denied. You ask my thoughts but at one hour; you will think me bountiful, I hope, when I shall tell you that I know no hour when you have them not. No, in earnest, my very dreams are yours, and I have got such a habit of thinking of you that any other thought intrudes and grows uneasy to me.

She filled the page until she had to sign it,

Here is hardly room for your affectionate servant and friend.
D. Osborne.

Harry returned from delivering Cousin Thorold to the next stop on her Royal Progress, and he brought Cousin Molle with him. Dorothy's resolve sagged. Was she never to have a moment's peace?

"Cousin Dorothy!" Molle exclaimed. "I was just telling Harry how ill my stomach takes all this traveling. I think I will have to stay at Chicksands for some time. By the by, do you suppose your cook has any of that delicate white cake he makes? I think it would be just the thing to settle me."

Cousin Molle wandered to the kitchen to harass the unfortunate cook, and Dorothy turned on Harry.

"I received a letter while Cousin Thorold was here, but I cannot find it now. Do you know where I might have mislaid it?"

"Who was it from?"

Dorothy hesitated. "I did not have time to read it."

"I don't recall you receiving a letter." Harry looked at her in concern. "Are certain you did not imagine it?"

"Of course, I really received it. Collins delivered it to me. Where is he?"

"I sent him to London on an errand. Come, a disappearing letter from you-know-not-who? Sounds like a strange sort of dream to me."

"'Twas not a dream," Dorothy protested. "And I think your groom was lurking around my room."

Harry put a heavy hand on her shoulder. "You need more rest, my sister. You sound irrational, and you are not looking well."

Dorothy stepped away from Harry's grasp. "Perhaps I will go sit."

She found her way to the cloister garden. She knew she had received a letter, despite Harry's slippery words. Had she forgotten where she placed it, though? A steel-gray heaviness wrapped around her, and she wished she could curl up and sleep. But she had to finish *Cléopâtre* so she could loan it to William. She was anxious to hear his thoughts on the characters, if he liked the same ones she did.

The sunlight shifted, leaving Dorothy in shadow. She shivered. How delightful it would feel to curl up under her covers and hide from everything. Not yet, though. The kitchen garden needed weeding to prepare it for spring.

"Dorothy!" Harry invaded the cloister with Cousin Molle in tow. "How pale you look. You *are* ill."

She shut her book. "I'm a little drowsy, but I was just going to work in the garden. A bit of sunshine will set me right."

"Sunshine!" Cousin Molle said, aghast. "Nothing of the sort! You need bedrest."

"Don't be such a coxcomb, Molle," Harry said. "The thing of it is for her to walk in the house for an hour, then rest for half an hour. And eat only weak broth. But, Dorothy, don't think of working outside. It is far beneath you."

"Is eating far beneath us? You've sent Collins away. Someone must help with the kitchen gardens, or we will starve. We could lose the estate."

Harry drew her aside. "Ultimately, 'tis John's estate at any rate. Let him worry about it. We must think of our future, you and I, and that means you must be healthy again. I know you have not liked the suitors who have come your way, but when Father is gone, we'll be cast out, and what will the estate matter to us then?"

Dorothy sat back. "It matters. 'Tis about our family. Our respectability. Our duty." She rubbed her forehead.

"Getting headaches?" Cousin Molle popped in. "I get the headache all the time." He picked up Dorothy's book. "Of course, in your case the matter would be somewhat different. Women are often subject to headaches when they study or think too much. And with your spleen—"

"You must care for yourself," Harry said. "You take on too much worry. Cousin Molle is right. Your place is to manage servants and make social calls, not try to run an estate. You are overworking yourself, misplacing things, letting your fancy run wild."

"And yet I did well when we first returned."

"You?" Harry chuckled. "I was the one who set the estate to rights, with help from Collins and Wright. What do you imagine you did?"

"I worked in the orchard and the garden. I found the chickens. We eat eggs from my hens nearly every day."

"Chickens!" Henry said, and he and Cousin Molle laughed.

"'Tis often the sign of a deranged mind," Cousin Molle said, "to imagine one's actions were more important than they were."

The throbbing in Dorothy's head turned to a piercing pain. She sank onto the bench and turned her face from the pain of the light.

"Now, now, my dear," Harry said. "I'll take care of you. Cousin Molle will know some good remedies."

"I don't want any of his remedies," she said weakly.

"Want them or not," Cousin Molle said, "you need them. You keep going this way, you'll end up mad—not even fit company for your dog." He waved her book under her nose. "Or so ridiculous the neighbors will all laugh up their sleeves at you as you wander about insisting you're Cleopatra or some other such nonsense."

"You don't want to be locked up," Harry said gently. "I don't wish to see you shut away from society. Come, be a good girl, and do as we bid. We will take care of you. I will take care of you."

Dorothy's head hurt too much to argue. What if her melancholy—that prowling wolf—did consume her? Would she even know she was going mad?

Harry escorted her to her room, where Jane helped her to bed with a great deal of fussing. Cousin Molle consulted with Harry in a whisper, and they left something for Dorothy to drink. She took it, not caring what was in it, if only it would make the headache stop and the confusion of her thoughts still.

Dorothy woke the next morning to the deep weariness that came when pain had ended and only the exhaustion of fighting it remained. Jane roused from her pallet and hurried to her side.

"Mistress, are you well?"

"I don't know. My headache is less, but my mind is tired. I… I don't trust myself, Jane."

"Why ever not? Your mind is as sharp as anyone's."

"Is it? I'm not certain."

"This is your brother's doing, my lady. Don't listen to him, I beg you."

"He is my brother. Why would he wish me harm?" Her voice caught, and she turned her gaze to the glass of wine by her bedside. A bar of steel had been soaking in it, giving the wine a strange, rusty odor. "They want me to drink this?"

"Aye, and exercise after, but I'm not sure you should," Jane said.

Dorothy studied the gritty-looking wine. She took a deep breath and swallowed as much as she could in one gulp. She gagged on the metallic taste, and it burbled in her throat. She held a handkerchief to her mouth, taking long, slow breaths until her stomach calmed.

"There," Dorothy said. "Now, for some exercise."

Jane frowned, but then a teasing smile twinkled in her eyes. "What about tennis?"

Dorothy smiled. "Perhaps something a little calmer. Shuttlecocks might be just the thing." She met Jane's worried gaze. "I will beat this. I will not let my own mind be my enemy."

Jane shook her head. "I'm not certain you know who your real enemies are."

Dorothy pretended not to hear but wondered if Jane might be right. If she were, though, what was Dorothy to do? It meant she was surrounded by people who meant her harm. But she could not believe that, not about her own family. William was a faithful friend, as was Jane, but her family—her father and her brothers—were her guardians. Whether she liked it or not, they controlled her life. If they chose, Chicksands truly could be her prison.

She and Jane played shuttlecocks in the yard, then Dorothy returned inside to write to William. She would not give him up. If the Fleet Prison had its clandestine marriages, like something out of one of her romances, Dorothy could have her secret correspondence as well. If Harry was stealing her letters, she would sneak her responses to William and burn his replies. Of course, if she did so, she might someday not be sure if William was real or just a dream she had invented to make her prison more bearable.

But Collins brought her another letter on his return from London. It was real, solid in her fingers. William spoke only of everyday things—his sister Martha recovering from a cold, the odd dream he had—but Dorothy read and reread the letter, trying to commit it to memory. She wanted to treasure it, but if Harry or his groom were spying on her, trying to keep her from William, she could not let them find it. Reluctantly, she folded it and fed it to the fire, and the flames licked it up. The seal with its unmoving anchor melted and blackened, and Dorothy turned away, unable to watch.

Dorothy ventured downstairs in the morning to join her brother and cousin for breakfast. They watched her drag her spoon through her oatmeal pudding and exchanged knowing glances. Their scrutiny made her fingers tremble. What did they see that she did not?

"Still suffering from the spleen?" Cousin Molle asked when she picked at her food.

"Just tired." Dorothy forced herself to take a bite of the thick oatmeal and smile a little.

"She's been daydreaming of William Temple, I'll wager," Harry said.

"What, that ne'er-do-well?" Cousin Molle asked. "A pretty face, perhaps, but I see nothing to moon over in that coxcomb."

Harry gave Dorothy a smug look. "He's a worthless young man. Arrogant, irreligious. Probably just toying with our Dorothy to get to her fortune."

"That's not true!" Dorothy said. "He's a good man, and he does not care about my fortune. 'Tis not enough to satisfy his father, anyway."

"Hah!" Cousin Molle said between bites of oatmeal. "Grasping family, too poverty stricken to ever rise above their station."

Harry leaned forward. "If he really cared for you, my sister, he would want to see you with someone who could provide for you. And if your affection for him was sincere, you would want to see him with someone who would give him the start in life he needs. They say he's courting Mistress Claybourn in earnest, and she could do that for him."

Dorothy squeezed her eyes shut, her headache flaring up to melt away her certainty. Perhaps they were right. She was deluding herself, reading too many novels. She was no heroine confined unjustly to prison, but a woman with too much imagination and an untrustworthy mind. Fate frowned on her and William. Their fortunes did not agree, and their families would never consent to the marriage. She should encourage him to pursue Mistress Claybourn. The thought of him with someone else shredded her heart. But if it brought him success and happiness, she would enjoy the moments they had shared and bid him farewell.

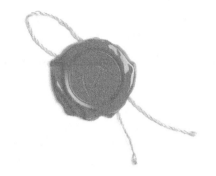

Chapter Eighteen

LONDON, ENGLAND

WILLIAM READ DOROTHY'S LATEST LETTER. Jane, who had delivered it to him personally on her visit to town, paced by the window of the parlor, wringing her hands.

Dorothy's words set William's teeth on edge, especially her cold analysis of his father's urgings to marry Mistress Claybourn.

> *In earnest, I know not what to say, but if your father does not use all his kindness and all his power to make you consider your own advantage, he is not like other fathers. Can you imagine that he that demands £5,000 besides the reversion of an estate will like bare £4,000?*

He swept a stubborn lock of hair from his face and turned to Jane. "How is she?"

"I am afraid for her, Sir. Her spirits are low, and her brother and Master Molle persecute her. They are near to convincing her that she is mad."

"She should not be alone with them." William stared out the window as though he could somehow pierce the iron gray fog and

187

see all the way to Chicksands. "I almost wish you had not come to London, but I am grateful to have her letter and to know she'll receive mine."

"My lady needs them. Otherwise, she'd have only her brother's word for anything happening outside Chicksands." Jane twisted a corner of her linen collar. "I'm always on guard to make sure they don't find your letters. If they knew, they would tighten the screws even more and probably send me away. I don't want to leave her alone."

"Nay, 'twould be monstrously cruel to leave her undefended with that viper." William clenched the arm of his chair. "If only we lived in the days of knights and damsels, I would attack the keep and carry her off, but that would not do today, I suppose."

"Sometimes I wonder," Jane murmured.

"'Tis a fanciful notion, but Dorothy would not approve, and I don't wish to carry off a lady while she scolds in my ear." He leaned back in his chair, tipping it onto two legs. "And she would be right. I cannot support her, especially not without my father's blessing. 'Tis one thing to say love is an all-powerful force, but we cannot eat love, and 'twill not keep the rain off our heads." He let the chair slam back onto the floor and rested his head in his hands. "If only I were not so useless! Had I applied myself more in school, made the right connection, perhaps I would have something to offer her besides the vague hope of Sweden."

Jane stood. "You are not useless, Sir. You will find a way. And you mean the world to my lady—don't forget that."

"You are a good friend to both of us, Jane."

She smiled and curtseyed. "Send me your response at my cousin's house, and I'll make sure Dorothy receives it. Collins is a good fellow, but I think Master Harry is watching him."

Jane had barely left when William's father slammed the door open. William jumped to attention.

"What is going on here?" His father stabbed a finger at the empty chair across from William. "Are you entertaining a mistress in the house, yet refusing to pay proper court to Mistress Claybourn?"

Pay court to her five thousand pounds and estate was more like it, but William kept those thoughts to himself. "I was visiting with an old friend. She is a respectable girl."

"Defensive of her, are you? Have you formed yet another *tendre* for a fortuneless, dispossessed girl? It just shows how unsteady your heart is, and how unfit you are to choose your own future."

William flushed. "If you would question my heart, Sir, I assure you it is still fixed. I prefer Dorothy Osborne over any other girl in Europe. And, her fortune is not so much less than Mistress Claybourn's!"

"She lacks an estate. Land is the thing that will secure you for the future. If this girl cared for you, she would urge you to do what is best for your family."

"As to that, Sir, she does!" William picked up Dorothy's letter and shook it in his father's face. "She urges me, as a friend, to consider your care for me, to heed your advice. It is not Dorothy Osborne who opposes you, but I, and my own heart."

"The heart is a fickle thing. It will lead you into ruin."

"As it did you? You married for affection rather than fortune! And you were happy! You cannot deny it."

His father's gaze softened a little, and he looked out the window, his eyes distant. "It was a happy marriage. But my beloved wife is gone, and we are left on the edge of ruin, pushed about by every change of fortune."

William stepped back, stunned as if he had been slapped. "You don't regret marrying Mother."

Sir John met his eyes. "For my sake, I do not. But what of you children? Did I not owe something better to you than this hard-scramble life?"

William shook his head.

His father squared his shoulders. "You will do your duty to your family."

He left the parlor, slamming the door behind him. William looked again at Dorothy's letter with a fresh wave of empathy. If stubborn William, who had been raised by an indulgent uncle, had trouble believing what his heart and mind knew were best for him, what of Dorothy always being told what to do and made to doubt her own sanity?

William wanted to shout defiance at his father, the Puritans, Parliament, and everything that stood between him and Dorothy. But what could he do? Write letters, play tennis, wait for Sweden. He had to cool off before he did the first, so he opted for the second.

By the time he had finished his game, he could barely hold his racket up, but his mind began to settle like muddy water caught in a bucket. He had a duty to his family. Duty! What a plaguy word. What had his cousin, Robert Hammond, said about duty pulling in two directions? Eventually, you had to choose a side.

Outside the tennis courts, William nearly stumbled into Mistress Claybourn strolling by with her mother as chaperone. Mistress Claybourn looked not at all surprised to see him. William groaned to himself.

The elder Mistress Claybourn gave William a predatory smile. "Master Temple! What good fortune meeting you here. Come, walk with us."

"I would…" But William had a letter to write to Dorothy before Jane left for Chicksands. A duty to a friend. "Yet I find myself quite exhausted. I think I might do better to rest a moment."

He meant to sit on the cool earth, but his legs betrayed him, and he found himself sprawled on his back in the park. Mistress Claybourn and her mother gawked. Let them think him mad. It might deter their persistence.

"Another time, then," the elder Mistress Claybourn said, hurrying her daughter away.

William chuckled. Now he had a story for Dorothy's letter. After filling his lungs with the grass-scented air and letting its coolness seep through his doublet, he forced himself to stand and made his way to the house where Jane was staying with relatives. He wrote his letter there, begging Dorothy to take better care of herself.

"I'll see she gets it right away, Sir," Jane said.

"You are a jewel, Jane," William replied. "Watch over Dorothy."

"Like a hound," she said with a sad smile.

Then there was nothing for William but the agony of waiting. At night, he dreamed of Dorothy caught in a deadly riptide that pulled her into a black, churning sea. He raced to her, but the wet sand and dark waters mired his legs, and he could only reach out helplessly as the tides tore her away.

In a few days' time, his landlady's maid brought deliverance in the form of a letter from Dorothy. He lapped up every heart-wrenching word.

> *The truth is, I cannot deny but that I have been very careless of myself, but, alas! who would have been other? I never thought my life a thing worth my care whilst nobody was concerned in't but myself; now I shall look upon't as something that you would not lose, and therefore shall endeavor to keep it for you. But then you must return my kindness with the same care of a life that's much dearer to me.*

That was something he could easily promise, though she scolded him for exhausting himself and fretted that he would become ill. His story of collapsing in front of Mistress Claybourn had made her laugh, though, and he would accept all the chiding in the world to know she had smiled for him. Yet she still defended his father.

> *He may be confident I can never think of disposing myself without my father's consent; and though he*

191

*has left it more in my power than almost anybody
leaves a daughter, yet certainly I were the worst
natured person in the world if his kindness were
not a greater tie upon me than any advantage he
could have reserved. Besides that, 'tis my duty, from
which nothing can ever tempt me, nor could you like
it in me if I should do otherwise, 'twould make me
unworthy of your esteem; but if ever that may be
obtained, or I left free, and you in the same condition,
all the advantages of fortune or person imaginable
met together in one man should not be preferred
before you.*

At least that sounded hopeful.

*Once more good-night. I am half in a dream already.
Your D. Osborne.*

If only she were his indeed! Was there any overcoming the obstacles in their way? It did not matter. He knew which duty he would serve, and it made his next step clear.

Mistress Claybourn finally claimed William for an outing to Hyde Park. William felt like a traitor with Mistress Claybourn's hand on his arm. She did not lean on him, almost hesitated to touch him, and her demure eyes hid behind long lashes. She expected his proposal, but nothing showed that she welcomed it. She was like many other women, he supposed, hoping for nothing more than a husband who would not abuse her while giving her a respectable position and the most comfortable life that could be hoped for in troubled times. But he had to believe life offered more.

"Mistress Claybourn," William said.

She turned her eyes to his. "Sir?"

"If I were to ask for your hand in marriage, I imagine you would say 'aye.'"

She drew a breath, her expression resigned.

"Nay, don't reply," William said. "That is not my question. Our families look on the match favorably, and you are a pretty, amiable girl, and ready to make someone happy."

She gave him a confused look. "Sir?"

"I apologize. Perhaps I'm being too blunt. But you don't actually wish to marry me, do you? If you were given the choice between myself and any other man?"

She hesitated, just for a beat. "It would be a pleasing match for our families, and I had thought you would be a dutiful husband."

William winced at the word *dutiful*. "I would intend to be. But I suspect your heart is not in it."

"My heart?" she asked quietly. "It rarely has much to say in marriages, Sir, at least among those of our station. I believe we would have affection for each other in time."

"And passion? Have you ever felt passion for anyone, Mistress Claybourn?"

She blushed deeply and said nothing.

"You have!" William exclaimed.

"Passion is folly, I have always been told. We are better to be guided by our elders."

"Passion alone is folly, but what of passion tempered by long-standing affection and a common vision?"

"You are speaking of Dorothy Osborne," she said quietly. "I have heard enough to know your attachment to her. I think your loyalty is commendable."

Guilt pricked at him. Poor woman, knowing he loved another all this time. He had a duty to her as well. "But?"

"But we don't often get those things we wish for in this world. We can only let reason guide our choices."

How much she sounded like Dorothy, yet how different she was.

"There is reason in my argument as well," William said. "Would not society be better served by allowing us to choose our own part-ners from the suitable alternatives, with affection and a common mind, rather than forcing us all into generation after generation of unhappy marriages, filled with discord and unfaithfulness?"

Her eyes widened, and she blushed.

"You see, my lady, I would always be making you uncomfortable. We live in an age of revolutions, and this is mine: I will not have a wife who does not have a place in my heart, and I in hers. Tell your father what an obstinate ne'er-do-well I am, and then find someone you truly care for." He kissed her on the cheek. "Much happiness to you, my dear."

A frown creased her forehead. "I don't entirely understand you, but I see you mean to do me a kindness. And I wish you well with your Mistress Osborne."

She walked back to her mother, who gave him a dark look, but he drew the easy breaths of a liberated man. If only Dorothy could also find deliverance.

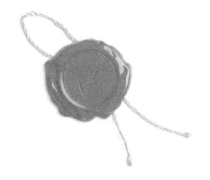

Chapter Nineteen

CHICKSANDS, ENGLAND

DOROTHY CROSSED THROUGH THE SHADED doorway of Chicksands after a walk with Jane and Ulysses. The warm touch of the sun lingered on her cheeks. In the daylight, with a friend at her side, anything seemed possible: even William's hopes for the future. Yet the dim stone halls of Chicksands whispered to her of responsibilities to her family.

Harry stood in the great hall, a letter held up to smoky fire of the rushlights. His face was bare, unreadable, yet in the firelight, a hint of triumph glittered in his eyes.

Dorothy stopped a few feet from Harry, and Jane paused behind her. Ulysses nuzzled her hand with his cold nose, sending an icy shiver up her arm. The handwriting on the letter was not William's. Who sent them news, then? Had Robin taken a turn for the worse?

Harry glanced at them. "It appears the Baroness Grey de Ruthyn has come to Bedfordshire to stay at her family's manor house by St Thomas Chapel."

Dorothy and Jane exchanged curious looks.

"They are quite nearly our closest neighbors, then," Dorothy told Jane, "When Chicksands was a priory, the St Thomas Chapel

195

was part of its property. Henry the Eighth split it when he seized the lands."

"And because we are such near neighbors," Harry went on, "and prominent ones as well, the baroness has invited me to visit this evening. She included you in the invitation as well, my sister."

"It sounds quite formal," Dorothy said. "I have not been feeling well—"

"It may be tiresome to us both, but I have decided to attend despite my many responsibilities around Chicksands, so you certainly can afford to as well. Being a baroness does not count for much under Parliament, but she could be a useful connection."

Dorothy winced from the thought of attending a large, formal event full of noise and gossiping. "I had rather stay with Father."

Harry cast a dismissive glance at Jane. "Leave us."

Jane looked to Dorothy for direction.

Dorothy leaned against Ulysses' warm coat. "I will speak with you soon, Jane."

Jane curtseyed and slipped out, shutting the door behind her.

Dorothy whirled on Harry. "Jane is my companion. You have no right to send her away."

"No right!" Harry's eyes flashed. "Don't forget your place, my sister. You are a dependent on me."

"On our father!"

"Who is too ill to know where he is many days. Who does that leave to watch out for your welfare?"

"Brother John."

"Ha! Banished from this house until Father dies and he inherits it. And that is only if he recovers."

"Recovers?" Dorothy had not heard much of her eldest brother since her mother died. Her father had still not forgiven John for abandoning the king's cause and marrying a Parliamentarian. A stark reminder of her fate if she chose William over her family.

"He has been ill for some time. If he should die, Chicksands will be mine. You must rely on me, Dorothy, until that day when I find you a suitable husband. And even then, ties of blood are stronger than political arrangements."

She took a step back.

Harry shook a finger in her face. "You will attend the baroness's party."

Dorothy gave him a stiff curtsey and stormed off to stop herself from screaming at him. The walls of Chicksands felt too close, too confining, as they never had before. She raced out to the gardens and threw herself down to the ground beneath her hawthorn tree. Ulysses whined and nuzzled against her, licking the tears from her face.

"My lady," Jane said softly.

Dorothy gave a start and sat up, trying to wipe her cheeks dry. Jane came around the tree and knelt in the shade.

"Oh, my lady." Jane embraced Dorothy. "I am afraid for you."

"I will be fine. Harry may bully me, but he will not hurt me." She sat up and plucked a leaf from her hair. "I suppose I had best meet this baroness to preserve the peace. She sounds horribly old and dry."

"I'll help you get ready. Perhaps 'twill not be so bad."

"There is one thing I want to do first," Dorothy said. "Something Harry said put me in mind of it."

Dorothy climbed the stairs to her father's room. The stale smell of sickness leaked from his chamber. Dorothy breathed through her mouth and stepped into the dim light of the curtained room.

"Dorothy?" Sir Peter called, but Dorothy could not be sure if he meant her or her mother.

"I'm here, Father," she said, taking his hand.

"My good girl. You have never deserted me."

"And I never will. Your children honor you, Sir."

"Not all," Sir Peter said weakly.

"Aye, Father." She tightened her grip on his hand. "I know you have been angry at John, but he is very ill now. I wonder if he would do better if he were allowed to come home."

"So he can gloat over the estate that will soon be his?"

"None of that talk, Father. We hope you will be with us for many years yet. But what if John does not have much longer?"

His hand trembled in hers.

"Do you remember how he would run the blockades at Castle Cornet to bring you news and supplies? It must hurt him now to be banished from your presence."

Sir Peter groaned and turned away, but Dorothy gently smoothed his sheets back down. "Mother would want you to part in peace with each other."

Her father sighed, a deep, rasping sound, full of long years of sadness and resentment. "Aye, let him come home."

Dorothy kissed her father's forehead. "Thank you, Sir."

She left him in peace. If John were seriously ill, he would not be reading his correspondence, so Dorothy addressed her letter to John's wife, Eleanor. When Dorothy finished, she entrusted the letter to Collins and went to prepare for the baroness's gathering.

Jane helped her into a green satin dress and pulled her hair up to show off her face.

"My necklace too, please—the glass beads that look like pearls," Dorothy said.

Jane fastened them around Dorothy's neck, and Dorothy put her mother's pearl earrings on. She smiled at her reflection. "That will have to do."

"You look beautiful. If only William could see you."

Dorothy sighed, and the mirror returned her sorrowful gaze.

"Sometimes I wonder if I will ever be happy," Dorothy said. "Or if I am just delaying the time until I give in to Harry's demands."

"Don't say that, my lady. For all God requires of us, he gives us the strength to overcome it, and the reward equal to it, if we endure it well."

Dorothy touched her mother's earrings. Would the reward come in this life, or the next?

Dorothy descended the stairs, and Harry bowed deeply to her. "You look lovely, my sister. Fresher than the flowers promising spring."

Had her brother been reading poetry? She returned a curt nod for his odd compliment, and they walked in silence to St Thomas Chapel Manor. The red brick building made good use of the local clay, matching the old St Thomas Chapel. The manor itself was a symmetrical building with large, leaded-glass windows—newer and more stylish than Chicksands Priory.

A footman opened the door and admitted them to a great hall bright with candle light and crowded with the local gentry in their best doublets and gowns. A consort of viols played on the far end of the room near the fireplace. Harry gave his name and Dorothy's to the steward, who guided them through the company.

"Master Beagle is in attendance," Harry whispered. "If you let Sir Justinian slip your net, he'll be waiting to slither his way in."

Master Beagle stuffed an apple tart into his round cheeks, sprinkling crumbs onto his dull brown doublet. Dorothy grimaced.

"The baroness needs more guidance in choosing her guests," Harry hissed in Dorothy's ear.

He gesturing with his chin toward their father's silver-haired nemesis, Colonel Samuel Luke, who was deep in conversation with another aged gentleman.

The guests shifted subtly and a young lady in bright yellow drifted forward, like a canary appearing from a flock of sparrows. Chestnut-colored curls crowned her head, and a hopeful smile brightened her eyes.

"Susan Longueville, Lady Grey de Ruthyn," the steward announced, "May I present Master Harry Osborne and Mistress Dorothy Osborne."

"Welcome," Lady Ruthyn said, her voice as sweet as a song. "It is a pleasure to meet my neighbors."

Dorothy curtseyed deeply to the baroness to hide her surprise. She had imagined a formidable old woman, but this lady could be no older than twenty.

Lady Ruthyn smiled at Dorothy and took her arm, guiding her away from Harry. "We are going to be good friends, I'm sure."

"Oh." Dorothy drew back from the young women's immediate intimacy. Did the baroness want something from her or her family?

"I'm so glad to find another young lady in this crowd." Lady Ruthyn lowered her voice, but her free hand fluttered as she spoke, punctuating her words. "Everyone else in the neighborhood is so old. I suppose all the young people have gone to London, but it is too crowded there for me, and the men in town seem quite silly."

Dorothy could imagine why. A beautiful young heiress with a title? The males of Bedfordshire would likely show themselves to be just as silly. Already Master Beagle followed Lady Ruthyn with a longing gaze.

Dorothy relaxed under Lady Ruthyn's warm smile. "I hope you enjoy it here enough to extend your stay for some time."

"Oh, I'm sure I will. Bedfordshire is so friendly. I was not sure many people would want to attend tonight, but look how many have turned out." She grinned unselfconsciously and gestured around the crowded room.

Dorothy would have doubted that anyone could be so unspoiled, but as Lady Ruthyn chittered on, Dorothy learned that her brother was supposed to be the heir. Only his sudden death, along with their father's, had thrust Lady Ruthyn onto center stage. The longer Lady Ruthyn talked, the more Dorothy felt a sisterly need to protect her from the world she did not understand.

When Lady Ruthyn stopped to greet another guest, Colonel Luke came forward and bowed to Dorothy. She drew back, looking for escape.

"Mistress Osborne," the colonel said quickly, "I have sought for an opportunity to speak with you."

"Oh?" Dorothy asked.

"I have heard you've done great work with your garden at Chicksands."

"I do find it enjoyable." Did the colonel want advice now on how to cultivate the lands he had stolen from her family?

He smiled nervously, deepening the lines around his eyes. "The beans you grow are complimented widely."

"That is…gratifying," Dorothy said, utterly confused. Colonel Luke was not seeking a wife, so this was not an awkward attempt at courtship.

"My own bean crop has not done well. I was hoping—might I buy some seed from you?"

Dorothy hesitated. Was it better to see their former lands lay barren, or to help them prosper under their enemy's plow? Yet it was hard to think of this old man as an enemy, as he stood before her with his imploring look. At least he was willing to pay, and they sorely needed the funds. "I suppose I have some to spare."

Colonel Luke bowed his thanks and moved back into the crowd as Lady Ruthyn returned to take Dorothy's arm again. As they walked, Dorothy noticed a dark-skinned girl following in their wake.

"Oh!" Lady Ruthyn beckoned the girl forward. "Mistress Osborne, this is Sheba. My mother sent her to keep me company."

"Sheba?" Dorothy repeated.

The way the girl's eyes tightened at the name, Dorothy guessed it was not her real one. She knew some of the rich kept African servants as symbols of their wealth, but she had never looked into the eyes of one of these servants. She felt a sort of sympathy with the girl, treated as a possession and a status symbol, though her hardships with Harry could be nothing to those of a girl torn from a far-away home.

"'Tis a pleasure to meet you," Dorothy said.

The girl curtseyed but said no more. Lady Ruthyn chatted on, seemingly oblivious to Sheba's discomfort. Dorothy considered how blissful it must be to know so little of suffering that one did not recognize it. Yet it also allowed one to do harm without knowing it.

When the music ended and it was time to depart, Lady Ruthyn took Dorothy's hand in both of hers and clasped them warmly. "Do promise we'll visit again soon," she said. "I will be delighted to have a friend so close."

"Of course," Dorothy said.

Harry frowned on the moonlit walk home.

"What is troubling you, Brother?" Dorothy said, unable to keep the teasing from her voice. "We are in the good graces of the new baroness."

"She is too pretty for my liking. Your solemnity gives you an extra air of grace that she is lacking, but she will turn the heads of your suitors."

"Why do you not marry her, then? Would you not like to know that your son or daughter would be the next heir to the Grey de Ruthyn title?" Even as Dorothy said it, she regretted it. Lady Ruthyn was too innocent for the harsh manipulations of her brother.

But he shook his head. "Not I. She would be too high-spirited for a wife. I would never have a moment's peace."

"So, it is up to me to marry, with none of the burden on you," Dorothy snapped.

"Precisely," Harry said, apparently oblivious to her sarcasm.

Dorothy wondered at her brother. Had he always been so distant, or was this another of the poisons of the war that Robin spoke of? For all his ambition, it was strange that he showed no interest in marrying and doing something other than managing their father's interests, but he kept his thoughts and plans to himself.

A few days later, Dorothy enjoyed a perverse satisfaction in hearing Harry complain loudly of their brother John's upcoming visit.

"He says you suggested it!" Harry said.

"I thought he might recover better here."

"Do you think we're still living in the days of the priory?" he asked. "You fancy yourself some kind of nun, and you're reopening the old hospital?" He gestured to the ruins east of the house.

"I'll be the one caring for him. I don't know why it troubles you."

"Of course, it troubles me. Having the house filled up with guests is such an inconvenience."

"I cannot imagine 'twill be more than John and a servant or two."

"Well, since you think Chicksands an infirmary, I told Cousin Molle he could visit, too. He imagines himself to have the ague or some other kind of fever. If you are going to be a nurse, you may as well have a full hospital to care for."

"You invited Cousin Molle?" Dorothy asked in disbelief. His imagined complaints would keep her more occupied than Brother John's real ones.

Fortunately, John arrived first. He looked pale and weak, but not as sickly as Dorothy had feared. She brought him broths and read to him and found him a reasonable patient. It took some time, but she also convinced him to visit with their father, and though she did not hear any of what they said, she thought both John and Sir Peter looked more at peace after the reunion.

Cousin Molle made his way slowly to Chicksands, but when he arrived, he staggered into the great hall, feverish and shaky.

"Cousin Molle!" Dorothy hurried forward.

"Cousin," Molle rasped, his teeth chattering.

For once, he had nothing more to say.

Harry's eyes widened at the sight of their guest, and he quickly excused himself, a handkerchief covering his mouth and nose.

Dorothy settled Molle in a chamber far from her father's, but it was too late. Ague burned its way through Chicksands.

Sir Peter fell into a feverish state, shivering and crying out in delirium as Dorothy tended him. He called for reinforcements from the king, told men who weren't there to catch the rats for a stew, and cursed the governor of Jersey for his cowardice. Dorothy's heart grated to hear that his nightmares still took him to Castle Cornet. It had ruined him—mind and body—and he was trapped there still, under siege against his demons. Death might be the only release from his suffering, but Dorothy would not let him go easily.

Dorothy sent Jane away for her own protection then stationed herself by her father's bed. Collins brought her meals to Sir Peter's room, and she only left her bedside vigil when the faithful servant warned her the post was expected.

Without Jane's company, she depended on William's letters to remind her that all the world was not labored breathing and the stench of sweaty linens. He worried that his letters were too long, knowing that she was busy, and asked how he could be of service.

Dorothy glanced at her father. Orange water might clear the foul miasma from the air and help them fight the ague. She begged William to send some.

She had to get the letter to Collins to sneak out of the house, then return to her father, but the effort to stand left her trembling. She leaned against the wall, grateful for its sturdy stone under her cold fingers, and stumbled off in search of Collins.

"You are ill, my lady," Collins said when she passed him the letter.

"Only tired."

Collins took her arm. "You are flushed, and your skin is hot to the touch. You must rest. I'll see to the others today."

Dorothy shook her head, but her body felt too heavy and awkward to break his grip.

"We cannot lose you, Mistress," Collins whispered. "You have held your father up and held Chicksands together, but I can help, too. I will not fail you, my lady."

She let him guide her back upstairs to her chambers, where she sank into an uneasy sleep. Harry wove in and out of her nightmares, roaring at her from the demonic, beaked face of a plague mask.

"Dorothy, wake up!" his voice called through her delirium.

"Shhh," Dorothy scolded.

"Dorothy!" Someone shook her shoulder roughly.

She opened bleary eyes and stared up at Harry, standing in his dressing gown like a king in his robe, with faint feverish spots reddening his pale cheeks.

"I have taken ill with this blasted ague. I need you to fetch me some soup."

Dorothy watched him in confusion for a moment, trying to decide if he was real or a nightmare.

"What are you waiting for, my sister?"

Real.

She pushed herself up and made her way down the stairs, depending on the wall to keep her feet beneath her. She gave orders in the kitchen for some broth to be sent to her brother's room, then stumbled back into the great hall. She lost her balance, and the floor roared up beneath her.

"My lady!" Collins caught her arm. "What are you doing out of bed?"

"Harry needed help."

"He could have called one of us. Sit here. I'll fetch a maid to help you back to bed."

Dorothy nodded and leaned her aching head in her hands. A rustling noise roused her and she looked up to see Harry looming over her, letters in hand.

"It looks like Collins is bringing the post to you instead of me," Harry said. "Why do you suppose that is?"

"I suppose because you are too ill to fetch your own soup," Dorothy said.

Harry held up a letter in William's firm script. "You will not want to read this drivel." He tossed it into the fire.

"Wait!" Dorothy scrambled after the letter, but the heat singed her fingers, and the flames consumed the paper. She rocked back and stared at her stinging fingers through tear-blurred eyes. "He was going to send me orange water for the fever," she mumbled.

"Mistress!" Jane rushed over, placing herself between Harry and Dorothy as she gently examined Dorothy's bright red fingers.

"You should not be here," Dorothy rasped to Jane.

"I heard you were ill, too, and came to help. We must wrap your hand."

Collins helped Dorothy up, and he and Jane half-carried her to her chambers.

"I'm sorry, mistress," Collins whispered. "I did not think he would be out of bed, or I would have watched the letters."

"But I have this," Jane said, holding out a bottle. "William sent it just in time, it looks like."

"The orange water!" Dorothy held it in her throbbing fingers, and a sob caught in her throat. "Thank you!"

Dorothy let Jane put her back to bed and fuss over her, promising to deliver the orange water to the other convalescents if Dorothy would take some herself. Dorothy did as she was told, but her mind itched with worry while Jane was away. Harry was trying to take William from her, and what could Dorothy do about it? Nothing, nothing, nothing.

Jane came up some time later. "Mistress?"

"I'm awake," Dorothy mumbled.

"I don't know what was in the letter your brother took, but here's one from Lady Diana."

"Thank you, Jane. You are a God-send."

"Just be well, my lady," Jane whispered.

Dorothy huddled in her bed and read Lady Diana's letter, each line cutting a deeper gash. Society turned its back on Lady Diana because of her red, swollen eyes.

> *I admit I wasted a tear over it, but I have dried my eyes, and none of my former suitors are not worth the trouble of more.*

"My poor, sweet Lady Diana." Dorothy wanted to rant at all the world for its callousness.

The letter continued. Not only had Lady Diana fallen out of favor over her appearance, but her sister, Lady Isabella, was at the center of a scandal. Her husband was a notorious brute, but not as notorious as Lady Isabella was for her less-than-clandestine affairs. Lady Diana made half-hearted excuses for her sister's conduct.

> *What do they expect, when they forced her to marry such a man against her heart? The heart will always win out.*

Lady Isabella's heart certainly seemed to have been broken, and perhaps not healed quite properly. It would only end badly for her—the woman was always the one who suffered the most for openly flouting the mores of society.

> *Do not let my sad tales discourage you, my dear. 'Twould be different if we could all have lovers as devoted as your William.*

Dorothy sighed. "He is not my William, nor is he ever likely to be."

> *The heart always wins. Remember that. Trust in your heart, and in Master Temple's.*

Dorothy nodded, but she was far from being able to accept Lady Diana's advice. She trusted her heart when it whispered that William would bring her the most happiness, and that she could please him best, but she did not trust in her strength. Especially not against Harry's stern determination, sharp eyes, and cunning. The heart, she had always been told, must submit to the mind, which for women meant bending to the mind of the men overseeing their well-being. With Dorothy's father so ill, that was Harry.

Dorothy hesitated, then burned Lady Diana's letter. She fell asleep with the embers still hot in the fireplace.

She awoke sometime in the night with the odd feeling that she was not alone.

"Jane?" she called.

Ulysses whined. A breeze whispered through the curtains around the bed. Dorothy parted them and pulled on her dressing gown. Something was not right. She slipped out of bed and across the rush mat on the floor to light a candle at the fireplace. Ulysses clung to her side, nearly tripping her. By the light of the candle, everything seemed to in order.

But not entirely. Her collection of seals, ordered before according to which she liked best, was now rearranged from smallest to largest. Had she done that when she was feverish?

She passed the fireplace again and noticed something on the hearth. Flecks of papers were neatly arranged on the chilly stones: scraps of letters that had escaped the flames.

Dorothy recoiled as though she'd found a snake. Someone had been in her room, digging through her secrets, and they did not care if she knew.

Harry.

John and Cousin Molle had no reason to and were both still ill and confined to their chambers. If any of the servants wanted to spy on her, they would not be so obvious.

How dare he! Dorothy had no privacy, and Harry wanted her to remember it—wanted her to know that his hand was in everything. There was no escaping him—not unless William's plans worked, and he found a position that enabled him to support a family. Even then, Dorothy would have to defy her own family to go to him and break her father's heart. Could she do that?

The black-edged scraps of paper taunted her from the hearth. Dorothy swept them together and held each one over the candle until it curled into ash. At least she would not let her brother violate her friends' privacy. She would not let him read the secrets of their hearts.

Chapter Twenty

WILLIAM FINISHED HIS LATEST LETTER to Dorothy and stretched, leaning his chair back to peer out the parlor window at the street. A lady's little lap dog darted into the traffic and nearly caused a hackney to tip over. The lady hurried through the tangle to save her tiny pet, which barked at the shouting driver as if it were a mastiff. William smiled. Was the dog brave, or simply too foolish to know its own smallness?

As the street settled down, William picked up his quill pen and twirled it between his fingers. Writing passed the time while he waited for news about Sweden, but Dorothy worried that his romances were too morose. He considered trying to put some of his more serious thoughts on paper, though his professors at Cambridge would have said he did not have the aptitude. And every time he considered it, he remembered his father's inflammatory pamphlet about the Irish inciting more violence there. Did he dare send words out into the world, knowing he could not take them back regardless of the trouble they caused? Yet the right words could also heal. He could help England understand what Holland knew about tolerance. The blank paper mocked him with its possibilities.

A wave of commotion rippled down the street outside: horses cantering along the cobbled road and men and women yelling.

William rushed to the window. People fled down the street or hurried into their houses to bar the doors.

"What's happening?" William called to the passersby.

"A coup d'état!" one of the men responded. "The army has disbanded Parliament and seized control."

William shuttered his window, for a moment feeling he was in Paris again during the Fronde. Was there no escaping the violence? He longed to fly across the ocean to peaceful Holland, but he would not go without Dorothy.

Dorothy.

Parliament had been more forgiving of Royalists than the radicals in the army. Would the army grandees exact revenge on families like the Osbornes now? William grabbed his coat. Dorothy had her Uncle Danvers to speak for her, but was he still in favor? William slipped out into the streets.

London was strangely empty, but a few brave housewives still fetched water from the wells, whispering their news to each other and keeping a wary eye on William as he jogged past. He wound his way to Westminster, and there the crowds thickened again. Vendors stood at their stalls, though they did not cry their goods to the citizens, and men and women jutted their heads out of upper windows, watching for any signs of action. William spotted the familiar abundant, brassy curls of Sir Thomas Osborne, in the thick of things as always.

"Sir Thomas!" he called. "What news?"

"Master William!" Sir Thomas motioned William closer. "Oliver Cromwell has taken control of England."

"So I gathered, but how? What happened?"

"Parliament was sitting as usual when Cromwell came in. At first, he listened to the debates, but then he stood and berated them for injustice and self-interest."

William snorted in disbelief.

Sir Thomas nodded and whispered, "Aye, there's some hypocrisy there. Cromwell called in his musketeers and they forced Parliament out. Algernon Sydney had to be dragged from his seat. But Cromwell locked the doors behind them, and that was the end of it."

"Then Cromwell is king now in all but name," William whispered.

"He managed what old King Charles failed at: he's the absolute master of England now, with no more Parliament and the army at his back. He'll have us all dressed in black and somber as a funeral procession every day of the week."

"'Tis a dark day." William glanced up at Sir Thomas. "You have an uncle who is close to Cromwell."

"Danvers," Sir Thomas said, his tone indifferent. "I imagine he's enjoying this day, in whatever way Roundheads have left themselves to celebrate."

William watched the angry and dazed-looking crowds milling about. Cromwell's musketeers patrolled the streets. No one dared spark a protest, but it waited like a keg of gunpowder just beneath the tension.

There was nothing for William to do. He turned away, his mind in a tumult. What did this mean for his chance to go to Sweden? As much as he did not long to be so far from Dorothy, it was a chance to make something of himself. He might show his father he was not such a disappointment and win over Dorothy's family, as Henry Cromwell had.

William stopped in his tracks. Someone coming up behind him uttered a curse and skirted around him.

What a fool he was! Even without her Uncle Danvers, Dorothy and her family were in no danger, as long as they had Henry Cromwell to speak for them. Henry was Dorothy's champion now, and William was powerless as always. Worse, Oliver Cromwell had just crushed William's opportunity for a career serving

Parliament—his means of supporting Dorothy. Was Fortune against them, as Dorothy feared, dooming any hope of their being together?

He wandered home, hardly noticing the extra soldiers in the street, and found himself mumbling an explanation to Martha of what had occurred. He stumbled up to his room to write the whole of it to Dorothy, including, in the interest of honesty, the truth about his uncertain future.

What am I to do?

He turned his eyes heavenward. "What am I to do?"

His gaze fell again on the blank paper awaiting his thoughts on Holland. Barricaded in his house, the future he imagined dissolving, he had nothing to do but pick up his pen and begin.

Chaos and lamentation reigned at Chicksands in the face of Oliver Cromwell's elevation to supreme power. Molle had recovered enough to spend the meals lecturing at length about God's wrath. Harry ranted about his glory days under Prince Rupert and berated Dorothy for failing to secure Henry Cromwell. Dorothy retreated to her father's chambers and did what she could to soothe him. Still too ill even to rise from bed, the news of Cromwell's coup struck Sir Peter back down into feverish delirium.

When Dorothy could no longer bear the sight of stone walls, she fled for the refuge of her garden.

The effects of the ague lingered in her weary head and muscles, but the peace of the outdoors soothed some of the aches in her joints. The sun warmed the earth after the cool, wet spring, and her chickens scratched in the dirt for worms. Best of all, Harry had finally left to hash over the news with his acquaintances.

Dorothy could still feel the echoes of despair in William's latest letter. She did not fear the threat to her family that William did. Oliver Cromwell was too high now to spare a thought for a sick, disgraced old Royalist and his children. But this disrupted all of William's plans. He asked her what he should do if he could not go to Sweden, and she did not know what to tell him. She did not let herself hope for a happy ending to their story, but their best chance lay in William gaining a steady position where he could support a wife and family. How could they ever have that when change crumbled every foothold they found? It was like climbing a cliff during a mudslide.

A shadow fell across Dorothy's garden plot, and she looked up, fearing Harry had returned.

But she blinked at the sun's glare and recognized Colonel Samuel Luke standing over her. Had he come to gloat over his Lord General's coup? Or was he gauging the Osborne's loyalties, looking for an excuse to gobble up more of their lands?

She stood and curtseyed, trying to dislodge some of the dirt clinging to her dress without drawing too much attention to it.

Colonel Luke bowed, the sunlight bright on his silvery hair. "How are you this morning, Mistress Osborne? It is good to see you out on this sunny day."

"Thank you, Sir. I am well."

They stood awkwardly for a moment.

"I know it is strange," Colonel Luke said quickly, "my visiting when things have not been at peace between our families, but I appreciated the bean seeds you sold me, and I overheard you telling the baroness you were looking for some pennyroyals. I had some in my garden."

He handed her a bundle of airy purple flowers in a basket, their roots still clad in soil. She hesitated. Was this some sort of test or trick? But his fingernails bore traces of dirt, just as hers did. She carefully took his gift.

215

"Thank you, Sir. This is very kind."

"Not at all. I would like us to be good neighbors. There has been enough fighting. It is time for peace, and I always find it in my garden."

He squinted in the sun, accenting the deep lines in his face. The sadness in his eyes reminded Dorothy of her father. Did Colonel Luke feel guilty, benefiting from the losses of his neighbors? Dorothy studied him for some trace of Puritanical fanaticism yet saw nothing but a lonely old man who liked to garden.

"There is something calming about being surrounded by growing things," she said. After another long pause, she added, "And where will the pennyroyals grow best, do you think?"

"They'll grow anywhere they can get a bit of sun, and they'll spread, so you have to give them enough room."

Dorothy drew him into a long conversation about his garden. He repeated much information that she already knew, talking to her as though she were a child, but it seemed grandfatherly rather than patronizing, and he taught her a few tricks to help her flowers bloom longer. By the time he began the short ramble home, their conversation had lost its stiffness, and they spoke as old neighbors might.

Dorothy studied the pennyroyals in their mound of fresh dirt. The air smelled clean and rich, like the soil, with a touch of mint from the pennyroyals. It filled her with a lightness she had almost forgotten. If Royalists and Parliamentarians could garden together, perhaps they could create more pockets of peace in their battle-scarred countryside. But a few pennyroyals, no matter how far they spread their stems, could not touch the discontent simmering in London.

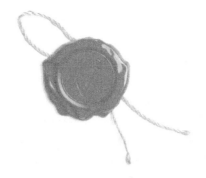

Chapter Twenty-one

WILLIAM SNUCK UPSTAIRS, CLUTCHING ANOTHER letter from Chicksands retrieved from the landlady's maid before his father saw it. Each line from Dorothy was a thread of sunshine pulled through the chilly blanket of London fog.

"William!" Martha called.

He gave a guilty start and stuffed the letter inside his doublet.

She crooked an eyebrow but did not comment on his behavior. "Father is looking for you. He says he has news."

"Thank you," William said. News from his father could not be good, but better to face it now. Aware of the precious piece of paper waiting next to his heart, he made his way back down to his father's study.

"Martha said you wanted to see me, Sir?"

His father stood and clasped his hands behind his back. Like most others in the city, he had changed his clothes for the somber colors preferred by the Roundheads. All of London looked to be in mourning.

"I've had news from Lord Lisle," Sir John said.

"Oh?" This was one piece of bad news William had been expecting.

217

"He will not be leading the embassy to Sweden. He claims his health prevents him."

"I see," William said. Lord Lisle's moral health was probably more to blame than any physical ailment. It was one thing to represent the shaky legitimacy of Parliament to another country, but not many men had the stomach to try to convince kings and courtiers to deal with a regicide and dictator like Oliver Cromwell.

"I don't have contacts in Cromwell's new government." His father's shoulders slouched. "I cannot help you secure a different position at the moment."

"I understand, Sir. Thank you." He could not blame his failures on his father. That rested entirely on his own lack of ambition and skill.

William left the room and quietly shut the door behind him. He respected and even agreed with Lord Lisle's decision, but this only cemented the fact that he had no prospects—nothing to offer Dorothy or anyone else.

He trudged up to his chamber and dropped into his chair. A stray tennis ball sat on his desk. He scooped it up and bounced it off the wall to catch it, again and again. Thump, smack. Thump, smack. A meaningless cycle, going nowhere, accomplishing nothing.

William hurled the ball into the corner and buried his face in his hands. Dorothy's letter crinkled against his chest. He unbuttoned his doublet to pull it out, smoothing each crease before reading it again.

> *I should not love you if I did not think you discreet enough to be trusted with the knowledge of all my kindness. Therefore, 'tis not that I desire to hide it from you, but that I do not love to tell it; and perhaps if you could read my heart, I should make less scruple of your seeing on't there than in my letters.*

He closed his eyes and inhaled, as though he could breathe in her words along with the scent of paper and ink, mingle them with his own longings. She loved him. She trusted him with her heart. What could he do to be worthy of such a gift? He pushed himself up and grabbed his tennis racket.

Martha met him in the hall. "Where are you going?"

"To play tennis," he grumbled, pushing past her.

"You're risking the Puritans' wrath?" She was teasing, but there was worry beneath it.

"I am not in a humor to be dictated to."

He jogged down the stairs and out the door, carrying his tennis racket over his shoulder and daring any of the passing soldiers to bother him. He could swing his racket faster than they could ready their muskets. Then he could flee to the Continent as an outlaw. Perhaps Dorothy's family would be proud of him then.

Few men braved the tennis courts, but William found an opponent in a foppish young man who continually consulted a hand mirror. William slammed the ball out of bounds a number of times and made wild runs to catch the hits that were returned to him. The fop beat him without knocking a curled lock out of place, while William was left shaky and out of breath. His opponent went back to his mirror, and William turned for home.

He walked along the Thames, the waters a swirling gray morass dotted with rotted turnip tops and cabbage leaves. William picked up a stick from the ground and hurled it out into the water. It churned in place a few times, then the current caught it and whisked it fast and far, off toward the Channel and freedom. For a moment, William imagined leaping after it.

But the Thames flowed away from Dorothy. Away from heart and hope and honor.

William put the river to his back and wended his way toward his lodgings. A shadow seemed to dog his steps, just visible in the corner of his eye. He glanced back and saw a man in a broad-brimmed hat behind him. The man pulled the brim lower over his eyes.

William quickened his pace and made a sharp turn. Were Cromwell's men watching him? Certainly, they had better things to do than persecute people for playing tennis. But if he fell afoul of Cromwell and the army, he'd have no hope of making a living.

He snuck another peek over his shoulder and recognized the face under the hat: Harry Osborne.

William slackened his pace, and Harry slowed, too. Had Dorothy's brother resorted to spying on him? William did not know whether to laugh or to call him out for a duel. He had lost his chance at Sweden—lost his best chance at Dorothy. His future seemed murkier than the stormiest day on the Thames.

He ducked around a corner and waited a moment, then stepped out in time to run directly into Harry slinking along after him.

"Master Osborne! What a pleasant surprise," William said through a tight smile.

"Master... ah, Temple is it not? You are a friend of my brother's, if I'm not mistaken."

William narrowed his eyes a little. "Indeed. Pray, tell me how he does."

"Robin is very ill, I'm afraid."

"I'm sorry to hear it," William said sincerely.

Harry grinned. "But I believe you know my sister as well. She's a merry flirt and spends most of her days writing letters to her suitors. We expect her to be married soon, though. Sir Justinian, of course, is her most ardent suitor. Then there's Master Talbot, a relative of the Baroness Grey de Ruthyn. But Master Richard Bennet has also taken an interest in her—his father is a London alderman, perhaps you know. We're placing wagers on which of them she will pick."

"And which is your money on, Master Osborne?" William asked.

"Oh, it hardly matters to me. They're all acceptable choices—wealthy and well-connected." Harry's grin hardened. "And how goes it with you, Master Temple?"

William turned his tennis racket around in his hands, sorely tempted to bludgeon Harry with it, but he suspected Dorothy would not approve. "I am well, Master Osborne, thank you for asking. Good day to you."

William stalked away, still rolling the tennis racket from side to side. Harry was a manipulator, there was no doubt, but William was not convinced he was a liar. He knew Sir Justinian still courted Dorothy, and he had to assume those other men did as well. Wealthy and well-connected. Everything William was not. He did not deserve Dorothy, and given enough time, she might realize that as well.

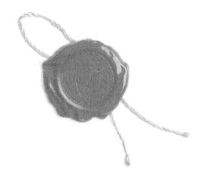

Chapter Twenty-two

CHICKSANDS, ENGLAND

DOROTHY REFOLDED HER LATEST LETTER from William and tucked it into the pocket in the waist of her skirt. She huddled under her cloak despite the sunshine. A garden spade sat forgotten at her feet. She plucked a sprig of rosemary and twirled it under her nose, searching for the familiar, piney scent. Nothing. Had the blues and yellows of the flowers not been brighter once, too?

She tossed the rosemary aside and rubbed her eyes. Between her own illness and her brothers' and father's, she could not remember a time when she had not ached with fatigue. And now, in his letters, William questioned why she did not write more. He dreamed that she would not say a kind word to him and insisted on sharing a chamber with Lord Lisle. His mind sounded as troubled as her own. If only they could see each other again!

The daily procession of milkmaids strolled along the main path to the village. They chased their cows and laughed and flirted with passing errand boys, unencumbered by massive skirts and tight stays. Free from the expectations of fathers and brothers, neighbors and strangers.

Dorothy should have been inside, but then she would have to face Harry and Master Talbot—Lady Ruthyn's cousin and the latest contender for Dorothy's hand. Harry had been singing his praises so long, she could hardly stand the sound of his name.

"Mistress Osborne!"

Lady Ruthyn traipsed down the path with only Sheba for company. Dorothy grimaced at her lack of concern for her reputation—not to mention her safety. The baroness folded her silk fan and beckoned Dorothy over.

Dorothy pushed herself up from her bench with a groan and joined the baroness and Sheba.

Lady Ruthyn linked her arm through Dorothy's and turned her like a dog on a leash to continue strolling. "I have been dying to speak with you. I just heard about the Marchioness of Newcastle-upon-Tyne, and I knew you'd have an interesting opinion on the matter."

"Do you mean Lady Margaret Cavendish?" Dorothy asked, spinning through the gossip she'd heard to pick out any bits about the marchioness. "I thought she was in exile in France with Queen Henrietta-Maria."

"She has published a book!"

"She what?" Dorothy pulled Lady Ruthyn to a stop.

"Aye, she published a book of poems, philosophy, and science, and under her own name."

Lady Ruthyn's eyes sparkled in excitement, but Dorothy shook her head, trying to make the strange news settle in her mind. "Have you read it?"

"Oh, aye. 'Twas marvelous. Better than any novel I've read for ages. Lady Newcastle-upon-Tyne knows she will be criticized, but she calls on us women to support each other and show men that we can write as well as they."

"Of course, we can," Dorothy said, "but 'tis immodest, to expose our private thoughts to all the world."

Exchanging barbs with men like a woman of the streets? How horrifying. How glorious. "One would have to be mad," she added. "Or French, which is nearly the same thing."

Lady Ruthyn laughed. "Perhaps you are jealous?"

Dorothy opened her mouth to deny it but could not. "Her husband allows this behavior?"

"He encourages it. He is enamored of her." Lady Ruthyn lowered her voice to a gossipy whisper. "They say it was a love match."

"I suppose this is what comes of not having proper examples to follow—no king or queen to set the tone. And when a husband is besotted with his wife, he makes a fool of them both." Like Master Smith rolling on the ground with his wife's little dog.

"Do you not wish to marry for love?" Lady Ruthyn asked. "Forgive me, but one cannot help but hear the gossip..."

"I don't know," Dorothy whispered. "I want to marry someone I love, but I also want to marry for mutual benefit of ourselves and our families—"

Lady Ruthyn's laughter trilled over the lane like birdsong. "Mistress Osborne, you are so grim at times! And yet, I believe your heart has been touched by Cupid."

Dorothy set her lips and refused to answer.

"Oh, very well, then. You can have your secrets. But I would very much like to fall in love."

Lady Ruthyn stared dreamily down the road, and Dorothy deepened her resolve to keep a watchful eye on the young heiress. Yet Lady Ruthyn did make her feel old. Had her melancholy robbed her of youth and joy? Or were Lady Ruthyn and the Marchioness of Newcastle-upon-Tyne ridiculous and wild, products of an age of unrest? She did not know what to trust—certainly not her own judgment.

"Ooh," Lady Ruthyn groaned. "Here comes my cousin, Master Talbot."

Dorothy wanted to groan as well, but she endured Talbot's empty compliments, focused as much on Lady Ruthyn as on Dorothy. Not quite as devoted as Harry believed.

She escaped back to Chicksands to find her father huddled by the fireplace and Harry looking smug.

"There you are, my sister," Harry said. "We have been discussing your situation." He turned back to Sir Peter. "I think there may be only one solution, Father."

Her father paled but said quietly, "What remedy do you see?"

"A marriage with a Parliamentary family."

Dorothy's heartbeat picked up at the words. Would her family finally drop their prejudice against William? Her gaze fell on her father. He looked empty and dry, as though the last spark keeping him alive had been snuffed out by Harry's words. Harry's betrayal. Was she betraying her father too, and all he had fought for, with her affection for William?

"Perhaps we will find a Royalist connection still," she said, trying to rekindle some sign of life and hope in him.

Sir Peter shook his head, a jerky, broken gesture. "I tried to defend the old world, where honor still had some value, but I failed, and now my children have to live in this new one. We will all do what we need to, to survive. If you must marry a Parliamentarian to secure your future, then you shall. At least it will give you more options. But, Dorothy," he said, his voice raspy, "seek someone in a position to care for you, to provide you with the security I could not."

"Father—"

Dorothy reached for him, but he stood and shuffled out of the room, leaving Harry looking as satisfied as a hound who'd cornered a hare. Dorothy lowered her hand. Was this final defeat of her father her own fault for not accepting Sir Justinian or any of the number of other Royalist suitors who had come her way? She rubbed her weary forehead.

"Have you overtired yourself, my sister?" Harry asked.

"Perhaps. I wonder, now that we're past the ague, if I might do well to travel to Epsom again. The waters helped last time with this scurvy spleen of mine."

Harry narrowed his eyes. "I begin to think your melancholy is an excuse to put off responsibility."

Dorothy stared at him in shock. He had never doubted her illness before. "I have been unwell for some time."

"And it is time for you to put this childish pouting behind you and make your decision. I think you will not be traveling anywhere until you have chosen your husband."

"What?" Was Harry holding her freedom hostage?

"Did Talbot catch up with you?" Harry smiled at her look of annoyance. "I thought he might. He is a determined suitor. Indeed, he has every characteristic to make him an ideal husband: wealth, position, tractable character."

"Why do you not marry him then?" Dorothy tossed over her shoulder, trying to make her way to her room.

Harry reddened and bounded up after her. "Do you think this is a game?"

"Not at all," she said.

Harry waved a letter behind her. "Your London suitor, Master Bennet is concerned about your recent illness. He says he will come with his coach and six to see you well again."

"Good heavens! How will his six horses make me well?" Pain throbbed behind Dorothy's eyes. "I shall tell him I am too ill for visitors."

Harry backed her into the wall. "You must choose one of them, Dorothy. Father's health will not last forever. You will need money to secure your future. Our future."

Dorothy wriggled away from him and continued up the stairs.

"Sir Justinian has written again," he called. "'Tis fortunate for you he is so strangely besotted. Don't chase all your suitors away for one made of smoke and flirtations."

Dorothy closed the door to her room, shutting out Harry, but not his words, or the frightening look in his eye when he loomed over her. Certainly, she had nothing to fear from her own brother, and yet she enjoyed the warm presence of Ulysses snuggled against her. She wished for a bigger dog, like the huge Irish hounds. Perhaps Henry Cromwell could send her one from Ireland. That would make her feel safer. Not from Harry. Just, in general. There was so much pressure coiling around her, and it would be good to feel secure again.

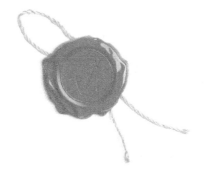

Chapter Twenty-three

LONDON, ENGLAND

MARTHA PRACTICED A GIGUE ON her lute, and the dark tones of the minor key suited William's mood perfectly. Dorothy's family kept her confined to Chicksands, though it seemed everyone except William was allowed to court her now. He began, like Dorothy, to curse the cruelty of Fortune. Nay, not Fortune, but their families.

A few fumbled notes caught his attention. Martha's fingers moved more slowly than usual over the strings, and she did not sing to accompany herself.

"Are you feeling well?" William asked.

She paused and cradled the lute in her lap. "Not entirely. This cough lingers."

William thought of Robin Osborne wasting from consumption and hurried to his sister's side to feel her forehead.

She giggled and batted his hand away. "When did you become a worried old maid? The physician says I'm recovering well."

William forced a smile. "I cannot have you taking sick on me. Who would keep me out of trouble?"

"I suppose you'd have to find a wife to do it." She studied him from under her long lashes. "I've heard Agnes Claybourn is engaged to a country gentleman. Are you sorry you did not marry her?"

"Not at all." William was not surprised that she had found a respectable match. He hoped she had found happiness as well.

Martha nodded. "She was not good enough for you. She did not love you enough."

"You would have me giddy with love, then?"

"The lady ought to be, though you must promise to still love me, too."

William laughed. "Of course. You will always be my sister."

Their father, Sir John, strolled into the room, whistling a cheerful tune. William drew back, as he often did lately in his father's presence.

"Well, children, you may congratulate me."

William and Martha exchanged a confused look.

"Why is that, Sir?" Martha asked.

"I have a new position in Ireland sorting out land disputes as Commissioner of Forfeited Estates."

"Has there been another coup?" William asked, only half joking.

His father gave him a stern look. "I have made my peace with His Highness, Oliver Cromwell, and with our new reality. You would do well to do the same."

William bit his tongue to keep from making a snide remark on his father's loyalty.

"Your gaze mocks me," Sir John said, facing William. "Understand this: Everything I do, I do for my children. Do you think I respect Lord General Cromwell? That I think him in the right? Of course not. But this allows me to care for my children. Your brother John will need good connections to succeed in law, Martha to secure a husband, and you will need them to find a direction in life. I'm putting myself in a position to help all of you."

William lowered his eyes. A man like Uncle Henry Hammond, who stood by his convictions, might do more for his family's moral well-being, but Uncle Henry was living in hiding now, unable to help his beloved parishioners, or even to attend his own mother's funeral. William had to admit the justice of his father's argument, even if he could not embrace it.

"John will stay here to continue his studies," their father went on, "but William, you and Martha will be joining me in Ireland."

William's stomach turned at the blow. Even farther from Dorothy than he was now. "Martha has been unwell," he said weakly. "Is it wise to take her to so dangerous a place as Ireland?"

Sir John studied his daughter. "You can bring her when she is feeling stronger."

"Maybe the waters at Epsom would help," William suggested. "I could take her."

"Are you still pursuing that Dorothy Osborne?" his father asked suspiciously.

"I am friends with Mistress Osborne."

"You are not to see her."

William drew a steadying breath. "She will not be at Epsom, if that's what concerns you." Dorothy could not be there, but he would feel closer to her, walking where she had walked. "Her family keeps her sequestered in Bedfordshire."

"As they should," Sir John said. "I have heard she is a merry flirt, passing her time with that silly baroness, Lady Grey de Ruthyn, and surrounded by suitors."

William gritted his teeth.

"You may take Martha to Epsom," Sir John said. "In the meantime, we must prepare for our journey."

William gave a curt nod. Martha watched their father stride from the room, then turned wide eyes on her brother.

"Is Ireland truly so dangerous?"

William wanted to shield her from it, but she was nearly a woman now and needed to know what she would face. "It is. The Irish fought bitterly for their religion and their freedom, and Lord

General Cromwell's forces have been vicious in their reprisals. Their country has been scarred even more deeply than ours by this war, and they have no love for Englishmen, especially those working for Oliver Cromwell's government."

"I see," Martha said. William was proud of her composed response.

"In the meantime, we'll enjoy ourselves at Epsom and be fortified for our coming adventure."

She smiled at him, but nervousness reflected in her eyes.

While their father prepared the house for his move, William and Martha retreated to the countryside.

Epsom was exactly the fresh country scene Martha needed after being in the foul air of London so long, but William still felt crowded by the visitors coming to take the water. He more than once heard his name whispered as he passed a group of gossiping ladies. It did not bother him much on its own, but when he heard Dorothy's name as well, it gave him a hot, sick feeling. Dorothy's well-being in society rode on her good reputation, and her name was too precious to him to hear on idle, malicious tongues.

He sat one evening, chaperoning Martha at a village dance and harboring gloomy thoughts, when a man called his name.

"William Temple!"

William turned to face his Cambridge schoolmate, James Beagle. The young man's round face was flushed with too much wine. "Master James. How do you do this evening?"

"A little more wine will set me right," James slurred. "But you've had the same affliction yourself."

"What's that?" William asked.

"Dorothy Osborne."

William drew back. "I think 'tis best we end this conversation. You are drunk, and we are in a public place."

"Ha!" James sniggered. "Still besotted by the little vixen, eh? I swear she's a witch, entrancing the whole countryside for her own amusement."

"Stop," William said, grasping the handle of his rapier. "Stop or I'll call you out now and let the laws against dueling be hanged."

James Beagle laughed too loudly, his jowls quivering. "Fool."

He staggered off, and William sank back into his chair. Half the room was staring at him, including his sister. Curse James Beagle and all the loose-lipped gossips.

A man approached and quietly asked, "You are Master William Temple?"

William took him in with a glance: a cavalier, moderately well off despite Oliver Cromwell and his Roundheads.

"Aye," he answered.

"I am Sir Richard Franklin, cousin to Dorothy Osborne."

William was uncertain how to respond, so he gave a nod.

"I don't approach you as an enemy," Richard said. "I'm interested in my family's welfare, and I was curious to meet the man who has stirred so much stubbornness in my good-natured cousin. I would like to know you better. I'd be happy to have you as a guest at Moor Park, just over in Hertfordshire."

William hesitated. A member of Dorothy's family being friendly to him? His experiences had made him suspicious, but it could be an opportunity, and he'd had enough of Epsom. "That sounds delightful."

"'Tis lovely!" Martha declared on seeing Moor Park from the carriage window.

William nodded his agreement. The land rose on a gentle hill, crowned by the manor. The rooms of the house opened to gravel-lined walks that passed through the levels of the gardens, under cloistered walks and through sweet-smelling beds of flowers laid out in geometric patterns. Dorothy must have walked these same paths, and William longed to share it with her.

Sir Richard greeted them warmly, though Lady Franklin gave William a shrewd look that warned him not everyone at Moor Park was inclined to like him. She fussed about the room, making certain everything was in its place as Sir Richard chatted with William and Martha about art and gardening until the steward called them into supper.

"So, Master Temple," Lady Franklin said at the table, "tell us about your prospects."

Martha gave William a concerned look.

William cleared his throat. "I am going to be joining my father soon. He is Commissioner of Forfeited Estates in Ireland."

"In Ireland? So far away." Lady Franklin dabbed her smile with a napkin.

"I have had many opportunities to travel. I hope to go into diplomatic service." William had never admitted his ambition to a stranger, and he felt strangely vulnerable, as if the smirking woman could snuff out his dreams like a candle. At least he had not mentioned his writings on Holland.

"Have you been on any diplomatic missions, then?"

"I have not. My first one was canceled due to the recent change of government."

"I see. 'Tis a pity my cousin Dorothy does not enjoy traveling. It worries her so. With her delicate mental state, it is always best not to upset her."

William took a careful sip of the hot soup, not sure the best way to respond.

Lady Franklin pressed on. "I think in seeking a match, one should look for a spouse whose humors agree with one's own. Do you not agree?"

Sir Richard redirected the conversation to safer topics, but William had fallen short of his opportunity with Dorothy's family. Diplomatic work seemed like his best opportunity, but would Dorothy be uneasy as a diplomat's wife?

Wandering the gardens one day, he overheard Lady Franklin speaking with her cousin Mistress Peters.

"This William Temple is nothing on Cousin Dorothy's other suitors. A foolish boy with nothing to offer."

"Nothing to offer, aye. She only wants him out of stubbornness, desiring that which she cannot have," Mistress Peters said. "'Tis a passing fancy, and she'll settle on one of the more acceptable choices soon enough."

"It hardly matters, anyway," Lady Franklin said in a low tone. "One husband is much like another, as long as one is comfortably situated."

William passed on, needing no more of their conversation. He came to a window that looked out on a statue of the mythical Leda twisting away from Zeus in his swan form. The artist had done his work well. Leda reached out a desperate hand, her face frozen in helplessness and sorrow.

"At least he will never actually catch you," William whispered.

Yet she was trapped forever in her misery. Safe but not secure. William wished he could rescue her, but he was not in a position to help anyone. Instead of being locked in stone, he drifted about with every new tide, never able to grab hold of anything stable.

"Which is worse?" he asked the statue, "to be always still, or always moving?"

Ladies' gossipy laughter drifted down the hall, setting his teeth on edge. He stared through the clear pane and smiled at the memory of Robin Osborne's defiant etching at the inn on the Isle of Wight—the one that had first propelled William toward Dorothy. Pulling out a pin with a diamond tip, he engraved his question into Lady Franklin's glass.

> *Tell me Leda, which is best*
> *n'ere to move or n'ere to rest*
> *Speak that I may know there by,*
> *Who is happier, you or I.*

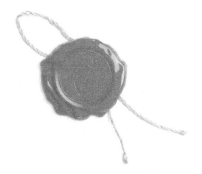

Chapter Twenty-four

CHICKSANDS, ENGLAND

DOROTHY LOWERED THE HOOD OF her cloak to steal a moment of sunlight on her face and air that smelled of hay instead of musty illness. The Sabbath was a delight, as Isaiah said, though Dorothy doubted the ancient prophet had been thinking of her escape from Chicksands when he wrote that verse. Even now, walking to the parish church, Harry shadowed her, walking with their brother John, and she felt his gaze on her exposed neck.

"Mistress Osborne!" Lady Ruthyn fluttered over, towing Sheba along. The baroness paid Harry no more heed than a brief nod of acknowledgment, but her dark-skinned companion shot him a nervous glance. Dorothy sensed Harry's tension, but he said nothing as the two young women came between him and Dorothy. Thank heavens for the authority of Lady Ruthyn's title.

"You have heard the latest news?" Lady Ruthyn asked, linking her arm with Dorothy's. With her light steps and airy gown, she seemed to float alongside Dorothy as they strolled to the church.

"I doubt it. My brothers keep me as sequestered as a nun," Dorothy whispered.

Despite her precautions and Jane's help, Dorothy had received one of William's letters with the seal broken, and one or two of her letters had gone missing, never reaching William.

"Then it is well you have me for your gossip," Lady Ruthyn said. "Lord General Cromwell has abolished church marriage."

"What?"

"He has proclaimed that none shall be married by any religious ceremony, and certainly not privately. The only recognized ceremony is to be a simple exchange of vows in public before an authorized member of the government."

Dorothy's steps faltered. "He not only thinks he is king, but God as well."

"'Tis shocking, is it not?"

"I suppose God still looks on what is in our hearts. He recognizes sacraments whether they are in a church or in the public eye."

"Will you marry before the government, then?" Lady Ruthyn asked.

"I doubt I shall ever marry at all, so I suppose it will not matter much to me."

"Don't speak so. I think you have been locked up with an ill father and that strange brother of yours too long." She paused. "I hope I don't speak too freely."

"Nay, 'twould be refreshing to have more time away from Chicksands, but what am I to do? They are my family."

Lady Ruthyn frowned, puckering her pretty forehead.

At the church, Lady Ruthyn's presence cowed Master Beagle, and it was one of the most gloriously peaceful days Dorothy had enjoyed in ages. She walked home slowly after the services, savoring each moment. If only she could share it with William, but it looked unlikely that they would be able to meet before he left for Ireland, and Dorothy feared they would not meet again in this life.

She returned home just behind Harry and John to find Collins waiting with a letter. "A special courier brought it," he said, his hand unsteady as he held it out.

Dorothy, Harry, and John exchanged worried glances, and then John took the letter.

"Does our father know it came?" John asked.

Collins shook his head. "I did not know what was in it, but I did not think—"

"It will not be good news," John said quietly. He broke the seal and read the paper, then passed a hand over his eyes.

"What has happened?" Dorothy asked.

"'Tis Brother Robin. He is dead."

"Oh!" Dorothy collapsed onto a seat, hardly aware of Ulysses' worried nuzzles. "Oh, poor Robin."

She wanted to cry for her brother, but no tears came, only a hollow disbelief. Robin's long suffering had ended. She wished she could sit shoulder-to-shoulder with him once more, see the smile he had not worn since the war, and hear him say he was at peace.

"It was not unexpected," Harry said.

"It always comes as a surprise." John's voice was subdued.

"Not so much to me," Harry said. "I have been spending time with him in his last days. You have your own affairs to concern yourself with, John, but Dorothy only thinks of herself, moping after her William Temple when she should have been concerned for her own flesh and blood."

Dorothy's throat tightened. Had she neglected Robin? She could not travel as freely as her brothers, but perhaps she could have written to him more often. She stroked Ulysses' soft ears and squeezed her eyes shut against the pain of Harry's accusations.

"Robin is gone," Harry said. "You and I must think of the future, John. This leaves each of us a larger share of the inheritance. Perhaps a more generous marriage portion for Dorothy as well."

"Hush, Harry," John said. "We can speak of that later."

After a brief pause, Harry stalked out of the room, and John's more quiet steps followed. Dorothy rose, moving automatically, and went to her chambers. She still had her mourning clothes from her mother's death. It seemed she had only recently traded them in for colors, but now she shed her green gown and slipped on the faded black wool. It scratched her skin, but its discomfort felt right somehow. She glanced at the mirror. The dark dress highlighted the circles beneath her eyes, making her the perfect picture of misery. She tossed a linen sheet over the reflection and turned away.

As she walked the halls, searching for peace in movement, her brother John caught up with her. They walked in silence for several minutes before John spoke.

"Harry is concerned for you."

Dorothy frowned. "He has an odd way of showing it."

"He lacks tact at times, but we do need to consider your future. I understand you were fond of William Temple, but you cannot pine after him forever."

"I need time to mourn my brother before I can think of marriage."

"There will always be someone to mourn, Sister. You must move ahead. Robin would have wanted that."

John was right, but Dorothy shook her head.

"'Tis a shame you did not marry Henry Cromwell after all. Think of the comfort Father would have in his last days, with his daughter connected to His Highness's family."

"I'm not certain Father would have found that comforting."

"Do you really still think of this Master Temple?" John asked.

"He is my friend; of course, I think of him."

"Ha, your friend. Men and women are not friends unless one of them fancies the other."

"So you say, yet I am still friends with Henry Cromwell, though he is happily married, and I am happy for him."

"Certainly, you would not still be friends with William Temple were he to marry someone else."

Dorothy gave the question honest reflection. "I would wish to see him married to a worthy woman with a great fortune."

"But Sister, would you have him love her?"

"Do you doubt it? He would not be happy in it otherwise."

John laughed. "You are such an unnatural creature."

Dorothy frowned at him. Perhaps she was unnatural, but after watching her family's mercenary ways, she was not certain she wanted to be as natural as them.

"Happiness in marriage is not unnatural," she said. "You are happy."

John shrugged. "I am comfortable. That is enough."

Dorothy shook her head. There was nothing natural at all about her family.

Harry gave Dorothy only a few days to mourn her brother and do her best to comfort their father before assailing her again over the breakfast table.

"Well, I hope you're satisfied," he said, tossing down a letter. "Sir Justinian has married Vere, the daughter of Lord Leigh."

"I wish them both happy."

"And what will you do, with your suitors losing interest? You've played your game too long."

"I suppose I shall have to choose a chain to lead my apes in Hell."

"You intend to die a spinster?"

"Perhaps." If she could outlast all her suitors and only William was left, her family might finally relent.

"We will not allow it. We'll have you married, Dorothy."

"You will have to chain *me* and lead me to the altar, and what a spectacle that will be."

Harry stormed from the room. Dorothy rubbed her forehead. Good riddance to another suitor. If she had really cared for any of them, or they for her, how many willow garlands she would have worn! She shivered at the autumn cold already creeping into the drafty halls of Chicksands. Better to burn her willows and keep herself warm. They would provide more heat than the professed warmth in her suitors' hearts and last as long.

She retired to the parlor to take up her sewing. Collins knocked lightly.

"Someone to see you, Mistress," he said with a grin.

Warmth spread over Dorothy, and she rushed into the room to find an unfamiliar man there with two great Irish hounds leashed at his side. Her dogs! Had William convinced his father to find the hounds she longed for? Did this mean Sir John Temple was softening in his opinion of her?

"A gift," the handler announced, "from Master Henry Cromwell, from Ireland, my lady. One of them lately belonged to His Highness Oliver Cromwell himself."

Dorothy's excitement fizzled. She was grateful to Henry, but if only they could have come from the Temples instead of the Cromwells!

"Thank you. And thank your master for me." Dorothy took the leash and ran her hands through the dogs' rough coats. At least she had them for company. After her brothers' coldness, these creatures, with their soft brown eyes, reminded her there was still affection in the world.

Harry's voice boomed behind her. "What is this? More dogs!"

"Gifts from Henry Cromwell."

"At least you could ask your powerful friend for something that would help the rest of us!" Harry shoved one of the dogs aside with his leg. "You collect suitors and dogs like the rest of your useless trinkets!"

Harry strode up the stairs toward Dorothy's room.

"What are you doing?" Dorothy ran after him.

Crashes sounded from her room. She reached the doorway to watch Harry sweep his arm across her collection of seals, scattering them over the rush mat. He kicked over her nightstand, and her buttons and shells crashed down. He ground the pearly shell from William to dust under his boot.

Dorothy fell to her knees, hands shaking.

"Stop! Harry, please stop!"

He whirled on her. "This garbage is as childish as your dreams of love and romance. 'Tis time for you to grow up and serve us—your family—as God intended."

He strode out of the room. Dorothy crawled forward and slowly gathered the wreckage of her treasures. Broken shells and seals from William. Coins and buttons she had collected with Robin. Foolish babbles. She let them clink through her fingers and sank beside them on the rush mat, curling around the pain behind her ribs. Family was all she had, and she had nothing.

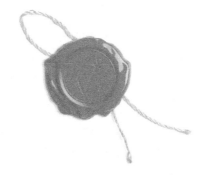

Chapter Twenty-five

LONDON, ENGLAND

DOROTHY WAS COMING TO LONDON. Her brother John decided she needed guidance from her Aunts Gargrave and Danvers. William knew John Osborne was not his ally, but he blessed the man's name.

He put on his best doublet and straightened his hair in the mirror. Dorothy would tease him if he did not care for it. Jane had tattled to Dorothy about his recent bouts of melancholy, and now Dorothy chided him in her most recent letter.

> *Can you believe that you are dearer to me than the whole world besides, and yet neglect yourself? If you do not, you wrong a perfect friendship; and if you do, you must consider my interest in you, and preserve yourself to make me happy. Promise me this, or I shall haunt you worse than she does me.*

She haunted him more than she could know. It seemed better than a dream that he would soon see her again. They'd had to wait on her brother Thomas Peyton's convenience, but finally he made his journey and brought with him all William's hopes for the future.

William grinned at his reflection and ruffled his hair. Dorothy would scold him about it and straighten his locks, and her gentle touch would feel better than a cool stream sighing over weary feet.

Satisfied with his appearance, he trotted downstairs, gave Martha a quick kiss on the cheek, and bounded over to Fleet Street where Dorothy's family were staying. Timber buildings crowded along the street, some home to taverns, while others offered novels, newsbooks, and pamphlets from the printing presses churning inside. The warm scent of ink momentarily overcame the stink of sewage bobbing down the River Fleet.

William ducked into one of the bookshops to find a collection of poems so he did not have to arrive empty-handed. He passed over John Milton—too Parliamentarian—and Robert Herrick—his stanzas on petticoats and loose lacings might shock Dorothy. He settled on the poems of George Herbert, a cousin of the Osbornes whom Dorothy admired, and continued on his way.

He paused at the site where Charing Cross had stood until the Puritans tore it down. He did not want Dorothy's family to see him. The shadows of an overhanging timber house offered him a place to watch unseen, reading Herbert's poetry until he spotted Jane.

"Psst!" William called and beckoned her.

Jane scurried into the shadows beside him. "My mistress will be so glad to see you, Sir."

"As I will be to see her. I brought this for her." He stuck a piece of ribbon in the book at a poem she would enjoy, "Love bade me welcome," and handed the volume to Jane. "Which window is hers?"

"Her window?" Jane giggled and pointed to one on the upper floor.

"You're an angel." William grinned and picked up a handful of small stones. After a few tries, he managed to thump Dorothy's window. A breathless moment of waiting, then she swung it open.

It was like seeing the sun again after many foggy days. Dorothy had grown thin and pale, the marks of her long illness and nursing duties etched into her face, but still beautiful, and even more so when she spotted William and broke into a shy smile. She waved, and he returned a courtly bow. She looked like she would call to him, but something made her look over her shoulder, and she pulled her head inside and shut the window.

"What are her plans?" William asked Jane. "I have to know when I can speak with her."

"We're going out tomorrow to Hyde Park, but I'm not sure what time."

"I'll spend all day there if need be. Thank you, Jane."

"Just make my lady smile again."

William bowed his assent and wove his way through the coaches and market stalls toward home. Dorothy was in London again, and only one night separated them. He was tempted to wander Hyde Park in anticipation, but he did not want to leave Martha alone for two entire days.

He returned home to find a letter waiting for him in his brother's handwriting. He lifted it with a sense of foreboding. John rarely wrote to him. He could pretend he had not seen it or that it had been lost. But he would not ignore his family. He broke the seal.

John begged him to join him on some business just north of the city that evening. William sighed. At least, whatever his brother needed, it could be dealt with that day. He returned his reply, and John sent back word that a coach would come for William after supper.

"What trouble are you in, Brother?" William muttered, imagining John in a duel or some other nonsense. But, duty called.

William hopped into the coach when it arrived, bringing his rapier and pistol in case they were needed. He endured the long ride through the city, and they stopped on the outskirts to change horses and meet John. His brother wore a dark hood pulled over his face and motioned for William to stay quiet. William refrained from rolling his eyes. Love had to be involved if his level-headed brother was acting so dramatically.

"So, what is the emergency that calls us away?" William asked once the coach lurched back into motion.

John pulled back his hood and met his eyes. "You are, William. Father heard your little inamorata was in London, and that you would be sneaking away to see her. He's not going to let you throw yourself away on some nobody. He sent orders for me to stop you."

William stared at his brother until the disbelief passed. He rested a hand on his rapier. "And so, you take the role of my jailer? I am the elder brother—"

"Then start acting like one!" John leaned forward, his face pale in the dusk light. "Do you know what people say about you—about us? Irreligious, rebellious, shiftless—"

"I am not the one who would sell my soul for political preferment. Let them say what they will about me."

"And what about the rest of us? Father and me, Martha, and your darling Mistress Osborne? Association with your name begins to carry a taint. And I don't just mean some social stigma, as if that were not bad enough." John leaned forward. "The army is watching us, William. You refuse to serve the Lord General's government. You associate with Royalists. The air is thick with conspiracies, and you are not immune from suspicion."

The coach walls seemed to close in on William. "Stop!" he called to the coachman, but the man ignored him and drove on into the night. A cold sweat prickled on William's forehead. "I am being kidnapped, then?"

"You are being escorted to Yorkshire for now. Soon enough we'll have you safe in Ireland, where you can do no more harm."

William pressed back against the seat, arms trembling with rage. He could try to jump from the moving coach, or upset it, but he risked hurting himself, his brother, and the driver.

248

He squeezed his eyes shut and pictured Dorothy again, standing at her window, looking pale but radiant, like the moon hanging overhead. Was he truly endangering her? He would write, explain what had happened, soften the blow as much as he could—for what greater insult could there be to a young woman than to find that her beloved's family disliked her so much that they dragged him away from her?

As furious as he was with his father and brother, he sensed another hand behind their actions. Harry Osborne. William wanted to rage against Dorothy's brother and the injustice of Fortune, but another part of him was afraid it was a battle he could not win.

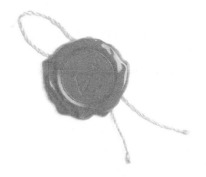

Chapter Twenty-six

Chicksands, England

THE DIM LIGHT OF WINTER barely penetrated the cloister garden at Chicksands, but Dorothy tried to sound cheerful as she wrote William a short note, hoping to find what had taken him from their meeting in London.

> *I shall hear from you a Thursday, and next week I shall be able to say much more than I can this, both because I shall have more time, and besides I shall know more.*

She hoped that was true. Harry had ripped her away from London, and she had heard no more than that William was detained by family business. Something had shifted, but she did not know what. The long, gray shadows of Chicksands cast a chill over her shoulders as she wrote.

> *If we do not take care of ourselves I find nobody else will. I would not live, though, if I had not some hope left that a little time may breathe great alterations, and that 'tis possible we may see an end of our*

misfortune. When that hope leaves us then 'tis time to die, and if I know myself I should need no more to kill me. Let your letter be as much too long as this is too short, I shall find by that how I must write. I do not think this is sense, nor have I time to look it over.

I am yours.
D. Osborne

What else could she say? She would know by what William wrote how their situation stood. She hurried to send the letter and return to tending her father, who had relapsed during her brief absence. Not only that, but Jane had taken ill in London as well. Dorothy was left to care for both of them, powerless to stop their suffering or help them fight the demons haunting their fevered dreams.

Outside her father's window, winter-starved birds stole the red berries from the hawthorn tree, stripping the last color from the garden. Her dogs clung close to her with their tails tucked low, and she imagined the ghosts of lonely nuns stirring in the shadows at the edges of her vision. Death stalked the gardens and ancient halls of Chicksands.

The days and nights dragged on, blurring together into a long stream of changing sheets, cooling foreheads, and catching short meals and broken naps at the bedsides of her father and Jane.

No word from William. Other than the servants, who went around on tip-toe, Dorothy was alone in her world of cold and sickness and pale rushlights.

When a figure loomed out of the faint dusk light on one of her trips to the kitchen, Dorothy gasped and dropped a half-empty bowl of porridge to splatter on her worn skirt.

"Hush, silly girl," Harry said.

Ulysses growled until Harry stomped in front of the dog and sent it into a cower.

Dorothy rested a hand on her tremorous heart. "I did not know you were there."

"Who do you think has been running the estate all these days, while you doze in your chair?"

Dorothy shrugged and picked up the pewter bowl, grateful it had not cracked.

"Aye, back to work. You'll forget your little romance soon enough, and then you'll see reason again."

"Forget my romance?" she asked, so tired the words jumbled in her mind.

"All this skulking about, acting as if you're a martyr. You'll move past it soon enough and see I've been right all along."

"What are you talking about?"

"William Temple, of course. He could not see how undeserving he was of you. No one will appreciate you as they should. As your family does." Harry brushed his thumb down Dorothy's cheek, and she shuddered and drew back. Harry rolled his hand into a fist. "I thought 'twould be enough to banish him from Saint-Malo and intercept your letters to him."

"*You* sent him away from Saint-Malo? You took my letters?"

"Of course. He was a distraction. But his father, practical man that he is, was more than happy to help me with the problem. As he was on this trip to London. William's family hates you so, they will do anything to keep you apart. You never could have been happy together."

"William loves me," Dorothy whispered.

"William does not know you, my sister. How could he love you? He only loves the idea of you. A shadow of his own imagination."

Dorothy shook her head, squeezing her eyes shut against the weary tears burning behind her eyelids.

"You will never see him again. You will never even hear from him again, now that I've rooted out your letter carriers." He held up a paper with William's seal, broken. "And he writes that he does not know when your misfortunes will end. He is giving up, Dorothy. 'Tis time you did the same."

Dorothy reached for the letter. Harry crumpled the paper and tossed it in the fire, which quickly licked it into ash. Dorothy groaned and sank against the wall.

"You will learn to rely on me now," Harry said. "'Tis a shame about Jane Wright, but in the end, I don't think she was good for you."

"What about Jane?" A cold sickness crept into Dorothy's stomach at the realization that Harry might be capable of harming her friend.

"I've sent her home where she belongs. We have to focus on our family. That is our safety and our security."

Dorothy held the bowl in front of her like a shield. "There is no security or certainty in this world. It is in God's hands."

"And yet we've seen that those who take control of their own destiny are the ones who prosper. Oliver Cromwell claims he is God's Englishman, and God rewards him for it. Well, I played the bold soldier with Prince Rupert in the late troubles only to see our fortunes wither, and now I watch over Chicksands just so our worthless brother can take it from me when Father dies." He closed in on Dorothy, his eyes fever bright. "God owes me my share of prosperity, and you will play your part in getting me my due."

"Nay." Dorothy backed away. "I will hide in these halls like a cloistered nun and care for the sick, but I will not be part of your plans."

"You will!" Harry grabbed her chin, his fingers pinching bruises into her skin. "And if you will not marry where it is wise, perhaps it is best to let you waste away here. Weak thing that you are, you will not outlast Father by long, and that will mean your inheritance may come to me as well."

Dorothy jerked away from Harry and ran, stumbling in her exhaustion. She fled for the refuge of the garden, but there was nothing green left there, no sign of life and hope. All was laid bare to winter's icy touch.

She circled around and snuck back up to Jane's chamber adjoining her own. As Harry said, Jane was gone, the room swept clean as though her friend had never been at Chicksands. Dorothy collapsed on the empty bed. Her tears would not come. There was only a gaping, black emptiness inside her.

Slowly, as if she were moving against a strong tide, she forced herself up and back to her duties. Her body was stiff and slow, but her thoughts raced in circles, wearing her mind down, like a frantic dog scratching and digging until nothing was left.

Nothing was left. Was this not what her mother had warned her about? There was no happiness in this world. Perhaps she had sinned in striving for something that God did not intend for her—in fighting against Fortune at every turn. It was a kind of madness, and her mind was fragile, unraveling like old cloth.

Sinful or not, she ached to speak with William one more time. At least she had to say farewell and set him free. She sat to write a last letter and ask Collins how to sneak it to London, if Harry had not sent him away as well.

Having tired myself with thinking, I mean to weary you with reading, and revenge myself that way for all the unquiet thoughts you have given me. But I intended this a sober letter, and therefore, sans raillerie, let me tell you, I have seriously considered all our misfortunes, and can see no end of them but by submitting to that which we cannot avoid, and by yielding to it break the force of a blow which if resisted brings a certain ruin. I think I need not tell you how dear you have been to me, nor that in your kindness I placed all the satisfaction of my life; 'twas the only happiness I proposed to myself, and had set my heart so much upon it that it was therefore made my punishment, to let me see that, how innocent soever I thought my affection, it was guilty in being greater than is allowable for things of this world.

William grasped Dorothy's letter. It crinkled in fingers, but it could not be real. He sat hard on the floor at Collins' feet to read it again and a third time, trying to make sense of it. This was not Dorothy's teasing. Her misery echoed in every word.

She was giving up. He would lose her. Not because she did not love him, but because she could not see past her despair. Because the demons of her own mind—and of her brother's—overwhelmed her. And William could not be there to help her fight them. He had to help her find the strength to fight them herself.

He yanked out a sheet of paper and scrawled a note.

I will not—I cannot—accept this answer from you. If I believed you did not love me, I would set you free to find happiness elsewhere, but you are consigning yourself to a state of misery, thinking to serve both of us this way. It will not do.

My love for you will not allow me to force you to anything, no matter how I desire it, but I will not break my word. I will love you and only you. I will renounce my father and my family name as surely as if I married you and he renounced me. I will wander the world, an adventurer. And if you die early, I will as well.

William glanced up at Collins when he finished. "You will make certain she gets this? Her brother will not take it from you?"

"I swear it to you, Sir," Collins said, clutching his hat in his hands, "as we both love her. She is a good mistress, and I would not see the cankers of her brother's spite harm her anymore."

William nodded and melted a few drops of wax onto the letter, then sealed it firmly with his anchor insignia. Now all he could do was pray that the light would reach her through her brother's shadow.

A quiet knock on the door roused Dorothy from her slumber at her father's bedside. For a moment, she felt only tired, but as she became more conscious and the sour scent of sweaty sheets reached her, the heavy weight of her misery pressed again on her shoulders.

"Enter," she called, not afraid to disturb her father, who slept deeply aided by a draught from the physician.

Rector Goldsmith pushed open the door, his brown hair newly chopped short in Puritan fashion. Dorothy straightened in alarm and glanced at her father. Who had called a priest for him?

"Quiet, my child," the rector said. "I have not come to see him. I came to see you."

"Me?" Dorothy sat straighter. "What have I done?"

"I am concerned about you." The rector pulled a chair up next to Dorothy's. "My sister Jane hinted that you were troubled, and we have not seen you at church of late."

"I have been caring for my father, though I suppose the rumor-mongers let their imaginations roam with my reputation. Do they say now that I have gone mad?"

"Do not fret, Mistress Osborne. You are not mad, though I think your mind is suffering from being so long locked inside."

Dorothy frowned. "My spleen often afflicts me, but I have determined to serve God as well as I can and let him ease my burdens as he sees fit."

Rector Goldsmith glanced at Sir Peter. "There is so much suffering in the world. I have often prayed to understand it."

"It is the nature of the world, it is not, Sir?"

"Perhaps. But there is much happiness in the world as well."

"Is there?" Dorothy lowered her face into her hands and whispered, "I wonder, then, what I am doing wrong, that none of it comes to me. Everything seems so...so difficult."

"Sometimes when our path is difficult, it is because God is trying to direct us a different way. But sometimes it is because the destination is worth the struggle."

Dorothy looked at him in surprise.

The rector studied her face, then pulled out a clay tobacco pipe and lit it. "Have you been tempted to end your life?"

"What? Never! That would be a sin."

"Why is that, do you think?"

Dorothy looked down at her clasped hands. "I suppose because we're meant to live as long as God wills it."

"I think that's probably right. But do you think He wants us to live as though we're already dead?"

"Sir?"

"If God wants us to live, do you not think that means He wants us to really *live*? He created things of beauty, so I have to believe he meant there to be joy alongside the sorrow. We are told that God is love. He has given you a share of trials, Mistress Osborne, but He will not give you hardships without giving you the strength to overcome them, and the moments of joy to sweeten the bitter. Do not reach only for the bitter, when you can also have the sweet."

"But we should not love the things of this world too much!"

"True. And what are the things of this world? Wine, food, fine horses, lofty titles. All dust and vapor." He waved his smoking pipe with a wry grin. "What are the things that outlast this world?"

"Our souls," Dorothy said.

"And the souls of others, and our love for them. I cannot solve all of your dilemmas, Mistress Osborne, but I would encourage you to think beyond the moment. We do have to suffer with dignity at times, yet when God calls us away from our suffering and we persist in rolling in it like a dog in its dung, is that not also a kind of worldly pride?"

Dorothy stared into the fire, stung by the accusation. Was she proud? The rector's chair scraped on the floor as he stood, and the door clicked shut behind him when he left, leaving Dorothy with her confused thoughts. She watched over her father and paced the room, staying close to the hearth where the embers warmed her cold toes in their slippers. When morning came, Collins entered the room with a tray of porridge and hot chocolate.

Dorothy called to Collins, "Wait! Where did you get this chocolate? We cannot afford such a luxury."

"A gift from the baroness."

Dorothy sank slowly next to the tray. Bless Lady Ruthyn. The bittersweet drink rolled over her tongue and warmed her all the way through as she swallowed it. It seemed to wake her from the long dreaming of the past few weeks. She lifted the porridge bowl and found a letter tucked beneath it.

William's handwriting stared back at her from the paper.

She turned the letter over and set it aside. What more could she say to him of their hopeless cause? What more could he say to her? She glanced at the folded paper. Did he have any sweet words as a balm for the bitterness of their situation? She grabbed the letter and broke the seal.

I will renounce my father and my family name as surely as if I married you and he renounced me. I will wander the world, an adventurer. And if you die early, I will as well.

Dorothy read his words again, her horror increasing. Could William really be so rash as to throw away his own ambitions—his life—for a hopeless romance?

She crammed her face into a pillow to muffle a scream. Since last writing to William, she had been more miserable than ever. The world had never looked so gray—not even when her family had been forced from their home. The peace she had sought through her decision seemed further away than ever, receding like mist as she pursued it.

The tears that had eluded her for so long came, and she sobbed until her throat burned and her eyes ached: for her mother and Robin and her father, and for herself.

The flood washed her denial away. She loved William. He was all the proof she needed that there could be happiness in the world. The home and peace she longed for—within sight, but forever out of reach. What was she to do?

She tried to write to him, stopped, tried again. Begged him not to be rash. Not to throw away his life or his salvation. Not for her or anything else.

Yet, was that what she was doing? Denying her own heart was slowing killing any love that might have dwelt in it, to say nothing of faith or hope. Hope was a painful remedy, though. How could she hope? What could she have faith in? God was all-knowing, but at times his wisdom seemed harsh.

She sat, trembling with the exhaustion of her fight. It was a choice. She thought she had chosen, but it had only made the pain worse. What if she chose to believe in William? Could the uncertainty of their future hurt any worse than the certainty of their mutual misery? Dorothy picked up her pen.

I see 'tis in vain to think of curing you, I'll study only to give you what ease I can and leave the rest to better physicians—to time and fortune. Here, then,

I declare that you have still the same power in my heart that I gave you at our last parting; that I will never marry any other; and that if ever our fortunes will allow us to marry, you shall dispose me as you please; but this, to deal freely with you, I do not hope for.

The truth of her feelings stared back at her from the page, and a weight dissolved from her chest. And yet, she had lied a little, because the hope of marriage to William bloomed in her once again. She struggled against embracing it. Hope was too a slippery ally, apt to turn on her in a moment when she was at peace and bring all the bitterness to drown the sweet.

No; 'tis too great a happiness, and I, that know myself best, must acknowledge I deserve crosses and afflictions, but can never merit such a blessing.

Dorothy finished her letter, and with her resolve never to give up on William again came a new sense of peace. At least she was no longer lying to herself. By admitting her feelings and embracing the truth of them, she felt freer than she had in months.

1654

TWO MONTHS LATER

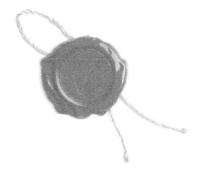

Chapter Twenty-seven

CHICKSANDS, ENGLAND

THE DAYS GREW LONGER, AND light and color slowly crept back over Chicksands. Dorothy continued her letters with William, delivered through various merchants and carriers suggested by Collins. It had to be someone she could safely leave a letter with—someone not in the employ of her brother. The constant worry rubbed at Dorothy like the handle of a garden spade raising a blister on her palm. She began to fear that everyone was Harry's spy, and no friend or neighbor could be trusted.

William had no encouraging news.

> *My father insists I join him in Ireland. I can no longer put him off.*

Ireland was in turmoil, and any number of violent accidents could take William from her if he went. If God willed that he survived, he would be so far away, and she so alone. Still, she could not hold him back. She banished thoughts of the dangerous Irish Sea crossing and sent a quick reply urging him to obey his father.

Of course, you must go. You owe not only duty, but love to him, and I would not have you cross him for my sake. But my brother plans to be gone from home next week. If I could see you again before you go, 'twould assure me that your love is not merely a dream. I remain

Your faithful
D. Osborne

William wrote back.

Nothing could keep me from you.

Dorothy feared a great many things might keep him from her, and especially Harry. He studied her sometimes when he thought she was absorbed in needlework or a book, and she wondered if he suspected her plans to meet William.

Though Harry finally left with Cousin Molle, Dorothy continued looking over her shoulder, expecting to see him creeping up on her. She straightened the pictures on the wall, rearranged the cushions on the chairs, and finally gave up any pretense of usefulness and paced in the garden, studying each plant for the buds that promised spring.

"Dorothy."

The whispered word sounded like something out of a dream. Indeed, how many times had she dreamed of hearing it, whispered in just those tones of longing and affection? She turned slowly, her hands over her mouth, while her mind grappled with the impossible joy of seeing William standing there. His dark hair was just tangled enough that Dorothy wanted to smooth his long locks, and a smile brightened his eyes.

"Well, my heart?" he asked.

She flew into his embrace. He wrapped his arms around her and folded her into his chest. His breath sighed through her hair, and his heartbeat sounded against her ear. She'd found her harbor. She could stay there forever, anchored and safe.

"I cannot believe...I did not know..." She held him tighter. "Oh, William. I am afraid. My heart whispers of all the dangers, all the impossibilities—"

"Shhh. That is not your heart. Listen more closely."

He was right. Her mind whirled with dread, but warmth filled her.

"I am so glad you came."

"I wish I did not have to leave again. Oh, Dorothy, if we could stay this way forever." He leaned back to look at her. "But we will find a way. I promise it."

"Don't promise anything we cannot control. Fortune is no friend to us."

"My heart is not governed by Fortune. I promise you this, Dorothy: I will love no one but you for all of my days. I will marry no one but you. Can you promise me the same?"

She lost herself in the hope brightening his eyes. "I can. I don't know what will happen, but I will marry you or no one."

"There. Then we are betrothed."

He smoothed back a loose strand of her hair, and she closed her eyes and leaned into his touch. It was too good to be real, but she never wanted to wake from the dream. His fingers traced her cheek, and she tilted her head back. His gentle touch paused on her throat, just over her quickening pulse.

William's lips found hers. She pulled him closer, and he kissed her more fiercely, his fingers wrapped in her hair as she sank into his arms. It was just him and her, alone in the world.

He pulled back, his breathing ragged. "Dorothy," he whispered and ran his fingers through her hair, sending pleasant shivers down her spine. "I need a lock of hair to take with me. I need something of you with me no matter where I go."

"I want of piece of yours too," she blinked away some of the blissful haze hanging over her mind. "And a ring. A simple golden ring, so no one will suspect what it is. But I will wear it always, in memory of our promise."

He drew her to his chest. "Anything you ask, my love."

"I fear I will lose you," she murmured into the musky warmth of his doublet.

"Never. I'll find a way back to you. That was not our last kiss."

She blushed and laughed through her tears.

Hoofbeats echoed across the yard. Harry, returned early from his business in London. Dorothy shrank against William.

"You must go," she said.

William glared in the direction of the stables, and Dorothy thrilled to know that she had a champion.

"Only for the moment—to keep you safe until I can protect you myself." William placed one more gentle kiss next to her ear and whispered, "Don't forget to send the lock of hair!"

And he was gone, jogging away from the house and leaving her arms empty and cold. Dorothy watched until she could not see him, then returned to the house, her nervous energy quickened by a jumble of ecstasy and fear.

Harry strode into the room, his gaze sweeping the empty sofas and chairs.

"Good morning, my sister. Not expecting me so soon, were you?"

"You told me you would not be gone long. I'm glad you made it back safely."

"Was that William Temple I saw?"

"It was." The words caught in her throat.

"He looked rather dejected."

"He came to say farewell. He's leaving for Ireland."

"Really?" Harry perked up. "A very dangerous journey."

Dorothy could only nod.

"'Tis for the best. I'm glad to see you holding up to the loss so well. You've come to your senses at last."

Dorothy was torn between laughing and crying. Here she had

promised herself to William, and Harry assumed they had just said their final goodbyes. But that was better for everyone. Now, Dorothy just had to play the part of Penelope, the faithful wife of the wanderer Ulysses, and keep her suitors at bay until her hero returned to her.

Dorothy sat with Lady Ruthyn, who daydreamed over her needlework while the sun made a halo of her chestnut hair. Harry had relaxed his guard a little since William left, and Dorothy would never again take for granted the joy of entertaining company. She had William to fill her imagination, but she needed someone of flesh and blood to remind her of the world beyond Chicksands.

"You are distracted, my lady," Dorothy said with a teasing smile.

"Oh! I suppose I am." Lady Ruthyn toyed with the creamy cloth in her lap. "Do you dread facing your suitors?"

"Is one of yours giving you trouble, my lady?"

"Well..." Lady Ruthyn blushed.

"Ah, not trouble, then."

"I'm not certain. Oh, Mistress Osborne, I'm so afraid I shall end up unhappy." Lady Ruthyn pouted at her unfinished embroidery.

"You have a bright spirit, my lady, but I would hate to see it crushed. What's concerning you?"

"I have developed a... a passion for one of my suitors, and now I cannot think clearly to know whom to choose. Everyone says that to marry for love makes one a fool, and I want to do my duty and make a good connection, but, ah, I cannot stop sighing over one of them. I suppose that means he *must* be the wrong choice."

"I don't think that logic quite follows, my lady." Dorothy said, trying not to laugh. "Can you confide in me the gentleman's name? If he is respectable, and of a good family, I don't see what the objection could be if you also have a *tendre* for him. I think an affectionate marriage would be the ideal."

Lady Ruthyn blushed prettily. "I will tell you, only because I know you will keep it in strictest confidence. You have such a wise look in your eyes."

Dorothy smiled again, sadly. "The war was hard on my family. I saw many years' worth of trouble, in a matter of days sometimes."

"Oh, and I am so sorry for it! Why must men be always fighting? But my Harry—"

She flushed again, and Dorothy's fingers went cold. Lady Ruthyn was not enamored of her brother, was she? She would not wish Harry on any woman!

Lady Ruthyn sighed. "What I mean is, Master Harry Yelverton."

"Oh!" Dorothy almost giggled in relief. "I don't know him. Does your family look kindly on the match?"

"I don't know. That is to say, they have not cautioned me against him. But perhaps they don't realize how strongly I have become attached to him."

Dorothy smiled. The Longueville family could not be unaware of Lady Ruthyn and Harry Yelverton's attentions to each other—even if Harry were subtle, Lady Ruthyn never could be—and as she was an heiress, they would certainly step in if the match was objectionable. Oh, to be so fortunate, to have a family smile on a match of affection!

"If they have not cautioned you against him, I would guess they do not disapprove," Dorothy said.

"Do you think so?" Lady Ruthyn grasped Dorothy's hand. "Oh, but could I be so fortunate? Nay, I fear I will have to set my heart elsewhere."

"Now, now, my lady." Dorothy squeezed her hand. "Don't make any decision yet. Give Master Yelverton the opportunity, and if your family approves, and your heart does as well, I think you can be very happy."

Not every romance had to end in tragedy or misery. Though Dorothy did not yet see the happy resolution for hers, it had to be possible.

Lady Ruthyn threw her arms around Dorothy. "Oh, thank you! You are such a friend. What would I do without you?"

"I'm certain you would survive, but I'm glad to be of service."

Collins entered the room. "A message, my lady."

Dorothy's heartbeat picked up as she took the letter, but it was not in William's handwriting. Instead, she recognized Master Beagle's prickly scrawl.

"Oh, a note from a suitor! Shall I leave?" Lady Ruthyn asked, her hands fluttering over her neglected needlework.

Dorothy chuckled. "No need. This suitor is one that simply will not understand his attentions are not wanted."

"Oh, it is not—" Lady Ruthyn bit her lip.

Dorothy met her embarrassed gaze. "It is not from William Temple. I admit, his affections are the only ones that interest me."

"I had heard rumors to that effect, but you are so calm about it! Can your heart truly be so far gone?"

"I suppose some people's hearts are quieter than others, though believe me that I have felt deeply."

Lady Ruthyn lowered her voice. "Then, you love William Temple, and no other?"

"I do," Dorothy said, warming at the words, and at the memory of his kisses.

"I see it in your eyes! And you believe matches of affection can ever be happy?"

"I think they can." Dorothy said, smiling to find she meant it. "I don't know that mine will have a happy conclusion, because our families object so, but how can Harry Yelverton's family object to you?"

Lady Ruthyn's cheeks turned a rosy shade. "But what of this servant?" she gestured to the letter in Dorothy's hand.

Dorothy sighed. "I will have to find better ways to discourage him." She opened the letter and groaned.

"What is it?" Lady Ruthyn was carefully not looking at the letter, but her foot bounced in place.

"These verses he sends me! I think in my courtships, I have seen every example of poor writing, and now he sends bad poetry!"

"Oh, may I?" Lady Ruthyn asked.

"Aye, I will not subject you to the worst of it. Here. At least this one rhymes:

A stately and majestic brow
Of force to make Protectors bow

Lady Ruthyn giggled into her hand. "Oh, dear! As if 'twere the Lord Protector Cromwell who had courted you, and not his son. Is this what you are subjected to? What shall you do with it?"

Dorothy paced over and tossed it into the fireplace.

"It seems so heartless!" Lady Ruthyn exclaimed.

"Would you have written back to him?"

"I would have felt obligated."

"At one time, perhaps I would have, too, but my mind and my heart are set. Why should I offer false encouragement?"

"That is true. I suppose it is kinder. Oh, to be as wise as you someday!"

Dorothy laughed, though the statement made her feel very old, and not at all wise.

Dorothy snuck her lock of hair off to William along with a ring so he would know what size to make her betrothal ring. Her skin prickled with pleasant tingles at the thought of it. A betrothal ring! Their love might never come to fruition, but the pledge was there, and the ring would be proof to herself when she doubted her own mind.

She waited each day for the packet from William, but the first delivery she received was not the one she hoped for.

"What is it?" she asked, observing the large box that Collins strained to haul into the room.

He opened it, and they stared inside.

"Coal, my lady," Collins said, brushing his fingers off on a handkerchief.

"Coal! 'Tis in short enough supply this winter. Who would send us such a precious gift?" Dorothy examined the note.

To warm your cold heart. -J. Beagle.

She and Collins glanced at each other and laughed.

"I ought to be insulted," Dorothy said, wiping tears of mirth from her eyes, "but I am so grateful for the extra warmth I cannot be. I suppose I shall have to thank him for the gift. Beagle is persistent, is he not?"

"He does not relinquish the scent," Collins agreed.

Dorothy smiled. "Even when he should."

Her polite and formal thank-you note elicited a return visit from Master Beagle. He strode into the great hall at Chicksands, his round face all smug smiles.

"I knew you would soften toward me. 'Twas only a matter of time."

"I believe you misunderstood my note, Sir," Dorothy said, standing.

"Nonsense."

Beagle took her hand and raised it to his cold lips. Dorothy yanked her hand free. He offered a letter with a flourish.

"I have poured my heart into this missive. I hope you will read it with the same affection it was offered."

Dorothy snapped it from his hand and tossed it into the fire.

Beagle cried out in protest.

"I am sorry to upset you, Sir," Dorothy said, "but I must make myself perfectly clear once again. I cannot return your affection. You waste your pretty words on me, and you would do better to turn your attentions to someone else."

Beagle shoved his hat on his head and stormed out of the room.

"Take care, my sister." Harry's voice came from the doorway. "You will gain a reputation as a shrew."

"Good! Then I will finally have some peace!" She turned from Harry, feeling his calculating gaze on her back.

Chapter Twenty-eight

FOG SAT HEAVY OVER THE hilly green countryside of Wales. Each mile William traveled west took him farther from Dorothy. He'd sent her a simple gold ring, inscribed on the inside with, **The love I owe I cannot show**. Dorothy would keep that line hidden against her ring finger—the one connected directly to her heart—while William stowed her lock of hair safe inside his doublet. He had hidden Dorothy's letters in a cabinet at his brother John's house, deciding they were safer there than on the journey. Even if he were lost, her words would survive. He could see the teasing curves of her parting thoughts when he closed his eyes.

> *I will not tell you the fears and apprehensions I have for you. No, I long to be rid on you–am afraid you will not go soon enough: do not you believe this? No, my dearest, I know you do not, what'er you say, you cannot doubt but I am*
>
> *Yours,*
> *Dorothy*

She was his Dorothy, and he belonged to her in every thought and every breath. He was going forward so that someday he would be able to come back. Yet as he wrestled to retrieve a boot slurped off by the muddy road, he wondered how long it would be before he returned to England. If this journey was a parallel of his quest for Dorothy, it did not bode well.

When he had time to raise his head, he was greeted only by the cold green hills, or the colder slate-gray sea waves that roared at the road when it meandered near the shore. Even Wales's isolated valleys were scarred by the brutality of war. Slighted castles blighted the hillsides—their mighty walls demolished by Parliament so they could never rebel again—and starving peasants crowded into the scattered towns, anxious to earn a few shillings.

Martha trudged beside him. Her cheeks were pale in the cold, and William worried that she had not recovered enough for the journey after all. There was no turning back now, though. She had ridden in the wagon until Conwy, but after that walled city, the roads became so rutted and muddy that their party had to disassemble the wagons and hire a dozen locals to help carry them to the Irish Sea. Two weeks from London, they were finally nearing the Menai Strait, where they would cross to Anglesey, and from there sail the Irish Sea to Dublin.

"I suppose a man could make a fortune renting wagons after the Menai Straits," William said to Master Lyons, the expedition leader.

"Aye." Master Lyons held his hand out to catch the icy rain drizzling over them. "But then you'd have to live in this, and who would want that?"

By the time they reached the Menai Straits, everyone in the party wore a brown coating of mud.

The strait itself was not very wide—William could make out the Isle of Anglesey across the choppy water—but the frigid winds of the Irish Sea lashed at them, as though determined to keep the English from crossing to the island, and from thence to Ireland.

"Secure your belongings!" Master Lyons called over the noise of the waves that battered the docks.

"Should we wait for fairer weather?" William asked.

The ferryman shook his head. "This is fair weather for Wales in March."

William made certain their trunks were lashed down and then touched his doublet, where his most precious possessions were secured: Dorothy's lock of hair, a miniature painting of her, and the latest draft of his essay on Holland.

William and Martha joined the others in the ferry, their wagons in pieces behind them. Martha clung to William's arm, and he held her close, keeping her as far from the gunwale and the vicious waters as he could.

They shoved off, the tiny vessel afloat in the violent sea like a baby chick at the mercy of an angry cat.

A large wave shoved the ferry nearly upright. William held Martha close and clung to the seat with his free arm. The ferry tipped forward, and he braced his feet, trying not to pitch forward into the water suddenly straight in front of him.

The boat slapped back down onto the sea. William smacked his head against the back of the seat. A spray of icy water showered down on them.

"We've lost some of the luggage," the helmsman cried.

"Keep going! For heaven's sake, get us to land," William ordered through chattering teeth.

The ferryman and his men wrestled against the might of the sea. William felt guilty not helping, but Martha clung to him, her ice-cold fingers digging into his arm with each yaw and pitch of the boat.

They nearly crashed into the dock on the other side, as if the sea were spitting them back onto land. William helped a trembling Martha off the ferry and turned back to survey the damage to their goods, ignoring the slight tremor in his own legs.

"How much did we lose?"

The ferryman sighed. "Most of it. 'Twas lashed down, but—"

William shook his head. "'Twas a miracle we made it across ourselves. We need to get warm and dry, and we'll do an inventory."

They crowded into an inn and gathered round the fire, warming damp clothes and chilled fingers. The reek of wet wool mixed with the smell of cooking fish turned William's stomach. He wondered if he would ever have an appetite again. He ate a little, just to have something warm in his belly, and to encourage Martha to do the same.

"We lost your wagon," Master Lyons told William, "and all the goods that were with it."

William's belongings were at the bottom of the sea, then. Wales giveth, and it taketh away. He had a sudden image of the Welsh merchants dredging the sad packages up to sell to the next poor fool who traveled by, but he shook it away. It would be good for no one but the mermaids now. Still, it felt like a bad omen, when they had only crossed the strait, and they still had to face the fury of the Irish Sea. She did not want more Englishmen, that was clear, and from what William had heard of the fighting in Ireland, he could not blame her.

He patted down his soggy doublet and pulled out his treatise on Holland. Ruined. Shreds of paper, reduced back to linen rags, came loose under his fingers, and the ink blurred into faded scratches. Hours of thought and labor—and his hopes for the future—gone.

"What is that, Brother?" Martha asked.

"Nothing," William said woodenly. "Just foolishness." He tossed the sodden scraps into the fire, where they smoked and hissed, then he wrapped his fingers around the locket with Dorothy's hair.

"We must be moving on," Master Lyons said to the company.

"Aye, we must," William whispered.

They gathered what was left of their provisions, restocked as best they could at mercenary prices, and continued to Holyhead. A grayer, sadder-looking town William could not imagine, as though the sea wind had wiped all the color from the landscape. Even the boats that sat waiting to carry them to Ireland looked beaten down.

With foreboding, William led Martha onto their boat. They pitched their way out of the harbor and toward the open water. The waves slammed the boat around with the noise and ferocity of a cannon volley. Nearly everyone—William and Martha included—lost their stomachs over the side. More offerings to the sea. With each boom that shook the hull, William was certain they were about to slide into the belly of the sea themselves. He clutched the locket through his doublet and prayed he would live, if only to see Dorothy again. The hours crawled by.

"What's that?" Martha pointed to the horizon.

At first William did not see anything, but then some of the hazy clouds resolved themselves into faint spires.

"Land!" One of the crew called.

William rested his head in his hands. His stomach roiled, leaving him too sick to enjoy the thought that their journey was almost over.

The waters calmed as they sailed into Dublin Bay. The boat thumped against the quay, sending another wave of nausea churning through William's stomach.

The port and city bustled with trade, and beyond the narrow streets and soaring church towers, the landscape rolled away, crisp and deep green. It was beautiful, but a sadness hung over it, like the smoke from chimneys in the distance. Or was the smoke from the destruction on some battlefield? William stepped ashore, an enemy in a hostile land.

Men and women in chains lined the dock, waiting to board a ship.

"Who are they?" Martha whispered.

William studied their faces: defeated, some marked by slit earlobes or brands, no hope left in their eyes.

"They are the ones who lost. The Irish. Cromwell is bringing English settlers to Ireland, and those who tried to defend their freedom and their lands are now being shipped off to the West Indies."

Martha was silent for some time. "And this is the government that Father now serves?"

"He's doing it for us," William said, and he knew it was true. His father was stubborn, but he was not actively cruel. He would not enjoy the sight of the Irish in chains.

As the defeated people trudged past him, William ached for them. For most, their only crime had been being Catholic—holding to the faith they had been born to. And refusing to rebel against their king. Oliver Cromwell and his Puritan army would squelch all those who dared to think differently, and that would lead to more war. People would fight for their beliefs until they were too broken to believe in anything. What England needed was the relative tolerance of Holland.

William touched his doublet where his essay had rested. He understood why his father made the choices he did, but William saw that he could never bow to Oliver Cromwell, not even to support marriage with Dorothy. She would not want him too. He had to find a more honest way to earn his livelihood. One that would also help people understand there was a better way. Not only his future with Dorothy, but perhaps also his life and the lives of Englishmen and Irishmen alike depended on his untested writing and diplomatic skills.

"Come Martha," he said. "We have to find Father and get settled in, and then I have a task to complete."

"What's that?"

"I need to buy a hound. The biggest I can find. I have an old promise to fulfill." He pitied the creature having to make the reverse of the trip they'd just endured, but he wanted Dorothy to have all the protection she could get for however long he had to be away from her.

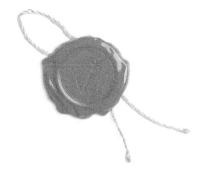

Chapter Twenty-nine

CHICKSANDS, ENGLAND

"OH, YOU ARE A BEAUTIFUL fellow!" Dorothy threw her arms around the neck of William's hound and ruffled its coarse fur. It took the attention in stride, gently licking her ear.

"He did not forget," Dorothy told the dog. She touched her golden betrothal ring. "What is it like in Ireland? Will he be safe?"

The massive dog beat his gray tail against the woven rush rug and watched his new mistress intently.

"Well, you'll do just fine, and I will make certain the others know their places. You are the new favorite, you know. I'll call you Brian, after the ancient Irish king."

She needed the company. Jane was in London with her family, and Lady Ruthyn had left to plan her wedding to Master Yelverton. Sir Peter's illness and Harry's pestering filled Dorothy's days.

If only her dogs could attend church with her as well, but she was left alone on Sunday to face the hateful stares and whispers of James Beagle. She knew some of what he was telling people: that she had gone mad as an ape, shouting and throwing things and laughing at nothing. She wanted to wilt under the curious stares but kept her head up. All she could do to counter the rumors was to show that she was not hysterical and attended church like a good Christian woman.

"I would think you would defend your sister's honor against Master Beagle's slander," Dorothy whispered to Harry outside of church.

"'Tis a good reminder of what becomes of an unnatural, disobedient woman. Your stubbornness is a great trial to me, but perhaps it will soften your heart to remember what it would be like if you did not have me as a protector." Harry strode ahead, leaving her to a solitary walk back to Chicksands. She wanted to stomp her foot and scream at him, but she took a deep breath, determined not to act like the madwomen everyone believed her to be.

Footsteps crunched on the path behind her. She turned to see James Beagle.

He stopped and glared at Dorothy, his round cheeks flushed.

"What do you have to say to me?" She advanced on him, and he stumbled back a step. "Have you not said enough behind my back?"

"I... 'Twas not my intention to besmirch your character, but you are not a rational woman. And you are so unfeeling. You have broken my heart, and you care nothing for it. I am so distraught, I would kill myself! But I do not have the nerve."

Dorothy took a steadying breath. "I am sorry your heart is broken, but I would not have been the person to mend it. I hope you find peace again soon."

She turned away and muttered, "I can hardly be expected to marry someone just to cheer him up."

Harry waited for her at Chicksands.

"Brother Peyton has written to you." He handed over the letter, making no effort to disguise the broken seal.

Dorothy took it with a stiff curtsey and left to read the message alone. She might not have any privacy, but she could maintain the illusion. She twisted the gold ring on her finger. At least there were some secrets she could keep to herself, and some joys even Harry could not take away from her.

Brother Peyton's message was full of enthusiastic plans for her future. He suggested she marry Sir John Tuften, a widower who, he assured her, would be an excellent husband, for he had been kind to his last wife, though she was very ugly.

"Oh, that is commendable of him," Dorothy told her hounds. "Is it too much to expect men to be kind to ugly women, too?" She paused and glanced at the mirror, studying the deep circles against her pale skin. "Yet have I faded so fast? Poor William. He will be lucky if he does not have to marry me after all."

She returned to her father's bedside. The dogs curled up quietly about her, seeming to sense the solemnness in the room.

Sir Peter's skin grew more ashen each day, and his breathing more labored. She had spent many hours tending him these last years, but this time a weighty foreboding hung in the dark folds of the bed curtains.

"Father." Dorothy roused him enough to try to slip some broth between his lips.

He coughed it back up, and blood came away when she dabbed his mouth.

"It is no use, Daughter," he whispered. "I know my end is near, and I am prepared for it. I only wish I could have seen you secure in the world." Tears trickled from the corners of his eyes. "I tried. I tried to make the world better for all of you."

"Shhh." She soothed his creased forehead. "You have shown us that there is courage and integrity in this world. What better legacy could you leave?"

He coughed up more blood, and his breath rattled in his throat. As she cleaned her father's chin, cold dread crept up her limbs. Her father's long years of suffering would soon be at an end, but the protection his presence had offered her would be gone. She would be at the mercy of her brothers.

Of Harry.

She shook off her own worries and concerned herself with keeping her father comfortable as the light faded in his eyes. Sometimes he called out for Dorothy's mother or others who had gone before. Her dogs whimpered and huddled closer to her. Dorothy wondered if there were visitors in the room whom she could not see, and her skin prickled at the idea.

"Dorothy?" her father cried out like a frightened child.

She took his hand. "I am here, Father. I will not leave you."

She held his hand long into the night. Other members of the household came and went, but she would not budge from his side, and her dogs stayed with her, as though guarding against the encroaching darkness.

Sir Peter whimpered and struggled for breath, his face lined with sorrow and struggle.

"I wish you did not have to leave me," Dorothy whispered, "but better things are waiting for you. You have earned your rest."

A few minutes later, he exhaled one last time, and his chest grew still. Dorothy tensed over him, waiting to see him move one more time, but he was gone. Gone back to her mother, to her older sister and her brother killed in the war, to Robin, to the king he had served so faithfully.

Dorothy felt as though her chest had crumpled in, making it difficult to breathe, but still no tears came. She wished there were someone to snatch her up in their arms and make her feel safe again, but her time for being a child was over.

"Go tell my brother our father is dead," Dorothy whispered to Collins.

He hurried out of the room. Dorothy straightened the blankets and began preparing her father for burial. A shadow fell over her, and she found Harry standing behind her, watching silently.

For a moment, Harry's gaze was fixed on their father, and Dorothy tried to read what she saw there. His gaze looked tired and hollow. A little vulnerable, perhaps. She had never seen him vulnerable before. What went on in his mind that made him as he was? Did he, like her, secretly want someone to hold him close and tell him that there was no need to fear?

He met Dorothy's eyes. They stood like that for several heartbeats, caught in an awkward moment of shared sorrow and uncertainty. Then Harry's vulnerability vanished, replaced with calculating indifference.

Dorothy drew back, her breath tight. Their father was gone. This was not the end of something between her and Harry, but the beginning. She pressed back against the bed curtains.

Ulysses stood and placed himself between Dorothy and Harry, and Brian and the other dogs followed.

Harry left without a word. Dorothy watched the empty doorway until her dogs settled back on the floor. She returned to preparing the body. Her mourning found no expression except a slight tremble in her fingers, as much from exhaustion as grief.

When Dorothy finally stumbled downstairs, it was so far past sunup that it felt wrong going to sleep. Instead, she found her book and curled up in front of the fireplace, not actually reading, but finding a quiet comfort in the weight of the book in her hands, a chance to escape her sorrow for an hour's time.

She was just on the point of dozing off when her dogs roused. She sat up, letting the book slide to the floor. Harry stood over her.

"Well, my sister, Father is gone."

"He is," Dorothy said. "It seems unreal, does it not?"

Harry shrugged. "In many ways, he has been gone since the war. Since the king failed to come to his aid."

"Something in him was lost then, but not all."

"His presence—his usefulness—was gone. But everything shifts now. This house is John's. Have you notified him yet?"

Dorothy shook her head. "I had not thought of it, with everything else."

"No matter. I shall do it. And do you suppose he will let us stay?"

"I had rather hoped he might."

"I doubt it will happen. He might, but that wife of his will not. Where do you suppose we will go?"

Dorothy made no reply. She had thought John's wife might look more kindly on her than on Harry, but she had to admit to herself that Eleanor was unlikely to want the old mistress of the house underfoot.

"You will *have* to marry now, or we will be sent from house to house as beggars," Harry said.

"Certainly, you can find work for yourself. I will be useful to my family members."

"Your only use is in marrying well. Why cannot you not understand that?"

"My marriage will be of no use to you. Surely you see that you cannot really spend your life tied to my petticoats? You have to stand on your own."

There it was again—that flash in his eyes—a sort of desperate fear.

"Of course, I will make something of myself," he said, "and you will help me to do it. You will marry whomever John and I instruct you too—and John will bow to my advice in the matter."

"I will do no such thing!" Dorothy said.

But John could force her to marry. She had nowhere to turn, and her only champion—William—was far away. Even friends like Lady Diana, Lady Ruthyn, and Henry Cromwell had no power against the wishes of her eldest brother.

Harry placed a hand on her throat and forced her face up to meet his eyes. "You will. You will obey."

"I will refuse," Dorothy said against the pressure of his hand. "If you toss me out, I shall become a companion or tutor in some household and throw disrespect on all our family, but I will marry no one but William Temple."

286

Harry released his grip to pace. "Temple! Temple! Temple! How sick I am of that name. Your single-mindedness shows how weak your wits are. All you can think of is one man who has left you behind without any hope or promise."

"He has not! We are betrothed! I will marry him or no other."

Harry paled. "A secret betrothal has no legal force, not anymore. The Lord Protector will have everything done above board, and I am glad for it."

"It does not matter. I will marry William Temple or die a spinster."

"You will be the laughing stock of the neighborhood. I will tell everyone you are mad."

"You already have by not speaking against Master Beagle. I no longer care!" She lowered her voice. "I am too weary to care."

Harry stepped closer, and his expression sent goose bumps over her skin. "Then I will tell them that William has compromised your virtue and left you in false expectation of his return."

"You would not dare lie so about your own sister."

"I would not have to. I need only drop the right words, and others will come to the right conclusion. You will be a spinster as you wish—no respectable man will come near you, and even the ladies will keep you at arm's length. You will be cut off from all society."

Dorothy's eyes stung, but she refused to cry. Those who were truly beloved to her would know it was not true.

"Then I can finally retire from the world as I have always wished. I see you for what you are now, Harry: a coward. You have not only lost a father this day, but a sister as well."

Harry stepped toward her, his eyes gleaming with hate. "You cannot disavow me. You are mine. *My* sister."

Dorothy sat upright in her chair, mustering the dignity of a queen. Or perhaps a king facing his executioner.

A thrumming growl reverberated through the room. Harry stopped and stared down at Brian. The big, gray hound rose to its feet, its hackles standing on end, its ears flat against its head.

Harry hesitated. The other dogs followed the lead of her protector, the four facing off against Harry. He glared at Dorothy and darted from the room. The dogs looked to their mistress.

"Good boys," she said, sinking in relief against their warm fur. "Good boys. Never leave my side. At least until John arrives."

Her eldest brother's appearance would end her sojourn at Chicksands, but at least his presence would stop Harry from doing something insane.

John arrived the next day on horseback. Dorothy came to welcome him, surrounded by her hounds, and he kissed her cheek in greeting.

"I came ahead of the others." He removed his hat and stepped inside, surveying his new home before turning back to Dorothy. "It will take some time to arrange everything, but I did not want to leave you alone at such a time."

For a moment, Dorothy thought he meant Harry's irrational behavior, but then he began rambling on about the funeral and the house. He thought of nothing but himself and his future.

Dorothy changed into her black again and stood with head bowed at the funeral, but her sorrow had already given way to numbness. Harry never spoke to her, but John took no notice of the tension between them. He showed only the most perfunctory grief for their father, then set about making Chicksands his own, drawing up plans to redesign Dorothy's garden. She made herself useful in the kitchen and parlor, occasionally resting under the beloved hawthorn tree that would soon make way for a new walk.

The village drew away from her, watching like a jury. A couple of weeks after the funeral, Master Beagle cornered her after church.

"My condolences," he said, looking almost smug.

"Thank you," she said uncertainly. "The loss of our father has been a heavy blow."

"But not so heavy, I imagine, as the loss of your good name." He was definitely smirking now. "I suppose, with your family casting you off, you will have to make your way to Ireland. I would wish you happy there, but William is not of a serious turn of mind. I'm sure he will only abuse whatever good is left of your nature."

Dorothy set her jaw to keep it from dropping open. She was sorely tempted to slap Beagle's insolent, jowly face.

"I am afraid that you have been most severely misinformed, Sir. My family has not cast me off, and if I travel to Ireland with William Temple, it will be as his wife and nothing else."

Beagle hesitated, then shrugged. "Well, it makes no matter to me, of course. But I cannot say I envy your position right now."

"Then we are even, Sir, for I will never envy yours."

She stormed away from him before he could work out if she had insulted him or not.

"Mistress Osborne!" a voice called behind her. Colonel Samuel Luke strode past Master Beagle, his back as straight as an officer marching into war.

"You should not be alone right now, dear," Colonel Luke said, offering Dorothy his arm.

She took it, not even able to thank him past the lump in her throat. He did not speak, except to bid her farewell within sight of her home.

She ventured inside to find a letter waiting for her, but it was not from William. Still, the tiny leavening of hope placed in her heart by Colonel Luke's kindness expanded at the sight of Lady Ruthyn's familiar handwriting, and even more at her friend's offer of an extended visit, if the current situation with her family became unbearable.

"Dear Lady Ruthyn, thank you," Dorothy whispered to her friend.

A few days later, John finally called her to see him.

"I nearly have everything arranged now. I see we need to provide for your future. That means marriage, of course."

Dorothy drew a deep breath. "I understand. I should tell you I have engaged myself to William Temple."

John gave a start, but quickly recovered his composure. "I see. Did Father know of this?"

"Nay, it happened just before his death, when Master William made his way to Ireland."

"And does his father know of it?"

"I don't know. But William will not betray my trust."

John sat back in his chair, studying Dorothy. "And what are Master Temple's prospects?"

Dorothy let her balled fists relax. If they were discussing this, there was hope that John would be reasonable.

"He has accompanied his father to Ireland, where Sir John is the Commissioner of Forfeited Estates, and Master William is hoping to work in the diplomatic service."

"Commissioner of Forfeited Estates for Ireland?" John steepled his fingers and stared off thoughtfully. "Is their fortune recovered from the war?"

"Somewhat. They are not wealthy, but also not impoverished."

"And in favor with the Lord Protector. I never understood why you turned down Henry Cromwell, but he's no longer an option."

Dorothy made no reply, sensing this was a question he needed to work through on his own.

He nodded. "Very well. If William Temple can make an offer with the approval of his father, I will entertain it."

Dorothy could not stop her grin, but she glanced down to hide it.

"Now, Sister, you must marry. William Temple is in Ireland, and it sounds like he may not return soon, if at all. Nothing is certain, and if another eligible offer comes along, you will have to accept it. We cannot have you bouncing around relatives like a shuttlecock."

"I am not to stay here, Sir?" Dorothy asked.

"Not for much longer. Perhaps Aunt Gargrave can take you."

A dire situation. "I have an invitation for an extended visit to the Baroness Grey de Ruthyn in Northamptonshire."

"I see nothing to object to in that plan. Perhaps a change of scene will... well, aye, 'tis a good plan."

Dorothy nodded. She would have to leave her dogs at Chicksands while she turned wanderer, but only until she had a real home again. She would find refuge with Lady Ruthyn, and William would rescue her. He would have to.

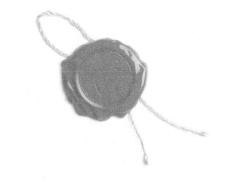

Chapter Thirty

DUBLIN, IRELAND

WILLIAM MADE HIS EVENING WALK back to the walled confines of Dublin from Trinity College on a fine April evening, his steps dragging. His father was ill, and it fell to William to look after their estate in County Carlow and to perform some of Sir John's duties as Commissioner of Forfeited Estates, searching through fragile historical records for answers in complicated land disputes.

Everything was complicated in Ireland, especially with England's attempts to drive the native Irish—it seemed—right to extinction. But the Irish refused to let their fire be quenched, and some fought in the courts for rights to hereditary lands and privileges recorded by monks in the distant past. William admired Irish tenacity and wished the need for it did not exist. If only there could be tolerance as there was in Holland. He had begun again to write of what he had learned there, but he feared his words were too clumsy to convey all he had seen. It was easier to brew violence than peace.

He entered Dublin through Dame's Gate. The uneven cobblestones of Castle Street prodded his sore feet, and the great round tower and crenelated walls of Dublin Castle cast a long evening shadow over the streets. He imagined instead he was in Hyde Park with Dorothy, listening to the sweet whisper of her rich voice.

One of his father's close associates, Godwin Swift, hailed him from his daydream, waking him to the briny scent of the Fish Shambles markets.

"How is your father?" Godwin asked.

"Recovering. Thank you, Sir."

Godwin glanced at the young man at his side. "Allow me to introduce my brother, Jonathan Swift. Another victim of Parliament."

William bowed to the younger Master Swift. There were many Royalists in Dublin, fled there after the ruin brought to their estates and families by Cromwell's rise to power. William was glad Dorothy's family had regained Chicksands, even as he longed to have her at his side, discussing the heartache and hope etched into the Irish landscape.

"I understand your family has been a great support to mine," Jonathan Swift said.

"Of course. We are happy to help anyone distressed by this war." William hoped, at least, that his father's motivations were selfless.

The Swifts looked as if they would say more but grew silent at the sight of Henry Cromwell approaching with his wife. Dorothy's friendship with Henry Cromwell demanded William's respect for him as well, but Cromwell was not a popular name in Ireland.

"Good day to you, Master Temple," Godwin said, leading his young brother away.

Henry pretended not to notice their sudden departure. In fact, from his distracted look, perhaps he truly had not taken note of it. He left his wife and drew William off the main thoroughfare.

"Have you heard the rumors?" Henry asked without preamble.

"I hear rumors every day."

"But these are about you and Mistress Osborne."

"What is the nature of this gossip?" William kept his tone light, despite Henry's seriousness. Had Dorothy let it slip that they were promised to each other? William had never been as concerned as Dorothy about keeping it a secret.

"I hate to pollute your ears with it," Henry said slowly, "but some claim you have trifled with her and left her to face the disdain of her neighborhood and be cast out by her family."

"What!" William raised his voice far more than he meant to, and Mistress Cromwell glanced up at him. He steadied his nerves. "I can assure you the rumors are untrue. Dorothy and I do have an understanding, but I love her far too well to do any harm to her. I would certainly never leave her in such a situation."

"I did not think you had. I only wanted to warn you what was being said. You may not be able to do anything to still the gossip, but at least you will be prepared for it."

William gave a grim nod. "I thank you, Master Cromwell."

"I hope you will take good care of her."

"I intend to."

The two men nodded to each other and continued on their ways. William hurried down through the market stalls of Fish Shambles toward the banks of the River Liffey, where his father and many other Englishmen built their fine homes and gardens. Nearby, the bells of Christchurch and St. John's rang out the hour, echoed by the more distant city churches. William took a deep breath and opened the door.

Martha greeted him with a kiss on the cheek and a warning look. "Father wishes to see you. He was in a foul mood after meeting with some of Lord Cromwell's English colonists today."

William nodded. He made his way up the narrow stairs to his father's chamber.

"Father, you asked for me?" he asked.

"William." His father struggled to rise.

William helped him up and placed a feather-stuffed bolster behind his back.

"I have been hearing terrible things," his father said. "Things that may put me in my grave."

"More trouble with the English colonists?" William asked.

"Trouble with you, my boy. I'm almost afraid to ask, but I must know the truth. What is the nature of your relationship with Dorothy Osborne?"

William sighed and sat by his father's bed. "I have done nothing to harm her honor or her position, if that is your fear."

"I am glad to hear that. I had not thought you would, and yet they said the news came directly from a member of the family."

William grimaced at the thought of Dorothy's gossiping relations. He had never met a looser set of tongues, and truth was the least likely thing to set them wagging.

His father coughed. "I sense there is more. Tell me the whole of it."

"There is," William said. "I am still determined to marry Dorothy Osborne."

"William..." his father whispered.

"We have promised ourselves to each other. We are betrothed."

"Betrothed!" His father rose from his pillows. "Without the permission of your own father or her family? Do you care nothing for duty, or for your future?"

"I care very much for both, Sir. We understood in promising ourselves thus that we would never marry without permission given on both sides. But we also know that we will never be happy married to any other."

"Foolishness! All the more proof that you are not able to choose wisely for yourself."

"I am sorry, as always, to disappoint you, Sir, but I have chosen and given my word. I will not go back on it. If you don't give me permission to marry, I will never marry. It will be up to my brother John to continue on the family name."

His father sank back into the damask bolster, his lips set in a thin, angry line. "Leave me now. I have nothing more to say to you on this matter."

William obeyed, his heart heavy.

"William?" Martha asked when he returned to the parlor.

"Oh, Sister, I have angered Father. I am sorry if it makes your task harder."

"I can handle Father. I am more concerned about you. You look as though you have been struck a blow."

"I have. I am determined to marry Dorothy Osborne, but Father does not approve."

"Your commitment to her has not wavered over all this time? How long has it been that you've known her?"

"Six years, and I have grown more committed to her with each one."

"What is Father's objection?"

"Sometimes I think it is only that I have chosen for myself, and he does not think me capable of doing anything right on my own. Dorothy's family connections are not ideal, and her fortune not tremendous, but she is a worthy match. She would make a good wife."

"And you care for her deeply," Martha said quietly.

"I do. And I don't understand how parents can expect a happy outcome for their children's marriages when there is no affection in the match—or even worse, when the couple's affections are engaged elsewhere."

"I hope Father relents."

"As do I. But what can I do?"

Martha shrugged helplessly. William knew what he must do, though. He must show Sir John that he was the responsible young man he needed to be, and not the careless boy he had once been. Once his father learned to trust his judgment in some matters, perhaps he would trust it in the most important one as well.

In the meantime, though, his father kept him in Ireland, and Dorothy was left alone in England to face the rumors and the spite of her brothers. All William could do was send his prayers flying across the water that she would be comforted and protected when he was not there to watch over her himself.

William ate a quick supper and returned to his chamber to pick up his pen. First, a letter to Dorothy. He rambled on, hating to finish, both because he longed for her and because he worried. He passed the letter off to the post-boy and returned to work on rewriting his treatise on Holland. As he watched the victims of civil war pass below him on the street, he ached to show the world that it did not have to be thus.

Several days later, after William returned from attending to his father's duties, he entered his study to find his father sitting at his desk, looking thoughtful. William gritted his teeth at finding his personal space invaded but said nothing.

"Godwin Swift tells me you helped resolve a case today."

"I did," William said. It had been immensely difficult, but it was satisfying knowing that justice had been served without regard to the religion or ethnicity of the plaintiff and defendant.

"You are pleased with yourself?"

"I am. It was rewarding."

"Do you regret not completing your studies and going into law, then?"

William walked by his father to stare out the rain-spattered window panes as he searched for an honest answer. "Nay. John will be an excellent lawyer, but I don't have the temperament for it. I would still like to pursue diplomatic work."

"You are such a headstrong boy. I never could imagine you as a diplomat."

William turned, ready to defend himself, and he saw that his father held his essay on Holland. He tensed. Would his father condemn his work? See it as childish? William was instantly aware of every fault in his writing. Once again, he failed to please his father.

"You wrote this?" his father asked.

"Aye, Sir."

"I thought all this time you were sitting in here mooning over that Osborne girl and writing her love letters."

"I do that, too, Sir. But Dorothy would not want me to waste my time or talents when there's something I feel passionately about."

His father nodded and flipped through the neatly written pages. "Your time has been well spent. The writing style is pleasant and engaging, and your observations are keener than I knew you were capable of."

William blinked in surprise. "Thank you."

"I'm not sure when you became so thoughtful."

"We learn much from suffering, do we not, Father?"

"Have I really been so unkind to you, in looking out for your well-being?"

"I know you think that's what you're doing, but my well-being requires more than wealth or land. Give me all the money in the world, and it would not make me wise, or happy. But in my wandering, I have learned something of people, and of myself."

"So, you defend your aimlessness?"

"I would not say aimlessness. I would say, in my quest to find myself, I may not have taken a direct route, but the path I did take has taught me things that, perhaps, will let me serve my country in a way that is my own."

"I am glad to see you turning to a more serious frame of mind." His father joined him at the window looking out on the cobbled street below. "I suppose you would give all the credit to your Mistress Osborne?"

The question was half-mocking, but William considered it seriously. "At first I would have. It was she who first gave me direction in thinking about myself—gave me reason to focus. But now that it has become something of a habit with me, I find that my thoughts don't drift so much, and I am more certain of what is right and what I want."

"You are stubborn, and your passion is dangerous."

"So everyone says. Yet, if passion is a fire, can it not also be tamed for a good purpose? Can we not be stubborn in defending what we believe to be right?"

"Do I sense reproach in your tone? Nay, do not object. I have followed the tides that seemed most likely to lead me to good fortune, and they have not always done so. Many men lost their heads in the war because they were stubborn, though."

"Yet they lived and died with conviction."

"Perhaps you should have been trained in religion like your uncle."

"I admire Uncle Hammond, but he is a homeless beggar at the moment for his convictions, and I cannot stomach the Roundheads and their soberness enough to side with them. 'Twould have been a poor use of me."

"And you think you have found a better use for yourself?" His father studied the pages of his essay. "Perhaps you have. You have a skill for understanding others that would serve a statesman well." He met William's gaze. "Very well. You have my blessing."

"To be a statesman?" William asked with a smile.

"To marry your Mistress Osborne, pursue your own course. You have grown up, and I will not interfere, though I will ask that you remain a little time in Ireland to finish your work here."

William stared, waiting to wake from this dream, as he had from all the others. Six years. Six years of secret letters and frustrated rendezvous. When he first saw Dorothy on the Isle of Wight, he never would have imagined what trials awaited them, and what defiance they would both have to muster against their families.

Yet now his father stood smiling at him in the strange stillness of reality while carts jostled and rattled outside the window. All those people out there, going about their everyday work, unaware of the joy spreading throughout William's limbs until he thought he must have blazed with it.

He started for the desk in a trance-like haze.

"Son?" Sir John called.

William spun around and bowed to his father. "Thank you, Sir! I have a letter to write!"

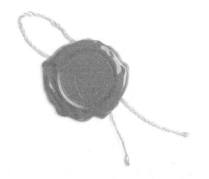

Chapter Thirty-one

LONDON, ENGLAND

DOROTHY REREAD WILLIAM'S WORDS SO often, she feared she would wear them off the page and erase their reality.

> *How hard 'tis to think of ending when I am writing to you; but it must be so, and I must ever be subject to other people's occasions, and so never, I think, master of my own. This is too true, both in respect of this fellow's post that is bawling at me for my letter, and of my father's delays. They kill me; but patience—would anybody but I be here! Yet you may command me over at one minute's warning. Had I not heard from you by this last, in earnest I had resolved to have gone with this and given my father the slip for all his caution. He tells me still of a little time; but, alas! who knows not what mischances and how great changes have often happened in a little time?*
>
> *Let me know of all your motions, when and where I may hope to see you. Let us but 'scape this cloud, this*

absence that has overcast all my contentments, and I am confident there's a clear sky attends us. My dearest dear, adieu.

I am Yours.
W. Temple.

A little time, and they would be together! But might Sir John change his mind? What would her brothers say? How many dangers stood between Ireland and London, ready to destroy her happiness before William could return to her arms? Dorothy read the letter again, trying to absorb some of William's confidence.

Lady Diana swept into Aunt Gargrave's parlor and perched herself on the chair next to Dorothy. Her eyes had the constant redness that scared away so many suitors, but her face still glowed with good humor.

"I hear I am to offer you congratulations," she said.

"Oh?" Dorothy asked, her voice squeaking. Had Lady Diana read her mind? It was such happy news, perhaps it showed on her face. "Is this a new piece of gossip? Every other says I am to be condemned."

It had not been so bad in the country as Lady Ruthyn's guest, but in London, the gossips seemed to be in fierce competition to produce the most enticing wares.

"Your reputation is saved," Lady Diana said. "You are to marry Lord St John."

"Lord St John! I don't even know him!"

"Gossip needs no sense, my dear, only enough details to make it interesting."

"Will I never cease to be a spectacle to all of my neighbors?" Dorothy rested her head in her hands.

"Come, I'm sorry to tease." Lady Diana rubbed her back. "In a week there will be something new to talk about, and you will be forgotten."

"'Twill not be soon enough for me. I'm afraid the rumors will frighten William's family away from ever accepting me." She took a deep breath. "But, as to that..."

"Aye?" Lady Diana scooted closer. "Dorothy, my dear, you have news! What is it?"

"William's father has consented to our marriage." The words sounded too beautiful to be real, even whispered to her friend.

"Oh, my darling!" Lady Diana threw her arms around Dorothy, who gasped out something between a laugh and a sob of relief. Lady Diana pulled back and held Dorothy's hands. "I knew God had some great happiness in store for you, after you endured heartache so willingly. When?"

"Soon, I hope. His father hesitates to begin negotiations with my brothers John and Peyton. I think he still believes William may change his mind, or my brothers refuse. But when the Temples can leave Ireland, they will go to Chicksands. And then—" Dorothy sighed, a deep breath scouring away her heartaches. "Then."

Lady Diana embraced her again. "And in the meantime?"

"I fly from relative to relative like some poor, bedraggled bird searching for a nest. Next I go to Knowlton Court in Kent to stay with Brother Peyton."

"Things will be more peaceful there, though I will miss you until you return."

Lady Diana could not stay long, leaving Dorothy alone with Aunt Gargrave.

"What is this latest nonsense I hear of you?" Gargrave asked when she returned from the market. "I am tired of hearing my relations' names dragged through the mud every time I step out to buy bread."

"I am sorry for it, but there's nothing I can do to stop the rumors, as I am doing nothing to start them. Speak to Harry about it, if you must vent your spleen at someone."

Aunt Gargrave shook her head. "That strange boy is another matter, but you know that you are not blameless. Defying your family for a young man whose family will have nothing to do with you. What can you be thinking?"

"I am thinking of the future. Of my future. Of my family's future."

"Your family? What can this have to do with your family?"

"Everything! William will do great things in the future, and I will be there by his side. 'Twill be a great advantage to my family, if I still have any left who will speak to me when that time comes."

"Do not pretend to me that you are thinking of duty to family."

"I am speaking from my heart as well, it is true. But I believe that is part of my duty."

Aunt Gargrave looked honestly taken back by Dorothy's words, and her expression lost some of its combative edge. "How so?"

"I believe families might be better guided by the heart. We would see stable marriages based on mutual position and on affection. No more scandals. No more bickering couples and unhappy children. I will not be like—" She caught herself short, but Aunt Gargrave took her meaning.

"Not like me, you mean, shackled to a drunk and a gambler I was only too happy to bury?"

Dorothy held out a hand, willing Aunt Gargrave to understand. "I admire your intelligence and your courage, but not your married life. You said that family was everything, but if a family is nothing more than legal bonds entangling two unhappy people together, how is that beneficial to anyone? Is family not also supposed to be about care and support?"

"You think I have not done my part to support this family?"

"You have, and that is when I have liked you best. That's when we felt more like a family. I almost think we were more of one when we were on the verge of starving in Saint-Malo than we are now."

Aunt Gargrave considered her for a long time, and Dorothy wondered if she had overstepped her bounds, but she would not back down.

Aunt Gargrave smiled slightly. "You have more wits about you than I realized. You also have a saucy tongue, and someone ought to have taught you to control it, but that will be your husband's role and not mine. I like *you* best when you speak your mind."

Dorothy smiled in return.

"This is not to say I think you're entirely right, but you were born to revolutionary times, and maybe you will have something to teach future generations from your experiences. If this William Temple of yours is a match for your temperament, you may fare well together after all. Mind you, 'tis none of my concern, and I will not be involved in it."

"Of course, Aunt," Dorothy said.

Bells rang outside in a great clamor and shouting echoed in the streets.

Dorothy and Aunt Gargrave hurried to the window.

"What is it?" Dorothy asked. A hundred terrible scenarios flew through her mind: fire, plague, attack. The crowded, dirty streets, the wooden buildings—it was begging for disaster.

"I don't know. Come, move away from the windows."

They retreated farther into the house, and the sounds of commotion faded. Aunt Gargrave's servant rushed into the room.

"Well?" Aunt Gargrave asked. Only her fingers, twisting a knot of thread this way and that, betrayed her agitation. Otherwise, she sat as still and calm as a queen.

"An assassination attempt by the Royalists on His Highness Oliver Cromwell. I cannot make any sense of the various rumors flying about, but I'm sure we'll hear more details soon, my lady."

Aunt Gargrave nodded severely, and the servant withdrew.

"A Royalist plot?" Dorothy whispered. "Do you think it succeeded?"

Aunt Gargrave's eyes twinkled mischievously for a moment, but she shook her head. "I do not know. Best to keep our mouths closed and our thoughts silent until we hear the whole of the matter."

News trickled in through the day. The Lord Protector still lived. The Royalists had plotted to assassinate him and return Charles II from his exile in France. Many Royalists were being arrested— anyone who might have known of the plot.

Dorothy took up a piece of needlework to keep herself distracted. She drew fine red yarn through the linen. If only the king were restored! Of course, then Henry Cromwell and Uncle Danvers would be in grave peril. And what of Sir John Temple, serving Parliament in Ireland? What of William? Her threads became tangled, and she set her needle aside, content to click her fingernails against the arm of the chair and wait for more rumors.

The arrest toll rose.

"Anyone we know?" Dorothy whispered to Aunt Gargrave.

"None we know well. But Lady Vavasour was arrested, in spite of her growing belly, because she was supposed to have heard some rumor of the plot and did not turn in her own husband."

Dorothy and her aunt exchanged concerned looks. Being women was not a protection. No one was safe from Oliver Cromwell's ire.

"He knows what a revolution means," Aunt Gargrave said, "since he started one himself. Blood leads to blood, and it will quickly get out of hand if he does not clamp down on it."

Dorothy shuddered at the thought of a volley back and forth between sides, more men and even women executed each time power passed hands.

The entire city shut down, the streets quiet except when a band of soldiers clanked by. No one was permitted to leave. Even the currents of breeze from the Thames stilled, leaving Dorothy and the rest of London to soak in the filthy heat of a London summer. Dorothy had the quiet she hoped for, but no peace.

"Be careful what you wish for," she reminded herself.

After a couple of weeks, the breeze blew again, and people began to venture from their houses.

"Cromwell is allowing people to move about the city again," Aunt Gargrave said. "Peyton is coming for you. Best to get you away before this powder keg explodes."

While Dorothy waited for his arrival, she was able to get letters through to William again. He was tired and frustrated with his father's delays. She tried to cheer him with upbeat accounts of her time in London: her Danvers cousins dragging her to Spring Gardens and the fortune teller William Lilly, and her battles with Aunt Gargrave.

> *I make it a case of conscience to discover my faults to you as fast as I know them, that you may consider what you have to do. My aunt told me no longer agone than yesterday that I was the most willful woman that ever she knew and had an obstinacy of spirit nothing could overcome. Take heed! you see I give you fair warning.*
> *Adieu. Je suis vostre.*

Dorothy had just finished packing and saying her farewells when Peyton arrived.

"I have excellent news for you, Dorothy," he said.

"Oh?" Had he heard something of William?

"I'm going to spare you the discomfort of the roads. We're going south by boat."

"By boat?" Dorothy glanced out the window at the looming storm clouds.

"Aye, all the way to Gravesend." Peyton grinned. "'Twill be an adventure."

Dorothy forced a smile in return. As ever, she was at the mercy of others. Water travel was common enough in and out of London, but she did not trust Fortune. Was this the cruel lady's way of snatching Dorothy from William before they could meet again? Dorothy dashed off one last letter as Peyton visited friends in the city.

> *If I drown by the way, this will be my last letter;*
> *and, like a will, I bequeath all my kindness to you in*
> *it, with a charge never to bestow it all upon another*
> *mistress, lest my ghost rise again and haunt you. I*
> *am in such haste that I can say little else to you*
> *now. When you are come over, we'll think where to*
> *meet, for at this distance I can design nothing; only I*
> *should be as little pleased with the constraint of my*
> *brother's house as you.*

Peyton escorted her to the wharves, where the watermen's cries of "Oars, oars!" greeted them. They boarded a barge that rocked on the choppy waters until Dorothy stomach pitched about and threatened her meager breakfast. She gripped the wooden gunwale of the little vessel. God, not Fortune, ruled over the waves. She would trust Him. Besides, if she were to be a diplomat's wife, she would have to learn not to dread the sea.

The tides bore them swiftly down the Thames. They docked at Gravesend, where the river widened out and approached the Channel.

"Was that better than the carriage?" Peyton asked.

"I suppose perhaps it was."

She had a fair chance to compare the two, since Cecilia had come to fetch them to Knowlton Court in the coach. Despite Cecilia's flurry of reminders not to lean and upset the coach, the ride passed without incident. They traveled along roads near enough to the sea to be touched by the salty breeze, and the scent stirred bittersweet memories of her seaside walks with William and Robin at Saint-Malo.

They passed through the ancient city of Canterbury and arrived at Knowlton Court. Peyton's youngest children ran out to greet Dorothy, nearly knocking her to the ground. They were followed by the Peyton hounds, until Dorothy was swarmed with paws and hands and kisses.

"Children! Leave Aunt Osborne in peace."

They turned their attack on their father, and Dorothy made her way up the stairs, ready for the peace of the house.

But Knowlton Court buzzed with activity. Young men dealt cards while the ladies laughed and played on the harpsichord and sang badly. Dorothy backed up into Cecilia.

"Oh, don't mind our guests," Cecilia said. "Let me show you to your room."

"Thank you," Dorothy followed her up another flight of stairs. At least she would find some quiet in her chambers.

Cecilia threw open the doors to a room strewn with gowns and stockings. "You'll be sharing this one with my daughter Dolly and a widowed countess. They will not be too much company for you, I'm certain."

"Of course," Dorothy said, a little dazed. The three of them crammed into the single bed? At least it would not be cold. And if Cecilia had shoved her in with a countess, each bedroom must be equally as crowded. How did one live in this noise? It was a much different place than when Dorothy's sister had been the mistress here.

Dorothy wrote to William and braved the company. The other ladies forced her to take part in a play, but she slunk away whenever she could, walking the garden and staring to the west, toward Ireland.

In her walks, she could not help but notice that, with all the chaos and drinking inside, many quiet, solemn talks took place in shady corners under the trees, with men slipping in and out hardly noticed by the general company, and Brother Peyton in the center of it all. He had not given up on the king, Dorothy realized.

He was still conspiring to bring Charles Stuart to the throne, and the chaos in his home allowed his fellow conspirators to come and go more freely. At least someone in her family thought of more than worldly concerns.

When courtesy forced her to stay inside, she sat with her eldest niece, Dolly Peyton. Here at least she had quiet companionship.

"Now you know why I enjoyed visiting Chicksands," Dolly said.

"My dear! I have no idea how you endure it here."

"One becomes immune to the noise after a time. But when you are established somewhere, do invite me to visit often!"

"I promise, dear, if I'm established in England. If not, you're still welcome, but I doubt you'll be allowed to travel that far."

"You think you would travel a great deal? I thought you hated it."

"Master Temple wishes to be a diplomat, and I wish to be with him. If that means traveling, I will do it. I think I can face any hazards, if he's by my side."

Her niece gave a dreamy sigh.

Dorothy shook her head. "I know it will not be a romantic life, but I would be perfectly content with it."

"Then I hope you have it."

"Soon," Dorothy said. "But William has to come back first. I dread knowing that he's must travel over such rough waters."

"And if you were with him, he'd be safe?" Dolly teased.

"If I were with him, I would be with him. Then nothing else would matter."

"Oh-ho!" One of the young men said, leaning in to their conversation. "These two beautiful ladies are speaking of love." He glanced at his companions. "Shall we woo them?"

"Do not waste your breath," another man said with a chortle. "That is Dorothy Osborne. She thinks she is above us all, and nothing will satisfy her in a husband."

Dorothy's face warmed. "I don't ask for so much. Only a marriage where I am loved and respected."

The men laughed uproariously.

"Ah, the fantasies of women."

"Your sweetheart will tire of you," the first man said, leaning so close Dorothy could smell the wine on his breath. "Especially once your beauty fades. How long do you think he will find you captivating once you are his? 'Tis the pursuit that men love. Once they have possession, they quickly become bored."

"You do better to marry for money. At least that lasts."

"Not always," Dorothy whispered, thinking of her father.

She held her head up, trying to silence her doubts. Was she foolish? Was William only interested in the chase, the romance of their impossible situation? He might tire of her quickly, especially as she aged. He often complimented her beauty. What if that was all that mattered to him?

The old wolf threatened to drag her back over that abyss that was so hard to crawl her way out of. Especially when the abyss itself told her she could not do it, that there was no point in trying. She touched her betrothal ring and shook off the darkness. She and William would prove these men wrong.

A few days later, as Dorothy strolled the garden paths, a page approached her with a bow.

"My lady, there is a gentleman here to see you."

Dorothy's stays suddenly felt too tight. William, here at last! She rushed through the garden and into the house.

"William?" she called.

"Much better, my sister," Harry said, smirking at her. "Your beloved brother has arrived."

Dorothy backed away, her heart trembling like a cornered rabbit.

"No greeting for me?" Harry asked.

Dorothy gave him a quick curtsey, never taking her eyes from him. "Why have you come?"

"Peyton is my brother, too. Or have you forgotten?" Harry traced his fingers over a gilt frame holding a picture of their deceased sister, Elizabeth. "This is such an interesting house. So many people coming and going."

His words were simple enough, but a threat that Dorothy did not understand lay under them.

"Sir John Temple and your darling William have come to Chicksands to treat with our brother John," Harry said.

Dorothy tried to hide the joy that news brought. Harry could not have come to bring her good news. He was toying with her.

He went on. "Sir John has written to Brother Peyton about the match, but he will not allow me to join in the discussions." He slammed his fist against the wall, and Dorothy flinched. "Me! The one nearest to my sister. They shut me out as if all of my care for you did not matter. 'Tis an insult to our family. Can you sit by and let them do this to me—to us?"

Dorothy slowly let out her breath. Of course, Sir John would not want the man who was an enemy to his son to sit in on the marriage negotiations. But Dorothy saw no great harm in humoring him.

"I will write to William and ask him to intervene with his father. After all, you will be brothers now."

"Aye, we will. And I suppose he is to be a great man." Harry's eyes had a distant, calculating look.

"He is. And I will not allow you to cling to him and drag him down."

"Oh, no fear of that, my sister." Harry smirked and left her alone.

Dorothy's hands trembled. What was Harry plotting?

Later that day, Brother Peyton found Dorothy sitting with his daughter.

"Congratulations, dear Sister, on your upcoming happiness." He kissed her cheeks. "I imagine we will have little trouble with the marriage contract, and you and your William shall be happily settled by Christmas."

"May it be so!" Dorothy said.

Peyton laughed. "Poor Dorothy. Life has taught you hard lessons, but sometimes things do go as planned. Are you certain you want Harry involved in the discussions, though? He has been a scoundrel toward you."

"He has, but I feel I must forgive him if I don't want his shadow lingering over my marriage."

"Aye, that is probably wise. Very well. But your brother John and I will make certain everything is settled in your best interest."

"Of course," Dorothy said.

She would be married to William. That was her best interest. She cared nothing for their talks of marriage portions.

"Only let it be soon," she added.

Peyton chuckled and embraced her once again, then left her to Dolly, who wanted to know all her plans for the wedding. Dorothy found herself a disappointment. She could not have the quiet church wedding she wanted, thanks to Oliver Cromwell and his Puritan cronies, but at least she could keep it a small family matter, no grand dresses or other spectacles.

More guests arrived later that day, including the famous Lady Sunderland and her Master Smith. Dorothy watched Master Smith hurrying to see to his wife's contentment. To Dorothy's surprise, he did not look foolish, especially when she cast a glowing smile on him. In fact, they both looked blissfully content.

Lady Sunderland drew Dorothy aside before supper. "I understand you are to be congratulated, Mistress Osborne. Your love story shall have a happy ending."

She gave Dorothy a sincere smile. Dorothy hated knowing how far the rumors of her and William had spread. But then, had she not heard Lady Sunderland's tale as well?

"Thank you, my lady," Dorothy said. "And congratulations to you as well."

Lady Sunderland smiled over her shoulder at her husband. "Thank you. You know, I was so certain after Lord Sunderland died that I had a long, lonely life ahead of me. God has been so kind to send me love twice."

Dorothy only nodded. It still seemed impossible to imagine loving twice. But Brother Peyton had managed it, too, as far as she could tell. From quiet, bookish Elizabeth to vivacious Cecilia, they both made him happy.

"I suppose some people are fitted for happiness," Dorothy said.

"We are all fitted for happiness, if we allow it in," Lady Sunderland said gently. "Though I know for many it is a struggle. After so much heartache and loss, it is frightening to take the chance and open one's heart to more hurt."

Dorothy nodded.

Lady Sunderland went on, "Fear made me less kind to my Master Smith than he deserved. I could not abide the mockery of the world, saying I was untrue to Lord Sunderland's love. I love them both, but I said I only pitied Master Smith." She squeezed Dorothy's arm. "I make amends now. They are different men, and I admire different things about them, but love is love. I am glad you did not give up on it."

"As am I," Dorothy said.

At supper, Dorothy sat next to Harry. She watched him from the corner of her eye. Had he ever felt love for anyone?

One of the new arrivals, Mistress Thornhill, sat across from them, an empty seat by her side. "For my husband," she explained through a strained smile.

They had started on the main course of roast pheasant in currant sauce when the porter announced another guest: Colonel Thornhill. His lady wife jumped at the announcement and wrung her hands.

The colonel stumbled into the room, reeking of ale. He slumped into the chair next to his wife and glowered, first at her, then at Dorothy and Harry, and finally at the meal on his plate. His grumbled something to Mistress Thornhill, who quickly asked the young man next to her to pass down the salt.

"Of course, Mistress Thornhill. It would be a pleasure."

She paled at his kind words. Colonel Thornhill studied the young man with narrow eyes.

"What's this?" he bellowed at his wife, bringing the murmur of conversation to a hush. "Already set yourself up as a flirt? I cannot let you out of my sight for an instant without enduring your faithless behavior."

Mistress Thornhill's eyes brimmed with tears, and she shook her head, clasping her hands in her lap as if in a prayer.

"I apologize," the young man said quickly. "Your wife has done nothing inappropriate. If I sounded too familiar—"

"Nay, I apologize to everyone here. I need to keep her under better control. Have I not told you to bridle your tongue, wench?"

Mistress Thornhill looked up, her eyes pleading with everyone at the table. "I did not—"

The colonel's hand flew across her face, knocking her back against her seat. The crack echoed in the silence. Dorothy clenched her hands, but there was nothing she could do. Nothing anyone could do. Mistress Thornhill belonged to her husband.

"To your chamber," Colonel Thornhill ordered.

His wife obeyed without a glance at the assembled company. The young man's face was red with embarrassment and anger, but he, too, was helpless against the rule of a husband.

Colonel Thornhill took a swig of wine and started a loud conversation with Harry. The talk slowly picked back up, though Dorothy remained in stunned shock.

As they left the table, Lady Sunderland touched her arm lightly.

"Not every man is a tyrant," she whispered. "Your William will not be such a husband."

Dorothy nodded. She could never imagine William striking her, though she wished sometimes that everyone who was thinking of marrying could spend an extended house party together. It brought out the truth of their personalities. Of course, some women did not have a choice in the matter, no matter if they knew their husband was a tyrant.

317

Later that night, Dorothy slipped upstairs while Colonel Thornhill was still playing cards with the other men. She brought some cold meat and a glass of wine, and gently tapped on Mistress Thornhill's door.

Her maid opened the door an inch, then wider when she spotted Dorothy.

Dorothy offered the food. "Supper for your mistress."

"Thank you kindly, my lady," the maid said.

"Is she...?" Dorothy hardly knew what to ask.

The maid straightened. "I'm watching out for her, Mistress. I'll keep her from any serious harm."

Dorothy nodded. "She is fortunate to have a loyal servant."

The maid smiled weakly and closed the door. Dorothy walked toward her room, but Harry waited for her in the hall.

"Well, my sister, you see what waits you in marriage."

"Not every man is like Colonel Thornhill."

"You deceive yourself. Every man wants power, and he wants the world to know he has it."

Dorothy shook her head, but Harry stepped closer and took her hand, stroking it. She tried to pull away, but he tightened his grip until her bones ached.

"I will not let you do this to yourself," Harry said. "I will protect you from your own foolishness. 'Tis the least I can do as your brother."

"What are you talking about?"

"I think I see a way to get you out of the marriage."

"I don't wish to get out of the marriage!" Dorothy wriggled her hand free, but Harry smiled.

"Luckily, I am wiser than you. I think I can argue in court that your marriage portion should have been part of my inheritance. The Temples will not take you if you are a beggar."

Dorothy backed away. William would not care, but his father? And his father would stop the negotiations if her family opposed the match.

"If you and Master Temple are stubborn enough to continue anyway, you should consider his future, and the future of your family."

"What are you saying?"

"Where do I find you tonight? In the home of a revolutionary plotting to bring young Charles Stuart to the throne. How many people in this household would hang if Oliver Cromwell heard a hint of what they speak about? And Master Temple would be questioned, would he not? After all, he must have known what his beloved was involved in. At the least, he would be out of favor and never find the lofty diplomatic position he craves. At the most, well, we know what happens to traitors."

"You would not!"

Harry reached out to touch her cheek, but she pulled away. He grimaced. "As I said, my sister, you must consider your future."

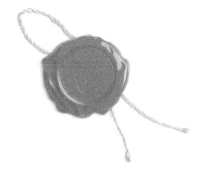

Chapter Thirty-two

WILLIAM TORE OPEN THE LATEST letter from Dorothy. The negotiations were not going well, with Harry doing everything he could to make himself obnoxious to Sir John. And Dorothy's handwriting was hurried and blotched.

In sober earnest now I must speak with you; and to that end if your occasions will give you leave as soon as you have received this come down to Canterbury. Send someone when you are there, and you shall have further directions.

I will not hinder your coming away so much as the making this letter a little longer might take away from your time in reading it. 'Tis enough to tell you I am ever

> *Yours,*
>
> *D. Osborne*

William read the letter twice. A meeting in Canterbury? It was not far from Peyton's house in Knowlton, but William did not like the secrecy. It reminded him too much of the earlier days of their courtship when all the world was against them. He traced the word "yours." He had to go to her.

Riding was the fastest way to Canterbury, but he had no horse. He rushed to a nearby stable and paid too much to rent a nag that he hoped could make the journey. William urged the mare south as fast as he dared, wiping sweat and dust from his eyes. Coaches rumbled past on the way to London, their guards eyeing him warily and presenting their muskets.

William arrived in Canterbury just before dusk and found a room at the old Fountain Inn.

"I need a message sent to Knowlton Court," he told the innkeeper.

The somber-clad man glanced out at the gathering darkness. "Now?"

"Aye, now."

"My boy cannot make it there and back tonight."

William hesitated. Dorothy would not have summoned him for anything less than emergency. "I'll pay extra for his lodging outside the city."

The innkeeper shrugged and called his boy to deliver William's hasty message.

The next morning, William was up at dawn, pacing the common room until the innkeeper's boy returned. William pounced on him and read Dorothy's response.

Meet at the market at eleven of the clock.

William paid his bill and wandered the market, counting the toll of the cathedral bells each time they rang. The yeasty scent of beer brewing rolled out from the timber-and-brick buildings, leaving him a little light-headed. Or was it that he would soon see Dorothy again?

It was not Dorothy he saw, though, but her niece Dolly, who motioned him over. William found Dorothy, wide-eyed and pale, sitting on a small trunk in a side alley.

She flung her arms around him and relaxed into his chest. He tightened his embrace.

"What has happened, dearest?" he whispered.

"I think—" She drew a deep breath. "I think we must flee to the Continent. We can be married after we reach France. But we must escape."

"Escape? I know the marriage negotiations are frustrating, but there's no need to flee them."

"Nay, escape from Harry! He is mad. He is determined to ruin us both."

"Shhh." William pulled her close again and soothed her hair. "Harry is not so powerful."

"But he is ruthless. He threatened to destroy your career, and your father and brother."

"And what weapon does he have that can do so much?"

"He would bring down Brother Peyton."

"Peyton?" William studied her face.

Thomas Peyton was an outspoken Royalist, and Cromwell was on the hunt for conspiracies.

"Harry will make certain you cannot find a position, and he will take my fortune." She gripped his arm. "Your father will never agree to the marriage."

William drew her in. "I will not let anyone separate us again."

"But what are we to *do*, other than leave?"

William glanced at the trunk she had brought along. She was ready to flee with him. They could leave behind all the trouble England had caused for them, but what would they be fleeing to? He would not have Dorothy regret a single day spent with him.

"Do you truly wish to go to the Continent? I could show you Holland and the Netherlands. You will love it there as much as

I do." William stroked her hair and traced his fingers down the back of her neck. "I'm not certain how I would support us, but I will find a way if you desire it."

She leaned into him with a weary sigh. "I wish for our trials to be at an end. But I hate to let Harry win! I hate watching bully-ruffians take the things I want and hurt the people I love."

"Then we will not let him win." William smiled sadly. "I will take you to the Continent someday, but not fleeing in the dark of night. Let us take this in steps. Harry wishes to lay claim to your inheritance?"

Dorothy nodded.

"Do you think he has a case?"

"I don't know. He managed my father's affairs these last years."

"Yet your father left a will and clearly allotted a marriage portion to you. My father and my brother are both familiar with the law, so I do not think your brother can match them in court."

"But what about his threat against your future—our future?"

"As to that..." William took a deep breath. "I have an idea I have not yet discussed with you."

"Oh?"

"I came to a realization in Ireland. I don't wish to work for Oliver Cromwell's government. His position is not legitimate, and his policies too brutal."

"I agree. But what will you do?"

"Live on my family's lands in Ireland as a gentleman farmer and work on my writing until the monarchy is restored. I know it will not offer much income—"

"I know how to live on little," Dorothy said. "And it puts you beyond the reach of Harry's threats. It sounds like a perfect plan. Except for brother Peyton. I don't wish to see Harry hurt him either."

"Thomas Peyton has chosen a dangerous course. I don't know how to put him out of the reach of harm," William admitted.

Dorothy frowned and stared into the distance. "I have an idea that may help. It would be simpler if only Harry would give me a moment's peace, but with your cooperation, we can take some of the pressure off Brother Peyton." She turned. "Dolly!"

Her niece had stepped a polite distance away, but she hurried back. "Aye, Cousin Dorothy."

Dorothy beckoned William and Dolly closer and laid out her plan.

Dorothy strolled the gravel path of the formal garden at Knowlton Court, Harry so close beside her she was surprised he never trod on her skirts. She scanned the deep green boxwood hedges. For the moment, she and Harry were alone. That would not do. She veered toward the house, where a group of ladies gathered the autumn-blooming musk roses.

Dolly wandered into sight and gave Dorothy a fleeting nod.

The curtain was up on Dorothy's performance.

Dorothy stumbled and caught herself on Harry's arm.

"Are you well?" he asked.

Dorothy snapped open her fan. "I feel... 'Tis difficult..."

She sat heavily on the turf-covered bench at the start of the path. Harry hovered over her. A few of the ladies glanced in their direction. Dorothy let the fan slip from her fingers. Her eyes rolled back, and she slumped into a swoon.

"Dorothy, my sister?"

Harry's fingers dug into her shoulder, but she kept her eyes closed and face slack.

"My sister needs help!" Harry called.

Boots and slippers disturbed the gravel, and murmuring voices gathered around.

"Oh, dear!" Cecilia's voice drew near. "What have you done to her?"

"I?" Harry asked. "I have done nothing! She fainted."

A soft hand touched Dorothy's forehead. Dolly, playing her part perfectly.

"She's burning with fever," Dolly said.

"Fever?" Cecilia's voice caught.

"Should we move her to my room?" Dolly asked.

Dolly was taking a risk there. Dorothy could not be trapped. She groaned and fluttered her eyes before opening them to stare at the worried faces gathered around.

"What happened?" Dorothy asked, keeping her voice raspy and low.

"You are ill, my dear," Cecilia said. "Only, I don't know what should be done for you."

"I cannot stay here. I don't wish to make anyone else ill."

"If you feel well enough, I could return you to London." Cecilia wrung her hands. "Oh, but travel is so hazardous."

"I... I feel I could endure it," Dorothy said.

"I will accompany her," Harry said.

That he must not do, but Dorothy did not object.

"Nonsense," said Cecilia. "This is a woman's work."

"She is my sister."

"She is also mine." Cecilia stared Harry down.

He glowered and backed away as Cecilia helped Dorothy sit up.

"I'll pack your trunk," Dolly said.

It would not take long. Dorothy had packed it that morning. She had made enough of a spectacle, so she took Cecilia's arm and shuffled away from the curious guests. Behind her, Harry called for a servant to pack his own belonging. He would find one of his trunks missing, and unless he happened to search in the deep end of the pond where William had disposed of it, he would not find it. It would take him at least half a day to replace it, giving

Dorothy time to get settled in London away from him.

Dorothy glanced over her shoulder. By now, William would be speaking with Brother Peyton in secret. Harry's careful guard had prevented Dorothy from speaking with Peyton or Cecilia, but William would warn Peyton of the danger so he could watch Harry and move his conspiracies elsewhere until it was safe to return. With Dorothy in London, Harry would soon forget Knowlton Court, and as long as he never knew he'd been tricked, he would not think of avenging himself on the Peytons.

Dorothy smiled to herself. It seemed that Fortune was finally turning in her favor.

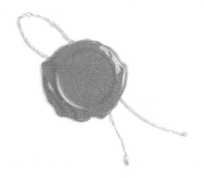

Chapter Thirty-three

DOROTHY STROLLED THROUGH HYDE PARK on William's arm, showing no signs of her sudden illness at Knowlton Court. Jane, who had come to stay with a cousin in London, and Lady Diana trailed a respectful distance behind, listening to Cecilia Peyton's chatter. The October sun hung low in the sky, but its light bathed the scene in a warm, golden glow.

"Wait, don't leave me!" Cecilia called. "I've caught my lace on this branch. Oh, dear."

As Jane helped Cecilia extract the delicate cream-colored threads from the grasps of a nefarious bush, William drew Dorothy aside a little. She glanced up at him expectantly. He trailed his fingers along the delicate skin of her forearm, raising pleasant goose bumps on her skin. Keeping his gaze fixed on hers, he raised her hand and placed a warm, lingering kiss on the inside of her wrist. She shivered and leaned closer, longing to kiss him in return.

"Soon, my dear heart," he whispered, his voice husky.

"It must be a dream," Dorothy said.

"Must it?" William smiled and drew her in, tracing a thumb down her cheek and across her lower lip.

"Oh, my!" Cecilia's voice sent a flush racing up Dorothy's neck. Jane and Lady Diana looked on with mischievous grins.

Cecilia smacked William's arm with her fan. "I admire your ardor, but Hyde Park is hardly the place for such displays. You will be one of those shameful husbands who kisses his wife in front of guests."

"I will." William grinned and pulled Dorothy in. "I will kiss her right now in front of strangers."

"You will not!" Cecilia scolded, but she was smiling. "The banns are not even read yet, so she is in my keeping. 'Tis well I did not leave her in the Danvers' hands. You require a great deal of watching."

"I am a scoundrel," he admitted, securing Dorothy's hand on his arm once again.

"You are a lover, and I am glad to see it for our Dorothy's sake."

Dorothy's friends grinned at her, and she blushed again. Here was family: those who loved her and wished her well. Not Harry, who followed her to London to badger her endlessly about William. At least Peyton and his conspirators were safe, and as long as Dorothy was surrounded by well-wishers, so was she. Nothing could touch her.

"We must hurry up our walk," Cecilia said. "We have so many preparations for the wedding."

Dorothy clung to William's arm, but she had to leave him temporarily to become his forever.

"I believe all these preparations are just to torment the groom," William said.

"Do you wish to set up house with no plates on your table and no sheets on the bed?"

"I suppose that would not do," William said with a teasing grin at Dorothy that passed by Cecilia.

"Not at all," Cecilia went on. "And with everything poor Sir Peter lost, we have much to make up for."

That was true enough. Dorothy remembered everything they had handed over to the merchants. It had all come to nothing. Yet it had brought William to her. They would make a fresh start. Already she had begun to set her collection in order: bowls and plates of pewter, crisp linens she would embroider herself, and even a set of forks to indulge William's love of Continental fashion. They would not have much to start with, but she would oversee every detail herself.

She allowed Cecilia to lead her away to their new lodgings on Queens Street. Their first inn had been infested with smallpox, so Cecilia had quickly moved them elsewhere, even procuring fresh bed linens in her concern. After sharing the crowded room at Knowlton Court, the clean, quiet chambers made Dorothy feel better than a queen.

Cecilia had friends over that evening for dinner and cards, and Dorothy did not wake until late the next morning, when the maidservant brought her a letter from William. She quickly penned her response.

> *You are like to have an excellent housewife of me; I am abed still, and slept so soundly, nothing but your letter could have waked me. You shall hear from me as soon as we have dined. Farewell; can you endure that word? No, out upon't. I'll see you anon.*

She spent another dream-like day with William and her friends planning her future. By the end of it, though, her head ached as though she were coming down with a cold. No matter, such a trifling thing could not dim the happiest days of her life.

The next morning, her headache was so severe spots swam in front of her eyes.

"I've been doing too much," she told Jane. "I just need to rest today."

"Can I bring up your breakfast?" Jane asked.

331

Dorothy rubbed her queasy stomach. "Nay, I'm not sure I can keep it down. Perhaps you can read to me after you've eaten?"

"Of course."

Jane came back soon and settled down to read. Dorothy tried to work on embroidering her wedding linens, but she could not focus. Aches gripped her arms and legs, and the light stung her eyes. She laid back in bed to listen, but even with a blanket, she shivered uncontrollably.

"My lady?" Jane put down her book.

"I'm just so cold."

Jane glanced at the fire and came over to touch Dorothy cheek. "You have a fever, my lady."

Dorothy groaned and squeezed her eyes shut. "I'm sure 'tis nothing serious," she whispered, but Jane's voice grew more distant. A hazy delirium wrapped around her and pain tore through her nerves. Her skin stung as though it were on fire, but her limbs felt too sluggish to rub or scratch away the misery.

She was only vaguely aware of the attentions of the doctor, or of Jane's muffled sobs next to her head. The words she did catch were, "I have to write to William. He deserves to know."

William rushed up the stairs. Jane paced at the top. He grabbed her by the arms. "Tell me!"

Jane's voice caught. "The doctors don't think she'll last the night."

William pressed back against the wall, trying to find something real to hold on to.

"You are wrong!" He pointed at Jane. "Tell me you are wrong!"

Jane sank to the floor. Sobs shuddered through her body. William watched in numb disbelief. The wooden stairway, the distant sounds of hackney carts, the sickly smell of boiling cabbage: he needed to shake them off, to go somewhere that still made sense. He needed Dorothy, but she was behind a closed door.

"Dorothy," William whispered—pleaded—the name that meant everything. All that was good and bright. All hopes for happiness. They had come so close. He squeezed his eyes shut. "She is not lost yet. I cannot lose her. What do the doctors say? What have they done?"

"Her fever is very high," Jane whispered. "They don't know the cause."

"I must go to her."

"I'm not sure..." Jane scooted back against the door and choked out, "It may be the plague."

The word hit William's chest like the slice of a rapier. "Nay. She is my betrothed. She was—she is going to be my wife. I will go to her."

Jane studied his face, her eyes swollen with crying. "Very well, my lord."

William burst into the room and fell to his knees next to Dorothy's bed. Her face was pale, with red spots on her cheeks, and her forehead glistened with sweat. William picked up the damp cloth from the bowl next to the bed and gently wiped her face. She showed no reaction. He finished washing her face and took her hand.

"Dorothy, can you hear me? 'Tis William. I am here. I will always be here. Please don't leave me, my heart. I cannot go on without you. Please."

He hoped for something—a squeeze of her hand or a flicker of her eyelids, but there was nothing but her shallow, rattling breathing, filling the room, filling his mind and sawing at the raw place in his chest that could not survive without Dorothy.

He stayed by her bed, wiping her forehead as the night slowly wore on. He breathed with her, his chest aching at the sound, but it filled his world. If it stopped, so did his heart.

In the morning, the doctor returned wearing a plague mask with a long beak nose. His eyes widened behind the demon's face when he saw William there.

"You should not have come, Sir," the doctor said, his voice muffled by the mask.

"I will not leave her side."

"Now there would be no point in it. If she has the Black Death as I fear, you have been breathing in the same foul air and will no doubt catch it, too."

William clung to Dorothy's hand. "I would rather die with her than live without her."

"You are young and foolish," the doctor snapped. "But it no longer matters. God's will be done."

William frowned at the man but did not protest. He had to give the doctor credit for even coming—many would not if they suspected plague.

The doctor gently looked over Dorothy's pale arms and felt her throat. William looked away as the man examined the rest of Dorothy's body.

"Hmm." The doctor straightened and looked again in her mouth.

"What is it?" William demanded.

"I do not see the swelling I would expect with the plague. In fact—" He lifted her hand and studied it in the light. "Aye, I see it now. The red spots? This is smallpox."

William gave a start and looked back at Dorothy's face. In the morning light, he could see it too: the small red dots starting on her fevered skin.

"What does that mean?" William asked.

"I do not have to quarantine the house, though anyone who has not had smallpox may want to leave to avoid infection." He glanced at William.

"I have not had it," William said, "But I'm staying."

"She could still die, and you could too, if you stay by her."

"I know," William said, "but I will stay. Someone will need to care for her, and why should anyone else risk exposing themselves?"

"Very well." The doctor removed his mask. A few smallpox scars pitted his clean-shaven chin. "You may want to smoke tobacco."

William wrinkled his nose. "I dislike the smell of it."

"Aye, but it may keep the air cleaner and prevent you from catching smallpox, too."

"Very well. What else must I do?"

The doctor gave some basic instructions, but William was disappointed by how simple they were: keep her fever down, get her to drink if possible. There was nothing he could actually do to fight this foe, to save his Dorothy. He could only wait by her side and be willing to share her fate, whatever it might be.

"I have had the smallpox," Jane said, once the doctor had gone. "I will not try to take your place, but I can help, too. You will need to sleep sometimes."

William did not wish to sleep, but he nodded his agreement. If Dorothy was going to be sick for weeks—and that was being hopeful, that the disease did not kill her quickly—he could not go so long without rest. "Aye, we'll care for her together."

They kept a long, quiet vigil over Dorothy's senseless body. The red spots spread and grew larger, turning into blisters that changed her face until William did not recognize her. Yet once, in her fitful sleep, she whispered his name, and it drew his heart out in pain and a longing to touch her, though he did not for fear of disturbing the blisters and making them worse.

Jane brought up meals, as well as news from outside. "The Danvers have smallpox as well," she whispered, though Dorothy showed no signs of hearing. "Her cousin, Henry Danvers—the one who once courted Lady Diana—has died. Harry is downstairs and will not go."

William only nodded at the news. He lit another pipe of tobacco, coughing at the smoke. Perhaps it would help Dorothy.

Still her fever did not abate. William read to her from the latest romances, in French, hoping something he said moved through the fog of fever to comfort her.

"You have to come back," William whispered into her blistered ear. "Please. Our story cannot end like this."

But Dorothy showed no signs that she could hear him.

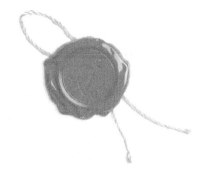

Chapter Thirty-four

LONDON, ENGLAND

AN UNPLEASANT, SMOKY SMELL LINGERED in Dorothy's dreams. She tried to open her eyes, but the light stung, and she was so tired she could not manage more than to roll her eyes back.

"What?" she croaked, her throat raw and parched.

"Shh, Mistress Dorothy," Jane's voice came out of the gloom. "You're safe. You need to drink."

Jane helped her sip some weak broth, and after a few moments, Dorothy felt that she could manage to open her eyes. She lifted her hand and it flopped onto her face. Her skin itched at the contact. Scabs covered her hand.

"What is this?"

"Smallpox," Jane whispered.

Dorothy gasped and coughed weakly. Jane helped her take a little more broth.

"William cannot see me like this," Dorothy mumbled. She imagined how disgusting she must look, disfigured by scabs and scars. "He cannot see me ever again." Tears dribbled from the corner of her eyes, stinging where they struck open sores.

"Dorothy." William's voice reached her from the doorway.

She fumbled for the sheet to block her face. "Please, don't look at me."

"He's been watching over you since you became ill," Jane whispered, then stepped back so William could take her place.

"I'm so sorry," Dorothy said, choking on a sob.

"Sorry, my heart? Don't be sorry. When I thought you were going to die—"

"If only I had! I am hideous!"

"Dorothy." He carefully smoothed her hair back from her forehead.

She longed for his caress but wanted to draw away from it at the same time. "You should not touch me. You should leave while you can."

"I will not."

She swallowed, and it felt as though sharp pebbles lodged in her throat. "My beauty is gone."

"You will have scars," William said, "but you are still the only one I want. No matter what happens to your body—when your hair turns gray, when your back stoops, when your eyesight weakens, I will still love you. If the mind that I love so well grows weak and confused with age. Even if your spleen overtakes you, and you grow silly or confused, I will be here to sooth your troubled brow. My heart and soul reside in you, and I will never stop loving you."

Dorothy sobbed into her sheet. "I love you, too. Always."

"Then that settles it. We will be married. Soon. As soon as you are able to stand."

"Still so disfigured?" She carefully touched the scabs on her face. "Do you not wish to present a more acceptable bride to the world?"

"I want to show the world that I love you and honor you in illness and in health. In spite of Cromwell and his laws. In spite of war and unrest. If I must fight my way through to clear a path to the magistrate, I will do it. We will be married, and nothing will stand between us again."

It was a small civil ceremony, as required by law, and held on Christmas Day. The Puritans refused to celebrate Christmas, treating it as any other day.

"I am glad of it," Dorothy told William. "Now it will always be a special holiday for us."

William grinned. He gently caressed her cheek and ran his fingers down to her throat, then bent to kiss her, making her forget all about her scars as she stood before one of Oliver Cromwell's stern-faced officials.

Harry Osborne was not there, already busy preparing his hopeless lawsuit to regain control of Dorothy's fortune. Her brother John attended, though, and Sir John and the Peytons. Lady Diana stood by Dorothy's side, as did Jane and Martha. Just the witnesses she and William needed, and the magistrate to make it legal.

At the invitation of Cousin Franklin, Dorothy and William honeymooned at Moor Park.

William showed Dorothy the etching he had made in the glass, asking Leda who was happier.

"And what is your answer, Master Temple?" Dorothy asked with a teasing smile.

"No one could be happier than I, Mistress Temple."

Dorothy would have argued that *she* could be, but he stopped her with a kiss that made her forget anything but the warm comfort of her husband's arms.

"Come." William kept an arm around her waist and guided her outside to the gently sloping garden of hedges and geometric flower beds. They followed the gravel walk past the trickle of fountains and through rows of evergreen bay laurels. Stone arches guided them to a little summer house secluded behind the laurels.

Inside the shelter, William pulled Dorothy in and kissed her once more.

"It is not Herm," he whispered with a smile, "but we can pretend it is ours alone for now. Is it not one of the most perfect gardens you have seen?"

"It is. I think we should have one like it," Dorothy said, settling her head against his chest. "Once the king is restored and you are one of his ambassadors."

William leaned back and arched an eyebrow at her. "You believe all that will come to pass?"

Dorothy plucked an errant laurel leaf that hung over William's shoulder and twirled it between her fingers, perfuming the air with the sharp, enticing scent. "We triumphed over Fortune. Everything else is possible."

He grinned and kissed her again, and even the perfect beauty of the gardens faded in comparison.

Historical Notes

IN TELLING DOROTHY AND WILLIAM'S story, I have done my best to stick to historical facts, but this is a work of fiction and contains speculation, especially about the motivations of various characters. We are fortunate to have Dorothy's letters from 1652 and 1654, and where I have quoted from them, I kept the modernized spellings used by her Victorian admirer and editor, Edward Abbott Parry. Because most of the letters were undated, I have also relied on Mr. Parry's arrangement of the letters, which are generally accepted as correct by modern historians. In order to prevent the novel from being cumbersome, I did omit elements of the historical timeline. For instance, Dorothy had many other suitors who don't appear in these pages. They play a minor role in the overarching story, so it felt safe to leave their names and details out of this narrative, though if you want to know Dorothy better, I recommend reading her letters for the anecdotes I had to leave out. The following notes give more details about the facts of each chapter.

CHAPTER ONE

We know that Peter Osborne's sister-in-law, Katherine Danvers, tried to get supplies to Sir Peter at Castle Cornet, was chased by pirates, and was then betrayed by Colonel Carteret as depicted here. There is no evidence of Dorothy's role in this adventure, but since her mother's health was already destroyed by the tolls of war, it is reasonable to assume Dorothy played some part in it.

Chapter Two

Martha Temple recorded the circumstances of William and Dorothy's first meeting, including Robin etching the scripture on the window and Dorothy taking the blame to save Robin, which deeply impressed William.

We don't know what either of them were doing on the Isle of Wight, other than traveling to France, but William did meet Charles I at some point, and this seems like the most likely time for it to have happened, while his cousin was the king's keeper. The uncle who raised him, Henry Hammond, was a close advisor to King Charles I, though. In fairness to William's other relatives, many men who had once sworn allegiance to the king changed sides during the war, and their reasons for doing so ranged from opportunism to complex moral dilemmas.

Dorothy's presence on the island at about the same time her cousin was arrested for attempting to free the king seems like too large a coincidence for her and Robin not to have been there in connection with him in some way.

Chapter Three

Dorothy and William were silent on the subject of their initial wooing, but they crossed to Saint-Malo together, and Dorothy does reminisce about her fantasy of life on the Isle of Herm in later letters to William.

Chapters Four, Five, and Six

We know little of the Osbornes' suffering in Saint-Malo, but it had a profound effect on Dorothy, dampening the natural cheer of her youth. She told William she did not smile much after France.

Her brother Charles was killed fighting for the king, and Harry (properly Henry, but Dorothy called him Harry, and it helped reduce the confusion with the number of Henrys in the book) went on a military mission for Prince Rupert, the king's cousin. Some of her brothers spent time at Castle Cornet during the siege, so I have assigned that role to Robin. John Osborne did marry his Parliamentarian cousin during the war and does not seem to have joined his family in exile. I don't know how upset Sir Peter was by this, but John appears to have spent little time at Chicksands during Sir Peter's lifetime, so I have assumed there was tension between them.

William's father did send him from Saint-Malo to get him away from Dorothy, right into Paris during the uprising known as the Frond. I don't know if Dorothy and Lady Diana spent time together in France, but Lady Diana's father, the Earl of Holland, was beheaded during a wave of retribution against the king's supporters after the execution of Charles I, despite the fact that Lord Holland was promised his life when he surrendered. At this time, England was ruled by the Lord Generals of the army and by the Rump Parliament, which had been purged of all moderates, including William's father.

Chapter Seven

The Osbornes would have returned to Chicksands to find it in disarray after being in Parliament's hands for so long. Their uncle Sir John Danvers, who signed King Charles I's death warrant, must have played a significant role in helping to restore them to their home. Many Royalists were not so lucky and had to live abroad, often in poverty.

Chapter Eight

The pressures on Dorothy and William to marry well were very real. Henry Cromwell stands out among Dorothy's suitors because he is clearly not a Royalist. Historian are uncertain where she and the youngest Cromwell might have met, but I think her Parliamentarian uncle Sir John Danvers is the most likely connection between them. Dorothy's letters allude to a meeting between her and William at some point at Goring House, the home of the Royalist George Goring, but since Goring was in exile at this time and there are no clear records of who held Goring House or what was happening there at this time, I set this meeting at Sir John Danvers' home.

CHAPTER NINE

William spent his time in Holland expanding his education, including learning Spanish, and polishing his writing by penning romances for Dorothy. His writing to her tapered off during this long separation, but it's clear his interest in her did not. While he did not meet the future King Charles II in Holland, it seems likely his travels to Breda might have been because of the young king's presence there, and he may have hoped to make himself useful to the future monarch.

CHAPTER TEN

Dorothy kept herself aloof from scores of suitors during William's absence. I have only included the most notable and persistent to avoid confusion, repetition, and an absurdly long novel. This is also the time period when Dorothy's bouts of depression seem to have become disruptive. Unlike some who stigmatize mental illness in modern times, most people in the seventeenth century recognized depression as a medical condition having a physical cause and being capable of treatment. It was, however, still seen as a mostly female illness. Dorothy's mother may have suffered from it as well, or from severe disillusionment brought on by the war, since she really did warn Dorothy that eventually everyone would let her down.

CHAPTER ELEVEN

Dorothy's brother-in-law, Sir Thomas Peyton, was a member of the Action Party: a group of Royalists who were willing to go to extreme lengths to restore the younger Charles Stuart to the throne. There is no record of whether Peyton ever tried to involve Dorothy in his plots, but she was close to him, and since almost all of her suitors were Royalists, it seems that Dorothy and her family was still seen as a good connection for those who backed the monarchy.

Dorothy did turn away a suitor who said he would marry her if her dowry were only a thousand pounds more.

We don't know all the details of Dorothy's refusal of her cousin, Sir Thomas Osborne, but they did have a volatile, family-wide falling out over the failed courtship. Sir Thomas went on to have a successful political career, eventually being elevated as the first Duke of Leeds after the restoration of the monarchy. He was known for being unscrupulous and was associated with several political scandals.

The waters at Epsom were considered a cure for a wide number of maladies, including "the spleen." In early modern medicine, a malfunctioning spleen was believed to contribute to depression and other mental health issues.

CHAPTER TWELVE

Seventeenth-century coaches were not very stable, especially given the terrible condition of the roads, and Dorothy relates elsewhere that her brother-in-law's second wife, Cecilia Swan Peyton, was a very nervous traveler. My account of their trip to Epsom reflects Dorothy's portrayal of her sister-in-law, though I'm not certain who actually chaperoned her at Epsom.

We know Dorothy visited Epsom in the summer of 1653 seeking treatment for her "spleen." Because Lady Diana was suffering from her "sore eyes" at the same time, I have allowed them to visit Epsom together, but there's no historical record of this. The exact nature of Lady Diana's affliction is unknown, but it was apparently long-lasting and eventually disfiguring.

We also don't know when Jane became Dorothy's companion, but it may have been about this time. While Dorothy doesn't mention Jane's last name in her letters, many historians believe that Jane is Jane Wright because of the Wright family's connections to Chicksands and the Osbornes.

CHAPTER THIRTEEN

While William apparently explained his long silence to Dorothy, because we have a letter where she forgives him for it, she did not keep the message with his explanation. She did chide him for coming close to Chicksands once without visiting. His reluctance was likely a combination of traveling and knowing the hopelessness of their situation, as I have portrayed here. The letters tell us his father wished for him to marry an heiress named "Mistress Cl." I chose the surname "Claybourn" as one of several possibilities based on the initials.

CHAPTER FOURTEEN

The Puritans really did cancel Christmas. Though they weren't all as dreary as tradition makes them out to be, in this case, they live up to the old stereotype of making certain that no one anywhere was having any fun.

Cousin Molle, or Henry Molle, was a retired Cambridge professor who, according to Dorothy's account, was also a severe hypochondriac.

Since Lady Diana was Dorothy's closest friend and staying nearby at the time Dorothy received her letter from William, I have given her the role of Dorothy's confidant. We don't know how Dorothy felt about Jane at this point in their relationship.

CHAPTER FIFTEEN

William seems to have become interested in a diplomatic career around the time that he was in the Netherlands and Holland, and his father would certainly have used any influence he had left to forward his son's career ambitions, and William was supposed to accompany Lord Lisle to Sweden. William felt that his father's refusal to consider Dorothy was due mainly to his distrust of William's ability to make his own decisions. Though she had a respectable, if not large, marriage portion, her connections would not have been favorable during the time of Parliament's ascendancy.

CHAPTER SIXTEEN

The titles of William's romances and his dedication note to Dorothy are his own words.

Collecting antique seals was all the rage in England in 1653, and William sent Dorothy a bountiful number, including those described here. Harry's strange gift to Lady Diana is also recorded in the letters.

William and Dorothy met in London in February 1653. It seems to be about this time that Harry's intense dislike of William took on an almost obsessive tone, and both families worked to keep the couple apart.

The incident with Jane in Hyde Park is fabricated, but she became a loyal friend to both Dorothy and William and an ally in their cause. Dorothy did see Colonel Hammond in London and was still afraid of him, or perhaps of the power that he might have over William or her own family.

CHAPTER SEVENTEEN

Dorothy's depression continued to plague her, and some of the cures described here are those she reported to William that she tried. The cruel taunting of her brother and cousin are also from her letters.

Chapter Eighteen

Dorothy did encourage William to think practically about his relationship with Mistress Cl., but he formally broke off his courtship of her in spite of his father's wishes. The exact circumstances are products of my imagination.

Chapter Nineteen

Susan Longueville, Lady Grey de Ruthyn, was a baroness in her own right after the death of her father and brother, and she was a near neighbor of Dorothy. She seems from Dorothy's accounts to have been cheerful and somewhat naive. I do not know that she had an African maidservant, but black servants were fairly common and often portrayed in the background of upper-class family portraits as a reminder of the wealth and status of their owners.

Chapter Twenty

Oliver Cromwell's takeover of England's government was a shocking event in an already tumultuous era, and would have been a blow to William's family, whose father was already on the edge of the political scene.

I don't know when William first moved from letters and romances to more serious essays, but his writings on Holland were later seen as revolutionary, as he was one of the first to write honestly and favorably about a country that was opposed to his in politics and religion.

The story of Colonel Samuel Luke visiting Dorothy's garden is from one of her letters. I don't know for certain how he offended the Osborne family, but they felt he had wronged them. Since he was a Parliamentarian, I have assumed he might had benefited materially from their fall, as was a common occurrence.

CHAPTER TWENTY-ONE

Dorothy's letters imply that William found Harry following him around London. This would have been a vulnerable time for William, losing his hopes of starting a diplomatic career and knowing that Dorothy had many other suitors.

CHAPTER TWENTY-TWO

Margaret Cavendish was an exceptionally bold Englishwoman for her time, being willing to publish her works under her own name. Though she did receive scorn and criticism for it—including from Dorothy, who said Cavendish must be mad to do it—she paved the way for future women writers in England, and it is easy to imagine that Dorothy, who had strong opinions on writing and such a love for books, might have been a little jealous of Cavendish's daring.

We don't have details on what softened the Osbornes toward the idea of Dorothy marrying a Parliamentarian, but that softening was not extended to William. At this point in history, though some couples did marry for love, it was considered unwise and almost immoral, especially among the upper classes.

CHAPTER TWENTY-THREE

Sir John Temple's return to Ireland would have improved his family's fortunes, but he might have also hoped it would separate his son from a match he viewed as undesirable. Dorothy's letters mention that Martha had a lingering illness, and I have assumed this is the reason for William's visit to Epsom in the summer of 1653, though William was also suffering through bouts of depression.

William also visited Dorothy's cousins, the Franklins, at Moor Park that summer, though I have speculated about the exact reason for his invitation. He was impressed and inspired by the design of the landscape, and he actually did etch the poem to Leda into the window. This seems extremely rude by modern standards, but given the fondness for window etchings just in William and Dorothy's tale, perhaps it was not viewed as vandalism by seventeenth-century standards.

CHAPTER TWENTY-FOUR

Dorothy reported that at the news of Robin's death, she was unable to cry. I have taken this to mean both that his death was not unexpected and that Dorothy was sunk deep in depression during this time.

Henry Cromwell did send Dorothy some "Irish greyhounds" (I would imagine more like the modern wolfhound). She expressed an interest in the biggest dogs she could find and seems to have bred them. She offered to send a "spotted dog" (likely a forerunner of the Dalmatian, as I have portrayed Ulysses) to William's sister Martha.

CHAPTER TWENTY-FIVE

We don't have the details of William and Dorothy's interrupted visit in London, but it's clear from Dorothy's letters that something dramatic happened to separate them, and that it threw both of them into despair.

CHAPTER TWENTY-SIX

I have abridged somewhat the letters that passed between Dorothy and William during this dark time to avoid repetition, but the heart of their falling out and reconciliation is still here. Dorothy was overcome by depression, frustration, and hopelessness, but finally reconciled herself to finding happiness where she could. It does sound like at some point she consulted with the local rector, who was Jane's brother-in-law, but I have invented the content of that conversation.

Chapter Twenty-seven

It appears from the letters that sometime early in 1654, around the time of William's hasty visit before his trip to Ireland, Dorothy and William formalized their engagement. The short note from Dorothy at the beginning of this chapter is my own invention, as she and William were secretive about their meeting and no letters planning it survived. They exchanged locks of hair, and William bought a ring for Dorothy. The family passed down a gold ring reputed to be their engagement ring containing on the inside the verse, "The love I owe I cannot show."

With newfound hope and energy, Dorothy continued fending off unwanted suitors and played matchmaker with Susan, Lady Grey de Ruthyn and Henry Yelverton. The stories of Beagle's bad poem, the expensive gift of coal to warm Dorothy's cold heart, and her burning Beagle's letter in front of him are all from her letters. As a side note, Dorothy called one suitor Beagle who he was an old university associate of William's. Some have suggested Beagle might not have been his real surname, but I chose to use the name that Dorothy gave him.

Chapter Twenty-eight

The British Civil Wars were a brutal and bitter time for the Irish, persecuted by the English for their Celtic ethnicity and their Catholic religion. Many were shipped off to the colonies in a status hardly better than that of African slaves (though not as long-lasting or as systematic) to make room for English settlers to take over their country. William's father, Sir John Temple, played a role in the persecution of the Irish—the pamphlet he wrote against them was later burned by the public executioner—and Oliver Cromwell is still a hated figure in Ireland. William Temple and Henry Cromwell, however, took a more fair-minded approach to their dealings with the Irish, and William never worked for Oliver Cromwell's government.

Chapter Twenty-nine

As 1654 wore on, the rumors about Dorothy and William became persistent, including those I have mentioned here. Sir Peter Osborne's death was both a blow and a blessing to Dorothy. It left Harry free to dominate her, but it also transferred her guardianship to her brother John and brother-in-law Sir Thomas Peyton, who were certainly better stewards than Harry. It also thrust Dorothy into the strange world of unattached women in the seventeenth century, with no real place to call her own.

Chapter Thirty

The Temples were influential in Ireland for several generations. Sir John Temple's father, William, had been provost at Trinity College, and both our William and his brother John would later serve in the Irish Parliament. Some say the district called Temple Bar in Dublin is named for them, since Sir John Temple had a house there, but it is more likely named for Temple Bar in London.

The Swift family were friends with the Temples in Ireland, which later led to the younger Jonathan Swift (the son of the man introduced in this chapter) to be secretary to William Temple and to flourish under his mentorship into the great satirist and writer responsible for "A Modest Proposal" and *Gulliver's Travels*.

The exact incident which caused William's father to relent to William and Dorothy's engagement is unknown, but it seems he eventually saw that Dorothy might not be the best financial match for his son, but she was the best match for his heart and mind, and William was not giving up on her.

Chapter Thirty-one

The letter included at the beginning of this chapter is one of very few we have from William to Dorothy.

There were many attempts on Oliver Cromwell's life, though it was eventually "ague," or malaria, that killed him in 1658.

Thomas Peyton, as a member of the Action Party, may have been involved in any number of these plots to restore Charles II to his throne, and his very busy house likely served as a base for some of the plotters.

The stories of the young men mocking Dorothy's notions of love and of the brutish Colonel Thornhill are based on Dorothy's letters, though I have filled in some details. Lady Sunderland may not have been at Knowlton Court at this time, but Dorothy was acquainted with her, and I wanted to give Lady Sunderland a chance to share her story. Dorothy did say that Lady Sunderland was more in love with Master Smith than her joking comments about him made it seem.

Why Dorothy allowed Harry to be part of the marriage negotiations is a mystery, but he was certainly still trying to manipulate her, and probably to prevent the marriage. The question of Harry's motivations also remains a mystery, and one that historians have debated. Some see him simply as an overly concerned brother, and others speculate he may have been a closet homosexual, but neither of these explain his extraordinary dislike of William or his fixation on his sister. He kept a journal where he wrote about Dorothy and William in code, which shows the depth of his obsession over them. I have tried to present him here as we see him through the lens of Dorothy's letters. Harry Osborne never married, but after the Restoration of Charles II, he found a position working in the administration of the king's navy, eventually helping to found a hospital for former sailors.

Chapter Thirty-two

The hurried and secret meeting of Dorothy and William in Canterbury is attested to in Dorothy's letters. We don't have the details about what emergency led to their rendezvous, but the outcome resolved any last obstacles standing between the couple. Harry Osborne was likely the root of their troubles, and he later sued the couple over Dorothy's marriage portion.

Chapter Thirty-three and Thirty-four

Before its eradication through vaccines, smallpox was one of the most terrifying and disfiguring diseases. Dorothy's severe illness was the final trial she and William faced before their quiet marriage on Christmas Day in 1654, six and a half years after they met on the Isle of Wight. Based on Harry's journal entry about the event, it sounds like he was not invited.

William and Dorothy honeymooned at Moor Park and later named their own home in Surrey after their favorite estate. They lived in exile in Ireland during the remainder of Cromwell's reign. After the Restoration in 1660, William had his opportunity to work as a diplomat, and he took Dorothy and their young family to the Netherlands and Holland for part of their marriage. Dorothy was known as the "Lady Ambassadress" for the role she played in helping her husband seek peace between England and Holland and for her bravery when the ship she and her children sailed on was under fire by enemy forces. William and Dorothy also helped arrange the marriage between the Dutch Prince William of Orange and the English Princess Mary Stuart, who would later rule England jointly as William III and Mary II.

Once back in England, William quickly became disillusioned with the dissipation and corruption of Charles II's court, and he and Dorothy retired to Moor Park in Surrey, along with a widowed Martha. William became well known for his essays—including his treatise on Holland—and Dorothy, we can imagine, remained an influence on his writing and thinking throughout their long life together.

Jonathan Swift later called William one of the last honest men and memorialized Dorothy in a poem as "Mild Dorothea, peaceful, great, and wise," a woman deeply in love with her husband for the rest of her days.

SELECT BIBLIOGRAPHY

David Cecil, *Two Quiet Lives*, Constable: 1967.

Thomas Peregrine Courtenay, *Memoirs of the Life, Works, and Correspondence of Sir William Temple, Bart.*, London: 1836.

Jane Dunn, *Read My Heart: Dorothy Osborne & Sir William Temple*, Toronto: 2008.

Jeffrey Forgeng, *Daily Life in Stuart England*, London: 2007.

Antonia Fraser, *The Weaker Vessel*, New York: 1985.

Martha Giffard, *Martha, Lady Giffard Her Life and Letters (1664-1722) A Sequel to the letters of Dorothy Osborne*, ed. Julia G. Longe, London: 1911.

Carrie Hintz, *An Audience of One: Dorothy Osborne's Letters to Sir William Temple, 1652-1654*, Toronto: 2005.

Dorothy Osborne, *Letters from Dorothy Osborne to Sir William Temple 1652-1654*, ed. Edward Abbott Parry, London: 1888.

Alison Plowden, *Women all on Fire: The Women of the English Civil War*, Cornwall: 1998.

Stephen Porter, *Pepys's London: Everyday Life in London, 1650-1703*, Gloucestershire: 2012.

William Temple, *The Works of Sir William Temple, Bart. in Two Volumes*, ed. Jonathan Swift, London: 1731.

A.T. Van Deursen, *Plain Lives in a Golden Age: Popular culture, religion and society in seventeenth-century Holland*, trans. Maarten Ultee, Cambridge: 1991.

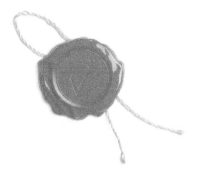

Acknowledgements

THERE ARE ALWAYS NUMEROUS PEOPLE who help an idea become a novel. I'm grateful to the Victorian writers and historians who fell in love with Dorothy while studying William's career and brought her letters to light.

Thank you to the Cache Valley chapter of the League of Utah Writers, UPSSEFW, and the Clandestines for your valuable feedback and support. A thousand thank yous to those who read early drafts of the novel and gave their input: Karen Brooksby, Britney Johnson, Lauren Makena, Keri Montgomery, Dan Wheeler, and Chadd VanZanten, who helped me kick it into shape. Also, to Lori Parker for making it pretty.

I'm grateful to my husband and children for their ongoing patience and encouragement.

And thank you to my readers for giving me an excuse to research and write. If you enjoyed this book, please take a moment to review it online or recommend it to a friend.

About the Author

E.B. Wheeler attended BYU, majoring in history with an English minor, and earned graduate degrees in history and landscape architecture from Utah State University. She is the author of *The Haunting of Springett Hall*, *No Peace with the Dawn* (with Jeffery Bateman), and Whitney Award finalist *Born to Treason*, as well as several award-winning short stories, magazine articles, and scripts. In addition to writing, she teaches history at Utah State University. She lives in the mountains of Utah with her family, various pets, and as many antique roses as she can cram in her yard.

You can find E.B. Wheeler online at ebwheeler.com and on Facebook at EBWheelerWrites.